WIND ON THE HEATH

IT is a beautiful and subtle relationship which has developed between herself and Michael Anderson, and Liz Tancred realizes that she must, however foolish and ill-judged it may seem, give it its true name: they are in love, though there are many barriers to divide them. In Michael Liz recognizes a rare spirit: though barely seventeen he is in many ways mature beyond his years and prepared and able to take upon himself the responsibilities of a man—and a man, too, in a country at war. Deeply attracted to him, she realizes also that to her has fallen the privilege of being the first love of his life: whatever the future may bring she will hold a unique place in his memory. Set in the Yorkshire countryside during the exacting years of war, this is an unusual human story rich in observation of character, in sympathy, and in tenderness. In Liz and Michael Miss Jacob has given us a touching pair of lovers by whose fortunes we cannot fail to be moved. It is a fitting novel from the pen of a very popular writer.

NAOMI JACOB
has also written

Novels:

POWER
JACOB USSHER
ROCK AND SAND
THE BELOVED PHYSICIAN
THE MAN WHO FOUND HIMSELF
"SEEN UNKNOWN . . ."
THE PLOUGH
ROOTS
PROPS
POOR STRAWS
GROPING
THE LOADED STICK
"HONOUR COME BACK———"
BARREN METAL
FADE OUT
THE LENIENT GOD
SECOND HARVEST
FOUNDER OF THE HOUSE
"THAT WILD LIE . . ."
YOUNG EMMANUEL

FOUR GENERATIONS
PRIVATE GOLLANTZ
GOLLANTZ—LONDON, PARIS, MILAN
NO EASY WAY
STRAWS IN AMBER
THIS PORCELAIN CLAY
THEY LEFT THE LAND
SALLY SCARTH
UNDER NEW MANAGEMENT
THE CAP OF YOUTH
LEOPARDS AND SPOTS
WHITE WOOL
HONOUR'S A MISTRESS
A PASSAGE PERILOUS
MARY OF DELIGHT
EVERY OTHER GIFT
THE HEART OF THE HOUSE
A LATE LARK SINGING
THE MORNING WILL COME
THE IRISH BOY

One-Act Plays:

THE DAWN

MARY OF DELIGHT

Autobiography and Biography:

ME: A CHRONICLE ABOUT OTHER PEOPLE
"OUR MARIE" (MARY LLOYD)
ME AGAIN
MORE ABOUT ME
ME IN WARTIME

ME OVER THERE
ME IN THE MEDITERRANEAN
ME AND MINE
ME LOOKING BACK
ROBERT, NANA—AND ME

General:
ME IN THE KITCHEN

Omnibus Volumes:
THE GOLLANTZ SAGA

Volume One
comprising
FOUNDER OF THE HOUSE
"THAT WILD LIE . . ."
YOUNG EMMANUEL

Volume Two
comprising
FOUR GENERATIONS
PRIVATE GOLLANTZ
GOLLANTZ
LONDON, PARIS, MILAN

TALES OF THE BROAD ACRES
Comprising
SALLY SCARTH
THE LOADED STICK
ROOTS

WIND
ON
THE HEATH

By
NAOMI JACOB

THE BOOK CLUB
121 CHARING CROSS ROAD
LONDON, W.C.2

MADE AND PRINTED IN GREAT BRITAIN BY
MORRISON AND GIBB LIMITED, LONDON AND EDINBURGH

For
JOYCE WEINER
with my love and admiration.
                    Mickie.

"There's night and day, brother, both sweet things;
Sun, moon and stars, brother, all sweet things;
There's likewise a wind on the heath. Life is very sweet, brother;
Who would wish to die?"

BORROW.

Chapter One

"Yes, I've had my ups and my downs," Ada Anderson said, not without a touch of self-satisfaction, as if implying that she had successfully surmounted all difficulties. "But generally speaking, things have not turned out too badly."

"I should say not!" her friend, Mrs. Brisco answered with admiration in her voice, "for never did a woman face adversity so bravely as what you have done, Mrs. Anderson. Never!"

The two women were seated in Ada Anderson's front room. A low-ceilinged place, where some excellent old pieces of furniture stood. The window with its small panes looked out on to a fairly small, but beautifully trim garden. The walls were panelled and painted a low tone of grey, against which the rich, polished wood of the beautifully kept furniture shone and gleamed. There was the Sheraton desk, dignified and satisfying, the good old Georgian chairs with their gracefully curved legs and restrained but elaborate backs, the Chippendale table, its wood shining like glass from much polishing.

Mrs. Brisco said, "Aye, this is a nice room. The polish you get on the furniture beats me, and I reckon that mine's kept pretty well."

Mrs. Anderson smiled, "Elbow grease and no French polish! I make my own polish and see that it's laid on with elbow grease, Mrs. Brisco."

Mrs. Brisco nodded, "Aye, a true Yorkshire woman, eh?"

"Nay, I'm not really a Yorkshire tyke," she laughed a small mechanical sound as if she tried to revive a joke which was long since dead. "Nay, I'm from Lancashire. Colne is where I was born. Just over the border. Yes, my father had a very good bakery business in Colne—Alfred Cawther. Very successful it was. People used to come from miles distant to buy my father's pies. Then," she smiled, "Enoch came over and we met at a dance—a church dance it was—and well," the smile widened and became somewhat deprecating, "we fell in love. My Enoch, a good husband if ever there was one. That's how I came to live at Huddersley, Mrs. Brisco."

The stout little woman said eagerly, "I'll lay that you've never regretted it neither."

"No, I've not regretted it." The tone was slightly pontifical. "Once I set my hand to the plough, I don't look back."

When Mrs. Brisco took her leave, Ada Anderson allowed herself the rare luxury of leaning back in her chair and closing her eyes. Not that she slept, but she found that with closed eyes she could come to a more accurate estimate of those things which demanded her attention.

She was a small, spare woman with smooth brown hair showing scarcely a trace of white, her closed lids hid eyes which were very bright and clear, her skin—though slightly weathered—was barely wrinkled, and her whole figure betokened tremendous activity and energy. She had come to Yorkshire as a bride, very much in love with her husband, Enoch Anderson. He was gentle and kindly, though there were times when she regretted his lack of forcefulness.

Yet, he had done well. In addition to the farm, not large but well kept, tended and productive, he had opened a general store in Huddersley. Ada, as yet unburdened by the claims of children, had taken over the management of the place. Each morning saw her, wearing a large, spotlessly white apron, ready to minister to the wants of customers. The phrase, "If you can't get it, Mrs. Anderson will get it for you" became current over half the county.

"Madam, I'm sorry. There's been no call for it, but let me write down the name and you shall have it by the end of the week. No, it's no trouble at all—it's a pleasure."

Then, when she was expecting her first child, news came that her father, Alfred Cawther, had died—suddenly. Ada went over to Colne, she arranged everything, she did her best to comfort her mother, and disposed of the business—at a considerable profit. She brought her mother back with her to Huddersley, and installed her in the farm-house where she and Enoch lived. It could not be said with strict truth that the arrival of old Mrs. Cawther brought actual joy and gladness into the old stone farm-house at Huddersley. She was a domineering woman, she had never hesitated to bully her husband and saw no reason why she should not now bully Enoch Anderson. Ada, during the first months of her mother's stay often remonstrated, "Nay, mother, don't for ever be nagging on at Enoch. After all it's his house you're living in!"

Her mother, spare, thin lipped, with eyes which seemed to see everything, paying particular detail to the very things you did not wish her to see, sat bolt upright in her chair.

8

"That's a bonnie road to talk to your mother! I wonder what your poor father would say if he had lived to hear my daughter talk to me that road? It's Enoch's house, is it? I wonder where Enoch, aye and you either, 'ud find anyone who'd do the thousand and one things I get through in a week—in a day if it comes to that. Never an idle moment. I'll teach you one thing, I'm worth my weight in gold—aye, gold to you an' Enoch!"

Finally it was Enoch, not Ada, who wore the old lady down. She enjoyed her verbal battles with Ada, but Enoch was in no way worthy of her steel. He was a mild man, with a quiet voice and very gentle blue eyes. When his mother-in-law grumbled at him, found fault, contradicted him flatly, or gave it as her opinion that he ran the farm in a way which "i' Colne we'd think was properly far back", he returned the soft answer which is reputed to turn away wrath.

"Why happen they would," Enoch would admit, "it's the road I find best for here, maybe in Lancashire they're smarter nor what we are in Yorkshire."

She snorted, "I wonder you like to admit it!"

"Nay," his eyes twinkled, "I didn't say that I *liked* it."

By the time Ada's baby was three months old, Mrs. Cawther decided to leave Enoch alone. She felt a half-formed grudge against him, felt that he was 'soft', she preferred Ada's temper, and enjoyed watching her flare up in sudden fury.

"However you came to marry that man," she said to Ada, "beats me. He's over meek and mild to say 'Boo' to a goose! No spirit!"

"He suits me," Ada retorted, "and seemly I suit him."

"I like men to be men, like your poor father was!"

Ada laid down the frock she was making for her son, Michael. "Now listen to me, Mother. Happen you've forgotten, happen it suits you to forget—Father scarcely ever opened his mouth, except to say 'Yes, Ellen' or 'No, Ellen'. You'd knocked all the spirit out of him years ago. Compared with Father my Enoch's a wild man of the woods, a roaring savage! Now, we'll have no more of it. I won't have Michael grow up in a house where there's always nattering and nagging. Leave Enoch alone, leave me alone and we'll get along all right."

"Leave Enoch alone!" The scorn which the old woman put into the words was the essence of bitterness. "That's exactly what I intend to do from now on. And you and all. Let's hope that blessed baby won't grow up to be a mealy-mouthed, poor-spirited creature—a worm, a milk and water——"

9

Ada went on with her sewing. "Don't worry, he won't."

Things did improve; true, Mrs. Cawther still looked at Enoch Anderson as if he were something beneath contempt; her attitude amused him, and there were times when he chuckled softly at the thought of the old woman to whom an argument—and for preference a heated one—was one of the chief pleasures of her life.

She was devoted to her grandson, and when Ada resumed her work in the shop, which she did at the earliest possible moment, her mother assumed full responsibility for Michael. He was, she declared to everyone with whom she came in contact, the most beautiful baby she, or anyone else had ever seen. When she had taken him in his perambulator into the town, she returned to recount long and slightly pointless stories of how people had stopped her, begging to be allowed to 'take a peep' at Michael, how they had exclaimed at his beauty, the colour of his hair and the smoothness of his skin.

"Mind you," Ada said to Enoch in the privacy of their own room, "I don't believe half of it's true."

"Half!" he smiled, "that's an over-generous estimate, my dear."

"Mind you, there's no denying that he's a lovely baby."

"Now, I'd say that is an over-generous understatement!" Enoch chuckled. "The lad's a picture, and bright as a button."

Michael was three when Ada's second child was born. The child arrived at a most inconvenient time, during the hay making, and when Ada at the shop was preparing for the annual stock-taking and sale.

"Miss Mellows will do her best," Ada grumbled, "but it's a poorish best. No method, that's what's wrong with Clarice Mellows."

The second boy, who was named James for no particular reason, was sturdy and strong, but lacking in the grace which his brother possessed. He was a contented, placid baby and gave little or no trouble to anyone. From the first it was obvious that Michael adored him.

Michael was twelve and Jimmy nine when Mrs. Cawther sat reading her morning post, which consisted of an appeal for funds for the new Methodist Hall, a catalogue from a drapery store in Peckham where she had once bought some stockings by post and they had kept her name on their list of customers ever since, and a letter.

She turned the letter over in her gnarled, stiff fingers, and announced to the company in general, "From my niece, my brother-in-law's daughter. You remember Uncle Joe, Ada, died four years after your poor father. Well, this daughter of his, Elizabeth—though she always gets Lizzie, married a chap from Barnsley way—a farmer."

Enoch said, "Why don't you see what she's got to say, Mother?"

"I shall—in my own good time, Enoch."

"That's right—hurrying over much never gets you anywhere."

"There's some as might well hurry a bit more! You lads 'ul be late for school, I'd not wonder."

Enoch looked at his watch. "Nay, they've gotten enough time."

"So've you seemly," she said tartly.

He laughed, "That's true—I'm getting old, like to take things a bit easier. Ada, luv, I'll have another cup of tea."

Mrs. Cawther made no reply, with dignity and unhurried movements she opened her letter and retired behind its sheets to read in private. Enoch finished his third cup of tea, rose and kissed his wife, then turning to the boys said, "Time you were both off to school. See that you behave yourselves," and with an amused glance at his mother-in-law, who made no attempt to speak to him, walked out.

The two boys gone, Mrs. Cawther sighed deeply, and laid down the letter.

"You'll be late at the shop, Ada," she said. "Seems to me that the whole family are taking things easy. Well, while you are here you might as well hear the news. Lizzie—your cousin—and her husband, George Tancred, have taken Cummings Farm."

"No!" even Ada was astonished for Cummings Farm was barely half a mile away from their own. A place which stood high in the estimation of the neighbours. A large, well-kept farm, with a fine Georgian house, good out-buildings and a couple of cottages. "No!" she repeated. "George Tancred's taken Cummings. Well, look at that!"

Her mother nodded, "Aye, it's what I expect from my family— or the chaps they marry. Not content to stick in a rut, always wishing to better themselves. If he'd enough smeddum your Enoch might have been moving into Cummings!"

Ada said sharply, "Now Mother, leave Enoch be! We've enough for our needs and we're satisfied."

"Well, it's nice to know as you're satisfied. Yes, Lizzie says they hope to be here quarter day. They're going in for graded milk!"

"It 'ul be no better than ours, that I will lay," Ada said.

"Happen it won't—happen it will."

Ada left for the shop, she knew that the housework, under her mother's capable management and the hard work of Violet, would be done perfectly, knew, too, that the dinner which would be served to Enoch and the boys would be well cooked and well served. She herself remained at the shop, lunching off a couple of sandwiches and a cup of inferior coffee sent in from the confectioner's next door.

She drove her little car—which Enoch had given her last Christmas—capably and efficiently. As she drove into Huddersley, her mind went back to her cousin, Lizzie Tancred. They were going to take Cummings. She was not jealous of Lizzie, but at the back of her mind there was a faint, half-nagging regret that Enoch had not had sufficient ambition to get the place. She knew the state of his finances, he was not wealthy, but he was safely, and comfortably off. What is called in Yorkshire, 'a warm member'. They could afford to live in a much more ambitious style, the shop was flourishing, and the farm did well. The boys —Michael and Jimmy—could be brought up as well, if not better than any brats Lizzie Tancred might have. Then and there she registered her determination. It was high time that the boys went to a good school, never mind the Grammar School—it was all right, but it didn't—she halted for the right word and found it— confer anything on the boys who attended it.

Michael with his good looks, and Jimmy with his alert mind were worthy of the best—and Ada Anderson decided—the best they should have. All day the thought was running through her head, while she attended to customers with her usual pleasant courtesy, when she watched the arrival of packing cases containing new goods, when she 'kept an eye' on the assistants—there were four of them and Ada maintained a certain distrust of them all except Miss Mellows—she was thinking of this new idea concerning the boys' schooling. It seemed providential that Mrs. Blenkiron—wife of Colonel Blenkiron—and always referred to in Huddersley as 'Mrs. Colonel Blenkiron'—should come into the grocery part of the store that morning.

She was a tall, haggardly handsome woman wearing a heavy linen suit, immaculate shoes, and a hat which was in itself a disaster. Ada watching her thought, 'That suit's four years old to my certain knowledge, and that awful hat looks as if she'd bought it at a jumble sale—yet how does she manage to look as she does? That's what's called—class, I suppose.'

She walked in, carrying a walking-stick, with her two Cairns at her heels. Ada hurried forward, she—whenever possible—attended to the 'County' herself.

"Good morning, Madam. How are the little dogs? Come for their biscuit?" She moved towards the rack where the biscuit tins with their glass lids stood.

Mrs. Blenkiron replied heartily, "Little brutes, all they think of is cadging food! Disgusting creatures."

It was well known that she would have sacrificed her life for one of the Cairns, but it was her—possibly only—affectation to disparage them in public. Ada gave then each a biscuit after which they took not the slightest notice of her, but lay down their heads on their paws, extremely bored and not taking the trouble to hide the fact.

Mrs. Blenkiron looked at them, her hard, good-featured face filled with sentimental affection.

" Selfish little beasts! Mannerless into the bargain. Well, Mrs. Anderson, have the things from Fortnums come? Good! Let's have a look."

Ada said, "I've scarcely had them unpacked yet, Madam. I'm thinking of starting a small—well, shall we say, side line? Dealing only in what you might called luxury lines. Nothing big, but the things which will appeal to people of taste. Caviar, pâté, cocks' combs, and the like. There's a make of curry powder which I believe is very special. If I might ask, how does the idea strike you, Madam?"

"As most of your ideas do, Mrs. Anderson—admirable. Now, there's my list, see that it's sent up, will you?"

Ada took the list, written in Mrs. Blenkiron's distinctive but sprawling hand on a sheet of grey note-paper which bore the address—Graystone Manor, and added the information that the telephone number was 26 Huddersley, the nearest station Huddersley, and the the telegraphic address was Graystones, Huddersley.

"It will be there just after luncheon, Madam. And now—" she hesitated, "I wonder if I might ask you a great favour? I shan't keep you long. Perhaps you'd take a cup of coffee—yes, I can send next door for it, though very soon I hope we shall acquire those premises and the shop on the other side—Baines.

My husband feels that we ought to expand. What with the drapery and the grocery, and it's certain that Huddersley can do with a nice, pleasant café—I think that he's right."

"I'm certain that he is!" Mrs. Blenkiron agreed heartily. "By all means let's have that coffee, if I can be of any help—well, you know how happy I shall be."

Ada sent for the coffee, adding in a whisper to the assistant, "Tell them it must be all right. It's for Mrs. Colonel Blenkiron"; then led the way into her small office. It was perfectly tidy if austere, Ada could not tolerate what she called 'muddle and mess'.

"Please take that chair, Madam." Mrs. Blenkiron with the two Cairns at her heel, nodded and sat down, the little dogs crowding as near to her as possible. "It's about my sons," Ada said, "I don't care for them to grow up with the kind of accent they'll get at the Grammar School, good though it may be. I'd like them to go to a school they could look back on—well, with pride. I've not much knowledge of such places, but that's why I ventured to speak to you about it, Madam."

"Ah!" Mrs. Blenkiron sat bolt upright, inflicting a slight kick on one of the Cairns as she did so, and crying, "Get out of the way you silly little ass!" then stooping to pat the dog and murmuring, "My angel, I didn't really hurt you! Gosh, what a clumsy mother you've got! Now, Mrs. Anderson," as the Cairn rolled over waving its paws in the air and exposing a well-filled pink stomach, "I wonder what you have in mind. Not Eton or Harrow?"

"Madam, no!" Ada's tone was reverential. "Just something with—well, tone."

"Umph. Ah, here's the coffee. Thank you—oh, and biscuits. Here, Timmy, here Tottie—here's a biscuit each. Greedy little animals. Always longing to eat something—then I have to exercise them like mad to work off their fat. Can't imagine why I keep the little beasts! That biscuit nice, my poppets? Well, I think that I can recommend the very place. Colonel Blenkiron is one of the governors. He'd put in a word for your boys. Blamey Castle! It's a school of good standing, not cheap but you get value for money."

She laughed, showing her beautiful if large teeth. "I'm a true Yorkshire woman! Healthy position, good modern buildings, and the food's good. I've often said to my husband that our boys—Gavin and Eldred—might have done very well there, and saved us money instead of going to Harrow! Mrs. Anderson, I

14

shall ask my husband to have the prospectus sent to you immediately. Go over and see the place. You'll be completely satisfied, I'm certain. Thanks for the coffee, come on you two idle hounds, stir your stumps. Good-bye, Mrs. Anderson, and in that order include a tin of pâté, will you? My husband adores it."

Ada saw her off, watched her bundle the Cairns into the shabby Ford car which she drove, and returned to her office to write down carefully—Blamey Castle.

That evening during the meal—high tea—which was served at seven, Ada listened to the two boys talking. Jimmy spoke with an accent which she deplored, Michael less so, but even his speech was tinged with the over-broad vowels of the West Riding.

She asked Jimmy if he would like another sausage, and his reply annoyed her.

"I don't mind," he said.

She snapped suddenly, "What do you mean—don't *mind*? Can't you say, 'Yes, please' or 'No, thank you'? And Michael, take your elbow off the table, and sit up! Don't lounge about like some farm hand for any favour. What's come to your manners, I cannot imagine. Father," to Enoch, "another sausage?"

"Yes, please, Ada," he answered primly, and Jimmy gave a great guffaw of laughter.

Grandma, pulling down the corners of her mouth, said, "It's time someone took you in hand, young Jimmy. I'd not like your mother's cousin to hear you behaving that road, or speaking rude."

Ada said sharply, "Never mind my cousin, Lizzie. I'll see to my own bairns, choose how."

That night when she and Enoch sat in the charming, if slightly stiff, sitting-room, she talked over her plans. First the boys must go to some school where they would learn to speak properly.

"Nay, they speak all right," Enoch said. "They both speak better nor what I do, Ada."

"Times change, Enoch. Education's a grand thing, and speaking nicely opens many doors. D'you think that I don't realize my own shortcomings? I do, y'know. I was talking this morning to Mrs. Colonel Blenkiron—yes, she stayed and had a cup of coffee with me in my office——"

Enoch gaped, "Mrs. Colonel Blenkiron did! I'll be damned!"

"Most affable she was too. I asked her about a good school for the boys. It appears that the Colonel is one of the governors of Blamey Castle. He's going to interest himself—and if you agree, that's where I plan for the boys to go."

Enoch whistled, "Making gentry of them, eh?"

"Nothing of the sort. Giving them a good start, that's the word I want—dash it!—I've gotten it—making them equipped for life. You'd not mind?"

"I mind nowt so long as brass is there. You know that, Ada luv. You're the headpiece, you've gotten the ideas. I'm just a working farmer, that's all."

She beamed at him, she loved Enoch dearly, true there were times when she wished that he would show a little more ambition, but she consoled herself with the thought that she had sufficient for both of them. She went on to talk about the shop.

She had told him that she had heard from Mr. Harrison, the auctioneer, that the café was coming on to the market, and not only the café but the nasty little haberdasher's on the other side of Anderson's.

"It's my idea," she said, "if you approve, to buy them both. To enlarge our place, we're fairly crowded out. The groceries do well, the heavies and the cottons do well, but we've no elbow room."

"Eh, you're a one," he murmured, but there was admiration in his tone. "You'll have us broke, Ada!"

"I'll not. Trust me. I'll have a property that 'ul be worth something. Oh, I was going to tell you, this morning while I listened to Mrs. Colonel Blenkiron, I felt that it was a treat to hear her talk. Really lovely. I thought, 'Well, to be able to talk that way will be an asset to our boys when they grow up.' So I just took the bull by the horns and asked her to come in and give me advice. Now tell me that you approve, Enoch luv."

He did approve, he approved of everything his wonderful Ada did. He often thought about her when he was going about his work, thought of her with admiration not completely unmixed with awe. He knew himself to be capable and hard working, his farming might not be spectacular but it was sound and—it paid dividends. Enoch never thought of himself as a rich man, or even as a man on the way to becoming rich, but when he made up his books he was mildly surprised at the balance in his bank. He was even more surprised when Ada brought home the auditor's report on the shop and its takings.

'Aye,' he would murmur softly, 'yon wife of mine has a headpiece on her, there's nothing more certain.'

The boys received the announcement that they were to go to Blamey Castle the following term. Colonel Blenkiron had taken the matter in hand, and had written and spoken handsomely of both lads and their family. They would enter the Lower School, Michael would pass into the Upper School when he was judged ready to do so, James would remain in the Lower School until he was twelve.

James grumbled a little, "I don't see why I want to leave Huddersley, Mum. It's not as if I was going to be a teacher when I grow up, I'm going into the shop along of you."

"Then you can learn to speak properly," his mother told him, "and not say—along of, when you can say—with. Anyroad, you'll need education in the shop or out of it. There'll be accounts to do, bills to check, and a dozen other things they'll learn you to do at Blamey. And think on, Jimmy, the shop now and the shop as it will be by the time you're ready to come into it won't be the same thing at all. Anderson's is going to be the best and most up-to-date shop between here and Bradford. Your Dad and I have our plans made, we've discussed it and he approves. Don't you, Enoch?"

He nodded, "Aye, that's right—it's all settled."

Michael watched and listened intently, his eyes grave, his fine hands clasped. He was excited, and didn't want that excitement to appear too evident. His father glanced at his serious young face.

"What are you thinking, Michael lad?"

"I was thinking that someone told me they have lectures on agriculture at Blamey, and a lab. where they show you how to experiment with all the new artificial manures, and they teach you how to fettle self-binders and tractors if they go wrong. Is that true, Dad?" He spoke rather breathlessly unable to completely conceal his excitement.

"I'd not doubt it," Enoch said, "does all that mean you want to be a farmer, lad?"

"More than anything, Dad. Jimmy can work with Mum and I'll work with you, eh?" He laughed. "There! The family's future is all settled!"

They lay awake in their old-fashioned low-ceilinged bedroom that night speculating about Blamey Castle. Jimmy gave it as his opinion that there'd be a 'school bully' who would be certain to attack them as new boys. Michael gave it as his that bullying was old fashioned, that it went out with *Tom Brown's Schooldays* and *Eric or Little by Little*.

James persisted, "I bet you there'll be fagging and tossing in blankets! And—whackings—they call them swishings. I'm not going to swot, are you, Mike? Other chaps despise fellows who swot."

"I'm going to get as much out of Blamey as I can," Michael said. "I'd like to play games well, and be good at sports, but I'd like to be pretty good—at any rate—at lessons. Dad and I are going to have the best farm here and hereabouts one day."

"I'm going to have the best shop—me and Mum! I'd rather have a smashing shop than a mouldy old farm!" Michael reflected that was typical of Jimmy, he could be passionately interested in anything which concerned himself, but he was inclined to deride things which interested other people and did not affect him.

The farm-house seemed strangely empty without them, even Grandma commented on it. She was chiefly interested in the prospective arrival of her niece—Lizzie Tancred—at Cummings Farm, and walked over several times a week to 'keep an eye' on the various alterations which were being made, returning with paeans of praise for the up-to-date methods and machinery which were being installed.

"I never thought such a lot about George Tancred but seemly he's made some brass, for what he's doing at Cummings must have cost a mint o' money. You oughter see the dairy! Like a palace! White tiles right up to the ceiling, an' all corners rounded. Aye, rounded!"

"Then they're not corners any longer," Enoch said.

"Nay, you know well enough what I mean. T' foreman told me as they're going to milk—listen to this—to milk by electricity. Did you ever hear the like."

"Enoch and me saw it being done at the dairy show. I can't say I liked the look of it over much. Michael was interested in it, he says it's hygenic. The things that lad says!"

Grandma nodded, "Aye, he's a clever one is Michael. Not that our Jimmy isn't clever and all. I'll bet the masters at Blamey are properly set up with getting two lads like ours—for they're as full of brains as an egg's full of meat."

Enoch smiled, "They get their brains from their mother."

Grandma eyed him sharply, "I could have told you that, Enoch."

"No harm in me saying it! Well, I'll just go round and see all's shut up for the night."

"Now, Enoch, can't you leave it to Wilson, why must you go trailing out every night?" Ada said.

He laughed; she thought what a pleasant, chuckling sound it was.

"You ought to know, aye and you *do* know, if you want a thing done right, the quickest road is to do it yourself. If I leave anything undone, then no one's to blame but me."

"Have it your own way—same as usual," she said tolerantly, not wholly displeased to have the chance to make such a remark before her mother.

As the door closed Ada turned to Grandma, "Eh, he's a masterful chap is that one!"

"There's some as like to keep dogs and do their own barking."

"Ah, well, if it pleases him! Mother, what do you think about asking Lizzie and George here while they're getting straight at Cummings? It was Enoch who suggested it. They could have the spare room, it looks very bonnie with the new curtains and bedspread."

Grandma, though secretly pleased at the idea, looked dubious.

"I doubt it 'ul all seem very simple to them after a place like what they're used to. Still—she's your own cousin, and—why, write and ask them."

Ada was excited at the thought of the visit from Mr. and Mrs. Tancred. She knew comparatively little about either of them, but she was determined that they should find Anderson's short of nothing which made for comfort and good living. She and Violet indulged in an orgy of cleaning and baking, even Grandma spent a whole day polishing silver which already shone and glittered. Ada took Enoch to the big larder, where food stood on broad stone shelves and asked for his opinion as to whether she had forgotten anything.

"Only one thing," he admitted, "so far as I can see."

"Nay, for any favour! What is it?"

He slipped his arm round her still trim waist, "You've forgotten that they're not bringing an army with them, and that they're only staying for a few days. They'd need to have ten meals a day and to stop for a month if they were to get through all this lot."

Their visitors arrived in the late afternoon, they drove up in a smart-looking touring car, Lizzie at the wheel. Ada and Enoch went out to greet them, Grandma remained seated in a dignified manner in the parlour.

George Tancred called, "Well, this is pleasant. It's awfully good of you to put up with us."

His voice, while unmistakably that of a North-countryman, was not marred by any hint of dialect. Ada couldn't imagine

Enoch saying "It's awfully good of you . . ." neither could she imagine him wearing that excellent suit of tweeds, well cut and obviously expensive, that clothed George Tancred's tall, slim figure. But the real shock was Liz, who descended from the car slowly, almost lazily, and moved over to where Ada stood, wearing tweeds not unlike those of her husband, a crisp shirt, loose, wrinkled gloves, and shoes which reminded her of Mrs. Colonel Blenkiron's.

Liz said, "Hello, Ada, this is nice! And what a lovely old house! Enoch, it's pleasant to meet you at last. Where's Aunt Ellen?"

Ada drew a deep breath, thinking, 'Oh, she's—elegant, that's the word. Looks like the people you see at a point-to-point. When I saw her last she was a dumpy little thing, far too fat. Now—well, I don't know.' Aloud she said, "Grandma's—we call her that, because of the boys—waiting for you in the parlour."

"The parlour!" Liz repeated. "How much nicer than—lounge. George will you help Enoch with the baggage while I go and visit the matriarch? Show me the way, Ada."

She moved easily, long limbs, slim hips and well-built shoulders. She was brown-haired, Ada suspected 'tinting' but had to admit that the effect was charming. More—Liz was 'made up'—it was done with admirable care, but it was evident just the same. Her voice was low, but full and quite charming.

"It's a lovely house, Ada. How old is it? You don't know! My dear, that must be put right at once."

Ada said, "I don't doubt that Enoch would know. Here's the parlour, and Grandma waiting for you."

Liz went forward, apparently her eyes were on the old lady, but Ada felt that she saw, and approved of, the Sheraton and the Chippendale; that she noted the curtains, the subdued carpet—in fact, that there was very little Liz Tancred did not see.

"Well, Auntie, this is nice. How are you? Isn't it kind of Ada and Enoch to allow us to intrude for a few days? We're both delighted."

She stooped and kissed Ellen Cawther's cheek. The old lady said, "How are you, Liz. You've got on a lot of paint and powder to my way of thinking. You're not on the stage surely!"

Liz smiled, unperturbed, "Oh, Auntie, everyone does it now. The only thing is that you must put it on really well. George likes it."

"More shame to him! I like clean faces myself."

Liz laughed, "But I assure you my face is meticulously clean. The time I spend cleaning it would surprise you."

"Good soap and water was the way o' cleaning it in my day."

"It is still. If I told you what I spend on soap—from Paris, you'd be surprised. Oh, keeping clean in these days is a very expensive business. Ada, what a lovely room this is. How do you get that exquisite polish on the furniture? It's out of this world. And that fireplace—what is it? Adams?"

Ada shook her head, "I couldn't really tell you." She made a mental note of that word 'exquisite'. She would use that with effect in business—but with care—powder, scent, the finer kinds of delicacies, even materials—but for more ordinary things, no, most emphatically—no!

Violet entered bearing a silver tray on which reposed tea-pot, milk jug—or rather the richest cream that could be obtained from Enoch's excellent cows, and sugar. Then followed cakes— "all made at home, Liz, I never buy shop cakes"—Enoch had wanted a couple of roast chickens but she had refused.

"They're not that 'high tea' kind, luv. They'd rather wait for supper."

George Tancred and Enoch returned, Ada determined that the next suit her husband had should be of some really 'classy' tweed. Liz was like a child, pointing out the various cakes on the table.

"Look, George, singin' hinnies, and there—fat rascals, and look at that cake—oh, Ada, it's all making my mouth water. Enoch, you're a lucky fellow to have such a wife!"

Enoch grinning, said, "Aye, tell me something I don't know."

Chapter Two

As she brushed her hair that night, while Enoch lay in bed watching her, Ada said, "Well, what do you think of them, luv?"

"I like him very well; mind at first you'd think he was a bit la-di-dah, but he isn't. He knows his oats does George Tancred. Most interested in everything. He's made plenty of brass it seems, and this farming is more what you might call a hobby. He wants to try this and that and hang the expense. Fancified way o' going on to my mind, but every chap to his own taste. No, he's all right, is George."

Ada plaited her hair neatly, and tied the ends with a piece of tape. "Aye, he seems nice—what do you think of her?" She had been longing to ask that question all the evening.

"I'd say that she was a lot more capable than she lets on. There won't be much misses that lady."

"Would you like me better if I looked like that?"

"Like you better!" he chuckled. "Nay, I gave over *liking* you soon after we first met. Since then—I've loved you, and no matter what you did or how you looked I couldn't love you more than what I do. I'd not care for you to plaster up your face like Liz does, I'd feel as if I was kissing a blancmange!"

In their room Liz and George discussed their hosts.

"It's a lovely room," Liz said, "Ada certainly has got cleanliness to a fine art. George, just smell these sheets! It's like sleeping in a lavender bed. Let's keep Cummings simple like this, farmhousey, shall we?"

George, brushing his teeth with almost frantic energy, spluttered: "If that's the way you want it, it's all right."

"These boys of theirs—" Liz sighed, "I can't wait to see them. I always feel that I've let you down, George. Just through wearing over-high heels and slipping! Oh, damn!"

He carefully dried his toothbrush, and then walked over to the bed, leaning down and putting his arms round her.

"Listen, sweet, what I wanted was—you. It would have been nice to have had babies, but I'd have been frightened to death. Let's just forget it."

"You do love me—tinted hair, make-up and all?" Liz asked.

"I love you tinted hair, you're the only woman I know who

22

knows how to put on make-up decently, and to make both essentially part of you. Now are you answered?"

"Bless you. I like both Enoch and Ada, don't you?"

"Yes, tremendously, but for God's sake don't try to model yourself on her and don't expect me to grow like him! As for that old aunt of yours—what an old warrior! She's got a tongue like a flail."

Liz nestled against him, her hand on his outflung arm. "And to-morrow," she murmured sleepily, "Cummings!"

It was a beautiful old house. Anderson's farm-house was good, the walls were thick, the floors laid with old wood, wide and strong, not the modern narrow planks of deal replete with knot-holes. The rooms were low, but sufficiently spacious, the staircase wide with low, easy treads. True, to Liz's ideas the bathroom was inadequate, with its bath enclosed in shining mahogany, and huge shining brass taps; but otherwise everything seemed to run like clockwork. If she had been asked to describe Anderson's she would have used one word, 'Safety'. It was one of those old grey stone Yorkshire houses, with the roof covered with thin slabs of the same material; it stood four square to all the winds of heaven, and instinctively you felt that no matter how those winds blew the house would stand up to them, brave and un-complaining.

Cummings was more ambitious; Liz thought that it was neither completely farm-house nor small manor house. That it was more attractive than Anderson's could not be denied. The house itself was built of old rose-coloured brickwork, and the chimneys were works of art in themselves. The front door massive and yet elegant, was decorated with a slightly over-hanging stretch of wood carved with a swag of fruit. A very simply designed double stair led to the front door, the steps on either side slightly concave in the middle, many feet had trodden them and left their imprint. The rooms were panelled on the ground floor, and the ceilings beautifully decorated with fine mouldings, the fireplaces were dignified and slightly austere.

George said, "The floors are good, but if you like we'll put down parquet."

She laughed, "We'll not change a thing, I've fallen in love with it. I loved it the first time I saw it, now I've fallen in love all over again. That's a heavenly newel post, isn't it, and these nice low-treaded stairs? When we're both ancient we shall still be able to creep up them easily—or moderately easily."

23

She was charmed with everything, and George Tancred, rubbing his small, rather bristly moustache, smiled with content. He was still in love with her; after six years he regarded her as the most attractive woman he had ever met—and George had not wasted his time.

"The only really modern things are the bathrooms," Liz said, "and let's praise the modern plumber for that. Ada's bath was completely adequate, but I felt as if I were in a rather splendid mahogany coffin with heavy brass fittings. It was essentially a bath in which to—get clean. I like a bath to luxuriate in."

The furniture was due to arrive at ten, it came at twelve, when the men had to 'knock off' for their mid-day meal. Ada had packed her guests a splendid luncheon of cold chicken, salad and crisp new bread with satisfying pats of golden butter. They ate it sitting on the wide window seat in the room which was to be their drawing-room.

"Think that you'll be happy here?" George asked.

She gave him one of her dazzling smiles. "Think! I *know*."

They worked until half past five, when the removers intimated that they had done enough, threw out hints concerning tea, and accepted George's cigarettes with the comment, "I ondly 'ope as it won't mak' me thirstier nor what I am. I'm as dry as a lime kiln!"

George recommended the small hotel just outside Huddersley, and pressing coins of the realm into their hands watched them depart. He turned to find Liz at his side, she was watching the big vans move slowly away, she laid her hand on George's arm.

"Now it's—all ours," she said, smiling.

They locked the doors and together, walking slowly, made their way to Anderson's. The day was fading, and all the landscape softened, the outlines blurred. There was a softness and gentleness everywhere. Once or twice a bird sang suddenly, then stopped abruptly as if it realized that the sound was keeping others awake. Here and there in the sky a star peeped out and then seemed to disappear until it finally asserted itself.

George said, "Nice place, I think, eh?"

"A wonderful place."

Again they walked in silence, George smoking his pipe contentedly, conscious that he was deliciously tired, and that the thought of a hot bath and a change of clothes were enticing; Liz allowing her mind, as it did so often, to wander back to the days before she met George.

Her mother had died when she was still a baby, and her

24

father when she was only a child of fourteen. Her father's sister, Aunt Alice, had swooped—Liz always imagined Aunt Alice as 'swooping'—down on Colne.

Alice had married an exceedingly well-to-do industrialist. He was a self-made man, and had made good. His bicycles might not be in the first rank, but they were popular and they were good. Aunt Alice lived at Buxton in a house which was a cross between a baronial castle and a villa at Surbiton. It was essentially comfortable, for her husband was completely devoted to improvements and even a small gadget for opening bottles more easily would delight him for weeks.

They closed and sold Cawther's house, and took Liz off to Buxton. There, Alice, who prided herself on moving with the times, 'took Liz in hand'.

Henry Goswell and his wife had no children, and the many specialists which they had both visited, gave it as their opinion that the chance of having any was exceedingly remote. They lavished everything on Liz Cawther. She was all they had longed for, she satisfied them in every way. That she was spoiled was undeniable, that it spoiled her—in her own character—was something which never happened.

She appreciated everything, she took nothing for granted. If her uncle brought her home a bunch of violets, if her aunt arranged that while they were away at Scarborough her bedroom should be completely redecorated, Liz showed no difference in the warmth of her delight. At school—and she was sent to the most exclusive and expensive school in Buxton—she was not only popular but she worked hard and gained the approbation of her teachers. Yet she did all these things without self-righteousness, without the slightest apparent self-satisfaction.

Harry Goswell, flushing slightly above the rim of his rather over-tight collar, when reading the school report on Liz's progress for the term, would catch her eye and grin.

"All right, Uncle?" she'd ask.

"Not too bad," smothering an expression of supreme satisfaction. "Might be worse."

"Conduct?" Aunt Alice would demand. "How's that?"

"Conduct, eh?" he would go through a farce of searching for the comment. "Ah yes—— Conduct—dear, dear—it says— 'shocking'."

"Harry Goswell, it does *not*! Show it to me, after all she's my niece. You're upsetting her."

Liz would giggle, "He's not, Auntie Al, he's only—kidding."

Goswell would pass the report over to his wife, still grinning. Alice would adjust her glasses, and scan the list. "Conduct, ah! *Excellent!* There, now you see what a fibber your uncle can be."

It was a pleasant household, and Liz was completely happy there, when she was sixteen they decided to send her to Paris.

Liz, grown now, tall and with a figure which promised to be quite beautiful, grumbled, "But why—Paris? I'm so happy here."

Harry, already weakening in his determination for Liz to be sent to Paris, said, "Now, Al, isn't that nice to hear?"

"Just the same, she's going to Paris. I want her—finished."

Liz said in dismay, "Finished!"

"Listen, my love, Alderman Bates's daughters have gone to Paris, so have Sir Gordon's two girls, and half a dozen others I can tell you of. Uncle Harry and I want you to have the best— for only the best's good enough."

Every year Goswell's firm paid better dividends. He dabbled in half a dozen things, even invented a patent stopper which expanded under pressure and usually exploded on to the floor, but which sold in its thousands.

Liz said, "People like to hear the—pop!"

Goswell and Alice were determined that Liz should become 'someone'. She had looks, her figure was wonderful, her brain above the average. In addition they were both completely devoted to her, and she to them. Accordingly they took Liz to Paris, having arranged for her to become a pupil at the most exclusive establishment of Madame Leroux. They spent a week with her at the 'Maurice', they both bought her far too many, and far too expensive clothes, and finally installed her.

Madame was charming. Alice said later, "Elegant, that's what I call her, elegant."

"She's that all right. Didn't care much for the name—Liz. Told me that 'Eleezabeeth' was more dignified. I said, 'Well, we like Liz, so that's what she'll have to be, Madame.' "

Liz remained at Madame Leroux's for nearly three years. She learnt to read and speak French excellently, a good deal of history, and covered a wide expanse of both French and English literature. She was taken to hear operas, to concerts and to such plays as Madame considered suitable for young girls. More, she learned how to wear her clothes, how to talk properly, and even how to apply a discreet amount of make-up.

Madame reported her to be a most satisfactory pupil, and a

26

credit to the establishment. Liz returned to Buxton to decide that her uncle must be richer than ever; the Goswell's had moved into an even larger house, there were two gardeners and a small, scruffy little boy who ran about after them and apparently did most of the dirty work. Her Aunt Alice had grown much stouter, and her calm refusal to allow anything to ruffle her in the least, had become positively impressive. She sat for hours in her own sitting-room where everything was draped in white-spotted muslin hung over pale pink silk, every piece of furniture had its pink bow, and in the wide window, which overlooked the garden, a canary swung in a gilt cage.

Alice Goswell sighed with pleasure, "I always say there isn't a prettier room anywhere than this one! That bird! What a singer, and so he should be. Harry bought him in Manchester, he's a champion, a Hartz Roller."

It struck Liz that almost everything in the house was 'the best of its kind'—the carpets were thicker and softer, the curtains richer and more handsome, the chandeliers glistened more brightly than she had seen, and both Harry Goswell and his wife exuded a slight aura of satisfaction which Liz found childish but amusing.

They had furnished two rooms for her, and as her uncle explained, whatever she didn't care for could be sent back to the shops from which they had come. He had obviously taken such pains to make both rooms eminently satisfactory, that Liz could only assure him that they were perfect.

That winter the Goswell's gave a ball for her, and there again everything had to be done on the most handsome scale. An orchestra was engaged from Manchester, an expert caterer was given a free hand, and the flowers and decorations were lavish in the extreme.

Liz enjoyed it all, but then she had a faculty for enjoying most things whether they were elaborate or simple. Several young men fell in love with her that winter, but she refused them all, only when George Tancred came on the scene, at a big dance at Buxton, did she realize that she was terribly attracted to him.

He was the son of a rich industrialist from Bradford, his father had died and George inherited a very large fortune. Farming attracted him and his model farm outside Barnsley was reputed to be one of the finest and most modern in the North of England.

When Liz first met him, George was a tall, slim young man

of twenty-seven, not strictly speaking handsome, but with pleasant rather blunt features and a charming smile. It was said that women found him irresistible, and Liz Cawther was no exception. George asked her to marry him, she accepted him, and after a stupendous wedding they left for Barnsley.

They had been married just over a year when Harry Goswell died, he left his affairs in meticulous order, his immense fortune divided between his wife and Liz. On the death of Alice Goswell the income from her share of the money was to revert to Liz. George and Liz went over to the great house at Buxton, and dealt with everything.

Alice protested, "I must get away. I couldn't face living in this great big place without my Harry. Everything here reminds me of him, it's too painful." She was almost distraught with grief, and completely unable to make decisions. The very sight of a document which needed her signature was sufficient to reduce her to floods of tears.

"It seems so heartless," she would protest tearfully, "to be thinking of signing papers when my Harry's scarcely cold in his grave."

Finally, Liz went with her to Bournemouth, and there in a hotel which offered every luxury, Alice Goswell began to take up the threads of her life again. Liz suggested that she should take a house, but she refused and for the remainder of her life lived in a large private suite, where she was given every attention, played a little indifferent bridge, visited the theatre, and attended concerts where the music was not too severely classical.

Liz and George were perfectly happy at Barnsley, the farm prospered and he was not above consulting her on matters connected with it. He had a great admiration for his good-looking wife; he admired her figure, her well-groomed appearance and even encouraged her to use a certain amount of make-up. Liz always remembered with gratitude that when she was carrying her baby, when her ankle twisted owing to the fact that she was wearing a fantastically high heel, when she was hurled down six stone steps, and when the doctor admitted to her that she could never hope for another child, George voiced no reproaches. He did not deliver a restrained if slightly regretful homily on the folly of wearing high heels when in a state of pregnancy, particularly when the streets were greasy after much rain. He merely leaned down, kissed her and murmured "Too bad, old lady. Never mind, we've got each other. Get well, I miss you terribly."

That had been five years ago, Liz was twenty-three, loving life, eager for new experiences, full of enthusiasms for the latest book, the newest incubator, the finest kind of electric churn. She was always busy, always interested. People liked her and admired her, for she was as particular over the cut of her country clothes as George was over his superfine tweed suits.

Had you asked her, Liz would have asserted that no happier couple existed than she and George, but something made her restive, she longed to get away from Barnsley—the place reminded her of something which she felt was slipping from her grasp. She could not have put a name to it, George was as kind and considerate as ever. She told herself that she *liked* George better than any man she had ever known, then started and wondered why she had thought of the word 'like' instead of love? They had had no quarrel, he was as attentive as always, apparently he enjoyed being with her as he had always done, but—there had been some change. A change so indefinable, so nebulous that she herself could not really put a name to it.

Now as they walked over the fields from Cummings to Anderson's, she turned and saw his pleasant, blunt profile, his good, strong teeth biting on to the stem of his pipe, his well-set shoulders, and his easy movement, and asked herself, 'What is it? When did it all begin?'

When she had shown him the advertisement that Cummings was for sale, he had agreed that they should see the place, and if it was suitable buy it. He had been delighted with the farm and so had she. For a few days after the purchase Liz felt that things had slipped back into 'the old days'. George was gay, lovable and ardent. Together they had interviewed contractors, plumbers, electricians, they had visited London and bought the most up-to-date machinery, and once when driving up the Great North Road, Liz remembered, he had turned to her, smiled and said, "Oh, Liz dear—isn't it all fun?"

Then slowly she had realized that not only had George changed, but that she had changed also. That was when she experienced the real shock. That was when she realized that no blame attached to him, when she could experience the same change. She still liked George, she would always like him better than any man she knew, she liked his easy walk, the way his hair grew, his kindliness and consideration, his ability to grasp new ideas. She knew that he liked her, that he had an affection for her. But—a line of verse ran through her head—'When love has changed to kindliness'. That was exactly what had happened.

So long as they were discussing furniture and where to place it, pouring over colour charts, discussing the relative values of two separators, or two incubators they were—together. Neither could have wished for any other person. It was simply that love —as they had known it—had died. There remained great friendship, even affection, but the old love, the intensely intimate relationship, was over.

She wondered vaguely if George had a mistress. She didn't feel that if he had she would be greatly affected. Then came another shock, as she knew that he had become—almost impersonal to her. Personal as regards material things, all those things which appertained to the farm, as someone who enjoyed good food as she did, who loved a house to be perfectly kept, and took a pride in the fact that whatever his land or his beasts produced should be of the best—only the best was permissible.

Liz felt suddenly wretchedly lonely. George was absorbed in his own thoughts, and she felt shut out, abandoned. Then irritably she told herself that she was being not only foolish but irrational. The change had been so gradual, it had come on her almost unnoticed. Only now, walking home in the half light of evening, where already the slight mist was beginning to lie on the wide fields, had she ever formularized it, ever admitted it frankly and openly.

She said—and her voice sounded strained in her ears—"I think that Cummings is going to be charming, don't you?"

He took his pipe out, and turning gave his wide, pleasant smile, showing those white teeth which she had always admired.

"Charming! Rather, once you get cracking with it. We'll open it to the public once a week, charge them half a dollar, I'll get myself up as a butler and show them round. Farmers will go home and commit suicide because they haven't got a farm like it, and their wives will leave them because they won't have a kitchen and rooms like yours."

"We'll make money," Liz said, "until everyone has ended in tragedy."

"Then we'll move and start somewhere else, eh?"

She said, soberly, "I shan't ever want to leave Cummings."

They reached Anderson's, Ada was still at the shop, but Violet brought them tea and Aunt Ellen regaled them with comments on the inhabitants of the neighbourhood which were acid but amusing.

"The boys 'ul be home for the half term—come the week end," Gran said. "Fine lads. I reckon as you'll like them. Jimmy's mad on the shop—he's nearly ten, but Michael's only got one thought —the farm. Clever, both of 'em, very intelligent."

George said, "How old is Michael?"

"Rising thirteen. Well-built lad an' all. Mind I don't set great store by good looks in men, but our Michael's a proper picture."

Enoch came into the parlour, Liz thought he looked disturbed, and that he sat down heavily.

He smiled, a rather wan smile, and said, "Well, how did it all go at Cummings?"

Grandma said, "Nay, you're home early, Enoch! Nout amiss, is there?"

The smile wavered and died. "Not really. I had one of my dizzy fits. Thought that a cup of tea might make me feel better. Not that there's anything wrong, but it leaves you feeling a bit shaky."

Grandma sat bolt upright. "This is the first I've heard of dizzy fits! What is all this?"

Enoch shook his head, and said nothing while Liz set a cup of tea on the table at his elbow. It was George who spoke.

"I can tell you," his voice came clipped and yet smooth, "only one thing—liver. And after I've seen the kind of food your wife gives you, candidly, I don't wonder. Better have the doctor run his tape over you, and give you something, and probably put you on a diet."

Enoch, sipping his tea rather noisily, said "Nay, I don't want any diet. As for doctors—they know less nor what I do mostlys."

"And that," said Grandma crisply, "is just talking sheer rubbish."

"Happen it is, happen it isn't." He set down his empty cup, and added, "I'll be back to finish off a few things. Thanks for the tea."

As the door closed behind him, Grandma shook her head, and said in the tone she might have used when referring to a slightly deficient child, "That's a queer one, is our Enoch. 'Thank you for the tea!' in his own house too. Well, they say there's nout so funny as folks."

"I don't like this giddiness," Liz said.

"Been standing about in the sun over long," Grandma assured her.

George laughed, "Enoch would have his work cut out to

31

find any sun to-day, Mrs. Cawther. The sky's been as grey as steel all day."

"Happen!" she snapped, "there's oftimes a *glare* behind the clouds, that can be more dangerous than actual sun."

As Liz and George climbed the stairs to their own room, he said: "That old lady would argue black was white! It must be sheer hell to have an argumentative wife. Thank God, you don't argue, Liz."

"I might, if I had anything to argue about," she smiled at him, and felt that the strange tension between them had eased a little.

On Sunday they were installed at Cummings, together they made a tour of inspection and were mutually satisfied. The old, well-shaped rooms had charm and dignity. The wide windows looked out on to gardens which were already showing the effect of care and attention. In the distance the river could be seen through the trees, a broad silver ribbon winding slowly through the lush meadow lands. On the horizon a dark line showed the hills. The sky was high and wide above them. George drew a deep breath.

"It's a pleasant place, eh, Liz?"

"I like it."

He smiled, "I'd like to hear you say that you—loved it."

"Perhaps you will—one day. I don't love easily, George."

For a second she met his eyes and felt that he was about to speak of their own relationship. A sudden sense of panic assailed her, she longed to say urgently, 'No, No, don't talk about it!' then as if he had felt emotion, he turned his eyes and continued to stare out of the window. Liz experienced a feeling of immense relief. To have begun to talk, to analyse, to search for reasons would have been to have acknowledged the change in their relationship—she didn't want to acknowledge it—yet. One day it might be necessary, until then—it was better to avoid any discussion, any admission that things had changed—slowly and imperceptibly.

That afternoon, Ada Anderson walked over with the two boys. Liz saw her sturdy figure accompanied by her two sons walking over the field path towards Cummings. George was writing letters in his study, and Liz watched them, reflectively, as their figures came nearer.

The smaller boy, with the head of thick fair hair, must be Jimmy; his father had said, laughingly, that "seemly he's a mathematical genius, that one—and only ten!" The other boy,

32

taller and very slim, must be Michael. She was conscious that she caught her breath. He was not only good looking, even at thirteen his beauty and ease of movement was almost staggering.

'If only I could have had a son like that!' she thought. Then there would never have been that change between George and herself, they would have been united by their hopes and plans for their son. Did childless marriages invariably go wrong? She remembered several of her friends who had no children, they had appeared to be happy enough. Mentally she gave herself a shake, and waved to the three people who were at the big wide gate, the boys pushing it open for their mother to pass through. Liz left the porch and walked to meet them.

"This is nice of you, Ada, to bring the boys on their first day at home." She turned and smiled at Jimmy, holding out her hand. Jimmy stared at her, his round face flushing with shyness, and muttered, "How do you do Mrs. Tancred."

Liz laughed, "Mrs. Tancred! I can't have that—just Liz, please."

Jimmy murmured rather loudly, "How do you do, Liz?"

Michael stood watching, his dark eyes shining with amusement. Liz held out her hand to him, he took it. "How do you do—Liz?" She was surprised to find how slim his hand was, firm and confident but narrower than his brother's.

Ada said doubtfully, "I'm not so certain that I approve of this —Liz. It sounds a bit cheeky to me somehow."

During tea Liz watched the two boys closely. They interested her, they answered sensibly and without embarrassment when they were spoken to, and she was thankful that George did not make the terrible gaffs so frequent among elder people when talking to boys. She rememberd how often an apparently intelligent lad had been reduced to gauche immobility by that question, 'And when do you go back to school?' or 'And do you like your school?'

George said, with a kind of tentative inflexion, "I don't know if you'd care to look at some of the improvements—well, we hope they'll be improvements—that we've installed."

Michael's face lit up immediately. "Oh, rather! I should like to see this electric milking machine. I saw it once at the Show, but I expect they've made improvements since then."

Jimmy followed them out, more slowly.

Ada laughed, "Jimmy's not got much interest in anything to

33

do with a farm. Now if you'd got a new bacon-cutting machine or something of that kind, he'd have been all agog to see it."

When they left, George told Liz that they were fine boys, and that already Michael had ideas—'and sound ideas'—about farming.

"He's a funny fellow too," he added. "I noticed their ties—surely the most hideous ever devised by misguided governors. That awful yellow and scarlet! I said, 'I should think you rather hate those ties, eh?' Michael drew himself up with the queerest hint of outraged dignity. He said, 'Oh, I don't know, sir, we're rather proud of them—they're distinctive.' I was covered with confusion."

The seasons slipped past, the years followed them. Life went on both at Anderson's and Cummings smoothly and easily. Liz knew that the breach between George and herself was slowly widening, the friendship, the mutal liking—even affection—remained, but she realized that love—as they had once known it—had gone for ever. Nothing could resuscitate it now; she told herself that nothing was so dead—as dead love.

She was not actually unhappy, she refused even to allow herself to speculate as to whether George had a mistress or not. If he had, she told herself, there was nothing she could do, except register her disapproval by leaving him—and she admitted that she did not want to leave him. She, as Ada Anderson, would say, 'enjoyed his company'. She felt assured that he enjoyed hers.

He only spoke once of their relationship. One winter evening, after dinner, when they sat comfortably on either side of the leaping, crackling wood fire, on to which from time to time he flung a handful of fir cones, he looked up suddenly, then with an obvious effort, asked, "You happy, Liz?"

"Why, yes," she answered, trying to keep her voice completely even, "what makes you ask?"

"It's a pity that things have to change."

"Do they have to change, I wonder?"

He shrugged his shoulders. "I don't know. I suppose, with people who are wise, if things do change, they accept substitutions."

" Substitutions can be very good after all."

"Providing—substitutions satisfy you, yes."

She thought wildly, 'Now if he asks if they do or don't satisfy me, what shall I say? Do I really want us to work to attempt to flog dead horses to their feet? Am I not really almost content?"

However, George only said, "Naturally—that's understood," and he turned to his paper again.

Michael was sixteen, tall and strong, still graceful, for he seemed to have missed entirely the coltish stage, when Enoch was taken suddenly ill. A farm-hand came running to George who was in one of the fields viewing with satisfaction a cow which he had recently bought. The man called to him, his voice loud with anxiety.

"Measter Tancred, can'st tha cum ovver. Our measter's bin taken prop'ly bad."

George found Enoch lying on the ground, breathing loudly and heavily, his face congested, even his hands looked swollen. They carried him home and telephoned for Ada. The doctor pronounced it to be a stroke, he gave his instructions calmly, and agreed that if they wished to consult a specialist from Leeds he was quite willing.

That evening Ada, surprisingly calm, though her face was white with worry and grief, talked to Liz and George.

"Seemingly Enoch may live for years, but he'll never be able to get about. He may be bedridden—mind it's hard, and him only just forty. His mind will clear, the doctor doesn't doubt, though it may be cloudy. I shall have to get a nurse for him. He must have the best attention, and"—she brought her broad, capable hand down on the table—"one thing I'm determined on—Enoch remains the master in his own house. Just as soon as he's well enough, I shall consult him about everything—as I've always done."

Liz leaning forward patted Ada's hand. "Well done, Ada," she said, "that's the right spirit."

Chapter Three

ADA ANDERSON kept her word, Enoch was given a place of supreme importance at Anderson's which he had never occupied before. The small, helpless man—for since his stroke he seemed to have shrunk—unable at first to speak at all, and later only to utter rather uncouth sounds which only Ada professed to understand, became the centre and focal point of not only the farm, but the shop.

If the hind came with a request for new sheets of corrugated iron with which to re-proof the Dutch barn, Ada would listen, ask for amounts, prices and the time necessary for the labour.

"Very well, Wilson, I'll speak to the master about it and let you know to-morrow."

"How might 'e be goin' on, missus?"

"Splendidly! The doctor is astonished at the progress he's making."

"Happen well 'ave 'im about wi' us afore so long."

She would answer brightly, "Nothing more certain, Wilson."

Her first real battle came when the boys returned for their summer holidays. They had, of course, been told of their father's illness, and when they arrived they were warned to go upstairs quietly as he slept so lightly, 'the least sound disturbs him'.

"Yes, come up and speak to him, but if he seems inclined to have a nap, we'll just go out quietly. He didn't have a very good night, so the nurse told me."

The big, airy bedroom had that look which rooms take on when they are inhabited by an invalid for a long time, an invalid who is most carefully and meticulously cared for, who is kept immaculate, well shaved—in Enoch's case a barber from Huddersley cycled over every morning for the ceremonial shaving of Enoch's pallid cheeks—and provided with clean linen at every possible opportunity.

Ada knew that her heart was beating heavily. Neither of her sons was lacking in intelligence, and she felt a sudden spasm of fear that they might realize that however well their father progressed he would never assume management of Anderson's again.

She opened the door softly, and laid her finger on her lips.

"I think that he's dropped off—well, we won't wake him. Later on you can come up and have a little talk with him."

Michael had seen all that he wished to know, he saw the yellow-white face, expressionless, as if someone had wiped all the character from it with a sponge. The head lolled a little to one side, and the mouth hung slackly open. The eyes were almost closed, but he caught a gleam of colour—Enoch had very bright blue eyes—and he saw too the heavy, laboured breathing.

They walked downstairs into the parlour, Ada talking with a slightly overdone brightness, Michael listening gravely, Jimmy looking puzzled and uncomfortable.

"Of course, it was a great shock," Ada said as she poured out tea, "a terrible shock. Except that your father has such an exceptionally fine constitution—well, I tremble to think what might have happened. Yes, Jimmy, have some more tea-cake. Grandma made them this morning. I must say that Grandma's been a great help. Of course, your father can't give me advice as fully as he'd wish to—he's far too weak as yet, and there *are* times—not so often now as at first, I'm glad to say—when his speech is a little blurred. I can understand him perfectly, but not everyone can. Still, time will put that right."

She leaned back in her chair and looked first at Michael, then at James with an air of triumph. She felt that she had been convincing, she had taken up her stand, and that stand she intended to maintain. She repeated, almost as if she uttered a challenge, "Yes, time will put that right!" as if she dared either of them to contradict her.

Neither of them spoke, James took another piece of heavily buttered tea-cake, and Michael fiddled with his tea-spoon. To Ada the silence was unbearable.

"I must say that both Liz and George have been most kind—most kind. At first, when the doctor wouldn't allow your father to be bothered or worried, George gave Wilson all his orders and went round seeing to everything. Liz offered to come down to the shop, if I wanted to stay at home to keep an eye on your father. Oh, most kind, they've been."

Michael looked up, and gave her his charming, disarming smile. "Mother dear," he said, "I'm sixteen. I'm taller than George Tancred, and I'm strong. I want to leave school and work here."

"Oh, I don't know. We'd have to give a quarter's notice!"

"I believe that they'd waive that, Colonel Blenkiron knows

the circumstances, he's one of the governors. And if they didn't waive the fees—well, I don't suppose they'd absolutely break—" he was going to say 'us' but with scarcely a pause said, "break Dad."

"I don't know," she hesitated, then took refuge in a phrase which was to re-establish her for many years, "I must talk it over with your father, we'll see what he says."

James pushed back the lock of fair hair which fell over his forehead. "I'd like to leave school too, Mum."

Ada turned quickly. "Now that I will not have," she said sharply. "No son of mine's leaving school at your age——"

"Boys do at the elementary school," his voice was sulky.

"You're not at the elementary school, and anyway, they don't all leave so young."

"I've done well, I was top in maths, wasn't I, Mike?"

"I think, with Mum, Jimmy, that you are a little young. You'd like to get into the eleven wouldn't you?"

"Oh, damn the eleven!"

"Well! Did you ever hear!" his mother exclaimed. "If that's the road you've learned to talk, we'd better see if we can't get you into Borstal! Never speak like that again, if you please."

That evening the boys walked over the farm, Michael viewed everything with the eye of criticism; he had worked hard at his theoretical farming, he had learned a good deal about soils, chemical manures, methods of increasing production, and what he saw at Anderson's pleased him. The place looked trim, prosperous and well cared for.

James showed no interest whatever; his pleasant face remained heavy and overcast. Finally he spoke, and his voice was sulky.

"You might have stood by me!"

"It wouldn't have been any good. Mum would never let you leave school at thirteen. She'd feel that it was a reflection on her —and Dad. It's different for me, I've taken Matric and School Cert."

"Mike, how do you think Dad is?" James asked.

"Pretty bad, I should say. It's bad luck."

"D'you believe that Mum talks everything over with him, gets advice and so on? Do you now—honestly?"

Michael stood and, turning, faced his brother in the falling dusk. His face and his voice were very grave, James thought that he seemed suddenly older and taller.

"Look," he said, "what you or I think doesn't really matter.

38

If he *does*, he is the guiding hand as it were—well and good, if he just lies there and she talks to him, even if he doesn't understand a word—well, it's something that gives Mum an additional sense of security. She's got a pretty tough proposition to handle, and if this—bit of imagination helps her, then we must just take it and accept it if that's how she wants it."

James wrinkled his forehead, puzzled and even disturbed.

"You mean—keep up this—pretence?"

"If it is pretence, yes."

"P'raps for years, Mike."

"For years, if necessary. It will be easier once we've got used to it. Personally I think it's a pretty gallant effort on Mum's part."

"I suppose it is, come to look at it. All right, Mike. I'll go back to Blamey."

When they got back to supper, Ada met them smiling brightly. "There you are! Here's the boys, Grandma. Grandma's been in Huddersley shopping. Dad wanted some new pyjamas. At first he was wearing night-shirts, but he grumbled that they were old-fashioned, so Grandma went to get some to-day."

They sat down to supper, plentiful and well cooked as all the meals were at the farm. Lamb chops, mashed potatoes and green peas. Grandma said, "These deep-freeze peas are a boon and a blessing. Just like fresh peas they are."

Ada nodded, "Wonderful invention. Well, Michael, I had a talk with your father, he woke up while you two were out. Very spry, he was too." She laughed. "He was funny. He said that at sixteen he'd left school over a year, and that if you liked to come on to the farm, he'd no objection." She beamed at her son, and Michael saw the whole thing, not as something slightly fantastic, but as profoundly pathetic. His mother was determined to see that Enoch was still acknowledged. He felt his eyes smart suddenly, and in the effort to overcome his rush of emotion, said in an over-hearty voice:

"I say, that's jolly decent. Tell Dad that I won't let him down."

"I'd have liked you to have a little talk with him," Ada said, "but what with the doctor, and these new pyjamas Gran's bought, he seemed a bit tired. The nurse has settled him down for the night."

James said, "And did you say anything about me, Mum?"

"I did not, and shan't either. You'll stay at school while you're sixteen—at least. So let's hear no more of it."

James mumbled, "All right, I only asked."

Next day Michael walked over to Cummings to see George Tancred. He found him in a serious mood, but ready to approve of the decision which Michael had made.

"Get on the land," he said, "there's going to be a war, and it will be the most devastating war in history. On the land, you'd be indispensable, they'd not drag you into the Army."

Michael asked, "And you, George? How about you?"

George shrugged his shoulders. "Oh, I should go." He grinned suddenly. "I'd leave you to carry on, Cummings and Anderson's. I'm a Territorial officer. Anyway—I should go. I'm under forty—" his grin deepened, "though not much! Oh, I should go."

"Why not me then—if there is to be a war?"

George stared at him. "Because I hope you'd not be such a bloody young fool as to stick your neck out."

Michael hoped that he might see Liz, his memory of her was vague. Someone who was slim, and beautifully groomed, who spoke in a voice which was indolent, and yet could quicken when the subject was anything which interested her. Her face, features and even the colour of her eyes eluded him. He only knew that he would like to see her.

"How's Liz?" he asked.

George said, "Very well and busy as usual. Now come with me, and I'll show you how we do things here."

He enjoyed his morning. George Tancred loved his farm, his stock and his mechanical contrivances. He talked well and lucidly, and Michael, eager and thirsting for knowledge, hung on every word. George introduced the farm hands to him. "Michael Anderson—this is Harris. Famous with hens—any kind of poultry. Only remember none of this new-fangled battery nonsense. The quality of the eggs isn't the same." Then, "Here's Willett, now what he doesn't know about stock isn't worth knowing." And so it went on, while Michael made mental notes of names and abilities.

To Wilson, Enoch Anderson's hind, George said, "Now, Wilson. Here's young Mr. Michael, coming to give us a hand when I've got to go marching off to the wars——"

Wilson shook his head, "Nay, Measter Garge, dean't be talkin' that road. Haven't Mister Chamberlain fetched home a sheet o' paper, writ i' yon Hitler's own hand to say as never 'ul his country an' ours fight battles agean."

40

"Germany!" George said. "That's not Hitler's country! He's an Austrian. However—there was another piece of paper—way back in 1914, and the Germans stated that was how they regarded it—as a scrap of paper. Well, here in Yorkshire, we'll be prepared and so I want Mr. Michael to have all the help which you can give him."

"Reight," Wilson said, "reight Mr. Tancred, he'll get it."

Back in George's study, he sat back in his desk chair and talked. Michael felt that in the last few months George Tancred had grown older, that there were new lines round his eyes, and that the eyes themselves looked tired—even a little anxious.

George leaned back in his desk chair and surveyed the room. "Nice room," he said inconsequently. "I've always liked it."

"A good room to work in," Michael agreed.

"Have you seen Liz yet?" Michael nodded, he had seen her for a few seconds only when she came over to Anderson's to ask after his father. "How d'you think she's looking?"

Michael smiled, "As always—charming and immaculate."

"She'll be a great help to you. Liz knows all the answers—or nearly all of them."

"George," Michael leaned forward, his slim brown hands between his knees, "you seem certain that there's going to be a war. Is it really as certain as you seem to think?"

"If you let a mad dog loose in a flock of sheep you can be pretty certain some of them are going to get worried. I'm not a clever chap, but I can remember the first war——" he laughed. "First war, no one knows when the first war was, do they? There have always been wars, the history books are crammed with them. I'm certain that they all spring from the same set of causes— greed, envy and fear. Get some hot-headed, shrieking idiot to play on those three strings, to know what is the right way to make a people hysterical, to forget everything except the fact that *they* want to be top dog—and you're all set for a first-class war. In '14 it was that mountebank, William the Second, play-acting, self-sufficient fool; now it's this scruffy little creature who looks a little like Charlie Chaplin with the brains left out. William and Hitler are using the same technique, and as I see it, they'll get the same results.

"Chamberlain has got a breathing space for us, but it won't be 'peace in our time', it will be just long enough for us to draw a breath, to get over our surprise at the impudence of this neurotic fellow actually—promising to be a good boy and play happily in

41

his own back yard." He threw back his head and laughed. "Gosh, it's amazing! However, until it does come—we must make as much hay as we can while the sun shines. Make plans, have a properly planned policy. . . ."

The sense of tension persisted, then slowly Michael felt that men's minds relaxed, they shrugged their shoulders and said that after all, as far as Czechoslovakia went there might have been faults on both sides, and anyway—what could Britain have done? Austria, well—Dolfuss might have been all right, but we didn't want the whole of Europe turning Fascists.

"Oh, yes, Dolfuss was a Fascist all right," a man told Michael.

"Well, what about Hitler?"

"Nazi, my boy, Nazi."

"It amounts to the same thing surely."

"Good lord no! Completely different!"

Michael was enjoying his work, he felt his muscles hardening, he no longer felt half exhausted at the end of a long day. It gave him a sense of pleasure to feel that he could work from early morning until the last light faded, and return home filled with a sense of well-being. Harris, Willett and Wilson all worked with him loyally, and always as a guiding hand was George Tancred. Michael's admiration for him grew every day. He gave his orders clearly and crisply, he listened to complaints and delivered judgement fairly and impartially.

One evening in August, Michael stood, his arms folded on the top bar of one of the good oak gates which were one of the small features of Cummings Farm, and stared out over the wide pasture. He started, for George Tancred had come up silently, and was standing beside him.

"It's nice," he said. "Nice, isn't it, Michael?"

Michael nodded, he felt his throat contract suddenly—the pasture, growing thick and green since the hay harvest, the trim hedges, the trees with their beautiful form and wide-spreading branches, the scent of meadow-sweet reached him, in the half light he could see the dim shapes of dog-roses in the hedgerow. There on the right, he could see Willett's cottage, there was a light shining through the curtains, and he could imagine how they were all gathered in their comfortable kitchen.

He said, a trifle huskily, "Yes, it's jolly nice."

"Not grand," George said. "Not magnificent like the Alps, or splendid like the Dolomites, we've no great gushing rivers like the Rhone, or the Danube, we've not got Canada's lakes—" he chuckled, "we shouldn't have room for them! We're small, but we are that 'precious stone set in a silver sea', and—by God, it's worth fighting for."

Michael sighed, "You're very sure——"

"You mean that I don't wear blinkers. Michael, look after Liz. Don't let her either over-work or—under-work, one's as bad as the other." After a pause he went on, "It's a pity things change, and yet I don't know. They say that change means progress. Anyway, it's no good going on with artificial respiration when you know the patient's dead. Come on, my lad, time that you were home. Look, there's the first star. . . ."

Two days later he said to Michael with something like quiet elation, "It's almost here. Germany has signed a pact with Russia."

Then Germany invaded Poland, and George shrugged and said, "That shows what guarantees are worth. Poor devils."

That night when he and Liz sat in the candle-lit dining-room, when the table had been cleared of everything except decanters and glasses, George chose a cigar with great care; then rose and lit her cigarette for her and returned to his chair. He sat, watching her intently, through the haze of his cigar smoke, so they sat in silence for some time. To Liz it seemed an eternity.

He watched her appraisingly. No, she wasn't beautiful, but she had an almost devastating attraction. Yet now that attraction, which had once made his blood run hot, made his temples pound, had gone. She was just—Liz, his good friend and companion, the woman he liked best in the world. Liked. A line of Wilde's ran through his head:

'Hadst thou liked me less and loved me more . . .' yet that didn't quite meet the case. Which of them had ceased to love first? He didn't know. Yet looking back, he thought that as love had died, liking, respect, admiration had grown.

There she sat, smoking quietly, completely mistress of herself, yet George had the impression that she was—waiting. Not with any apprehension, not fearfully as if expecting a sudden blow, but waiting for the inevitable from which she knew that there was no escape.

He said, "Liz, I've got to talk to you. You don't mind?"

She met his eyes, and smiled. "No, George, of course I don't."

"There'll be war to-morrow. We shall hear it. That thin, impersonal, honest voice of Chamberlain's. On the radio. Then, I shall have to be off. I have papers warning me. You don't have to worry, I've left everything in order, and there's oodles for you."

Her smile seemed a little wintry. "I have plenty of my own."

"I know that, I'm glad of it, but I'd like Cummings kept up properly. "The war may take a long time to win——"

She interrupted, "But you believe that we *shall* win!"

His still youthful grin broke out. "We shall lose practically every battle except the last. Oh, we shall win it all right. Only, I don't somehow believe that I shall be here for—the Victory March."

"George, what nonsense! Why should you think that?"

"I don't *think*. I *feel* it. Liz, this part isn't so easy. There is omeone—well, someone of whom I'm very fond."

"I thought so, my dear."

"She's not, not your sort. She's kind and nice, she's pretty and—yes, she's good. The whole thing was my fault. Not that I regret it, except for the fact that it may hurt you, it's been worth it. But—here's the rest of it. There's a little girl, she's two."

For the first time he saw Liz move, she stubbed out her cigarette with a movement which was almost convulsive. A little girl. If she could have given him a child, he would still have loved her, and she might still find him the ideal lover. As things had worked out she was the barren wife, no matter how efficient, how companionable she might be, while this other woman—fruitful, able to bear his children, held him because of that one fact alone.

She tried to remember phrases which she had heard—'Men live to produce and reproduce their kind', and 'A man who had a child to a woman he loves, feels that he can never be completely obliterated', 'Men long for children because they cannot bear the thought that their personality is . . .' mentally she cried, 'Stop! don't go on stringing silly, cynical sentences together. Come down to facts. Face everything.'

George was sitting, his shoulders humped a little over the broad shining table. He looked heavy and dispirited. He was watching the blue smoke of his cigar, intently but idly. She looked at him, kindly and without passion. Only regretting that her own disability—a disability which she would have given everything she possessed to escape, had prevented her giving him what it was obvious meant so much to him.

She said, her voice very low and warm, "Yes—tell me."

"You don't mind, Liz?"

"Only that I couldn't give you children."

"You mean that, you really mean it?"

Her steady eyes met his. "On my word of honour I mean it."

44

He sighed, "She's a dear little girl. Well, I've left sufficient if I'm for it, to attend to her education and bringing up. No, not finishing schools in Paris——"

Liz laughed and was surprised to find how easy it was to laugh. "And now I speak French so atrociously, George."

He continued as if she had not spoken, "But to make it possible for her to earn a good living. I don't mean as a shop girl, but something that will give her—opportunities. You don't mind, Liz, don't mind that I've provided for her—decently?"

"My dear, it's your money. I have plenty. I shall have more one day—though I hope it won't be for many years—you've done what is right. And—her mother?" That had been more difficult to say.

"She'll be all right. She's young——"

Liz thought, 'I'm not really young any longer!'

"She's pretty——"

'I was never that,' she thought, 'people used to say that I was attractive, and smart and even amusing.'

How queer it was to be sitting opposite to George discussing the future of his mistress and his child. Yet it didn't seem to matter very much. Liz felt no particular sense of loss, only a regret that —everything was finished. No! everything wasn't finished, she and George still had that wonderful sense of companionship, that was why he could talk to her—frankly—as he was doing.

One of the candles in their silver holders guttered.

She said, "Snuff that candle, George, please."

He stared at it, there was a long trail of wax winding down the candle. She saw his intent expression, and said, "What is it?"

"What in the West Riding they call a—winding sheet in the candle. Perhaps it's an omen."

She felt suddenly irritated, it seemed that George was determined that he was going to be killed, was almost deriving some satisfaction from the thought.

"Don't be so childish! Because the draught catches the soft wax in a certain way, what on earth can that have to do with— winding sheets? Anyway, they don't use winding sheets any more."

Carefully he snuffed the candle, his eyes still sombre.

Liz thought, 'How men love to dramatize themselves!'

She said, speaking carefully and evenly, "If—I say—if with emphasis, anything should happen—and it might happen to me just as easily as to you—bombs and all the rest of it. Colonel

45

Blenkiron talked about a 'civilian war'—would you like—this—this lady to come here?" She wished that she had possessed the courage to say 'woman'. Somehow 'lady' sounded so patronizing.

George lifted his head and stared. "Come here. Mavis! She'd loathe it. She knows nothing of the country beyond Blubberhouse Moor, the Red Lion at South Stainley and the Bolton Arms."

Mavis! Liz smothered a sense of hysterical amusement—that George should have a mistress called—Mavis! She thought that she was growing a little hysterical, the whole scene had played too long. It was time that the curtain came down.

"You'll leave early in the morning, then?"

"Yes—early in the morning. No, Liz, if anything should happen to me or to you—young Michael might not be a bad bet. He's keen, I think he'll be efficient." He rose and leaving his cigar to burn itself out, came round to where Liz sat. He laid his hand on her shoulder, and looking up she met his rather tired eyes.

"It's been a good time, Liz," he said, "maybe it hasn't lasted —as we hoped that it might, but there's been friendship, and a community of everything, and friendship—and well—thank you for everything. You've been a grand pal——"

She took his hand and laid it lightly against her cheek.

"One day when this infernal madness is over—we'll have other good times, George."

He drew his hand away almost abruptly. "Good-night," he said. She sat alone for a long time, listening to the measured ticking of the big clock in the hall. A nice, steady, reassuring sound. The chapter was closed—it had opened at a dance, when she wore pale green—which didn't really suit her. He had looked so well groomed, so friendly, that she felt her heart go out to him. Then the excitement of being engaged, Harry Goswell beaming with satisfaction, and saying, "He's a nice lad, and a clever lad. More than that he's got enough brass—aye, and more to do the things he wants. As we say in Yorkshire, 'Don't marry for money, but go where money is!' "

Liz remembered that she had cried indignantly, "Uncle Harry, I'd not care if George hadn't a bean!"

Their wedding, the whole thing was as if seen through a haze, or like a photograph which has faded a little. The scent of flowers, a tiny piece of buckram in her sleeve which scratched and irritated her. The heavy scent of flowers, herself standing with Uncle Harry in the porch, conscious that the arm which he offered her was shaking. Her own whisper, "You're more nervous than I am!"

46

His hoarse reply, "Don't talk such rubbish, Liz!"

Then the Bridal March from Lohengrin—which she never liked—and she pressed her uncle's arm, whispering, "Our cue!"

The aisle which seemed like a mile walk, faces turned to watch her, all slightly out of focus. Then George and his best man taking shape, standing out clearly, the white carnations in their button-holes looking startlingly distinct.

The smooth, rather unctuous voice of the officiating clergy-man, then moving into the vestry and wishing that it was larger. She felt stifled in the crowd. In the car with George, who held her hand and assured her that he'd not go through it again for all the tea in China.

She laughed, "You won't be asked to—unless it's with some-one else, and I shan't let you go!"

Standing with George under a huge bell of white flowers, thanking people, shaking hands, leaning forward to kiss cheeks which smelt either of expensive scent or equally expensive shaving cream.

George groaning softly, "Lord, these damned boots pinch!"

She whispered back, "Slip upstairs and change them—Hector will show you your room."

"Could I? By Jove, I will, this is agony!"

The moment he had gone everyone was asking, "Oh, Liz dear —such a lovely wedding. Why where's George?"

Liz attempting to look faintly embarrassed replied, "George? Oh, he won't be a minute."

Old Aunt Cawther who had come over from Colne, attired in purple—the hottest shade of purple imaginable, and a bonnet which waved with purple 'tips'—like an old-fashioned funeral hearse, said, "Aye, it's the excitement and the fizzy wine that does it."

George returned, wearing the most shockingly old pair of shoes, grinning and murmuring, "That's sheer heaven! I've had this pair for seven years—good as new."

"Their looks belie them," Liz assured him.

Finally changing, coming down the wide stairs, seeing George standing waiting, holding out his hand, smiling.

"Good thing we're getting away. I should have had one glass too many in another five minutes!"

"Sure you haven't had it already?"

"Oh, Liz—look at that!" as he executed a particularly neat turn. The town was left behind, they drove through little peaceful villages, where houses, washed the colour of good cream, nestled under wide eaves, standing in gardens gay with flowers. They crossed old stone bridges, which spanned chattering, shallow rivers; and once came to a water splash, where, George told her, when the river was in flood you had to go five miles out of your way to find a bridge. Finally as the bright daylight was beginning to fade, they drove through Barnsley and out into the country again.

She had visited the farm-house several times, but thought that she had never seen it look so attractive. Not unlike Cummings, she rememberd, though smaller. Two-storeyed, with gables set in the fine grey stone roof. Everything meticulously kept, borders trimmed exactly, the window frames shining with bright new paint.

George said, "Well, we're home, Liz. Now don't walk in, I've got to carry you over the threshold. My domestic staff rule me with a rod of iron and warned me gravely about that before I left."

He carried her easily, and she went into her new home laughing and half protesting. Some servants were waiting—a very stout, elderly woman. "Mrs. Robbins, our invaluable cook—Maude, and Ellen. This is Fred Mullins, who looks after the garden for us, and this is his son, Young Fred. Now, Mrs. Robbins, where's that champagne?"

"All laid out ready, sir. This way if you please, M'um."

They filed into the quiet room, George talking all the time. "Glasses—that's right. Liz dear, here's your second wedding cake. Mrs. Robbins insisted on making it, so you can cut it now."

"Mrs. Robbins, how kind of you——"

"Nay, M'um, it's not all I could wish. T'cake itself is over new. I began to mak' it the morning as Mr. George told us as he was engaged—I'd have liked it kept a bit longer m'self."

"If you'd told me, Mrs. Robbins, we'd have postponed the wedding," Liz said.

They drank her health; gradually the health of everyone present was drunk, when Mrs. Robbins, glancing at the clock on the tall mantelpiece, changed from being a red-faced, stout countrywoman into a martinet.

"Luke at the time! M'um, you must excuse me, there's my dinner to think about. Fred have you an' Young Fred got the luggage up? Maude, take Madam up to her room, maybe you'd like Maude to unpack for you? That's right, Maude. Ellen, get all this cleared away and start laying your table. You sent the flowers in, didn't you, Fred?"

It all came back so clearly, the dinner—eaten at the same table as the one she sat at to-night. Waking to turn and look at George, his hair tumbled, and the bristles on his cheeks showing golden in the morning sunshine. He looked very young when he slept, and Liz felt a rush of tenderness sweep over her. He stirred as if conscious through the mists of sleep that she was watching him. His eyes opened, he blinked hard, then stretching out his hand pulled her down beside him, murmuring, "It's all true—it's not a dream."

"It's all true, darling."

And now, he had gone merely saying, "Good-night". He was in love with someone called Mavis, had a little girl—she must remember to get the proper address, because—her mind baulked at the thought—if anything happened, someone would have to let—Mavis know.

She went up to her room, there was a light in George's study as she passed, for a second she wondered whether she should go in and say 'Good-night' again, then decided against it. He might be writing last-minute letters—might be writing to Mavis as he used to write to her—letters which were invariably short, not very well expressed and yet filled with affection. Liz went up the stairs, and to her own surprise felt suddenly not only unbearably tired but terribly sleepy. When she woke in the morning Maude brought in her early tea, on the tray was a large square envelope—the kind George always used.

"The master went off about seven, M'um." Maude sniffed tearfully at the recollection. "Wouldn't have you wakened, not was it ever so. 'Let Madam have her sleep out,' that was what he said. Not many gentleman 'ud have that much thought, as Mrs. Robbins said, 'It just goes to show the kind gentleman 'e is.'"

Liz slit open the envelope, it was like George to have slipped away without waking her. Whether it was consideration, or his dread of a possible scene, tears, reproaches, she didn't know—she didn't really care. She only knew that she was going to miss him deeply, that life would be lonely without him.

She was glad that they had moved to Cummings, not so very different from the old farm, and yet not crowded with memories of those days when they had been so much in love. Here, George had become her friend, her close and much loved friend, but the other George—her lover—had been left behind in the old house.

49

She drew out his letter. *My dear Liz—I didn't want to wake you. Don't worry and as for that matter I spoke of last night—Claygate has all instructions. He'll see to it all if necessary. Take care of yourself. It's been a grand time taking it by and large, and thank you. My love to you, G.*

Chapter Four

GEORGE had stopped the car for a moment at Anderson's on his way. He had shaken hands with Gran, taken Ada in his arms and whispered, "Carry on, hold the fort, old girl!" accepted a cup of tea and a slice of toast, had asked Michael to walk back to the car with him, shaken hands firmly and without any trace of emotion, then as he got in and banged the door, he had leaned out and said, "Mike—here, just a minute." Michael came nearer, "Take hold of everything. The men are all right, but they need direction. Back your own fancy. You're young but you can study, and I believe that you will. Everything's tiptop now, see that you keep it that way. And—Liz, look after Liz. She thinks that she knows it all—well, she knows a whole lot, but remember the farm's your business. Claygate, my lawyer knows all about it. When you see Liz, give her my love. She's a grand scout. Well, s'long Mike, and all the best."

Michael walked back to the house, he felt depressed and yet elated. Depressed because George had gone, and gone with that queer certainty that he would never come back, and elated because he was now, a 'master man'. He knew that George, with his orderly mind, would have made every possible arrangement, and that Claygate had his instructions. But he had—he smiled at the thought—a mandate from the reigning monarch, and he walked back to Anderson's, his shoulders squared, determined that whenever George returned to Cummings, he should find it kept as well as careful direction and hard work could keep it.

Since Enoch's illness Ada had taken to returning home at mid-day; she stayed for an hour and then rushed back in her little car to grapple with the business at the shop. During the last year, she had improved the place out of all knowledge. She had bought the café, and also the haberdasher's; always insisting when customers commented on the improvements, "Well, it's what I always say—my husband may be laid by—temporarily—but he's a fine business man, and I'm fortunate to have his advice. In fact, what I should have done without his invaluable—for invaluable it is—help, I scarcely dare think! Lost, I should have been—completely lost!"

A few days after George's departure, Michael came into dinner, hearing as he always did, Grandma's warning voice, "Mind your boots now, if they're clarty—don't go messing up our clean passage." He called back cheerfully, "They're not clarty, Gran— I'll watch your precious passage."

They were just about to sit down at the table, when his mother burst into the big, bright kitchen. Her usually high-coloured face was drained of all colour, she pressed one hand to her breast as if the heavy beating of her heart oppressed her.

Gran said, "Nay, our Ada—whatever's wrong now?"

Michael took her gently by the arm and propelled her towards the big arm-chair which stood by the shining oven. "There, there, Mum," he murmured, "shall I run up and see if there's anything I can do for Dad? He's all right, isn't he? Come now, Mum— try not to be so upset. Tell us what it is."

She raised her eyes, he saw that they were swimming with tears. "Nothing wrong—that's just it—everything's right! Oh, dear—lend me your handkerchief, Mike——" she wiped her eyes and leaned back in the chair, while Michael stood watching her affectionately.

"Tell us, dear," he urged gently.

"He's spoken my name! He has—plain as plain—A-da, just like that. Quite clear, just a bit of hesitation, but his eyes bright and his voice steady. Oh, what it did to me! 'A-da,' he said, like that."

Neither Michael nor old Mrs. Cawther spoke, they had for months tacitly accepted Ada's stories as to what Enoch had said, what Enoch had advised, and they had made no comment. Whatever their thoughts had been, they had kept those thoughts to themselves.

Michael said, "Now that's wonderful news, Mum. You'll see it will be full steam ahead from now on! Now, come and have your dinner."

She caught his hand and held it tightly. "I don't know that I want anything—I'm just so full of happiness."

"Just the same," Gran said, "you'll come and eat your dinner, and keep up your strength. And as well as being filled wi' happiness, I'd like to hear you mention—thankfulness. Thankfulness to One Above—yes, Michael, I'll have a few more peas, and another potato."

That afternoon, when Ada went forward to attend personally to one of her 'specials', she had reverted to her old method of referring to her husband. Just for the length of that brief scene in

52

the kitchen at Anderson's had she admitted the true state of affairs; now, mistress of herself once more, she fell back on—pretence.

"Good afternoon, Mrs. Rawsley—the curtain material. Certainly, it came in this morning, it will be up at the Grange by tea time."

"Splendid—though from what I hear we shall all be forced to hang dreadful dark curtains at the windows to prevent any light showing. Our houses will look simply awful! Still—we shall have to get used to it. What about food, Mrs. Anderson? People say that it's going to be terribly short. Is it?"

Ada pursed her lips. "I was discussing that with my husband only this dinner time. There'll be a shortage of certain commodities, he says, but—oh, we shan't starve, Madam—that's his considered opinion. Certain things will be—so he thinks—rationed pretty carefully. But on one thing he is determined, while we have the stock we shall be—these are his words—completely impartial. There'll be no preferential treatment for anyone."

Mrs. Rawsley nodded, "I suppose he's right. Still, there are *some* things that *we* are accustomed to, things which make no appeal to—to well, the lower classes. Take those delicacies you have in that case there——" she waved a well-gloved hand in the direction of Ada's huge case which held 'specialities'. "You don't expect your servants to appreciate things of that kind, surely? They wouldn't *want* them!"

Ada disliked Mrs. Rawsley, and when she left, though Ada accompanied her to the door reassuring her that the curtain material would be delivered "on our next delivery", she walked back to her own office her expression grim, and her lips pursed.

'If they want them, if they can pay for them, they'll get them, Mrs. Rawsley or no Mrs. Rawsley! *They!* as if working people belonged to a different breed. They're British, they'll go out to fight for their country, they'll run the risk of being killed—same as Mrs. Rawsley's sons.'

It seemed to Michael that at last his father was making progress. He thought that his skin looked less pallid, his eyes were certainly brighter, and held the light of intelligence. Even the useless hand appeared to show faint signs of life. It was Michael who had the idea of giving his father a little soft rubber ball to hold, and showed him how to try to press it gently with his fingers. He watched Enoch's eyes, and felt that he was comprehending what Michael said.

A few days later, when Michael visited him, he turned his eyes to the bedside table where the little ball lay, and with an effort, enunciated, " 'All. 'All."

"You want the ball, Dad," his father's eyelids drooped, his son felt that he wished to signify acquiescence. "There you are!" He folded the still chilly fingers round the rubber, and waited.

Faintly the fingers moved. It was so small a movement as to be almost imperceptible, but—they moved.

Enoch met his son's eyes again. " 'Ook," he said, " 'ook!"

Michael exclaimed, "Splendid, Dad, splendid. Go on at this rate and we shall have you playing for Yorkshire next year!"

He fancied that he saw a sudden gleam of amusement in Enoch's eyes, and went away well satisfied.

He thought that his mother was experiencing a second blooming; with each day after her visits to her husband she came down smiling and obviously well content. Michael wondered how much personal satisfaction she was deriving from the firm belief that her prognostications regarding Enoch showed signs of being fulfilled, if not completely at least sufficiently to prove that she had been right.

His admiration for her had grown ever since his father's illness. She had shouldered burdens, faced problems, dealt with various difficulties and had never forgotten, what George called, her 'Spenlow Jorkin's role' making Enoch always appear to be the power behind the throne.

For himself, he was quietly happy. He loved the land, loved efficiency and ability. The men who worked with him were generous, faithful and loyal. If suggestions were to be made, they were made tactfully and without the least hint that they knew better than he did.

"I 'ad thought, Mister Michael, if you approved——" or "D'you know I was thinkin' last neight, as if we was to——" Never teaching him, always suggesting that here was an idea which might appeal to him.

His knowledge was growing, he was making plans against the time when the greatest need of Britain would be food. He planned to have the lawn at Anderson's dug up and planted with potatoes, he thought that they might do the same with the lawns at Cummings. True, it was a pity, for those smooth, velvet green lawns were the result of years of rolling and watering, but—if potatoes were worth more than the beauty of vividly green lawns—then the lawns must go.

54

He saw very little of Liz. After George had gone she went off to visit her Aunt Alice, she brought her back to Cummings for a time, and appeared to be immersed in looking after the elderly woman who was in failing health. From time to time Michael met her, asked for news of George, gave his quick report as to the running of Anderson's and Cummings, receiving from Liz her enchanting smile, and the assurance that George was completely happy that he was 'at the helm'.

"That's pretty generous of him," Michael said.

She smiled, "George is generous, but never without reason to back his generosity. Michael, why don't you come over to dinner one evening? There are so many things I want to talk to you about, and—without promising you a gala evening, at least you'd have a chance to talk over your plans."

He said, "That sounds lovely, Liz. I'd like it. Thanks a lot."

"To-day's Tuesday—say Thursday. Yes?"

"I shall look forward to it."

He watched her walk away, her beautiful, long legs encased in well-cut slacks; her shoulders square, her small, neatly shaped head erect.

That mid-day he said to Gran that he had seen Liz. She nodded.

"Poor lass, I'll lay that she misses George."

"She seemed pretty cheerful. Looked nice too."

"Wearing those trousers wimmen wear these days, eh? Well, I will say this for our Liz, most of 'em looks proper sights. Either they have the bottoms that tight that you see—everything, or they have 'em that slack they look like wasps—aye, you know how a wasp's bottom always seems to hang down! Liz gets them right somehow."

"I expect that she goes to a good tailor, Gran."

"Happen."

On Thursday Michael experienced a real sense of pleasure. He bathed luxuriously, shaved meticulously, and gave a little shiver of pleasure as he drew on his silk socks, and felt that smooth linen of his shirt slip over his shoulders. His dinner-jacket felt light and distinctly pleasant.

Gran said, "Eh, look who's here! All dolled up no less."

Ada looked at him lovingly. "Mike, slip up and say 'Good-night' to Dad."

"Of course, Mum."

Enoch was propped against his pillows as usual, but his

colour was better, his eyes brighter, and when Michael entered he raised his head and sent a smile—a rather lop-sided smile—but a smile nevertheless.

"Hello, Dad, I've just come to say, 'Good-night'."

Enoch moved his head a little. "'Ook smar'. 'Ike to see man 'ook smar'. Have a goo' time."

"Good-night, Dad."

"'Oo' ni'."

When he went to the parlour, Ada said eagerly, "What did he say?" Michael smiled, "Said that I looked damned smart, that he liked to see a fellow look well turned out; he hoped that I'd have a good time."

Ada shot a glance at Grandma. "Always one of the noticing ones, our Enoch. Nothing misses him."

He walked over the field path to Cummings. Although it was only the end of May, the light still lingered. He walked slowly, savouring the soft air, sniffing the scents of flowers and blossom with appreciation. He knew that his love of the country was growing and deepening every day, he felt that he was putting out roots into the very ground, roots which would hold fast for the rest of his life. Country sights and sounds tugged at his heart strings, stirred him emotionally, made him stronger month by month in his determination to give the land of his very best—his brain, his sinews, his energy should all be dedicated to the land.

True, if the war continued he would do his military service as soon as his age permitted it. No use George telling him not to be a bloody fool and stick his neck out, to explain that he would be able to get exemption on account of his work—he couldn't do that. Not that he wanted to be a soldier, not that he had any wild dreams of winning fame and glory; he had no illusions about modern warfare, it would be exceedingly unpleasant, excessively uncomfortable and remarkably dangerous, but Michael could not imagine himself trying to hide behind his trade while other men went out and risked their lives.

He was nearly seventeen, in another year—if the war lasted so long—he would have to leave this land to the care of others. It seemed idle even to try to believe that his father would ever be able to take an active part in the running of Anderson's and Cummings; he might improve sufficiently to give advice—and sound advice—but that would be the extent of his activities. The men would do their best, he knew that he could trust Willett implicitly—and he was over age for the Army. And Liz—George admitted that Liz 'knew the answers'. The men admired her ability, and their innate loyalty to George Tancred would be a further influence.

Michael felt his heart warm towards Liz Tancred; he had never known her particularly well, though her looks had appealed to his youthful and slightly romantic taste. He liked her crisp, clear voice, the air of poise and certainty which was so much part of her. He could not imagine Liz fumbling about anything— whether it were physical or mental—her movements, and her decisions would always be quick, exact and clear cut.

He reached the gates of Cummings, those oak gates pleased him. He felt that there was something essentially suitable in the gates of an English farm being made of English oak. One day, perhaps, since his land and George's marched together, he might be able to afford oak gates for Anderson's.

George had said, "Yes, I know what they say—that I've more money than sense putting so much money into gates. Let them say what they like, my gates will be standing, as good as ever, when theirs are needing painting and repairing, and half of them rotting to pieces."

Michael swung open the gate, and entered the short drive which led to the house. He remembered how George had told him that a good farmer had to have eyes at the back of his head, "and the more like gimlets they are—the better". Michael was training himself not only to see but to observe and to remember. Nothing was too small, nothing but must have its rightful place in the general scheme of things.

The drive was well kept, the edges of the lawn exactly and meticulously clipped, the bushes properly tended, he heard a dog bark and wondered where it was kept, if it was properly exercised every day. The idea of a dog being kept continually on a chain always infuriated him. No, Liz would never allow that, he felt certain.

The house pleased him, it looked elegant for all its simplicity. He smiled. As if it had taken on Liz's habit of always looking immaculate! The door was opened to him by Maude, and the impression which she gave of neat efficiency pleased him. The hall was cool and gave a rather fictitious air of space, for in reality it was very little larger than their entrance at Anderson's. Michael wondered why they never used the front door but invariably came in through the door which opened on to the farm-yard.

"Good evening, Master Michael, Madam is waiting for you in the parlour," Maude said, and again he liked the old-fashioned word—parlour.

Liz rose as he entered, her hand outstretched. "This is nice!"

"It was nice of you to ask me."

She was wearing a dress of some lacy material, rather long. It looked light and fragile, Michael thought, and her neck showed very white against the dark material. Her hair was smooth, cut short and waved closely to her head. To Michael she seemed the epitome of elegance.

"A cocktail?" Liz asked.

"I'd like one."

She handed him the small glass, then sat down on the wide sofa, saying, "I've got a lot to say—I hope you're willing to listen. It's all—a dead secret. You know what is happening in France?"

He nodded, "Nothing very good, they say they're going to evacuate the British — yes, and the French. It's pretty awful."

She looked him squarely in the eyes. "It will be slaughter!"

For a moment he wondered if she was trying to show him that he ought to join the Forces, lie about his age, enlist somewhere where he wasn't known, where they'd accept him.

"Do you think that I ought to——"

Almost irritably she answered, "Go and join up? No, no most emphatically. Stay where you are, go on with your job, you're doing it very well. Listen, I went down to see my aunt—she's at Bournemouth. I felt that this was coming. The Dutch surrendered, the Belgians surrendered this morning! I don't blame them, they have their own skins to save, but"—she leaned forward, so that the light caught her hair and made it shine with new lights—"it's going to be hell for our men. The Maginot line! I always suspected that it was overrated, as if any 'line' can hold back such an inrush, particularly when their hearts—the French —aren't in it. They've had no help from their own people—and so now they'll blame us, because we didn't send them the troops we—hadn't got.

"I'm leaving in the car the moment dinner's over. I bought a boat when I was staying with my aunt. It's being taken to Dover. That's where it will be at the moment. She's a good boat, and I've managed—that means anything you like—to get a supply of petrol. How I wangled!" Her eyes were alight, and a flush showed in her cheeks. She looked very young, excited. Michael frowned.

58

"I don't understand, Liz," he said. "A boat, a supply of petrol?"

"Listen!" she ordered, suddenly tense, all the excitement subdued. "Boats—hundreds of boats, they'll be wanted to take the men off. Transport—poof! German bombers overhead, everything that floats a target. They'll be there, small boats, rowing boats, motor boats—if they can only take a couple of men —they'll take them. I can take eight, ten at a pinch."

"You don't mean that you're——"

"Don't be an owl, Michael. Of course I'm going. Dover to Dunkirk. As many trips as I can make—always provided the Huns don't get me. I shan't be alone, every bit of small craft on the South coast will be there. Now what I want you to do, is to keep quiet about it. If I get back—well and good, if I don't— then you can talk if you want to. I'm not doing it just for an adventure, but I owe a debt and I want to pay it."

"A debt?"

"To George. Years ago, when we were married, I realized that he wanted children, wanted them desperately. Because I was conceited, because I wanted to dress as all other women did, wear heels which were heaven knows how high—well, I had a nasty fall. That meant, so I heard later, that George would never get his children. That's when I contracted my debt. I don't suppose that I shall find George on the beach at Dunkirk, but if I can manage to get half a dozen men away—I shall feel that I've wiped out my obligation—in part anyway."

Michael stared at her. She looked so exquisite, so beautifully groomed that the idea of her launching herself off into desperate danger, discomfort, and acute peril seemed fantastic.

"Liz," he said, "Liz, you can't!"

She smiled, and said, "Mike, Mike—I can! Another cocktail. I make them rather well, don't you think?"

Absently he replied, "Magnificently." Then he said impulsively, "Liz, you can't do this. Let me go instead. I can handle a boat. You can say you wanted me to go to London to get machinery, permits, anything you like—but don't go."

"Haven't you heard the warnings?" she was still smiling. "That we're all in the front line in this war—which up to now people have called 'phoney'. Well, here's a civilian who wants to get to the front line."

"Then let me come with you."

"To take up a precious place in my boat? No, my dear. You'll stay here, and do your job, and look after the letters I've written

59

—just in case. Remind me to give them to you before you go. Now—dinner, and I hope that you're hungry."

He followed her into the rather austere dining-room, where the table glittered and gleamed with silver and glass. As they seated themselves, Liz gave him a quick warning glance, and laid her finger on her lips enjoining silence.

Michael knew that all appetite had left him. He saw that the cold soup was perfectly prepared, that the roast duck was crisp and browned to a nicety, the orange salad would have tempted him at any other time. Now, he could think only of what Liz had told him, allowing his anxiety to take away his appetite and make him feel irritable and nervous.

Liz driving to London through the night, Liz going to Dover or wherever it was she had the boat waiting. Liz setting out, roaring across the Channel in company with other small craft, the beaches crowded with men, the air filled with German planes, the sights, the sounds which Liz must inevitably see and hear. The thought of it all made him feel physically ill.

Liz said, "Mike, you're eating nothing, and Mrs. Robbins remembered that you once told her that you liked roast duck, with—what she calls—a 'lid to it'."

"I'm sorry, I do like duck and the salad is delicious, but—oh, Liz, don't do this crazy thing!"

She answered very quietly, "It's not crazy—as I see it. If I didn't do it, I should regret it for the rest of my life. I'm not a girl longing for adventure, I'm a woman—who is going to do a job of work, and I hope do it decently."

"What am I to say when they ask where you are?"

"I've told the servants that I am going to see my aunt—you can say the same, or—" she laughed, "if you want to keep your conscience completely clean, say, 'She told me that she was going to see her aunt'."

"My conscience!" Michael exclaimed. "What will lie most heavily on my conscience will be the fact that you're going alone."

This time her laughter was more than her usual chuckle, she threw back her head and let the sound of her mirth fill the room. As she dabbed her eyes, while Michael sat stiff and offended, she stretched out her hand towards him.

"My dear, I didn't mean to hurt you, don't be angry. Only you were allowing yourself to grow so—yes, pontifical. Go alone! Of course I must go alone—it's not a day excursion to France!"

"You won't be able to let any of us know if you're all right," he grumbled.

"Michael!" Liz cried in a tone of humorous exasperation. "Do stop! You're just racking about in your mind for objections. You'll soon hear if I'm not all right. There, finish your wine while I go and change. A cigar? Would you like one? Then the cigarettes are there in the box."

Michael sat staring gloomily at the flowers which stood in the centre of the table. Of course it was wonderful of Liz to go, but he felt that he selfishly wished that she hadn't told him. No matter what they might read in the papers, hear over the radio, he must keep his mouth shut, must not betray undue anxiety at any cost. The thought of the responsibility distressed him. What if George came home on leave, if George was waiting to embark at Dunkirk, if he arrived to find Liz absent?

'Madam's with her aunt at Bournemouth, sir.'

'I'll telephone to her—' then later, George striding over to Anderson's. Demanding news as to Liz and her whereabouts.

'She's with her aunt, George—Michael, didn't you say that Liz had gone to visit her Aunt Alice?'

He could imagine his own distressed face, the rush of colour in his cheeks. 'She told me that she was going to her aunt, George.'

Oh, damn it, a nice mess they'd all be in! Then he remembered what Liz had said about paying a debt. It had stirred him deeply, until he had allowed his irritation to get the better of him and make him forget everything but his own annoyance and apprehension. He had often wondered why George and Liz had no children, he felt that George in particular was so evidently the kind of man who would like children. Liz—he didn't know—anyway it was hard luck on her, and something which she must feel strongly about to have evolved this idea of paying off a debt.

She might be doing something which was foolhardy, but it was a gallant thing to do, to plan alone, to face the dangers—known and unknown. He could picture her, steering her boat, driving it at full speed, her eyes bright, her lips parted in excitement. He believed that she'd laugh at the danger, that she'd have a joke ready for whatever men she could take aboard. Michael, at that moment, felt a pang of envy for the men who might scramble into Liz's boat, hear her voice—light yet always so distinct, her assurance that she'd get them back—somehow.

He stubbed out his cigarette and walked back to the parlour. A moment later Liz entered. She was wearing dark blue slacks,

W.H.—C   61

they made her long legs look very boyish and beautifully slim. Her blue sweater came high up with a turtle neck, and he caught the gleam of a bright scarf which she had twisted inside the collar.

He stared at her in frank admiration. "You look stunning!"

She said, "Thank you, Mike," as if he had pleased her. Then handed him a letter, saying, "Put that somewhere safe, if I get back you can give it to me, if I make a mess of it, or something makes a mess of me, open it."

He put the letter away in his inside pocket, moistened his lips, suddenly dry at the thought of 'something making a mess' of Liz, and said, "All right, I'll do that."

She pointed to her haversack. "Talk about travelling light! Only it's not really very light—bottles weigh such a lot! George's best brandy. Rather amusing if I met George and gave him a drink of his own brandy."

"Your clothes——?"

"I don't anticipate that we shall change for dinner," she smiled, "a toothbrush, tube of paste, hairbrush and comb, and some soap—oh, and a towel. Quite a small towel because I can't believe that the arrangements for washing will be particularly extensive. Some Elastoplast, a few rolls of bandage, tins of Brand's Essence—and that's the lot. Oh, I have a compact in my hip pocket—I couldn't resist taking it. After all a shiny nose never kept up anyone's morale."

Michael sighed, "God, I wish I were coming with you, Liz."

She shook her head. "In this case, your room is more valuable than your company, bless you. There, I've got the car waiting, I'll drive you back to Anderson's." He helped her into her big driving coat, picked up the haversack and followed her out.

The night was dark, but the sky was spattered with thousands of stars. Liz looked up at them. "My uncle always said that to 'take a star bath' was a splendid cure for vanity. He was right; to stare up at those stars does make you feel how insignificant you are."

She swung the car through the gates and into the road, Michael watched her hands on the wheel, capable as well as beautiful. He had always admired her hands.

They didn't talk, Liz drove in silence, until they were nearly at Anderson's, when she said, "I won't drive right in, your mother might ask questions, and I'm certain that your face would give away too much. There! Will that do?"

"Splendidly. Good luck, Liz, and come back soon—or I shall come and fetch you."

She turned and put her arm round his shoulders, then leaning forward kissed his cheek. "Thank you so much, Michael. God bless you."

He got out in silence, he could not have trusted himself to speak, the tears were pricking his eyelids. He heard the car purr into motion, turned to see the lights vanish into the darkness, then—his hands deep in his pockets—began to walk slowly towards the farm. He thought that the world felt—suddenly—empty, and very lonely.

He let himself into the house, using the back door as always. Everyone had gone to bed, and Michael felt glad of it. He didn't want to talk, to answer questions about the dinner, he wanted to follow Liz in imagination as she drove down the Great North Road towards London. He lifted his hand laid it against his cheek, where her lips had rested. It was the first time that a woman, other than his mother or Gran, had kissed him. He thought that it was like having a cool, scented flower laid against your cheek—he imagined that he could still smell the scent which Liz used—distinctive and elusive.

He put out the lights, saw that the door was properly bolted, and then went quickly upstairs to his room. There he leaned on the sill of his window and tried to imagine where Liz had got to —he pictured her driving, keeping up a steady pace, neither pressing the car nor slowing down unnecessarily. The long, low, powerful car eating up the miles, carrying her nearer to her goal every moment.

He sighed and turned from the window; Liz had gone to pay her debt.

Chapter Five

MICHAEL had never worked so hard, he woke in the morning after Liz had left feeling feverish with anxiety. He asked himself as he dressed if he could have done anything to prevent her, then if he could have exerted any influence would it have been right to do so? Could you interfere with the destiny of other people? Had not every person to work out their own, to stand by it, accept it, make the best of it?

The early morning was beautiful, cool and clean. The world looked as if it had washed and groomed overnight. He stood at his open window sniffing the scents of early morning; it was barely seven and he could hear the sound of Wilson's voice, shouting his good-natured "Hoop! C'm hoop!" to the cows as he drove them to the milking shed. A dog barked, the happy carefree bark of a dog who is enjoying freedom and the morning sense of well-being after a good night's rest. A cock crew, and somewhere a hen, proud of her newly laid egg, clucked and announced her achievement to the waking world.

Michael sighed, a sigh which held only pleasure that a new day had begun, a day which he would fill with work, even unnecessary work, so that he could forget where Liz was and what she was attempting to do.

George had left him in charge, and Liz too had told him that she trusted him and his ability. He settled his shoulders into the shabby jacket which he wore on the farm, and descended the stairs. He swallowed the cup of tea which was ready for him, and ate a thick piece of bread and butter—he would come back later for his proper breakfast. He nodded his thanks to Violet, refused a second cup of tea and went out to begin the day's work.

Willett met him. "Mornin', Mister Michael. Noos bean't soa good!"

"No! Dunkirk, I suppose."

"Must be summat terrible, I ondly 'ope as Mister Tancred bean't standing theer on then flamin' beaches. Death an' destruction, they say. Men prop'ly mowed down. Hun planes as thick i' the sky as bram'mles in autumn. Nay——"

Michael, conscious that the sweat had broken out on his forehead said, "Horrible. Now, I've been thinking—the lawn at

Cummings, and ours at Anderson's, what about ploughing them up for crops of some sort?"

Willett said, "Nay, them bonnie lawns!"

"They're luxuries, and we can't afford luxuries at the moment."

"Have you axed your dad, Mister Michael?"

"Not yet, I shall when I go back to breakfast. And as for Cummings when Mrs. Tancred left—" he hesitated, then went on steadily, "to visit her aunt, she gave me a free hand. My father will be quite willing, so let's get cracking."

"Seems a terrible pity—taken years to get them lawns lukeing right——"

Michael said, "Aye, lots of things are a pity, but there you are. Now what about catch crops in the orchard? Plenty of room between the trees—Anderson's orchard and Cummings is even bigger."

Willett scratched his chin. "I don't reckon as them catch crops does the trees a lot of good."

"I don't believe that they do so much harm. Anyway, we'll risk it. I'll see about setting Harry on to it when I come back from breakfast. And—if this weather holds, what about starting cutting?"

"Full early——"

"It looks ready to me. Anyway, we want it cut in good time. We may be able to get a second crop of something if we're early."

"Aye, happen. But, Mister Michael, it don't do to overwork the land. The lands need rest same as 'umans do. Rest an' refreshment."

Michael laughed, "I've thought about that. Why do you suppose I've laid in all those artificial manures? Don't worry, I won't starve the land, I think too much about it. I'll tell you something, there'll be farmers who'll be damned greedy, who'll force every possible blade out of the land, who'll starve it, they'll make money while the war lasts. When it's over, they'll be left with tired, starved land, and they'll grumble that farming's no use to anyone. Just wait, Willett, and see what our land 'ul be like at the end of the war—as good as it is now? Or damned nearly as good."

Willett nodded, "Right! Then them's orders, eh? Start ploughin' up the lawn at Cummings—and you'll see young Harry about the orchard?"

Michael went on to talk to Wilson, he gave orders that the

big barn should be cleared, that the roof must be looked to for fear of any leakages. All roofs were to be seen to.

"Why Ah dean't knaw as mooch is wrang wi' onny on 'em," Wilson assured him.

"I want them looked over just the same," Michael insisted. "I don't want even a hint of a cracked or broken tile or slate. Let me know what you need and I'll get it—" he grinned, "while the going's good."

He walked back to breakfast, Gran was waiting for him. The good smell of fried bacon filled the kitchen; to Michael it seemed that coming into the big, spotlessly clean room, with its shining ovens and gleaming stove, its meticulously clean sink and draining boards, and glittering brass taps, and the long table laid with a clean white cloth, war was an impossibility. This was how English people had lived, how English kitchens had been kept for hundreds of years—surely it was unchangeable.

Gran said, "Nay, it's baddish news about this Dunkirk. I listened to the early news. What a set on!"

Michael felt his hands clench. Liz might be there by this time! He moistened his lips and said, "Tell me. . . ."

"Why seemly all these poor soldiers is crowded together on this beach. The Germans is shelling them the whole time. Sheer murder it is. But there's 'undreds—for all I know, thousands— of small boats going to the rescue, apart from the Navy. Aye, right little boats, some as 'ul ondly hold two or three—but they'll all be there. Men, aye, an' wimmen. Think of that, Michael. Wimmen going to the rescue. It makes you feel—well, makes you feel glad you're English."

"It's—it's magnificent," he said.

He filled that day with work, filled it so that at the end of it he was astonished at the amount which had been accomplished. All the time his brain was working, trying to devise ways and means by which he might provide for the time when things became in short supply. Pigs—surely there was a big possibility there, poultry—all kinds of poultry, a sufficient stock of fertilizers and chemical manures, everything must be put in perfect order, repairs done immediately before extra labour became difficult to obtain. It never occurred to Michael that he was preparing to assume heavy responsibilities, responsibilities which were in reality too much for a boy who was not yet seventeen. He had an active brain, imagination, and physically he was in perfect condition.

66

Farming was his job, he had chosen it, and when George Tancred joined the Army, Michael accepted the additional work as a matter of course. No one appeared to think that the work was beyond his powers, and while he was not in the least conceited or self-confident, he never thought so himself. The work was there, it had been handed to him so far as Cummings was concerned by its owner; Anderson's—well, surely it was the obvious thing that when his father could no longer direct farm matters and policy that the work devolved on his elder son.

So, all through that long day, Michael worked and planned and tried not to think of Dunkirk and 'the little ships', tried not to speculate about Liz, or make mental pictures of her driving her boat into the region of hideous danger in the endeavour to save a few lives from the mass of men gathered on the beaches.

That evening he listened almost unwillingly to the account of the evacuation on the radio, the calm voice of the announcer, with its perfectly enunciated phrases, brought the whole scene so vividly to him. Gran listened, her hand cupped round her ear so as not to miss a single syllable, his mother listened, her lips compressed, her eyes shining, even Violet—who always declared that she "wasn't really one for t'radio"—stood twisting a corner of her apron, her rosy, shining cheeks, which Michael always thought looked like apples, a little paler than usual.

He thought, 'All over England, all over the world people are listening to this; it's Saint Crispin's Day all over again. As long as the world lasts people will talk about Dunkirk, tell stories of the bravery, the determination and the courage. "The little ships" will go down to history, another Armada!' He wasn't a particularly religious youth, but he knew that he was praying silently as he had prayed so often during that long day, 'God, take care of Liz.'

Another day dawned, another day during which Michael flung himself into work; the harder, the more arduous, the better he liked it. Gran said, as she gave him his breakfast, "They're still at it, over there, seemly. They say as we're not only fetching away our own lads, but a lot of Frenchmen an' all."

"They're our allies, Gran."

"Fat lot of use they seem to have been—up to now! Lukes to me as if we're bad pickers when it comes to picking allies."

Michael was astonished at the change in his father during those Dunkirk days. Enoch had pointed to the newspaper, and had managed to enunciate a few blurred words, indicating that he wished to have the accounts of the evacuation read to him.

"Won't it be too much for you, Dad?" Michael asked.

"No—no—read it."

He read the account, slowly and very distinctly. His father's eyes were fixed on him, he was obviously listening intently. When Michael finished, he saw that tears were on his father's cheeks.

"You mustn't let it upset you, Dad."

"No—'onderful. Grand." Then quite suddenly, "Liz—where's Liz?"

"She told me that she was going to see her aunt." As he spoke Michael felt that the words came mechanically, without any actual conviction.

Enoch shook his head, "Not Liz—no." Then as if the effort had been too much for him, "Read more—to-morrow."

"Yes, whenever you wish, Dad."

" 'Ood boy—'ood ni'."

On June 3rd, they listened to the announcement, the evacuation was accomplished, nearly 350,000 men had been brought to England.

Grandma said, "I'll lay as plenty of 'em's left there, poor lads, killed by them 'Uns."

Ada sighed, "Now they'll think out some fresh devilment!"

Michael went out into the farm-yard, he felt that he must fill his lungs with air, he realized what a strain the past days had been, how difficult it had been to keep silent concerning Liz and her whereabouts. Now it was over—unless—he shivered—some ghastly catastrophe had happened, Liz would be coming home.

He went off to work filled with conflicting emotions. Relief, thankfulness and then following quickly uncertainty and a sense of apprehension.

Willett said, "Well, it's over, seemly, Mister Michael."

"Yes—a wonderful job!"

"Aye, but what a cost. Equipment, stores, and lives. I read as some of the poor chaps who got away hadn't a stitch on their backs. Mind, you couldn't help but smile thinkin' what they must have luked like, nobbut a tin hat!"

At dinner time, Ada beamed at him, "Never saw anything like it. Your father's properly set up about Dunkirk—when I told him about it, he fairly laughed. He did indeed. I've never seen such a change in anyone! Go up and have a word with him, Mike."

She was right too; when Michael entered his father's room, Enoch nodded and smiled, a smile which seemed to Michael to be less distorted already.

"Good news, eh, Dad?"

" 'Ood—damned 'ood. We've s'own t' buggers! *'Uts*—that's what our lads 'v' got."

Michael threw back his head and shouted with laughter. He could not remember ever hearing his father swear before—not even when he was in good health, and to hear him now seemed to mark a definite milestone on the road to his recovery.

Downstairs his mother asked—with that faint hint of jealous possessiveness, "What were you shouting with laughter about?"

"Something Dad said. Expressing his opinion of the Germans."

"Mike—you're making it up. He never!"

"He did, Mum, I swear it—I know you'd approve of his sentiments, though I'm not certain that you'd approve of the words he used."

"You don't mean to tell me as Dad was swearing!"

"Just that, Mum. A good, rather dirty swear word! Two as a matter of fact."

"Well, and he was never given to using bad words! That's what Dunkirk done—started your dad off swearing!"

Later that afternoon, Michael was watching the unloading of a lorry and checking the load, he smiled happily, for this was the first delivery of his precious fertilizers and chemical manure. The big barn was waiting, cleaned and swept, the tiles had been inspected and repaired where necessary.

"Nothing much to do, Mister Michael," young Harry told him. "Mr. Tancred keeps his buildings in tiptop order, not like some as puts off while the places is half ruined."

"You know the old saying about a stitch in time," Michael said.

"Aye, an' it's trew, nothing surer."

Wilson came across the field. "Yes, Wilson—want me?"

"Message, Mister Michael, would you kindly step over to the house?"

"Nothing wrong is there?"

"Not as I knows on. That was all that weer said—would you kindly step over."

Michael was conscious of a dreadful anxiety. Had a message come concerning Liz—or George? Would some terrible message have come, an orange envelope which already was sufficient to strike terror into the hearts of anyone who had someone near and dear to them in the Forces. He hurried away, and once out of sight of the barn broke into a run. That was how Liz Tancred saw him, wearing shabby flannel slacks and a rather faded blue shirt, running up the drive.

She stood at the window, watching him come nearer and nearer. How handsome he looked, with his head thrown back, his arms pressed to his side, moving swiftly, almost mechanically.

Her thought was, 'How fit he is, this Michael. Trained to a hair.' Then came a rush of thankfulness as she remembered those other boys—many only a few years older than Michael—who she had seen left on the Dunkirk beaches. She remembered, too, the men who had scrambled on board her motor boat, men who were grey in the face with fatigue, who had scarcely eaten or drunk anything during those long hours every one of which held sixty seconds of immediate danger. Men who were half naked, many wounded, some had clung to their rifles but all were ready to strain their lips into a grin, and to voice some words which showed that, weary though they might be, they were beaten for the time only.

" 'Baffled to fight better, fall to rise and sleep to wake,' " she had quoted to one immense Scotsman with a shock of untidy red hair.

He blinked his tired eyes, "Aye, that's reit, m'aam. We'll fight given the tools to fight wi'. Yon Hun's not done wi' us yet. We'll show him!"

A little, very thin Cockney flinging his skinny legs into the boat said, " 'E's sed it, m'aam. Coo! Just a breather, that's all we want. Then 'e'll get what's comin' to 'im, the So and So."

And almost startlingly, a voice saying, "It's awfully good of you to do this, m'aam. These little boats have been marvels. Can't thank you enough."

Then the door opened and Michael rushed in. His hair was ruffled, his eyes shining, he was panting a little after his run.

"Liz——"

She held out her hand. "Hello, Mike. You shouldn't have hurried."

He laughed, "All I got was a message—would I kindly step over! How was I to know what it meant? I had horrible visions of messages from the War Office. Oh, Liz—thank God you're back. Was it awful?

He was still holding her hand in his, very gently she withdrew it. "Parts of it were—yes, grim. I was petrified with fear. Oh, and so filthily dirty. Other parts were wonderful. The boat was an angel, never put a foot wrong. I gave her to a fisherman at Dover! Never talk to me about the Channel—I know it better than my own garden!"

"How many trips did you do?"

She shook her head. "I've no idea—you just went out and came back, then went out again." Liz laughed. "And tried to hope that you'd get back. One Lancashire lad said to me, 'Better'n Blackpool any day—can't help laffin',' though God knows what the poor devils found to laugh at. But laugh they did."

"Tell me—when did you get away?"

"Last night. I was so dead beat that I went to London, found a hotel—by Jove! they were kind. Bathed and fell—literally—into bed and slept until this morning. Oh, and George is back. He must have been at Dunkirk, I didn't see him. You might as well hope to find someone at a League football match. He must have got away early, his telegram was sent from—" she paused, then said, "England. He'll be here to-morrow he says."

"Where is he?" Michael asked, "not coming until to-morrow?"

"Maybe he had to get some clothes—probably he was like the rest of them, or most of them, half naked." She spoke very rapidly, and Michael had the impression that she was worried that George had not come directly to Yorkshire. Liz went on, "Michael, what about a drink? I'm still tired to death, and one might put a little life into me. Yes, ring! Then if I so much as mention Dunkirk—hit me!"

They sat together on the big chintz-covered sofa, Michael watching her as she sipped her drink. She looked tired, her face seemed to have lost all its colour, though she had always been pale. Her eyes were a little sunken and her hands—those beautiful hands—were still grained with dirt. Two of her nails were broken, he noticed.

"Everything all right, Mike—on the home front?" she asked.

"Splendid. I've lots of plans, Liz. I won't bother you with them, if George is coming I'll talk them over with him. My father was asking after you——"

"Enoch? Tell me."

He told her carefully, repeating the words which his father had used. He added, "I told him that you *said* that you were going to your aunt. He didn't believe it, that was quite obvious." Then he repeated what Enoch had said when he heard that the evacuation

71

was complete, and it was good to see her face relax and to hear her laugh whole-heartedly and without restraint.

"I'll come and see him to-morrow. He's a great fellow that father of yours. Another drink, Mike, and I'm going to send you away. I want a hot bath—oh, I had one last night and another this morning, and look at my hands—it will take weeks to get them clean. Then I'm going to bed and to sleep the clock round."

He stared at her, and for a moment wondered why his heart suddenly began to beat so heavily. He was happy, relieved, thankful that she was home, but surely there was something more than those emotions which almost overcame him. He took her hand in his, and lifting it to his lips, kissed it gently.

"Dear, dear Liz. These past few days have been endless. I've never worked so hard in my life, never. I wanted to fill every second so that—Dunkirk couldn't intrude."

She laughed softly, her familiar chuckle which always delighted him. "If ever I think that you're slacking, I shall know what to do. Take myself off to some impossible place where there are a few Hun planes, and—see if the trick works. Oh, Mike, don't tell everybody where I've been. If you do make them swear not to talk about it. I don't want the *Huddersley Chronicle* coming out with a dreadful photograph and a lot of rubbish. Promise."

He nodded, "I promise—but I can't promise for them—the people I talk to. I'm afraid that you're in for it, Liz—local heroine makes good and so on."

"Oh, damn!" She yawned and stretched her arms. "There, I'm going to bath and bed. See you to-morrow, Mike. I don't know what time George will be here, he'll telephone to you. Good-bye."

He hoped that she might lean forward and kiss him as she had done that night in the car, instead she laid her hand on his shoulder, and said very gently, "Thank you for standing by me, bless you."

She walked slowly upstairs, pausing at the wide window on the stairs to watch Michael's figure as he walked with that swift easy stride back to his work. Liz sighed, she was still terribly tired, what a relief the quiet, peaceful atmosphere of Cummings was after the roaring inferno in which she had spent those last days. She felt that the noise was actually shattering her brain, and towards the end of the evacuation she had worked automatically, scarcely conscious of what she did, only going through movements which had become part of a mechanical routine. She could not remember that she slept, the most were snatches before she turned round to go back to Dunkirk, brief spells when she closed her eyes and sank into blessed oblivion, only to wake with a start and set off again.

In her own large, cool bedroom she felt almost too exhausted to undress and revel in a bath. She sat at the window, staring out, barely conscious of the scene which lay before her. Well, she had paid her debt, to the best of her ability, that was something. George was safe, she realized that he had gone first to Bradford and the thought left her unmoved—he was safe, she was thankful, and if his first thought had been to go to his mistress, to see her and his child, what right had she to blame him?

'If only he won't try to invent lies to account for his absence,' Liz thought. 'Somehow in the world to-day there ought not to be room for unnecessary lies. I understand somehow, since I was out there, why Michael hated having to tell lies about where I had gone. So many tremendous things are happening, and lies are at the best small, petty, rather mean things.'

Her thoughts wandered to Michael, it had been pleasant to see him racing up the drive, a joy to watch his easy movements, to see his eyes shining so brightly because she was safely home again. What a handsome fellow he was! Vaguely she speculated as to where he got his good looks—Ada, though a nice-looking woman, the picture of health and energy, she was not and never had been outstandingly handsome, and Enoch, he had always seemed to Liz to be rather colourless, a nondescript type. Good, hard working, honest as he could be, but nothing like this undeniably handsome son of his. How old was he now? Nearly seventeen, or was he already seventeen? He looked older. If he suddenly decided to join the Army they'd take his word that he was over eighteen.

Liz shuddered, she didn't want Michael to go, didn't want him to run the risks she had seen men taking, the thought of his fine, slim body being mangled and defaced made her feel as if someone had clutched her heart with a cold hand.

Making a violent effort she stood up and stared at her reflection in the big mirror.

'What a hag!' she said softly. 'Liz, my girl, just remember that you look a hag, won't you? You're not old, but you're too old to lose nights of sleep, too old to snatch food at unlikely

73

hours, to rely on cigarettes to prevent you feeling hungry. Too old to be able to do without decent face creams, hot water, and efficient shampoos. And'—she hesitated because she was trying desperately to face facts with courage—'and, remember that he's years younger than you are, he may look older than he actually is, but even then it doesn't make him your age or near it. You've lost George—and it doesn't really affect you a great deal, you're still good friends with him, that's all you want from him— and evidently all that he wants from you. Keep your thoughts away from this boy, except in the matter of work—don't be a fool, Liz. Nip it now, in the bud before you let the whole thing get out of hand. You're not in love with young Anderson—' it gave her a sense of reassurance to say 'young Anderson', the words made it all seem more impersonal. 'You do feel a physical attraction towards him, he's young, handsome, and probably romantic. Boys of that age often fall in love, or imagine that they fall in love with rather haggard women years older than them- selves. Now—go and have that bath, and do something to that face—Heaven knows it can do with any help you can give it.'

She bathed, Mrs. Robbins sent her up a tray of attractive, light food—cold consommé, chicken, a few slices of beautifully made toast. Liz tried to eat, knowing that her eyes were heavy and that all she longed for was sleep—sound, dreamless and undisturbed. She had been too utterly weary the previous night to savour the exquisite comfort of clean, smooth sheets, to-night she lay there thinking that she had never enjoyed such luxury in her life.

She woke to find Maude waiting with her early tea.

"Seemed a shame to wake you, m'um, you were sleeping so sound."

"Oh, what a wonderful night," Liz smiled, "the bath, the bed, Mrs. Robbins's wonderful little dinner, and—sleep." Then realizing that Maude was watching her with puzzled eyes, she realized that the girl must be wondering why on earth—if Liz had been staying with her aunt in a comfortable hotel—these things should be rated so highly. She laughed, "All right, Maude—as soon as we have time, we'll all congregate in the kitchen and I'll make you all blink your eyes with surprise! There, run my bath, will you?" She looked better, the marks of fatigue had almost disappeared, her skin looked smooth, and her eyes less sunken. She flexed her muscles and was thankful that the unbearable aches had gone.

'Just the same,' she murmured as she applied her make-up carefully and discreetly as she always did, 'you don't look eighteen, my girl, or anything remotely like it.'

She busied herself with small duties about the house, she ordered the meals which she felt George would appreciate, she cut flowers and arranged them, she was glad to be home, she'd be glad to see George, and she would be completely sensible—about everything.

Mrs. Robbins, vast, kindly and innately curious asked after her aunt. "I 'ope as you found 'er in the best of 'ealth, m'um."

Liz looked at her, eyes twinkling. "Mrs. Robbins—as far as I know she is in the best of health. I've not got time to talk to you now, but I will—as I promised Maude this morning."

"Maude did say something about you making us blink our eyes."

"I'm too busy just now to make them blink, so you must just be patient."

"I didn't think as you luked any too grand last night, if I might say so, no mower did Maude nor Ellen. Prop'ly tired out, we all said."

Liz laughed, "You were all completely right—only this is—to-day, that was yesterday. There, you inquisitive old woman, I must fly."

George arrived before luncheon. He was wearing a very shabby uniform and a service hat which was palpably new. The sleeve of his tunic had been torn and it had been mended inexpertly.

He looked tired, thinner than Liz remembered, he kissed her warmly on both cheeks, and said, "Oh, it's nice to be back. Liz, I could use a drink without the slightest effort."

"They're waiting, and the fatted calf is all prepared. When did you get back?" She wished she had not asked, for George flushed.

"A couple of days ago. I had to see about a new kit." Liz thought 'The implication being that he stayed in London, well, let it go at that!'

He drank with deep appreciation. "That's good. Well, that was a wonderful picnic at Dunkirk! Whew, what a mess up, and as usual the French beefing that they didn't get proper attention!"

She said very calmly, "I looked for you——"

"You looked for me—when—where? In London?"

"No, at Dunkirk. I went doing a ferry service with a motor boat. I got back last night."

75

He stared at her. "Go on—quickly—tell me, Liz. I can't believe it."

She told him, making light of nothing, exaggerating nothing. He listened intently, neither asking questions nor making comments. She ended her story, "And when the show was over—I came home." He laid his hand on hers, and she knew that he was profoundly moved.

"Liz, if I'd seen you—I'd, damn it, I'd have sent you packing back home. You might have been killed!"

She laughed, "Dear George, what a fertile imagination you have! There, that's the gong, come and eat."

Chapter Six

GEORGE was appreciative, he listened to all Michael had to tell him, listened attentively and nodded approval. His comments were always brief, and his suggestions crisp and reasonable.

"You're still determined to go and join up when you're eighteen?" Michael nodded. "You're a damned fool, but I can't stop you—only, remember this, if you try any sneaking into the Army by telling a pack of lies—I denounce you, or if I'm not here, then Liz shall."

"That's all right, on the day I'm eighteen—I go. Until then, I've got my job here. You're not angry about the lawn?"

"To hell with the lawn! What this country will need is food! Grow it in the bath if that's the only place possible—but grow it."

It was pleasant to walk round the two farms with George, to listen to his comments, to hear him talking to Willett, Wilson and young Harry; pleasant when he and Liz came over to Anderson's and were delighted at Enoch's progress.

Liz said, "Cunning old fox that he is—he knew I wasn't with Aunt Alice!"

Gran said, "Then for pity's sake let's hear where you were Liz. There's some very queer stories flying about let me tell you that."

"She behaved like a crazy person," George told them, "rushing off and doing a ferry service." He smiled at her, "Crazy, but damned plucky."

"And where on earth did you get that tunic mended, George Tancred? It's a disgrace. Whoever mended that must be about as handy as a cow with a side pocket! Tak' it off and give it me, I'll fettle it. Michael, lend George a coat to go home in, you can take this over in the morning. Tut, tut, it's a fair botch!"

Liz watching George's face, sensed in some way that the unknown Mavis had attempted to mend it. Gran was right, it was 'a botched job'.

It surprised her that she cared so little; even when the week-end came and George made some excuse about going off to see Claygate, she felt no shock, no distress and most certainly no jealousy.

She said, "George, don't make up stories about Claygate to

tell me. Lawyers don't keep their offices open at the week-end. You've a right to go where you wish."

He flushed, "I didn't want to hurt you, Liz."

"My dear, this *doesn't* hurt me, only I loathe being treated as if I were a child or a half wit."

Half sulkily he said, "Very well, I won't—I'm going to——"

Impatiently Liz cut him short. "I know where you're going."

"Then there's no more to be said."

"No necessity to say anything. Only, George, do get it out of your head that you're behaving like a criminal, or that I'm sitting at home nursing a broken heart. We talked all this over before you went to France."

"I'm sorry about it——"

"Then you've no right to be—sorry. If you're happy with this girl, what have you got to be sorry about? That side of our life together finished years ago. We've been over all this before! Let's accept things and get the best out of life."

He looked at her intently, his pleasant face sombre. He did love Mavis, he adored the little girl—he wished that Liz could see her—but withal he felt regret that he and Liz had ceased to be lovers as well as friends. There would never be anyone quite like Liz, no woman would ever satisfy him as completely as she had always done, he would never have so much in common with anyone, not even with Mavis.

Indeed, Mavis and he hadn't much in common. She was pretty, good-tempered, she kept her small house beautifully, cooked delicious meals for him, she was loving, even passionate. He sighed, it was just that Liz was—different. Liz was interested in so many things, did so many things well, could discuss matters appertaining to the farm, stock, new hen houses. Liz was interested in most things, Mavis was interested only in those things which affected her, things which were included in her immediate circle.

He sighed again, then shrugged his shoulders, feeling that even to indulge in such thoughts and speculations was to be disloyal to Mavis. He knew that she accepted him as he was, she might regret that they could not marry, but she would compare him as he had been comparing her with Liz.

Liz had been watching his changing expression. She thought, 'Poor George, it's all puzzling him terribly. He really feels that he's doing me a kindness, making everything easier for me by telling lies about old Claygate. We're both puzzled—George

78

because he really loves an ordinary, conventional life, he's rather ashamed of having a mistress tucked away in some small villa in Bradford; I'm puzzled because—oh, because I'm afraid of being hurt, or else making some frightful error that I shall regret all my life.'

She said abruptly, "George, would you like me to get a divorce?"

He stared. "A divorce? What on earth for?"

"For the same reason that most people sue for a divorce."

"Good Heavens, Liz—don't do that! You don't want a divorce, I mean, not really, do you? There isn't—isn't anyone else?"

"You mean—am I having an affair with anyone? No."

The look of relief on his face amused her. She laughed, "George, what an irrational, illogical creature you are. You can have an affair—a very complete one apparently—but you'd hate me to do the same."

He nodded, "I admit it, I'd hate it." He ran his fingers through his hair as he invariably did when anything presented a problem. "I don't know, I suppose it is illogical—confound it, Liz, it's all so difficult. I've thought about it all until my brain feels addled. If I'd read in some book about a man loving two women I'd have said it was simply rubbish. But here I am——"

She smiled at him, kindly, tolerantly. "But you don't love two women, you love one—I hope—the other you like—I hope—very, very much indeed."

"It's difficult to say where friendship stops and love begins," he said.

This time her smile changed to a laugh. "If Grandmother were here she'd tell you not to talk like a penny book with the pages torn out. It's no good talking about these things, we're neither of us metaphysical types; we'll accept things as they are, get what happiness we can."

So George Tancred went off for his week-end and, Liz spent her time divided between the house and the farm. She rarely saw Michael for more than a few minutes at a time, once or twice she wondered if he purposely avoided her, then took herself to task for imagining things. Why on earth should he avoid her? To him she was probably positively elderly. She had told George that she was not in love with anyone, that was true, she wasn't in love with this good-looking boy, and yet she was allowing herself to behave like a schoolgirl, imagining that he 'avoided' her, allowing her pulses to quicken if she caught sight of him on the farm.

When they met she knew that whatever she said sounded stiff and artificial. "How beastly the lawn looks!" or "What are you going to plant there?"

"You and George will leave me just a few flower-beds, won't you?"

Michael nodded, "Of course—we'll not rob you of them."

"Come to luncheon on Sunday."

"That's very kind of you—I should have to get away pretty early."

"Not working on Sunday surely?"

"Playing tennis—Mercy Blenkiron's home on leave, she's in one of the women's services, I forget which."

"Make it dinner then—supper on Sunday."

"Awfully sorry, Mercy's asked me to stay for supper."

"Some other time then——"

She walked away, trying to assure herself that she didn't really mind, that she had only asked him to prove to herself that she could face sitting through a meal with him alone, talking in a perfectly ordinary way without the least difficulty.

Mercy Blenkiron! Tennis and supper doubtless with a crowd of other boys and girls. She could hear Mrs. Blenkiron's loud, cheerful voice announcing that she liked to see 'young people enjoy themselves'. She could imagine comments on Michael's looks, and the decision on the part of other people coinciding with that of 'young people' that 'Young Anderson is really exceedingly presentable'. Young, young, young! There would be more tennis parties, she would hear Ada say that Michael was always being asked out to play here and there at the houses of 'the gentry'. Gran would no doubt add her comments that 'Seems as if Michael is always being asked to——' or 'Lukes to me that Michael's seeing a lot of that young Miss——' He'd go and do his military service, and when the war ended he'd come back, settle down, marry and—that would be that!

'You fool!' she told herself, 'you crass fool. Of course he'll marry, and what has it got to do with you? George will come back and farm again, you'll settle down with him, and you can grow elderly and then old together. Watch the young generation growing up!'

Michael went back to work, feeling bad-tempered and disappointed. He'd rather have gone to have luncheon with Liz

—or supper—or any other meal, than go to the Blenkirons'. He didn't particularly like Mercy, but she'd met him in Huddersley and had pressed him to come. He didn't think that either Mum or Gran were too pleased about it. Mum said that Mrs. Blenkiron was all right, but that her voice was enough to give anyone a headache; Gran said, "Prop'ly taken up by the gentry, Michael, aren't you? It 'ul be tuppence to speak to you next I'd not wonder!"

Anyway, it was probably a good thing that he was not going to Cummings. He was thinking far too much about Liz, there had been times during the past week when he felt disloyal to George for letting Liz occupy his thoughts so much. He wondered what George would think if he realized the almost painful fashion Michael's heart beat whenever she came to speak to him. He'd either stigmatize him as a young fool or feel that he had betrayed the trust which George had placed in him.

So he went to the Blenkirons' and played tennis furiously, and tried to believe that he was enjoying it all tremendously, that Sir George Fowler's daughter—Tonette—was half as pretty as she obviously believed herself to be, and that Mercy Blenkiron played tennis as well as she, too, obviously believed to be the truth.

Harry Rawsley, who rode home with Michael after a hilarious cold supper, said, "Isn't Tonette a smasher?"

Michael contrived to say with feigned sincerity, "By Jove—" as if words failed him.

"I think Mercy likes you quite a lot, Anderson."

"Mercy? No, I've known her all my life."

"I've heard some of these girls talking——"

Michael thought, 'So have I! I've heard them talking enough to-day to last me for quite a time!' Aloud he said, "Oh, they say anything!"

He was glad when Rawsley said, "My turning. Goo' night, Anderson" and he could ride on alone in the cool dusk and think quietly. He had another year to go through before he could join the Army without breaking his promise to George, without leaving Anderson's in the lurch. Twelve months—twelve months when it might not be a bad thing to get into the set of young people with whom he had spent the afternoon. Perhaps he could develop a sentimental feeling for Mercy, write long stupid letters to her when she went back to the A.T.S. She was a couple of years older than he was, he didn't think that she was particularly attractive,

81

but—one nail could drive out another. Always supposing that Mercy Blenkiron would feel any interest in him.

As he rode past the gates of Cummings he saw that the lights were still on, and pushing open the gate wheeled his bicycle up the drive. He told himself that he was being unutterably stupid, but the urge to see Liz, to talk to her if only for ten minutes was too strong. The thought of seeing her made him feel shaken and unsure of himself. He propped his bicycle against the pillar of the porch, and rang the bell. While he waited he turned to look at the already ploughed-up lawn. Gone was the soft, beautifully cut and rolled grass, in its place were the scars left where to-morrow young Harry would begin to plant turnips for the winter feed. The stout figure of Mrs. Robbins stood in the doorway, crying, "Why if it's not Mister Michael. Oh, the mistress will be pleased, she's all alone, the master won't be back while the morning. Come in."

Liz came out into the hall, she stood in the hall, saying, "Who is it?"

Michael said, "I hope you don't mind—I know it's late."

"Of course I don't. Have you enjoyed your party?"

He followed her into the drawing-room, trying desperately to keep his voice even. He always admired her in the slacks which she wore during the day, but to see her again in a long, rather elegant dress which looked soft and smooth though he had no idea what the material was, which seemed to cling to her figure, to accentuate its curves, and enhance its beauty, filled him with a pleasure so exquisite that it almost amounted to physical pain.

"Tell me about the party—get yourself a drink and sit down."

He went over to the table, poured himself out a drink and returned to the fireplace, resting his arm on the broad mantelpiece. He looked very tall in his flannels, soft white shirt and his old Blamey blazer. For a moment he did not speak, just looked at her, treasuring every second that the French clock—all gilt and enamel—ticked out.

Liz said with humorous insistence, "Well—tell me!"

"Some shocking tennis," he said, "there was only Harry Rawsley who played any game at all; Mercy Blenkiron isn't too bad, but the rest—whew! Pat ball!" He relapsed into silence again.

"Tell me about Mercy—she's in the A.T.S. isn't she?"

Michael nodded, "Working for a commission. She's quite nice."

82

He saw Liz's beautiful eyebrows lift a little. "Attractive?"

"I don't know—perhaps. Liz, do you think that George will let me off that promise. I mean about joining up. I'm seventeen next week. I look older. Will you put it to him?"

She spoke very slowly, as if she weighed each word carefully. "Why do you suddenly want to go, Mike?"

For a moment he hesitated, then said, his voice very young and boyish, palpably not speaking the complete truth, "Oh, well, you know how it is. Other fellows who look younger than I do, go and get commissions, even go overseas. It's pretty damnable to feel that they go while I stay here safe in Yorkshire."

"But you know that you're doing a very, very good job."

She saw him shrug his broad shoulders. "A good job! I don't know. I admit that I work pretty hard, but I fancy that there are plenty of people who could do what I'm doing as well, yes, and better. Anyway, I want to have George let me take back my promise." He said the last sentence with a kind of defiance, as if he resented the fact that he had ever given his word to stay on the farms until he was eighteen. His eyes, watching Liz intently, were clouded; his young mouth was set in hard, determined lines. He repeated, "I want to have George release me. I want to get away."

"Are those all your reasons?" Liz asked. Her voice was cool, even detached, yet she felt that she was facing a crisis. The whole idea was fantastic but she was in love with this boy, not only because he had beauty—the beauty which belongs not only to good looks but to youth and health; more—she knew that he loved her. It might be the immature infatuation of seventeen, but he was older, more thoughtful than his contemporaries, and watching his set face, listening to his voice made sharp and clipped by something which meant desperation, she knew that despite his years this was all real and serious to him.

She viewed the whole thing from the vantage ground of her greater years, she knew that she loved him, was conscious of many things which she desired but would not admit even to herself; she knew that the whole thing was folly no matter how real and vital it was now. Michael was different. To him she was the first love of his life, no matter what the future might hold for him this love would always remain as something precious. He might —he would—marry some pleasant girl, live a hardworking life, watch a family of handsome sturdy children grow up round him, but in his innermost heart she—Liz Tancred—would always

83

remain as a memory—growing frail and indistinct with the years —which brought with it colour, and a sweet savour. She remembered a couplet—who wrote it?—Tom Moore surely—'You may break, you may shatter the vase, if you will, but the scent of the roses will hang round it still.' No, Michael would have a memory of her as she was now; by the time she had grown middle-aged, elderly, even old—he would have ceased to care, he would only remember her as he had known her now.

"Are those all your reasons?" she asked again, still speaking very gently.

He shook his head as if to clear his mental vision.

"No—not all."

"Can't you tell me the others?"

He stared at her, then said quietly but with great intensity, "No!"

"Shall I tell them to you, Mike?"

His voice had regained its youthful, half-sulky quality.

"You don't know them, you can't know them."

"We'll disregard them, if you'll listen to what I'm going to say; you may realize that I *do* know, more than that, you may understand. As soon as George's leave is over—that will be at the end of this week—I am going to London. I want to work. Someone—who was it? Napoleon, Bismarck, I've forgotten said of London, 'What a city to loot!' They won't loot it, because they'll never get a foothold in England, but they'll be out to destroy it. I can find work there, driving ambulances, serving in a canteen, doing a dozen things—but I shall do them in London. Mike, stay here, just for another year. You're not evading your duty, you're doing it."

"Why should you leave your home? Why should you go to live in some beastly hotel in London? You could be doing work —yes, war work if that's what you want—here."

Liz held out her hands, he stood uncertain for a moment, then came forward and sat beside her on the sofa.

"Do you want me to answer those questions, Mike?" she asked.

"Yes—yes, I do."

She spoke very slowly, unemotionally, "Because, my dear, as things are it is better—wiser—that I am not at Cummings while you are at Anderson's. That's why I shall go away. The farms need you, they can get on quite well without me. Another year, who knows, the war may be over, or George may have been

84

invalided out, you can't tell. Only, Mike, let me be wise for both of us."

He watched her, frowning a little, then said: "Liz, you do understand?"

She nodded, "Only too well, don't let us put it all into words. To do that makes it seem additionally fantastic. I'm ten years older than you are, I'm married, my husband is a soldier—ready to go back on active service. Well, I'm going to London!"

She said the last words with decision, throwing back her head as if she challenged anyone to prevent her doing what she had determined. Michael saw the long line of her neck, the set of her beautifully shaped head, and obeying a sudden impulse laid his hand on hers.

"Liz, don't go—stay here—I'll stay here. We'll see each other. Talk together. Liz, I love you so much."

She withdrew her hand very gently, it was such a smooth movement that Michael barely felt it. She smiled, a smile which went to his heart. It held so much regret, so much tenderness and yet the firm resolve still remained in her eyes.

"My dear, I wish that you didn't. I could wish that you'd come and told me that you thought you were in love with Mercy, or that little girl of Fowler's, what's her name?—Tonette." Then impulsively, "I should have hated it, hated it, but I could have seen some future for you in either of them—a home, warmth, affection—I've nothing to give you that I could give you cleanly and decently. Then, Mike, age does matter—when you were thirty, I should be forty. If it were——"

He laid his hands on her shoulders and twisted her round so that she faced him directly. "Stop talking about age!" he demanded furiously. "Age, age, age! What the hell does it matter? What does matter is that you've filled my heart, God knows I've tried, harder than you'll ever know, to drive you out. All the time you were at Dunkirk, I fought against even thinking of you—I didn't succeed. It was hell. How do you suppose that I can go on working here for another twelve months knowing that I could take the car and drive to London just to get a sight of you, just to hear your voice? You ask what's impossible. I can't do it."

"You *will* do it, my dear," she said very quietly.

He dropped his hands, she thought that he looked beaten, as if the spirit which had driven him to work so hard had died. Yet she knew him sufficiently well to realize that he would conquer and continue to do the work which had been allotted to him bravely and conscientiously.

"You want me to do this?" he asked.

"I want you to—and you want to do it," Liz said.

"Can I ever come to see you in London?"

She knew that here at this juncture she might steer the whole discussion into smoother waters.

"Why, yes, provided that you weren't—playing truant from your work!" she smiled.

"Just come as a nice, hard-working lad, only seventeen, doing a job of work to release George for the Army, and you to drive canteens or ambulances, eh?"

She flinched at the bitterness in his voice, and knew that her defences were cracking. He was so young, so sincere, and so beautiful. Liz felt her strength ebbing away, she leaned back against the big cushions and breathed rather than spoke the words, "Oh, Mike." She felt chilled, felt that she was of her own volition pushing something precious out of her life. George had his Mavis, and here she was offered the love of someone young, truthful and sincere, a boy who might be young in years but who had already proved that he could face the responsibilities of a man.

Again she said, "Oh, Mike . . ." and covered her face with her hands. His arms were round her, he was drawing her very close to him, whispering softly, all the bitterness gone from his voice.

"Liz, dearest Liz, don't. Just tell me—I won't ask for anything else—that you do love me a little."

"A little—God! a little! That's why I must go away—simply that, because I do love you so much."

He still held her to him, she could feel his heart beating.

"You must go to London," he said, "and I must stay here. I'll come and see you—at long intervals, and you shall take me to—to the pantomime, if they have them in war-time! Don't worry, Liz, my darling, wonderful Liz. Only take care of yourself, don't run into any danger. I'll see that everything goes well here, you can trust me, I swear that you can trust me."

She lifted her face from his shoulder, pushed him back so that she could see his face, his expression was serious and very tender and he looked almost pathetically young. She took his face between her hands and drawing it to her kissed him. Kissed his lips, feeling them firm against her own. She knew that his breath came quickly, that his arms round her were very strong, straining her to him.

"Again," he whispered, "Liz—kiss me again."

"Oh, my darling——"

He kissed her lips, her cheeks, her eyelids, kisses which were full of ardour and passion; she wished that the embrace might go on for ever. For years she had longed for such kisses, for years George had kissed her with a temperate affection, this was something she had not known since the early days of her marriage."

At last he let her go, his hands fell and he sat looking at her silent, and smiling softly.

"It is worth having lived—just for those moments," he said. He lifted her hands and kissed them, then rose. "I must go, my wonderful Liz. That was—good-night. I won't even quote Romeo and Juliet to you, though the lines are hers not his. Don't worry, my darling, I'll stick to my work. I don't think that I'd better see you very much before you go away. Only let me know where I can always find you. There, good-night, and have wonderful dreams."

Her eyes filled with tears, "I've had my wonderful dream."

"Ah, but you shared it—that makes it only half yours."

He stooped and kissed her very softly, without a trace of passion, then without speaking went out, closing the door softly.

Liz sat there, she knew the time was past when she could tell herself not to be a fool, when she could ridicule herself for falling in love with a boy ten years her junior, these things had lost their efficacy. She loved him, she had admitted it, she had known peace and happiness as she lay in his arms. She could still recall the faint scent of his hair which had lain so softly against her cheek, the scent of fresh air which seemed to cling about him. He had asked for nothing but her kisses, he had not even hinted at anything further. He had been kind, he had realized that her love was as great as his own and that had contented him. For how long, she wondered? Well, the future, with its possible complications, must take care of itself.

She could not have formulated her hopes, her fears—for even at that moment she knew that there must be—fears. That was where the problem of age entered into everything. They could all wait, they could be dealt with when they became pressing.

In her bedroom she stared at her reflection. Her lips curved into a smile. This was the 'hag' who had come back from

87

Dunkirk! Her cheeks were a little flushed, her lips parted easily and softly, her eyes were bright yet seemed suffused with tenderness.

'I can't call you a hag, my dear,' she said softly, 'I only hope that it won't be evident to everyone that—I'm in love.'

Chapter Seven

MICHAEL wheeled his bicycle towards Anderson's. The night was clear and cool, sometimes he heard the rustle in the hedgerow as a benighted mole or rabbit scuttled for home, once he heard the bark of a fox, and at intervals some bird roused for a moment from its sleep uttered a last call and then allowed sleep to claim it once more.

He tried to order his thoughts, to come to some clear understanding with himself. Liz loved him, and he knew that he had given her his heart. It was almost unbearable to recall those moments when he had held her in his arms, pressed kisses on her face, and felt that she shared his momentary happiness.

He had always disliked chance embraces, even when he was a child, and at children's parties when games were played which entailed the giving of kisses as forfeits, or in 'Postman's Knock', he had withdrawn into himself, and wished passionately that no one of all the little girls would choose him. He knew boys of his own age who had swaggered that they had been for a long evening walk with some girl or other and implied that they had indulged in wild bursts of kissing. He liked girls—except when they played bad tennis, and expected him to praise them for volleys which were inefficient and futile. When almost a year ago he had been given the charge of two farms, he had worked for it, he had enjoyed the sense of responsibility, he had tackled problems and —he admitted it—the praise which George had given him was very sweet.

Now, he had fallen in love with George's wife—and he felt immediately a sense of guilt that he had betrayed the trust which Tancred had placed in him. He felt unbearably tired, and he laid down his bicycle in the grass verge, and flung himself down to make an attempt to—see things straight.

The grass was cool, it smelt sweet, and Michael lay there his hands under his head, relaxed, and with the sense that he was emptied of all emotion. His mind, still filled with the knowledge that Liz loved him and that he loved her, accepted the fact as something accomplished. He knew that he had loved her for months, but that putting the statement that he loved her into words, had crystallized and made everything clear.

It was better—certainly wiser—that she should go away. He dared scarcely imagine what life would be without her, a drawn-out repetition of the days when she had gone to Dunkirk, filled with anxiety and apprehension. He had not seen very much of her, since her return, but those passing glimpses, those brief meetings had been sufficient to send him back to his work filled with new courage, and fresh determination. Liz—going to London for twelve months, that was a different thing altogether. That meant not only deprivation but intensified longing and loneliness. What if she was right? What if the Germans attacked London, showered bombs on it, dealt destruction everywhere? How could he face remaining safely in Yorkshire, growing food while he knew that she was in danger!

He stirred restlessly, a heavy dew was falling and he felt chilled through the thin flannel of his trousers. He stood up, lifted his bicycle, and rather stiffly because the cold had cramped him, began to walk home.

His mind was still dealing with his future problems. His father was improving, every day showed that he was acquiring strength, that his mind was growing clearer and more active. Even his speech had become more distinct. That Enoch would ever be able to lead a completely active life, Michael realized was impossible. He might dictate, give orders, make plans, but a farm needed someone who was active, who could go out and *see* what was happening.

In twelve months—for he never wavered in his fixed determination to join the Army on the very day that he was eighteen—who would take over the direction of Anderson's and Cummings? It was true that George might be invalided out—but even so, he might not be sufficiently fit to take a really active part in the work of the farms. Liz would come back, but after all Liz—his beloved Liz—might know a great deal but did she know sufficient to take over two largish farms? There had developed in Michael an almost passionate love for the land, it gave him real joy to watch a field being ploughed, to see the even furrows of rich, dark earth being prepared to receive the grain which would eventually produce a crop which meant food for the people of the country. To see the grain gathered, the stooks arranged in neat lines in the fields, to hear the threshing machine at work, to see the fine, well-built stacks waiting to provide food for cattle gave him thrills of intense pleasure.

It never occurred to him to think that he was still barely

seventeen, young, immature, practically untried; he had taken on a job which he felt certain that he could do, and he had done it. Many times when he began to take over, he remembered that he had been forced to flog himself. His muscles had not set, his frame was too light for the tasks which he set himself. He had won! He was trained to a hair, his thews and sinews were like whipcord and wire, he could tackle the hardest and most gruelling day with nothing more than a normal, healthy weariness. The times when he had flung himself on his bed utterly exhausted were over. Not Willett, Wilson, young Harry or the labourers could put in more hours of hard work than Michael Anderson.

Now, he pushed his bicycle wearily. He knew that the last talk with Liz had exhausted him as no day in the harvest field, no hours spent at the market—how he loathed the market!—no long stretches of scattering chemical manure on heavily ploughed fields could ever have done.

Looking towards the east he knew that the sky showed lighter. His heart bounded. 'The dawn!' The thought of it seemed an omen to him. This night he had kept his vigil with the sweet grass as his bed and the stars for company. Then the slight lightening faded, the sky was dark once more.

'The false dawn,' he murmured.

Was that an omen too? He was almost dizzy with weariness, with the effects of the emotion through which he had passed. Once or twice he staggered a little as he walked.

He reached the farm-yard of Anderson's, there was the solitary light which Mum always left for him. He—walking mechanically—pushed his bicycle into the shed, then with his hand on the latch, looked up at the still darkened sky, and turned his head towards Cummings.

He stared over to the dark shape which held the woman he loved. Liz was there, asleep, dreaming it might be of his kisses. Young and romantic he sighed and remembered the words given by Shakespeare to young Lorenzo,

> . . . in such a night as this,
> When the sweet wind did gently kiss the trees,
> And they did make no noise; in such a night,
> Troilus, methinks, mounted the Trojan walls,
> And sigh'd his soul toward the Grecian tents,
> Where Cressid lay that night.

Momentarily intoxicated by the lovely words, he let his mind run on, repeating softly the answer to Jessica, the further fancies of Lorenzo, until the end of the beautiful scene, when Michael sighed again, looked again towards the dark mass of Cummings, then entered the farm-house, put out the light and crept to bed.

During the week which followed he saw Liz only once, then she came with her long, easy stride—with George—to where Michael was weighing out fertilizer. He contrived to keep his hands steady—it would be dreadful if young Harry noticed how they suddenly became less certain—and said in a normal voice, "There! That's enough for the lawn, get cracking, Harry."

"I will that, Mister Michael."

Michael straightened up from the big scales, and smiled. "Hello, George. We've made a mess of your beautiful lawn, eh? Good morning, Liz. Have you seen 'Molly's' baby? Lovely little heifer."

Liz said, "Yes, a little beauty. Does you credit, Mike."

George laughed, "Come, credit where credit's due. 'Darlington Duke' did have something to do with it. Well, Mike, I'm off at the end of the week. If there's anything you want to talk over, come and have dinner—come early—then we can get down to cases."

Have dinner! Sit in George's study and discuss stock, crops, developments—that was fairly easy, but to sit at that shining dinner table, and later to go back into the drawing-room—the room where he had told Liz that he loved her—where she had admitted that she loved him, where she had lain in his arms while he showered kisses on her upturned face—that was too difficult.

He said, "That's nice of you, but honestly, George, by the time work's over for the day, I'm dead beat. Couldn't we meet during the day—immediately after luncheon, I'll bring the books over and we can—get down to cases."

George nodded. "That's all right by me. Don't kill yourself with work. Don't be over keen."

"Oh, believe me, I'm not likely to do that."

He never met Liz's eyes, was only conscious that she was there. Conscious of her slim figure, her poise, her usual appearance of being perfectly groomed.

George clapped him on the shoulder. "Right! Let's say to-morrow immediately after luncheon."

Michael grinned—it was surprisingly easy to grin—"We call it dinner."

Then Liz spoke, "In that case come over in time for a cup of coffee! Dinner or luncheon makes no difference, we drink coffee after both."

For the first time he met her eyes squarely, and thought again how beautiful she was—possibly not by the rules of strict loveliness, perhaps her features were irregular, but to Michael Anderson, she was the most wonderful thing he had ever seen. Again he managed to contort his face into a smile. It had been easy when talking to George, now—his face felt stiff and cold.

"Thank you, I'd love to."

George said, "See you soon," and the two of them walked away while Michael tried to collect his wits and refrain from turning to watch Liz walking for the sheer pleasure of watching her.

The cows were coming back for milking, he watched their slow progress, easy and unhurried, it was soothing to watch them. So many things about a farm were soothing, Michael thought. The soft cooing of pigeons, the whirr of the cutters, the drowsy buzz of bees heavy with their loads of honey, even the sharp bleating of sheep as they called to their lambs which strayed too far from their mother's side.

A good life, he felt, a life which gave opportunities for development, for hard work which promised results, which held the rewards of attainment. The endless round of the seasons, each bringing its particular work to be done, each promising its special harvest whether grass, grain or the fruits of the earth.

He saw the last of the herd disappear into the milking shed, then walked off to do some task which was waiting. They'd begin hay-making next week if the weather held—next week, the thought came like a sharp stab of pain, for next week Liz might have left Cummings, might have gone to London and he dreaded to think of the blank life which her departure would mean.

Willett said, "Looks good that crop, eh?"

Michael started, he had been immersed in his thoughts. "If the good weather holds we'll start cutting to-morrow. The four acre is ready, don't you think?"

"Aye, that's the result of the last two'three days." He glanced at the clear sky. "I reckon it 'ul hold all right. Wonderful the difference a few days make."

The difference a few days could make! A few days ago he had told Liz that he loved her, she had admitted that she loved him; a few more days and she might have gone.

"We might see if we can turn on another couple of men," he

said, forcing his mind back to the hay-making. "D'you know of anyone in Huddersley?"

"Happen, I'll go down this evening."

"I'll have a look at the cutter." The thought of working on the big mowing machine pleased him. He welcomed the idea of doing a job which meant getting greasy and dirty, sweating a little, using his hands and concentrating fiercely on the work. He had chosen his job and nothing must interfere with that; he must take himself in hand, use sufficient self-discipline to prevent himself growing moody and absorbed in things which were outside the work of running the two farms.

He ran back to the farm, and put on his boiler suit; that was what he needed—action, hard physical work. He looked in at the kitchen where Gran was preparing dinner.

"Now lad, come for a drink or something?" she inquired.

"Might be pleasant, thank you."

"Give it a name, I can't do wi' ditherers."

"Stone ginger."

"Gassy rubbish. Well if that's what you fancy, you know where it is—i' t' larder."

Michael drank the cool liquid, and heard Gran's injunction to "Swill out that mug before you go"; obeyed her with a smile, and then went out turning towards the shed where the mower was kept. He stripped off the cover and set to work, whistling a nebulous tune which had no particular beginning or end.

He was completely absorbed in his work, so absorbed that he did not see Liz Tancred standing at the entrance of the shed.

She stood watching him, quite motionless. She saw his intent face, heard the whistling which was the outcome of complete concentration, once she heard him mutter at some recalcitrant nut, "Damn it!" then wipe his forehead with the back of his hand, leaving a smear of grease on the tanned skin.

'Why on earth,' Liz wondered, 'should it seem almost touching to see him making himself dirty? No reason at all—just sentimentality.'

She spoke, "You're making yourself filthy, Mike."

He started, then looked up. "I didn't know that you were there."

"I came to tell you that I've told George that I'm going to London when he leaves."

"Have you definitely settled what you're going to do?"

"Yes. I'd practically settled it all before I told him."

94

He turned back to the machine, saying with apparent inconsequence, "We start cutting to-morrow."

Liz moved a pace forward, she spoke as if she had not heard what he said about the hay-making.

"Mike, George goes on Saturday, would you like to drive up to town with me—or I'd do the driving—then you could bring the car back in the evening?"

He stared at her, pushing back a lock of hair which had fallen over his forehead, making another grimy mark.

"If it's fine, the chances are we'll be cutting. Anyway we shall start at five on Monday, Liz."

She nodded. "The hay-making comes first," she said.

For the first time he spoke with some feeling in his voice, very quietly, very distinctly. "The work must come first," he said, "I'd be letting down everyone if it didn't. You must see that."

"The work first—I come in as a bad second—or third."

"You know where you come," Michael said speaking fiercely but still very quietly. "You know that, nothing can change it. Play fair, Liz. It's hard enough anyway."

For a brief second she let her fingers rest on his oil stained hand, then sighed, "You're right—I was wrong. I shan't see you for months. Still——"

His boyish grin came suddenly. "I shall come up to go to the pantomime," he said.

Liz shook her head. "Oh, Mike—what a mess it all is."

Then she turned and left him, he watched her figure, then picked up the wrench and bent to his work again.

In the distance she heard that indefinite whistling begin again.

The weather held, Michael was out at five. Willett had managed to find two additional men in Huddersley, neither of them very young but sufficiently strong to rake the sweet-smelling grass, to spread it to dry in the sun and with Michael driving the mower, they cut the field, and he promised himself that the following day should see a start made on the large field at Cummings.

He rushed back to Anderson's, ate his dinner, washed and changed and tore over to Cummings. He snatched up his account books, and with them under his arm ran over the field.

The drawing-room—the parlour—was cool and smelt of roses, they stood everywhere in bowls and vases, filling the air with their scent. He thought that Liz looked not unlike a rose herself, a pale beautiful rose, with a long stem.

She smiled. "Coffee, Mike?"

George, standing near, said, "And then when you've drunk that, what about a—man's drink?"

"I've got to get back to the field. We've put in a good morning, it's going to be prime hay. Long in the stalk, just the kind of stuff we want. You don't mind if we work on Sunday, George, do you? Means double time for the men, but it's worth it if we can catch the good weather."

George—Michael thought that he looked depressed, he was growing heavy about the jowl, though his face was still pleasant and his smile kindly—pursed his lips.

"I've always been against Sunday work, except the bare necessities. I've never felt that it paid in the end. Still, I suppose it's different while there's a war going on. Use your own judgement."

Liz said, "Another cup of coffee, Mike? No? Then, George, what about a cold drink, and you can get down to your work."

How cool she was, Michael thought, her voice level, she had discarded her slacks, and wore some kind of a flowered dress. She looked, as always, immaculate, beautifully groomed. Gran always grumbled that she used too much make-up—but she used it so well, with such good and restrained judgement. He remembered that Mercy Blenkiron had looked as if she'd drenched her face with a flour dredger! He supposed that you could tell that Liz resorted to all those aids which women used, but the finished result was so smooth, so well done. She smelt so pleasant too— a hint of lavender as if her clothes were laid up in it; he could imagine the piles of beautiful, fine garments, meticulously neat, filling her chests and cupboards. Instinctively he knew that Liz was extravagant over her linen, that everything she wore had to be crisp and fresh. Then there was some other scent which he imagined that she sprayed on her arms, and neck, perhaps her hair. It reached you when she moved—elusive, scarcely defined, and yet individual.

George's voice at his elbow said, "C'm on, Michael, you're dreaming. Forget the hay for five minutes," and handed him a long tumbler in which chips of ice chinked against the tall glass. "See how you like that."

As he took the glass, already frosted, he thought that he saw a bright glance in Liz's eyes, as if she shared with him the secret of his lapse into dreams. It was no actual laughter, more a

96

recognition that she understood and was glad that he could become so absorbed in her.

He drank the contents of the long glass with appreciation.

"Wonderful! Now, George, give me half an hour and I must get back."

In the study, at Tancred's big desk, they became immersed in the accounts of Cummings. George was astute and his praise—though temperate was none the less sincere. He let Michael see that he appreciated all he had done, was doing and would do in the future.

"A damn good show," he said, his hand on Michael's shoulder when the explanations, plans and suggestions were ended. "I'm grateful. You've heard that Liz is going to town. I don't see why not. Always provided that things don't get too hot there—which they very well may. That won't deter Liz, she's got sufficient pluck for twenty. If they do, if the Hun starts bombing—as I believe he will—try to get her back."

Michael said grimly, "I should have a hope, shouldn't I?"

"A pretty poor one, I'll admit, but do what you can."

Michael collected his books. "I'll cut along. Glad that you're pleased with the way things are going."

He walked back to deposit his books, to change quickly into working clothes, his mind again disturbed and troubled. He was not a youth given to self-analysis, but the thought of George worried him.

He had always liked Tancred, had even admired him, he was fair and just, 'decent' was the word which came to Michael's mind. George had trusted him sufficiently to leave him in charge of the farm, to keep the accounts, spend money wisely; he wondered what George's reactions would be if—he knew. Then he asked himself—'if he knew—*what*? What was there to know?' People did fall in love, and how far they could control that emotion was a matter of conjecture. Admittedly they could keep quiet, they need not blurt the state of their mind to the other person as he had done. If he had done wrong, if he had any reason for feeling that he had let George down it was when he had lost his head, felt suddenly desperate and told Liz—or tried to tell Liz—what she meant to him.

As he drove the mower round the big field, the scent of the sweet grass, hot in the sunshine rising to his nostrils, he tried as he did so often to hammer the whole thing out. What would the future hold? Would he go on loving Liz as he did now, would she

97

continue to love him, or would the whole thing fade and die like those field flowers which were lying now in the cut grass, already fading and beginning to wither?

Michael was ignorant of the development of a love affair, he had never experienced even the mildest form of sentimental feeling for any of the girls he had known. He was not completely innocent in common with most boys who have been educated in a large school. The various entanglements, the intricacies and the very furtiveness of school intrigues had never interested him, he had realized them, but he had shrunk from participating in anything which he felt was scarcely worth the risk.

He remembered discussing the matter with a boy called Randolph. Randolph was—in Michael's opinion—making an ass of himself over a junior fellow, a little chap with very curly hair.

Randolph said, "There's no harm in it, Anderson."

"There's precious little good in it! That's your affair, it's not my pigeon, but it's the damned *risk*. We both know what it means if Manders finds out and tells the head. You'll both be sacked, and—it's not worth it."

His friend shrugged his shoulders. "Plenty of chaps do it."

"More fools they! If people want to risk being expelled, then take a risk for something worth while. I'm not preaching, God forbid, it may be that I'm one of those cold-blooded types. When I first came there was a big chap in the Fifth, it was his last half. I was flattered because he made it obvious that he—well, liked me."

Randolph regarded him gravely. "I imagine plenty of other men have—liked you."

"I hated hiding everything. Furtiveness. Sneaking into the box room, meeting down in the spinney and all the rest of it. I'm not pie but—I felt *dirty*. I told this big fellow so. I remember how furious he was." Michael laughed at the remembrance. "He used words that I didn't even know the meaning of—then. I do now!"

He let his thoughts run on, unchecked. He scarcely knew what he was trying to disentangle, only felt that if he worried over everything sufficiently he might get things straight.

He remembered during last winter going to a dance at Huddersley; most of the people were his seniors, though because he looked older than his years they treated him as their contemporary.

"Had a good time this Christmas, Anderson?" Frank Clayton had asked.

"Jolly good. And you?"

Clayton winked. "I should say so. Had a couple of nights in town. Did we hit the high spots!"

Larry Mason grinned. "I only got to Manchester, but believe me, you can have a pretty hot time there if you know the ropes."

Clayton said, "I take it that you know 'em, Larry."

"I should do. Now, we'll see what life in His Majesty's service offers. I started when I was fifteen! I thought it was damned dull."

"Still hold that opinion?" a tall young man in uniform asked.

"Not likely. Do you, Anderson?"

Michael hated and despised himself for flushing hotly. "I don't know."

"You don't know! What! d'you mean that you've never——"

The flush, he remembered, died. "No, never."

"Good lord! Strapping, great chap like you! One day when we're all on leave we'll meet in town. We'll show you—life, eh, Mason?"

It hadn't shocked him that they went with women, he just wondered how they could possibly show the slightest interest in some woman—they probably didn't even know.

Even now, he had never allowed his mind to wander along such paths regarding Liz. He turned the mower neatly at the end of the field and began to drive back cutting fresh swathes of tall, rich grass.

It would be wonderful to hold Liz in his arms, to feel her soft smooth skin—he thought it must be very cool, perhaps faintly scented with the faint perfume which she used so carefully. For the rest—he dared not think. With fierce determination he forced himself to turn his thoughts into other channels. He felt the sweat on his forehead, and wiped it away with his shirt sleeve. He brought the mower to a standstill, and called to Wilson.

"Come and take over, will you?"

Michael got down, he felt that his legs were weak and inclined to shake. Confound it, he must take a firmer grip on himself, not allow his mind to stray into dangerous paths.

Wilson climbed on to the driving seat. "You've bin driving over long, Mister Michael, you luke all done in. It's heavy driving, this is."

Michael nodded. "I'll take your place raking. Carry on."

Resolutely he forced himself to think out plans, to remember the various suggestions which he had made to George. Friesians —George said, "I've always regarded them as a rich man's beast. But if you believe in them, try a few—not a herd, just as a trial. Study the milk yield first though." Pigs—they had discussed the merits of Large Whites and Gloucester Spots. Michael fancied the Large Whites. "Get a couple of nice gelts," George had said. "See how they come on. You'll need some new sties. Get them done before labour gets difficult." Poultry, the merits and demerits of Light Sussex, Leghorns, Rhode Islands; keeping semi-intensive, a new type of house, roomier and better ventilated. Crop rotation, catch crops.

There was plenty to think about. There would be more forms to fill in with these new government departments. George, grumbling, said they'd all be clerks not farmers very soon the way things were going.

"I must see if my mother can't find me a room to use as an office."

"No sense in that," George objected, "while I'm away come here and use this room, everything's to your hand."

There, his thoughts had taken the bit in their teeth and bolted back—to Liz. To use George's study, to have a good and valid excuse for visiting Cummings every day—then he remembered that Liz wouldn't be there, Liz was going to London.

Michael set his teeth, he felt frustrated and disheartened.

Then he caught sight of Violet coming into the field, carrying the tea. He waved to Wilson. "Tea—knock off for a break."

Chapter Eight

GEORGE left on Saturday morning. Michael had read of men who going overseas commended their wives to the care of some special friend. He walked across the yard to where George had halted his car, in an agony of mind that George might ask him to 'take care of Liz'. George didn't, he looked preoccupied, and seemed anxious to get away.

"S'long, Michael," he said.

Michael shook his hand. "Good luck, George."

"Thanks. My love to them all. No, I haven't time to come in. All the best." Then glancing at the sky, "It's going to rain, there'll be no hay-making for you to-morrow. S'long."

"It's going to rain," the words rang in Michael's head long after the hum of Tancred's big Sunbeam had died away. Going to rain, no hay-making. He went back into the house and looked at the barometer which hung in the narrow hall. He had set it yesterday, it had been steady enough, now—true enough—it had fallen.

In the kitchen he asked Gran if she had heard the news.

"Nay, I've no time to be twiddling knobs all the time i' the morning. I listen at night when work's over."

He went up at dinner time to see his father. Enoch now sat in his big chair for several hours each day. His improvement was a miracle the doctors said. His face looked pale but it was almost normal again, the dreadful twisting of his features had almost disappeared. Certain letters still presented a difficulty to him, but his speech was sufficiently clear for anyone to understand.

"'Lo, Michael. How's the hay? Wilson says—rain i' 'orthern distric's. 'Et's hope it won't 'ast long. Good crop?"

"Splendid. I wanted to work to-morrow—if it rains—well, we shall have to lay off."

Enoch chuckled. "I used to have a piece o' seaweed I got at Whitby—someone's 'aken it away. Used to hang behind that door."

Michael said, "I'll take a trip to Whitby some day and get you another piece."

His father chuckled again. "When I was young, 'ere used t' be a song, 'As 'oon as I 'ouched my seaweed, I knew it was 'oing to be wet'. Funny how you remember daft things 'ike that."

They had started carting the small field's crop. The hay was bone dry, and with every load Michael watched the sky. The rain was holding off. Strange that you could be divided between the carting of hay and the longing to drive with Liz to London.

He told Willett, "If it's fine we'll work to-morrow. That's all right, I spoke to Mr. Tancred—double time. He's willing."

Willett sniffed the air like a gun dog. "It 'ul not be fine. Look at those hills, you never saw hills so clear as yon unless rain was coming. Still let's hope it 'ul take up quickly."

"Let's hope so. This field will be clear by dinner time." Clear it was, the field left shorn, denuded of its grass, already showing a little harsh and rusty looking, for the sun was still strong, though the clouds were gathering. Michael walked back to dinner, hurried through it and walked over to Cummings. As he crossed the field great drops of rain fell splashing on his face. In the distance he heard the low rumble of thunder, this was the end of hay-making for to-day and probably to-morrow.

Ellen said, as she opened the door to him, "Madam's still having her coffee in the parlour. Will you walk in, please?"

Liz looked up as he entered, he thought his heart missed a beat when he saw her sudden smile, and the light in her eyes. "Mike——!"

He stood some paces away from where she sat. "See the rain?" he asked jerking his head towards the long windows. "That's put paid to my hay-making for the week-end."

Liz still smiled. "So as you can't make hay—you'll take the second best and drive to London, is that what you've come to say?"

"Don't be unkind, you must know how it is——"

" 'I could not love thee dear so much, Love I not—hay-making—more', never mind, I'm teasing you. Drive to London, and bring the car back in the evening. Let's make an early start—rain or no rain. Eight, then we can lunch at Stamford. You know the George? Nice old place."

Michael saw that her face had taken on new animation, she looked younger and more vital. Was it possible that she was happy as he was at the prospect of spending a few hours together?

"May I sit down?" he asked.

"Darling, in my delight that I've won a victory over the hay, I forget my manners. Have a cup of coffee—a drink——" he shook his head. "Then smoke."

He said, rather heavily, "Liz, what about George?"

"What about George?" he heard her voice sharpen a little.

"I mean—do you think he'd mind? I mean mind about my driving with you?"

Her eyebrows shot up, she looked intolerant. "Mike, are you growing tender-hearted about George, imagining him reporting at some dreary depot? George doesn't have to report until Tuesday at mid-day. At the moment George is in Bradford—ostensibly having some momentous interviews with Claygate. I've reminded him once that solicitors don't keep their offices open after mid-day on Saturday."

"I suppose that he's seeing him early on Monday," Michael said, he felt disturbed, worried over George Tancred's whereabouts.

Liz leaned forward. "My dear, George is spending the week-end with someone called 'Mavis' and his small daughter. I don't mind, I forget if I told you that everything—like that—is over between George and me. He's still convinced that he won't come back, just as he felt when he went to France. Poor George, he'll hate leaving Mavis—I don't know her other name, probably she is known as 'Mrs. Tancred'—and the child." She sighed. "He was very sweet, he said all kinds of nice things to me, but I'm—like you and your hay-making—a bad second." She glanced at the window. "Look at that rain!"

Michael stood up, the rain was pouring down, the peals of thunder were growing louder, the flashes of lightning more frequent and brilliant.

"It will wear itself out," he said, "there'll be sunshine to-morrow—but—" he turned and held out his hands, "it won't be possible to work. Liz—dear, dear Liz. How I've hated this past week—these past two weeks."

She came to where he stood, and laid her hands on his shoulders.

"I'm a fool to admit it—but I never knew that I could love anyone so much."

"And yet you're going to London."

She took his face between her hands and kissed him gently. "We've got to be wise, Mike. We're caught in the machinery, if we stayed here someone would suspect, then someone would whisper, and I won't have you—or myself—for that matter, though I matter less than you—dragged into a welter of scandal and general beastliness.

"Either this love of ours is going to last, to grow and be very lovely and wonderful, or—oh, I know that it seems impossible now—die down and fade out of existence. No, don't look like that—these things happen, I'm not really old, but you're young, terribly young." She kissed him again. "My beloved Mike."

He caught her in his arms, holding her close. "Liz, I shan't change. I *know* that I shan't. Only while you're away try to always *believe* in me. I know that I'm young, time will put that right——"

"But," she said sadly, "even time won't allow you to catch up with me, darling."

"Then you must concentrate on growing younger!" he smiled down at her upturned face. "Now there's your war work, ready to your hand—then when you're about nineteen, perhaps you'll feel that this frightful gap which stretches between us can be bridged. Silly, silly adorable Liz, I must go."

"Kiss me again."

For a moment, time, the pouring rain, the thought of the farms left him, he was only conscious that he held her to him and pressed kisses on to her face. At last, when it seemed that time had stopped, the ticking of the French clock held no significance whatever, she pushed him away, and said—her voice shaking a little—"At least we shall have to-morrow."

"To-morrow. I'll be here—just before eight." He knew that his voice was not quite steady. "I shan't be late. Good-night, my dear, dear love."

He went home and told his mother and Gran, both bemoaning the rain, that Liz wanted him to drive to London with her and then to bring the car back.

Ada said, "Nay, in one day! It's a longish drive."

"The car's powerful, Mum, it eats up the miles. A Humber Snipe."

"Even then it's a long drive, and if it's fine on Monday you'll want to start early."

Michael laughed. "Dear Mum, with this downpour it would have to be a blazing day to-morrow to make it possible to make hay on Monday."

She rose and pushed back her chair. "Just the same, I shall pack a bag for you in case you have to stay the night anywhere. Now, if Liz wants you to stay in London, and wants to go to one of these grand restaurants—would you like your evening suit—and all the rest of it put in?"

Michael shook his head. "Don't bother, Mum. I shan't stay the night in London and I shan't go to any swagger restaurants."

She rubbed her nose reflectively. "You never know."

Michael went to her and slipped his arm round her waist, already ample; he drew her close, what Gran called a 'right luving hug'.

"*I* know," he said.

Gran looked up from her knitting. "It's a strange, queer thing to me that George Tancred couldn't have driven Liz up to town himself. I know where his depot is—Bedford. Unless my jog'-raphy's all wrong, that's not so far from London." Her keen old eyes behind their steel-rimmed glasses peered at Michael. "I say it's a queer, strange thing."

"It's not, Gran. I don't know, but George may have had to make a call on the way. He did say something about his solicitor."

"Tut! Of a Saturday afternoon——"

"George is a valuable client, Gran."

"Happen he is, happen he isn't." She returned to her knitting, murmuring, "Two purl, one plain—slip one, two purl. . . ."

His mother returned, she had blossomed since Enoch's recovery and Michael understood—now, as he had never done before, what that nice little man meant to her. What a fight she had put up, when everyone else would have wagged their heads and predicted that Enoch Anderson was—finished. His mother had clung to her faith, more, she had—and she was not an imaginative woman—created a legend that even though he was bedridden, Enoch still was the controlling hand. Now, it seemed that her faith was to be justified, and Michael saw her, as he had not seen her since his father's illness, smiling, with the colour returning to her cheeks, and the spring to her step.

"Dad's ever so pleased," she said, "he says the drive will do you good. He's a bit tired—been up in his chair quite a long time to-day, but he's sent you this. If you stop on the way for luncheon or whatever it might be, he says, 'Tell Michael to pay, I can't do with young men letting women settle the bill.' There."

She handed him a five-pound note.

She sat down, took up her knitting and said, "And your bag's all packed. Dad's loaned you his nice pigskin one. Oh, and Miss Fowler telephoned to know if you'd go over to-morrow. It seems they've gotten a hard tennis court. It dries quite quickly. I asked her to telephone—or you'd telephone her in the morning. I didn't know then about your going with Liz."

Michael, lounging in the big chair, soothed by the quiet, friendly atmosphere of the parlour, enjoying resting his eyes on the beautifully polished table, the gleaming bits of brass on the mantelshelf, had already begun to feel sleepy. He forced himself to attend. Tonette Fowler, the girl who young Rawsley regarded as a 'smasher'.

He said, "Mum, be a darling and telephone for me in the morning, say I've had to go to London."

Ada laid down her work, and looked intently at her elder son. "Michael, I want you to listen carefully. Oh, Gran knows because we've talked it over. Last week you were at Colonel Blenkiron's, now here's an invite from Sir George Fowler's daughter."

Gran interpolated, "And think on, he's not some jumped-up knight, isn't George Fowler. He's a baron-ite. I've heard that he's the sixth or seventh of 'em."

Ada moved impatiently. "All right, Gran, let me talk. You're going to be here for another year, even then maybe they won't take you, as being more use on the land, and I don't want you to get—well, ideas above your station.

"There's no sense in not admitting, even if I am your mother, that you're a taking looking lad; you speak nicely, you wear good clothes—Dad's always insisted on you and James being well dressed—and—well—there'll be a shortage of nice, good-looking lads. These young girls—they get fancies, and I don't want you to get fancies too. Neither Colonel Blenkiron, Sir George nor any of the other families you've come to know, would welcome Michael Anderson as a son-in-law.

"We're not gentry, we're not even yeoman farmers, we're in trade and your Dad, before it pleased God to strike him down, was a working farmer. We live in a farm-house! So just be wise, my dear, about mixing over much with these people. They're nice folk they're friendly, but—they'd never want you as one of the family not was it ever so."

She spoke so earnestly, her face was so full of affection and real concern that Michael leaned forward and patted her hand.

"Mum, what on earth are you worrying about? They're nice girls—Mercy Blenkiron, Tonette Fowler, Kathleen Broadwood, and the rest of them but—you're allowing your imagination to run away with you, dear. I'm just an extra male to make up a party—that's all there is to it. They're nice, kind, friendly, but— there it all ends."

He thought, 'How could any of them attract me after—Liz!'

Ada nodded. "I hope that you're right." Then her voice taking on a slightly higher note, "Neither Dad nor me would take it kindly if you got—entangled with any of those young ladies. Remember, to Mrs. Colonel Blenkiron, Lady Fowler and the Honourable Mrs. David Broadwood, I'm—Mrs. Anderson who serves them in the shop!"

He watched her kind, serious face, saw the little line which always showed between her eyebrows when she was worried, and wished that he could have told her that he had given his heart completely and irrevocably to Liz Tancred.

He smiled at her. "Mum, don't look so serious, and don't talk about being 'Mrs. Anderson who serves in the shop' because you're so many other things as well. Anyway, what's wrong with serving in a shop? I expect that once upon a time Lord Woolton served in a shop."

Gran reminded him, "There's shops and shops, my lad."

"Gran, your logic is too much for me!" he laughed, and felt relieved when he saw that his mother's face cleared, that the little worried line had disappeared. She folded up her knitting, and sighed, a sigh of content.

"It's been a longish day," she said. "I could fancy a cup of tea before I go to bed."

Michael sprang up. "Sit still, I'll make it."

He was glad to have something to do, even if it was only setting out cups on a tray and making tea in the squat, brown pot that his mother declared made better tea than any other.

Gran said, "That's what I always say, give me a brown tea-pot and you can have all your silver ones; as for those metal things they give you in tea shops—nay, they make me feel right badly, mucky things."

He whistled softly as he warmed the pot, measured out the tea—'one for each person and one for the pot' that was the formula—then carried it back to the parlour.

Ada said, "There's a good lad. Yes, milk first."

"Give it time to draw," Gran warned, "or it 'ul be only blash. I can't stand blashy tea."

Michael slept fitfully, he was afraid of sleeping late for he was very tired and the thought that he must be up at seven made him restless. He lay awake, staring at the dark square of the open window, not completely dark for in June the nights were very short, and dawn came almost before the sky had completely lost the last light. There was a smell of rain-washed fields, for the heavy rain was over, and had left the world scented and fresh, as if it was relieved to have had the refreshment of the cool rain after days of heat. On Monday he might be able to get back to the hay-making.

He woke with a start, afraid that he had overslept, his watch showed that it was nearly seven. He leapt out of bed, went to the bathroom and had a cold shower, shaking himself like a dog, and enjoying the sudden shock of the water. He shaved carefully, using the new safety razor which his father had given him for his seventeenth birthday a few days before.

As he dressed, he wondered if a bridegroom felt as he did, a kind of wonderful elation, not unmixed with nervous tension. He selected a tie carefully, not his school tie, Liz had once said that she thought it hideous—he supposed as a matter of fact that it was ugly. His suit was immaculate, old Bealby might be a country tailor but he knew his job. He boasted that he 'built for half of the nobility and gentry in the Riding'. He put his brushes in Dad's pigskin bag, and carrying his shoes in his hand because Mum and Gran always had a 'bit of a lie in' on Sunday mornings, he crept quietly down the stairs.

The fresh, clear air of the early morning was wonderful. He stood for a moment savouring it, drawing great draughts of it into his lungs, rejoicing in its sweetness.

He wondered if Liz would miss this clear air, cooped up in London, hedged in with tall houses, breathing petrol fumes, missing the wind blowing in from over the moors, the cool nights, and all the beauty of the countryside. As he walked over to Cummings he realized, as he had done so often, that he had chosen the life which suited him as no other could have done.

The car was standing at the door, he put his bag on the back seat where Liz's luggage was already stacked, and walked into the house. She was coming down the stairs, and as she caught sight of him looking even taller than usual in his dark suit, she thought that her heart missed a beat. How good looking he was, smiling up at her, his teeth showing unexpectedly against his tanned face.

"Good-morning," he called, "I'm early—I was so afraid of being late that I rushed everything."

"You're in time to have coffee with me. Have you had breakfast?"

He laughed. "I'm afraid I forgot to have any."

"I take that as a compliment," she assured him. "Well, come and have some now. What a heavenly morning, we're going to have a wonderful drive—I love the Great North Road."

As they drank coffee, Liz reminded him that she hoped he'd use George's study, and have a word now and again with Ellen and Mrs. Robbins. She was so lucky, she said, to have them, both past 'calling-up age' and with no wish to find other work.

"They'll always get you anything you want—coffee, or a drink. And anyway, I shall try to get here from time to time, though they are so trustworthy they don't need supervision. Still, I'd like to think you talked to them sometimes. Come, let's be off."

She said good-bye to her servants, both inclined to be tearful at the parting, Mrs. Robbins—incredibly stout—giving a warning of the dangers of London, the wickedness of South country people as compared with the sterling integrity of those fortunate beings born North of the Humber. Ellen, sniffing a little, said that she'd never been to London, and never wanted to go.

"I ondly went once on an excursion," Mrs. Robbins told them, "That was enough for me, for a dirtier place I never did see!"

"Go along with you," Liz laughed, "pair of Job's comforters."

Mrs. Robbins answered, "Well, m'ùm, I ondly hope as London won't get you down. We shall be thinking about you!"

In the car, they sat silent, but Liz felt that their silence was not due to the fact that they had nothing to say, but because there was such a complete understanding between them. Michael sat, turning a little sideways so that he could watch her face, and once or twice she turned and smiled at him.

He gave her back her smile, saying very softly, "Dear Liz."

A whole day stretched before them, the first day they had ever spent together; the thought filled her with content; not only content but a great wave of tenderness swept over her. She longed to—give him things, lovely things. She would have liked to take him to Sulka's, to buy him expensive shirts, pyjamas, to lavish on him everything which would give him satisfaction.

Then she smiled, she could never imagine Michael being content to see her order and pay for clothes for him! She knew instinctively that at the very suggestion he would shrink, and refuse—politely, she didn't doubt—but quite firmly.

There were other things which were equally impossible. She had seen his pigskin case on the back seat. For a moment she had wondered if he had decided to stay the night in London, and leaving very early, drive back to Anderson's to-morrow. If so—but she dismissed the idea, she could never make any proposal to him, and she knew him sufficiently well to know that the advance would never come from him.

She said, her eyes still on the road ahead, "Is that your very smart case on the back seat?"

He answered readily, "No—well, it's only lent to me. It's my father's. Mum insisted that I brought things for the night, in case I was marooned somewhere on the North Road."

"You don't think that she—knows about—us?"

He spoke very gently, "Dearest, of course she doesn't, and there isn't really anything *to* know."

"Happy, Mike?"

"I'm with you, Liz dear."

They drove on in silence, moving swiftly, Michael filled with admiration for the way she drove, so surely, taking no risks, but somehow contriving to pass everything on the road. That was typical of her, he thought, she was so *sure*. He could never imagine Liz fumbling, being indecisive; always she would be in complete control of whatever she undertook.

For almost the first time in his life he did not watch the passing landscape, did not look at farms and speculate on the kind of crops they would produce, did not note which stacks were well built, which cattle showed the effects of care and attention. He was conscious of great trees, of here and there the glimpse of some big house, or picturesque cottage, but it was all absorbed into his consciousness without any particular attention on his part.

At Grantham, Liz turned to him after one of their long silences, and said, "The Angel and Royal, I think. Could you use a drink?"

"I'd love it."

She turned in neatly under the old archway, and parking the car with a precision which delighted him, went with him into the old hotel.

Michael asked, "Why Angel and Royal?"

She laughed. "I'm an ignorant person, Mike. I confess that I don't know. All I do know is that it dates back to—Henry the Eighth I think—look, there's a bit of the old carving. Yes—I'll have a sherry. And you—also a sherry. Dry, waiter."

He asked where they were lunching, she told him that she

planned to make The George at Stamford. He said that he'd put a call through to tell them to keep something, "we might be late."

Liz sat in one of the big chairs, she could hear his voice asking for telephone numbers, and thought what a pleasant voice it was.

'What a pleasant person he is too.' She thought, 'If only everything could be different. If only I were not ten years older than he is! If only George would decide that he wanted me to divorce him so that he could marry his Mavis! If only—if only— Oh, it's all going to be so difficult! Mike has such integrity, he'd never accept an—affair, particularly as he is working Cummings for George. He'd have scruples, and then in a year—he'll go to the Army. I don't know how I shall be able to bear that.

'I've seen them at Dunkirk—' she shivered, the very thought of Mike being wounded, disfigured or the worst of all—which she would not even imagine or formulate in her mind—made her feel physically sick. 'Perhaps the war will be over——' but in her heart she knew that the war would not and could not be over. Michael would go, because for all his gentleness, for all the love which she knew he felt for her, he had determination and once having made a decision he would abide by it. The thing had become a point of honour, a principle with him. He would never be content to remain in safety while his contemporaries faced danger, disease, and hardship.

He came back, scattering her thoughts. "That's all right. Even if we're rather late, there will be something. I've even ordered the wine!"

"You don't know what we're eating!"

His smile widened. "Indeed I do! Cold duck, salad, and a bottle of Margaux." Then anxiously, "You like Margaux?"

Liz chuckled, "You'll tell me next that you know the year!"

"I do! I wanted '19 but they offered me '20—and it's quite good. At least I've read that it's good. You see we had a master at school who was very knowledgeable about wine and food in general. He lent me books, and told me about wine and the best kinds."

"I feel that I know so little about you and your interests," Liz said regretfully, "one day I shall want to hear everything about you, from the time when you were quite a small boy. You must have been a very nice small boy, Mike."

"Like most small boys, I expect, a bit scruffy, not too clean, and with hair generally standing on end."

"I don't believe it! Come, we must be on our way, I mustn't miss that duck!"

He followed her to the car, and sat with his arm along the back of her driving seat. They were out into the country again, when he said impulsively, "Liz—dear Liz, I do love you so. Couldn't we steal five minutes—only five—turn into some quiet lane. Please, Liz dear."

She nodded without speaking, then turned the car into a lane overhung by tall chestnut trees, and stopped. She turned and faced him, "There! Kiss me, Mike."

He put his arms round her and kissed her almost hungrily; then very gently released her, and sat watching her.

"You stare me out of countenance," she said.

"I'm trying to make a picture of you—as you are now—as we are now. Just we two in a country lane, in a complete small world of our own. That's what we'll make one day, dearest, a world of our own. God knows when or how—but we will. There, I promised five minutes, the time's up, and my materially minded and adorable Liz is allowing the thought of roast duck to take first place in her mind." Once more his arms went round her, and she knew the joy and sense of peace which always filled her when she felt those wonderfully strong yet gentle arms.

"Bless you!" he whispered. "Oh, how I am going to miss you."

Chapter Nine

THEY drove on through the lovely, green country, and Liz thought if nothing good ever happened to her again she would still be able to say 'At that time, on the summer Sunday—I knew what happiness was!' They spoke very little, glancing at him she saw that Michael's face was grave, set in lines too old for his years. He was not watching her now, he was staring out at the long, black ribbon of road, immersed in thought. Again she remembered—as she had done so often—that they had caught him and put him in harness while he was still only a colt. He had assumed, and assumed willingly responsibilities which were far too heavy for him. No wonder that he looked older than seventeen. Now the love which they felt for each other, wonderful though it might be, had laid an additional burden on his shoulders. Instead of being able to enjoy this strange thing called 'being in love', it was something which he must guard and hide. Her poor Mike.

She said, "When is your birthday, Mike?"

He smiled. "I was seventeen four days ago—four? Yes, no, three."

"And you never told me!"

"Darling, you don't rush about telling people when your birthday is! It would be like a child hinting that it wanted a present."

"But—" indignantly, "I should have loved to give you a present!"

"I know, I know you too, Liz. It would have been something stupendous, and everyone would have raised their eyebrows, and said that you had more money than sense."

"Which is probably true, my dear. I'd love to give you a gold cigarette case," she was hurt and the fact could be heard in her voice.

He put out his hand and laid it very lightly over hers for a brief second. "My sweet, my mother gave me a cigarette case, a silver one. She went to enormous pains to get a nice one, and it is very, very nice. My father gave me a superlative new razor— it appears to do everything except play tunes——"

She interrupted him, "You shave!" The idea made her feel happier, then he was no longer—a boy.

"Of course, every day; you wouldn't like me to go about looking all fluffy like a newly hatched chicken!"

Liz slowed the car down, and said, holding out her hand, "Let me feel." He put her fingers against his cheek, moving it gently up and down. She said, "Real bristles! How exciting. I feel that your shaving has lessened the gap between our ages. Yes, and what else did you get?"

"My brother sent me a book token, and Gran gave me a dozen—mark that a dozen—wonderfully fine handkerchiefs. Oh, Liz, I do love *fine* things. I get a kind of sensuous pleasure from them—fine handkerchiefs, good Yorkshire cloth, Macclesfield silk ties—a sybarite, that's me."

"Yet I've seen you whistling happily while you cleaned the mower and got great smears of grease all over your face—to say nothing of your hands. They were filthy!"

"Only what Gran calls—clean muck," he said.

"I shall find something in London, it will be late but that's your fault."

Michael said, very gravely, "My darling, don't, I beg you, send me anything. You've given me so much, made me so happy— oh, yes, and unhappy too, but that was inevitable. But extravagant presents from Bond Street, I don't want them. I mean that. Gran's eyebrows would go up, my mother would say, 'Liz has spread herself!' and I should loathe it."

She said suddenly irritated, "But I *want* to! I've more money than I know what to do with, thanks to Uncle Harry. Why can't I spend it as I want to!"

His hand tightened a little on her shoulder. "You said just now that I made you feel that the gap—if indeed there is a gap which matters a row of pins—between our ages—had been bridged because I use a razor. Now, when you talk as you are doing, I realize that you are years, and years younger than I am. Let me be wise for you, darling, I know that I am being wise."

Almost pettishly she said, "Oh, very well!" and drove on in silence. Michael still smiled.

"Stamford!" Liz exclaimed, then, "Sorry that I was cross."

They drove into the courtyard, and turning to him with a smile, she said, "I can positively smell the roast duck! I am gloriously hungry and we can spend a whole hour over luncheon." The old place seemed to exude friendliness, they both felt its charm, its kindly antiquity. The martinis were beautifully cold, and later they sat opposite to each other and Liz realized that they were both sufficiently young to enjoy excellent food and good wine with no chill to it.

She told him of her plans for London. She would share a flat with a friend, in a big block of modern flats in Knightsbridge. She had joined a women's corps which drove ambulances, mobile canteens, and had plans—if their operation was necessary—for taking food and hot drinks to the docks. She gave him her address and he wrote it down in his diary.

"Monica says they are most modern flats, and that their air-raid shelter is considered the very last word in safety."

"If you're driving about with mobile canteens, or working at the docks that air-raid shelter won't be much help! Liz, will you promise that if—if there should be bombing raids—George thinks there will be—will you promise me to come back to Yorkshire?"

She looked at him, her face very tender. "Michael, *you* to ask me that!"

He frowned, puzzled. "You would!"

Liz laughed, not her soft chuckle which he loved, which meant a quiet but real amusement, but a definite laugh—a sound which held at once surprise and disbelief.

"My dear, do you have such a poor opinion of me? Thousands of women will be needed, and thousands will be there, ready to do what they can. Would you really like me to—run away, to save my skin? Mike dear, be yourself!"

He nodded. "You're right. One-half of me would like you to say that at the first sign of bombing you'd catch the next train north; the other half of me knows that—you couldn't and wouldn't even if you could."

Luncheon over, Liz said, "Tell the waiter to bring me the bill, will you?"

"It's my luncheon, Liz."

"It most definitely is not!"

"As a matter of fact it's my father's—Enoch's. He insisted that if we had a meal together I was not to allow a girl to pay the bill. He was very emphatic, and sent my mother down with the —the wherewithal. I'd got plenty, my father pays me a very good salary, and so does George. Your country bumpkin is quite a well-to-do young feller. No, please, Liz—you'll hurt me terribly."

She sighed humorously, "Oh, I can see such *rows* in the future!"

"The future—one day it will be—the present. We'll have rows just for the sheer joy of making up our quarrels afterwards."

As they drove into London, down the crowded Finchley Road, Michael said, "It's exciting to be driving into London with you."

"We've got to get to the other side of the Park, and won't a cup of tea be pleasant? Then I must send you away on your return journey. Promise me that you'll stop somewhere and have a meal."

"It will taste like Dead Sea fruit after our last meal together." He was allowing the thought of the coming parting to over-shadow everything. Depression was descending on him, and the sight of the huge block of flats where Liz drew up, with several liveried porters waiting, did nothing to raise his spirits. He was used to simplicity, even at Cummings—where everything was done much more elaborately than in his own home—there was not the air of luxury and expense which this great block of modern flats seemed to convey.

It was in such places that Liz and her friends presumably lived. He knew that Tancred was a rich man, that Liz's Uncle Harry had left her a large income, he had taken those things for granted, now they seemed to loom terribly large, to have become dreadfully important. Suppose—suppose that in the future, whatever it might hold and whatever circumstances might shape it, people shrugged their shoulders and said that Michael Anderson had done well for himself. Then, as he busied himself in handing out luggage to the uniformed porter, he tried to reassure himself, that whatever anyone said, or thought, Liz would understand and dispel any cloud which might threaten them.

He followed Liz into the big elaborate hall. The porter, his manner slightly over-respectful, escorted them to the lift. "The luggage, Madam, will be waiting for you, it will go up in the service lift. Miss Power's flat is on the third floor. Very fine building, sir, don't you think? One of the finest in London, all reinforced concrete and steel girders. Here you are, Madam."

An elderly woman, wearing a black dress and immaculate apron, opened the door. Liz said, "I'm Mrs. Tancred. Is Miss Power at home?"

"No, Madam, she was so sorry, she's on duty until ten this evening. She told me to ask you if you'd like tea."

Liz turned to Michael, smiling. "There! Just what I was hoping! Nothing could be nicer than tea."

"The kettle is on, Madam. May I show you your room? And perhaps the gentleman would like a wash. I always say to Miss

Power, 'whatever drawbacks these flats may have, there are plenty of bathrooms!' Yes, we've one each, Madam. This way, sir."

Michael followed her, she fussed about. "You'll find plenty of towels, sir. There are hairbrushes."

He thanked her, and stared round the bathroom. Their own at Anderson's was effective, he doubted if it had ever occurred to either his father or his mother to install two bathrooms. Here was a perfect battery of porcelain taps, gadgets and contrivances for a shower, an electric heater and a special lamp which he imagined to be one of the 'ultra-violet' things he had read about.

Bath towels like great sheets, smaller ones, fine linen towels, and small coloured and embroidered hand towels. They had all these things at home, but they were not dealt out in this profusion.

He washed, brushed his hair and his jacket and felt better. He sniffed the soap, and hoped that he didn't smell so strongly after using it, he'd hate to go back to Liz reeking of carnations.

She was waiting for him in the big, light drawing-room. She had changed her clothes, and Michael felt a new wave of depression sweep over him. In these sophisticated clothes, in a dress which was almost long, he felt that she had transformed herself from his companion of the Great North Road into someone who had definitely moved into a different world.

He said, "It's a marvellous flat, isn't it?"

"Um-m. I'd rather have my rooms at Cummings any day."

"Dear Liz." His depression lifted a little. "That's a nice frock, it suits you."

"It's quite old, but, yes, it is a nice frock. I hope that you paid attention to what that porter said about the building."

He nodded. "I did indeed, and felt suitably relieved."

She poured out the tea. "Is that as you like it? To-morrow I must go and see about my uniforms——"

"You're not going to wear uniform! Oh, Liz—and you look so wonderful in pretty clothes." His dismay showed plainly.

"Wait until you see me in uniform," she told him. "You'll see how smart it *can* look." She talked, speaking very rapidly, as if she could not bear the silence which might ensue if she stopped. Michael thought, 'She's talking trivialities, talking for the sake of talking. I don't care a damn about Miss Power, I don't care a damn about who the Commandant of this Corps may be. I'd rather sit silent and just watch Liz. She's afraid of a silence at this moment, yet as we drove here, we both sat silent for miles and I—at least—was utterly content.'

"You're not saying much, Mike."

"Dearest, forgive me, but you've not given me the chance, unless I flung my manners to the winds and interrupted you."

She sighed, "I shouldn't have minded. Oh, Mike—I wish you hadn't to go. The thought of you going back to Yorkshire makes me feel so—tired. Yes, mentally and physically. At home, even if I didn't see you—except in snatches—there was always the chance that I might catch sight of you, striding over the fields, cleaning a machine and getting very dirty, or even hear you calling to Willett. Now—" she made a helpless gesture, "I feel deserted, marooned on a desert island. Will you write to me, Mike?"

He sat down near to her. "Angel, I don't believe that I'm very good at writing letters, but if you want them you shall have them. Will you mind dreadfully if it's about the hay, and the turnips, and how the hens are laying, and how the baby heifer is doing?"

"No—so long as at the end you put 'I love you and miss you.' "

"And you'd know that—even if I didn't write it," he said.

The clock on the mantelpiece struck the hour. Liz started. "Quick, another cup of tea and you must go. You'll meet so much traffic, people coming back after the week-end. It will take you an endless time to get out of London. Oh, and Mike, you'll have to get a fill up, make them fill the tank, and charge it to the farm account. Use the car whenever you like, won't you? Forward any letters, and open any telegrams. Come and see my bedroom —I can't say good-bye to you here, Florence—that's her name— might come in."

He followed her into the light, airy room, with a big window looking out on to some gardens. Her bags were scattered about, she had evidently snatched up the first dress which came to her hand. Vaguely he wondered if she was a tidy woman, and then wondered again what had made him think of that at this particular moment.

He drew her to him. "Liz, my dearest, dearest Liz. Take care of yourself, you will, won't you?"

"Mike, I'll try. Kiss me and go—I believe I'm going to cry. I don't cry very often, nothing's worth crying about—except—this. Leaving you, you leaving me—whichever it is."

He kissed her, many times, gently and tenderly. "My beloved Liz——" he whispered. "God bless you, and take care of you."

"Good-bye, darling—now—go, Mike."

He drove away, feeling that he was steadily moving back into another life. The day which had been perfect, filled with companionship, love and warmth was over.

To-morrow he would take up his various tasks and duties, he would work harder than ever, he would not allow himself to moon about thinking only of Liz. Only when he wrote to her would he allow the thought of her to take complete possession of him. He hadn't written many letters in his life—to his father and mother when he was at school, occasionally to Gran, and now he wrote a short, rather stiff letter to James every week. He must try to write naturally to Liz, there should be no striving for an effect, he'd write as he talked to her—if he could. He stopped once and had a drink and a sandwich, then drove on again into the gathering dusk.

The hay was in, the weather held, Michael was so tanned that he looked like a native. James came home for his long summer vacation, James grown taller and broader, at fourteen still immersed in mathematics, yet finding time to play cricket and football and to play them both well.

George Tancred wrote at long intervals, he was well and 'somewhere in Africa'. The place was hot, incredibly dusty and the smells were something which neither George—nor anyone else, he added, except the natives—had ever either experienced or imagined.

Michael had driven over, in their own rather rattling and distinctly elderly Morris, to Colonel Blenkiron's. The colonel had a fine herd of Friesians, and Michael longed to begin one.

Blenkiron boomed, "People tell you that they're a rich man's beast. Rubbish, Anderson, sheer, unadulterated rubbish. They're not cheap, tell me what—worth having—*is* cheap. Study the milk yield! Stupendous! Come into my study, I'll show you the charts."

Two beautiful heifers. They were the pride of Michael's heart. So, too, were the two gelts, large whites of impeccable pedigree. He had built two new sties, and there they lived growing, with each week, more handsome—as handsomeness goes in pigs.

The poultry he had sorted out. George had kept far too many 'barn yards', many of them had been allowed to run free. They had interbred, more than that they were not even first-crosses. Leghorns for laying, Light Sussex for table birds. He even had one pen of Rhode Islands—they were heavy, their flesh was inclined to be yellow, but they were good layers, and the people who said that they were 'forever going broody', obviously didn't keep them in the right way.

He had new movable houses, with their own runs, they were kept exquisitely clean, and the houses moved from time to time in case the grass grew sour. Then it was raked, and re-sown, and the hens kept healthy and in fine condition.

Young Harry went to join the Army, and Michael engaged three 'land girls', they were housed at Cummings, and gave no trouble, indeed he thought that Ellen and Mrs. Robbins welcomed their company.

His father was growing stronger with each month. He was able to come downstairs and on fine days to sit outside and watch what he could of the work on the farm, his expression, Michael felt, full of longing to be able to take part in the life.

Michael's own days were filled with work, with projects, and with the everlasting forms which gradually came in greater and greater quantities. James made light of them.

"Let me have them, Michael. Just show me where all your figures and returns are kept—they're nothing!"

Michael said, "Nothing, Jimmie, if that's all I had to do, but undeniably *something* when you've a farm—two farms for that matter—to run. I'll be grateful if you can deal with these damned forms for me, very grateful."

"Easy as pie!" his brother returned.

Every morning he went over to Cummings, if there were letters for Liz, he liked re-addressing them, enjoyed the feeling that he was entrusted to do that for her—and he made it a duty to see that they caught the first possible post to London. Even if he had to send off one of the land girls on the farm bicycle to Huddersley.

Liz—he had limited himself to three letters a week to her. At first they were difficult to write, he wanted to say so much, and resented the knowledge that, while he longed to write words which could convey in some measure his love for her, when he read the letters they seemed stiff and mechanical. Once he wrote, almost in despair, *I leave wide spaces between the lines, hoping that you can read between them.*

She wrote to him regularly, letters on thick, blue paper. Her writing was large, generous writing Michael thought, and the letters were not really as long as they appeared. Those were his happiest moments when, seated at George's desk, he opened them and read what she had written. To Michael it seemed that he could hear her voice, even sometimes hear that chuckling laugh which he loved. There were times when he longed passionately to go up to London and spend a few hours with her. He loved his mother, and loved—in a lesser degree—his grandmother, his father was growing to mean more and more to him, his advice was invaluable, and when the Friesian heifers were installed at Cummings, nothing would satisfy him but that Michael should drive him over to see them. James was a fine fellow, but all the time he felt the longing, the tugging at his heartstrings to see Liz.

Crops were ripening; day by day he watched the wheat, barley and oats change from green to a soft gold, saw the ears fill and felt again the joy of the harvest. It filled him with content and pride, 'England needs food!' well, Michael Anderson would see that she got every grain that he could produce for her.

On August 9th, when he went back to breakfast, he felt as he entered the kitchen a sense of tension.

James looked up, "Michael, they bombed London last night. I heard it on the news at eight."

Gran said, "Imagine the impudence of it!"

Michael repeated, his voice dull, "They bombed London! Where?"

"Didn't say."

He sat down, drank a cup of tea, and said, "I've got to go into Huddersley. No, I don't want anything to eat, thanks, Gran."

Huddersley—no, everyone knew him there, he would go over to Cummings and telephone from there. Ellen met him, she looked distressed and worried.

"Eh, Mister Michael, I am glad you've come. Think of it—them brutes bombing London, and madam there an' all. There's a telegram for you, on the desk in the study."

"Thanks Ellen, it may be from Mrs. Tancred."

He picked up the orange envelope, and wondered if he dared open it. The sweat ran down his forehead and into his eyes, he sat down heavily, still holding the unopened telegram. Ellen watched him, making little clicking noises with her tongue. She was to tell Mrs. Robbins later, "That poor lad, for say what you like that's all he is—was prop'ly upset. Couldn't bring his'self to open the wire."

With an effort he slit the envelope.

Perfectly safe nasty experience but courage of everyone wonderful writing immediately Liz

Ellen said, "Excuse me, Mister Michael, everything all right?"

Michael looked up and smiled. "I'll read it to you," he said. He read it slowly, doing so seemed to make it more real, as if Liz were talking to him.

Ellen exclaimed, "There! They won't beat us, Mister Michael."

There followed dreadful days when the raids were an everyday occurrence; every day Liz telephoned to Cummings, if Michael was not there she left a message when and where he could speak to her. Sometimes Michael's hand shook so much that he could scarcely hold the receiver, and only the sound of her voice—that light, clear voice—stabilized him. Many times he urged her to come home, protested that there was work in plenty for her waiting at Cummings.

She always gave him the same answer, "Michael, you're inciting me to run away!"

She wrote to him, in that rather sprawling, easy handwriting.

My dear, there are several millions of people in London. They can't leave. I took on this job, and apart from everything else, in common decency I can't leave it—until it's finished. Meanwhile although I won't pretend that it is very pleasant, it has got moments which are wonderful. Florence, who is not noticeably humorous, said the other day when it was raining, and there was a raid going on, "I'm glad to see the rain, that will give those horrid Huns a good wetting. I hope they catch their deaths of cold!" I think of you so often, my dearest, and even when I do get a little 'windy' the thought of you and your love for me is a wonderful help.

Then there was a breathing space and from August 31st to September 7th, the raids ceased, the 'Battle of Britain' was apparently over. On September 7th, the night raids began, and Michael wondered which terror was the more dreadful.

Liz wrote:

It's not every night, there are some nights when everything is quiet, and they say that each day our defences are growing stronger. But it's going to be a long war, a grim one, my dearest. The poor East End! But offset that—the pluck of the Cockney! Not all the aeroplanes in the world can break or even shake that. They're marvels, it's a privilege to do anything for them.

He found that talking with his father helped him in those days. Enoch, coming down every day for several hours, had made further improvement, his speech was clear, only at intervals did

122

some letter prove difficult. Michael had never realized the amount of clear thinking that his father did. To sit with him and discuss the affairs of the farms, to talk of the war, to speak of the hundred and one things which were part of the daily routine, made Michael relax and gain assurance.

One evening, as they sat together in the garden in the cool softness of a late September evening, Enoch looked at his son, frowning a little.

"You've gotten over thin, Mike. About time you 'ook a holiday."

"Holiday, Dad! We're harvesting!"

"Tut, tut! You'll not be harvesting for ever, lad! You're like a rail. Our James 'ould make two of you. No sense in killing yourself. I'd say go to 'Ondon and see Liz, but 'ats no place to spend a holiday just now."

Michael set his teeth, as if he didn't know that! As if he would care about the night raids if only he could be with Liz. Still, she wouldn't 'run away' from her work, and neither would he.

"It's not going too well, Dad, is it?" he said.

Enoch sighed, "How much do we know, Mike, folks like you and me? Damned little. We're just private soldiers, an' I mind a man tellin' me that in the last war. The one as was to end all wars!" He laughed. "Aye, that's what they said—a war to end all wars, an' make the whole world 'afe for democracy! That bet didn't come off, by God, it didn't!

"'Es, this chap said we're like private soldiers. Each one—i't' last war knew his own bit of line and no more. That's like us now, Mike. We're not doing the directing, and we don't know what plans are being made. Those who know aren't going to send us notice what's being 'lanned. Churchill, Roosevelt, Wavell, and the rest of them.

"Now you read me a bit out of a letter from Liz about the spirit of the Londoners. Liz is seeing with 'at you might call a—limited vision. It's not the spirit of Londoners, it's the spirit of the whole of England." He raised his hand, and brought it down on the arm of his chair. "It's the spirit of the whole of 'loody England! Think on, lad. Let the Russians, and Rumanians, and damned this and that country put their money on the Germans! They think they're on a safe thing, they find 'easons for thinking so. We're not sufficiently trained, we're not so well 'quipped as the Germans, we're one thing an' another. Good! It 'ul be a long struggle, but who'll be past the post first—i' the end. You know, an' I know."

Michael said, smiling at him affectionately, "You sound like Winston Churchill! You put heart into a chap."

"You've never needed to have heart put into you, it's always been there. Mike—" Enoch's voice was wistful, "let me—come in on things. I was a pretty 'ecent farmer, and I've got everything back except just the strength to get out and do a good day's work. It's a bitter 'hing, lad, to feel that you're—laid aside. Let me feel 'at I can still be a bit of use to you, as a farmer and—" he paused, then continued, "and as your Dad, who loves you, an' admires you."

Michael longed to tell him about Liz, to admit that so long as the raids lasted he would go in fear, fear for her and for himself, because without Liz nothing—not even his much-loved land—would matter. This small, pale-faced man, who had suffered so much and who had won through with his courage unimpaired was, in spite of his bodily weaknesses, a strong prop and stay. He knew that it was impossible to speak of Liz and his love for her, but he did feel that when the time came—if ever it did come—he could speak to his father as to no one else.

He loved his mother, admired her, and respected her, but he had never felt so close to her as he did to Enoch at that moment.

He said, rather huskily, "Thank you, Dad. There's nothing much to admire."

"No? Listen, I know a bit about horseflesh, an' I know that it's wrong to shove a youngster into harness over 'oon. 'At's what we've done. Only, this partic'lar youngster's got staying power we didn't know of. Well, Mike, I reckon it's time I was goin' in. No, no!" suddenly testy, "I can get up by myself. I'm not a cripple!"

Michael laughed, "Who said that you were? I'll have you out for the hay-making next year, see if I don't."

Enoch, moving towards the house, said laconically, "Happen."

Chapter Ten

THE harvest was in, and a good harvest too. Michael had driven Enoch down to watch the threshing machine at work, and his father had been obviously content with all he saw.

"Next year's harvest," he said, "you'll have an extra chap working, it 'ul be me, my 'ad."

"I can well imagine that, Dad, only by next harvest—unless by some miracle the war ends—I shan't be here. I'm joining up the day after I'm eighteen."

His father slanted a glance at him, then sighed, "Aye, Mike, I see it your way, that's why I'm so set on being a well man agean. I don't say that I'll ever be one 'undred per cent fit, but I'll be able to 'et round, an' you—nor George Tancred neither—shan't have anything to 'umble about when you come back—as please God you both will."

There was a silence between them, Michael felt its tenseness, felt too an admiration for this small, unimpressive man who had fought through his illness, and was now determined to take his place in the world again.

He smiled. "There are more heroes, I honestly believe, out of the Army and Navy than in them, and one of them is you, Dad."

Enoch plodded on in silence, the sound of the threshing machine was growing fainter as they approached Anderson's; he still walked stiffly, and leaned heavily on his ash-plant, but there was determination in every line of his face, his whole, spare body was filled with it.

"Sometimes, Mike," he said, "folks mak' me sick, yes, sick. We started off with a lot of silliness—'Run Rabbit Run', and ' 'Eng Out the Washing'—'Roll Out the Barril'—there was a lot of daftness! Then this new one, ' 'Hat a Surprise for the Duce' an' something about he's had no spaghetti for weeks. It's time we stopped those vainglorious songs. Every time we've started to bawl 'em, we've had a set-back.

" 'Land of Hope and Glory'—that's different, so's that nice song by this young feller Iver Noveller—though he can't be all that young for they tell me he wrote a song in the first war— 'Keep the Home Fires Burning'—well, he's written another. I 'eard it on the wireless a few nights back. 'Rose of England.' That's a song that is!"

They walked back in silence, Enoch had never been a talkative man, and the fact that he talked now to his elder son, was proof to Michael that a new bond, a fresh link had been forged between them. It would have made him very happy to be able to speak to his father about Liz, but Liz was his 'secret garden'—he walked there, and must always walk there alone.

He was happy, happy because he knew that the year had been a success, because his father was better, because his mother was happy and confident concerning the future. He was even happy in the knowledge that Liz—although unattainable—loved him, and wrote to him very often.

The night raids went on, but not always made on London. Gran said, "Aye, we're all in it this time! Birmingham got it last night seemly. Never mind, they'll get what's coming to them, those Huns!"

Ada nodded, "I had a traveller in this afternoon—eh, stuff's getting bad to get hold of!—and he told me that the rate we're building aeroplanes is something—stupendous. That was the very word he used, 'Stupendous, Mrs. Anderson, I can't say more and I couldn't say less with truth'."

"Aye," Gran breathed, "there it is! We're not prop'ly started yet."

The rich days of October passed, the apples were picked and stored, the winter pears hung ripe, and in the fields the men were making 'potato pies' ready for the coming winter. The wonderful scent of burning leaves—'smudges' they call them, hung in the air. Gran was drying herbs, refilling the bags of lavender for the linen cupboard, her jams were made, her fruit bottling finished, she talked of marmalade.

Ada said, "I doubt there'll be no Seville oranges, Mother."

"Then I must make sweet marmalade, or use lemons."

"They're growing bad to get."

"Nay, my girl, if we can't snow white we'll snow as near white as we can get."

Michael wrote to Liz, *Can't you get leave? Is there any chance of your getting home for Christmas?* She answered, *Not a hope, my dear, not a hope. I'm well, working like a horse, and we do get a quiet night at intervals.*

He had been out doing one of the odd jobs which never cease on a farm, the day was cold, and even in his thick coat and the woollies which Gran and Mum made for him, Michael shivered. The countryside looked bleak, the fields had lost their green, lost even the golden hue which came immediately after the reaping. They were grey, asleep until the spring should wake them. Even the moors, those moors which Michael loved, were drained of their splendid purple. Here and there a bush of gorse showed brightly yellow, and in the hedgerows the red berries of hips and haws shone like rubies. There was still some colour left in the countryside, and Michael's heart felt lighter for the sight of it.

He entered the farm-yard, how trim and well kept it looked! Even to the step by the back door, with its yellow-sanded surface which Violet rubbed and smoothed every morning. Mechanically he glanced at the roofs of the steadings, and thought of the stacks, now thatched by old Bill Turner, who boasted that he was the best thatcher 'i' all Yorkshire'. He had made good his boast, for the stacks were beautifully done, and would stand up to any bad weather which might be in store.

Michael opened the kitchen door, and the smell of baking bread reached him. What a comfortable smell it was too, not only comfortable but it carried with it a sense of well-being, of homely things, heart-warming things. He scuffed his feet on the mat, and closed the door behind him. The kitchen was warm, and he felt his cold hands begin to tingle.

Violet looked up from the loaves which she was tilting in their shining tins preparatory to standing them aside to cool.

She said, "Mister Michael, they telephoned—Ellen did—to say there's a telegram over at Cummings, seemly it's bad noos. When Tommy Carter delivered it, 'e said as they was sorry at the post office about it."

"How sorry—why sorry? Is it about—Mrs. Tancred?"

"I couldn't rightly say—and them at post office 'as taken a' oath not to tell what's in them telegrams. I couldn't say—I don't reckon soa, it's for Tancred. Mrs. Tancred—well, if it 'ad bin about 'er, surely it 'ud have come here."

Once more he raced over the fields, there would be a frost later, he could feel the grass crisp under his feet. Violet was right, if it had been about Liz it would have come to Anderson's. His heart was thudding hard, he tried to reassure himself that it was to say that George was coming home on leave. That would mean he must telegraph to Liz—would she get leave too? He wondered if he could bear to see her with George, when he so longed to be alone with her, to talk of their own affairs—oh, what a tangle it all was.

Ellen was waiting for him, the unopened telegram in her hand.

"Mister Michael, please God it's not bad noos."

He opened it, the words stared up at him, the phrasing which had grown so familiar to so many British people since that fateful day in last September. *The War Office regrets—Major Tancred—killed in action——*

Ellen, watching Michael's face intently, whispered, "Oh, what is it, Mister Michael? Tell me, please."

"It's—Major Tancred, Ellen," he heard his voice shake and grow hoarse.

"Wounded?"

"No, Ellen, not wounded."

"Not—not killed?"

Michael nodded. His throat was dry, this was the first time that death had come so near to them all. George dead—they had known that he had been in Africa, with General Wavell's army, his recent letters had been filled with confidence, while he could give little or no exact information there had been a new spirit of hope and expectancy. Now George was dead.

Ellen said, "Oh, the poor missus! Who's to tell her?"

He answered tonelessly, "I don't know."

"Mister Michael, come into the kitchen and let uz give you a cup of tea. It's shook you. Well, it 'ul shake all of us."

He followed her, listened while she gave the news to Mrs. Robbins, they both cried, and Michael watched them dry eyed. Not only Liz, there was this girl George had loved—and a child. She'd get no official telegram, she wasn't the next of kin. He would telephone to Claygate. George might have left instructions with him.

He drank his tea, grateful for its strength and warmth. Mrs. Robbins, rocking herself backwards and forwards, murmured, "Oh, our pore missus. 'Oo'll tell 'er. You can't telephone to 'er, can you, Mister Michael? The shock!"

He put down his cup. "Thank you, Ellen, that's done me good. I'm going to telephone to Mr. Claygate—the solicitor."

"Now that *is* a' idea! You've gotten a 'eadpiece!"

He gave his news to Oliver Claygate, and heard the rather thin, precise voice answering.

"A terrible shock, Mr. Anderson. A very fine fellow. And Mrs. Tancred? In London, yes, of course. Are you going to inform her?"

"Not by telegram. It's one thing the War Office doing it, they've got to. I shall go myself."

"When? You don't want her to see it in the lists!"

"Immediately—yes, immediately. And, Mr. Claygate—" he hesitated, "if there is anyone—if there are people who should be told, can I leave that to you?"

"Indeed, yes. Most distressing, most distressing. It might be well if Mrs. Tancred could come North for a short time—business matters, you understand, business matters. Pray offer her my most sincere condolences. I shall of course write to her—to London?"

"No, to Cummings. I'll try my best to persuade her to come back with me. Good-bye, Mr. Claygate."

He went back to the kitchen, Ellen and Mrs. Robbins were drinking fresh cups of tea. He told them that he was going to London, and that he hoped to bring Liz back with him.

"What did I say," Mrs. Robbins exclaimed, "I said to Ellen, I said, 'Leave it to Mister Michael, he's got a 'eadpiece on 'im.' Send uz a telegram, won't you, when to expect madam?"

Ellen, sniffing, suddenly added, "Everythink 'ul be ready for the pore dear, be sure of that."

He walked back to Anderson's, his feet felt heavy, it was an effort to walk quickly. His mind was surging with thoughts, thoughts which intruded and which he tried with all his might to drive away.

George was dead, Liz was free. What was that going to mean to them both, how would it affect them? Then he clenched his hands, and tried to banish the ideas which rushed through his mind. He must not allow himself to think along those lines— surely he must feel sorrow, pity for George who had so enjoyed life and was now lying dead in some grave so far from his own land. To speculate concerning his own future at such a time was infamous!

He was sorry, terribly sorry. He had liked George, George had believed in him—trusted him. The thought of that trust came with a stab of something which brought regret with it. Yet, George had loved a woman other than Liz, he had a child by her, and it was evident that Claygate was in his confidence.

He could imagine Gran saying, 'Nay, lad, two wrongs don't make a right, and wrong's no man's right, think on.'

Had he betrayed the trust which George had placed in him? Or could he take unction to his soul, that George's trust was that he would do his best for the farm, the Friesians, the beasts, and the like. Well, he had betrayed no trust there! The farm now was as good if not better than it had ever been, he had never spared himself, he had poured out time, thought, and determination.

Then he knew that he was indulging in wishful thinking, in seeking for excuses, self-justification. He tried to tell himself that he had *done* nothing wrong. Then he remembered some words he had learned in Scripture lessons, about whoever had lusted after a woman in his heart had already committed adultery. Then again he defended himself, he hadn't 'lusted after' Liz Tancred. He had held her in his arms, he had kissed her, loved her nearness and the delicate scent which she emanated. Once more his sturdy north-country honesty asserted itself. He *had* lusted after her, but he had sufficient will-power not to actually formulate his thoughts, purposely he had kept them nebulous. The desire had existed, all the same, and now he was indulging in sophistry, trying to make himself out a kind of Sir Galahad!

Michael knew that he felt no actual shame, how far could you control—love? That was why the phrase had been coined—falling in love. That was exactly what it was, falling, unable to save yourself, facing something immeasurably stronger than you were. How far was anyone blameworthy? No, not for falling in love, you could excuse that, or whatever powers governed the lives of men and women would surely understand that, but allowing emotions to overcome you, to 'take the goods the gods provide'—there you could, if you had sufficient strength, sufficient integrity, retain command.

He was going now to tell Liz that her husband was dead, killed fighting for his country, defending the very ground on which Michael trod at the moment. Liz might not have loved him, Liz knew everything about his mistress, his child, but Liz had—his mind halted for a word—decency. It was impossible to mourn with a particularly personal sense of loss, the death of every soldier who was killed. Only George had, at some time, meant a great deal to Liz, she must have loved him, or she would never have married him. Some of the fragrance of those early days might still cling around his memory. That would be the time when Liz mourned for him.

Liz must be given time for decent mourning for George, she must have time to realize that she no longer had a husband. Michael had seen them together, it had been evident to him that they were friends, and good friends. She might have condoned his affair with another woman, Michael felt certain that she envied that other woman who had given George a child, but the friendship had remained. Michael loved her, completely and absolutely, but in the days which lay ahead—immediately ahead —he must demand nothing, ask for nothing. They must not even return to their former moments of embraces, passionate kisses, to do so would be almost as if they admitted a certain relief that George was dead, and that they were free.

Michael's mouth twisted a little. It seemed that George Tancred dead in North Africa exercised a more restraining influence than he had done when he was still alive.

He walked into the warm kitchen where the smell of newly baked bread still hung in the air. Violet looked at him, her round face showing curiosity.

"Everything all right, Mister Michael, over at Cummings?"

He hesitated, then said, "Major Tancred has been killed."

Violet flung up her hands. " 'Lor, that's 'orrible, isn't it? Oh, poor Mrs. Tancred—'im and 'er always so happy together. It's shocking, isn't it?"

Michael nodded. "It's bad. Is my mother back?"

"No, she's still at the shop, and Mrs. Crawther an' all. The master's i' the parlour. Be careful, Mister Michael, be careful not to gie' him a shock."

"I'll be as careful as I can," he said, and walked along the long, cool flagged passage to the room where his father sat.

Enoch looked up from the farming journal he was reading. "Hello, Mike. Join me in a cup o' tea? It's here, only just brought in." Then looking at his son more closely, he frowned.

"Nout wrong, is there?"

"I'm afraid the news is pretty bad. Dad, there's a telegram from the War Office, they sent for me to open it at Cummings."

He heard his father draw a sharp breath. "George wounded?"

"It's worse than that, Dad."

"Nay! Not killed!" Michael nodded. "Eh, that's terrible. Now, 'at's to be done? Yon poor Liz, alone there i' London. With none of her own wi' her. You've not telegraphed?"

"No, I thought that it might be better if I told her."

Enoch's face lost some of its distress. "Right—aye, you're right. After all you're one of her own kin. Noo, let's see what's to be done. Let me think, Mike." He sat silent for a few moments, and Michael felt a sudden rush of gratitude that his father should feel that he could take control and direct.

"Listen," Enoch said, "get on the phone to London. You know the name of a decentish hotel. I don't. I'll pay all exes. Take a sitting-room an' a bedroom, then you can ask Liz to come an' have 'inner with you. If she shares this flat wi' someone, well, it might be difficult to break 'ad noos i' front of others. That's the first job. Then get Liz's car, it's faster'n what yours is. Drive down, can you get plenty o' petrol?" Michael nodded.

"Then go and get this 'otel fixed. I'd do it mesen, but I'm not over handy with phones. And Mike, tak' yon nice bag o' mine. An' put on a black tie, lad. It's respectful."

"Right, Dad. What a help you are! I'm damned grateful."

"An' go to my bedroom, find my wallet i' top left-hand drawer. Here's the key. Bring it here. Mind, it's your job to do everything, don't let yon poor lass have to 'ink of a single thing. Mind that!"

Michael went out to telephone to London, he tried to remember the names of 'decentish' hotels, every single name—except Claridges—seemed to have faded from his memory. He would telephone to Colonel Blenkiron!

The husky, friendly voice reached him. "Hello, hello, Blenkiron here. Yes, yes, Colonel Blenkiron. That's right."

Michael explained, "Urgent business—rather bad business, sir, calls me to London. I've some distressing news for Mrs. Tancred. Yes, sir, the worst. It's pretty awful. My father wants me to get a bedroom and a sitting-room in some—decentish hotel. He feels that it would be easier for Mrs. Tancred—you see she shares a flat with a friend—if I saw her alone."

"Umph. He's right of course. I'll tell you the place—Green's, in Dover Street. Mention my name, no—on second thoughts, I'll ring up for you. Mind it's not a cheap hotel, Michael."

"That's all right, sir. It's awfully kind of you. Don't bother to call me back, I'm driving to town, I pass your house. May I just come in and hear that it's fixed?"

"Do—yes, most certainly do! I sympathize deeply. Good fellow, poor Tancred."

He went back to his father and told him what Blenkiron had said. Enoch gave it as his opinion that there were plenty of worse folks than Blenkiron. He opened his wallet, saying, "Had that a few 'ears, Mike. Your mother gave it to me the day we were married. They don't make 'em to last like that i' these days."

132

He gave Michael four five-pound notes. "See Liz has everything she wants."

"I'll get back as soon as I can, Dad, until then——"

His father's eyes twinkled suddenly. "Until then, the old crock will try not to make a botch of things. I'll try my wings at being a farmer again."

Michael ran Liz's car out of the locked stable where he kept it, he hadn't driven it since that night he came back leaving Liz in London, though he had washed and cleaned it meticulously.

He found both the colonel and his wife waiting for him in their big, light drawing-room, which always seemed to Michael to be far too full of chintz-covered chairs and small tables.

Blenkiron said, "That's fixed, mention my name. Bad business."

Mrs. Blenkiron held out her hand. "Dear, dear—what a dreadful thing. Poor Liz Tancred. Take no notice of that little brute of a dog of mine, he won't bite," for the little dog had come snuffing round Michael's boots. "Come here!" The little dog took not the slightest notice and was almost immediately joined by its brother.

"Can't imagine why I keep 'em," Mrs. Blenkiron boomed, "they're neither use nor ornament. Well, tell Liz how grieved I am. Good fellow, poor Tancred."

Her husband, whose voice boomed exactly as hers did, snapped his fingers at the two dogs, who paid no more attention to him than they had done to their mistress, and said, "Anything I can do? Notice in the local paper—yes—well, let me know if there is. Have you telegraphed to Mrs. Tancred? No? Possibly you're right."

Michael thanked them both, stooped to pat the dogs, who immediately fled to their mistress.

"Cowardly rats," she said, beaming at them, her broad face filled with an expression only just short of idolatry. "Good-bye, Michael, hope you have a good run."

Out on the road, heading south, Michael's mind went back to that last drive when he and Liz had set out together. Now there was no happy expectancy, no delight as there had been when she sat beside him. There were only miles and miles to be covered before he would see her and deliver what must inevitably be a blow. She might have ceased to love George but even admitting that only friendship remained, his death must come as a shock, and would make changes in her life.

As he had done so often when his thoughts turned to Liz, Michael made an almost physical effort to drive his mind into other channels; he tried to plan his work for the following week, to think out a scheme for next spring, to congratulate himself that he would have his father's help and good counsel to deal with any problems.

It was half past eight when he reached Green's Hotel, he had not stopped driving for a moment and felt tired, travel stained and apprehensive. When he asked for the number, they greeted him, "Oh, Mr. Anderson—Colonel Blenkiron's friend. Yes—he telephoned about four. A garage? If you like to give the car keys to one of the porters he'll take it round for you. Wilfred!" she called, "take this gentleman's car round to the garage. Tell Frank to take up Mr. Anderson's bag."

In his sitting-room he telephoned to Liz's flat. She answered it herself, and the sound of her voice, heard for the first time for so long, for he only telephoned at long and rare intervals, sent his heart pounding fiercely.

"Mrs. Tancred speaking——"

"Liz," he said, "Liz—it's me—it's Mike."

"Mike! Where are you? What, here in London!"

"Liz—I'm up on business, at Green's in Dover Street. Will you have dinner with me? Please say that you will. I know it's late, but—even if you've had dinner——"

He heard her laugh. "I have had dinner, mercifully I'm not on duty to-night, and there's a moon nearly full so perhaps it will be a quiet night. But I'll come and watch you eat yours. Yes, at once. Oh, Mike, how lovely to see you—yes, now. No, don't come for me, if you've driven down you must feel dead tired."

"I feel terribly dirty!"

"I shall be there before you've taken off the dirt of the North Road."

He washed, ordered sandwiches and drinks to be sent up. He wished that he had sent out for flowers, then remembered that this was not a festivity, and flowers might be out of place. The telephone rang. "Mrs. Tancred to see you, sir."

"Please ask her to come up to my sitting-room."

Liz! She was here, and now he must tell her about George. He longed to go and meet her at the lift, felt as if he were rooted to the ground. Someone knocked on the door, mechanically he moved to it, and opened it.

Liz—looking very tall, very slim and wonderfully smart in

134

her uniform. She had told him, he remembered, that he would be surprised at how smart a woman *could* look in uniform.

She nodded her thanks to the porter, and came into the room.

"Mike——" she held out her arms, and put them round him. "Mike, such a long time—since I saw you last—when you left me at the flat."

He kissed her, holding her to him, only murmuring her name again and again.

His resolutions were forgotten, he was with Liz again, she still loved him. He said softly, "Liz, darling, darling Liz—such a long time—oh, such a dreadfully long time."

She slipped out of his arms, taking his hand led him to the rather stiff, typical hotel sofa.

"Let me look at you! Mike——" suddenly dismayed, "you're too thin. You're working too hard, worrying when one of the Friesians had a chill or one of your wonderful Large Whites goes off its food——"

"Neither the Friesians nor the pigs are ever anything but well," he said, "I had to come up to town, Liz darling——"

She was looking at him intently, not at his face but at his tie. "Mike—your father's all right?"

"Wonderful, quite wonderful. He'll be out and about in time for the hay-making next year. Liz, let me get you a drink." She nodded and he walked to the table and prepared drinks, then brought them and set them on the small, spindle-legged table near the sofa, moving it nearer to her. Although he felt that his whole body was shaking, his hands were steady.

"No, it's not my father—Liz dear, it's George."

She breathed, "George—killed?"

"Yes, there was a telegram from the War Office," he pulled it out of his pocket and smoothing it out handed it to her. She read it, and laid it down on the sofa.

"Poor George," she said, "and Mike, that poor girl and the little child. Does Claygate know?"

"I think that he knows—everything."

"You've spoken to him—since this?" she tapped the telegraph form with her finger. Michael nodded.

"He hoped that you'd come home—come back to Cummings."

"I'll ask for leave—but I can't stay there, I shall have to come back. How long can you stay? I could get leave quite early to-morrow. You'll drive me back. Oh, God! poor George, he always felt that he'd not come back, he felt that in France, then when he went back I think, he still felt it. He wasn't old, and he did enjoy being alive. You know, my dear, that we were not in the least in love any more, but we did have a great liking for each other, there was a certain companionship, friendship between us. But that poor girl—Mavis. I'm certain that George has provided for her—and the little girl; he was generous, poor George. He was very fond of you, Mike—he trusted you, believed in you. Yes, I'll come back with you to-morrow," she smiled and laid her hand on his, "not gay like our last journey together, eh?"

"But you won't stay?" he said wistfully.

"I can't, darling, I can't. I've watched other women bereaved, heartbroken, women who have lost husbands they adored, sons —even daughters—who were all the world to them, but they only snatched a few days' leave to—to get their grief under control, and they've been back. Tighter lipped, more silent, but filled with determination, and the intention to 'carry on'. I've lost a —good, kind friend who was my husband. I loved him a long time ago, Mike. He was good looking, gay, amusing—yes, George was amusing when I first knew him, it was later that he grew, well, heavier. I never quite realized how much he wanted children until he came to see me after the doctor told him that I could never give him any. I can see his face now—trying to sympathize and yet showing that he was going through the most ghastly disappointment. He never said one word of reproach, only gave me—me, and the whole thing was my stupid fault— all the sympathy he could offer. Poor George. He'd have been far happier with his Mavis, living in some nice villa, having a family of children growing up round him——"

"Don't think on those lines, Liz," Michael begged. "Don't ever blame yourself. You say that—you told me—you slipped because you wore high-heeled shoes—you might just as easily have slipped on a bit of orange peel! Dearest, drink that drink— it will pull you together. I know that it's been a bad shock——"

"Yes, it is a shock."

"Do you realize, Liz, that you're free now. I don't want to say things which might hurt you, or even things which seem, how can I say it?—disrespectful to George, but I love you, I'd give my life for you, if it would do you any good, but I'm as much your lover—for now and always—as if—as if we'd lived together in the fullest sense of the word. We live in a small community in Yorkshire, and—" his mouth twisted suddenly, "we've got to conform to what are regarded as—the decencies. Maybe they're

136

right, maybe it is decent to mourn the dead for a certain prescribed time, but one day—one day, Liz darling, I shall be able to come and ask you to marry me."

She watched him, her face grave. "I'm too old, Mike. Anyway, it doesn't make sense to try and plan ahead in these days. God only knows how many of us will come out of this alive. Only one thing I do know, that I love you. Entirely and completely." She sighed, "I'm so dead tired. Mike, give me another drink and then take me back to the flat. I think we're going to have a quiet night, I pray so. I'd hate to think of you in one of these damnable raids. Then I'll telephone to my C.O. and get leave first thing in the morning; let's leave as soon as we can."

"I shall be waiting," he said, "not only this time, but all the time until—there's nothing else left to wait for."

Chapter Eleven

HE was waiting when Liz telephoned saying that she would come to Green's at half past ten. He protested that he would call for her, but she refused. "No, I'd rather come to you."

He had paid his bill, distributed tips, and ordered coffee to be served in his sitting-room by the time she arrived. She looked immaculate, but there were shadows under her eyes, and her eyes themselves looked heavy.

"You didn't sleep," he said regretfully.

"Not very much, Mike. I'd too much to think about. Yes, I should love some coffee. It's cold this morning, there was hoar frost on the grass in the park."

He held her hands in his, gently but very firmly. "Liz, you're not to worry. It's all pretty dreadful, but it's happening to so many people——"

She cried almost wildly, "And you—you say that you're going the moment that you're eighteen! Mike, you can't, you mustn't."

Speaking slowly and rather heavily, Michael said, "Liz, my dearest, I promised you, I promised George that I'd wait until then. I'll do that, but then—it's no use, Liz darling, I can't hide behind other chaps. Maybe the damned war will be over by then, who knows?"

Impatiently she replied, "Mike, don't be a fool! You know and I know that it won't be over—Churchill knows, Roosevelt knows, that beast Hitler knows. It may be mopped up in the desert, then it will break out somewhere else. Half the world will be in it before it ends!"

"Drink your coffee," he said very quietly. "Then we'll be off. I'll drive——" his mouth flickered into a smile, "this time."

"You're tired after your drive yesterday——"

"And you're tired after a bad night, darling. Come, let's go."

In silence they drove North, Liz sat almost huddled in her seat, and Michael refrained from speaking. The long dark road was slowly—far too slowly—being eaten up. He wished they could go twenty times as fast. Once he turned to look at her, her eyes were closed, he wondered if she slept.

Liz, her eyes closed because she longed to shut out the thought

138

of the last time she had taken this drive, only then it was from Yorkshire to London, and now the direction was reversed, tried to order her thought.

Back at Cummings, there would be letters to answer, there would be kindly people who called, and she would have to—pretend. They would go away and say that she was admirably controlled as a soldier's widow ought to be. In her heart she knew that all she longed for were Michael's arms round her, his kisses, his words that he loved her more than anything else or anyone else in the whole world.

And Michael was already planning to leave her—to leave them all, perhaps as George had left them. Not that George's death meant a great deal to her, she had liked him, even at times admired him, she was sorry that he had died, that his Mavis and her child were left desolate. That was sincerely her thought, her belief. She would see Oliver Claygate and find out if Mavis were properly provided for—if George had not done that—but she felt certain that he had, George wasn't the man to evade responsibilities of that kind—then she would arrange something.

It was the prospect of facing all the pretence, all the assumption that she had returned as a heart-broken widow that irked her. It had been sufficiently difficult to tear herself away from Yorkshire and come to London, to cut herself off from Michael, but while George lived she had been determined that she would run no risks. She had flung herself into her work, work which had been, and would be both arduous and dangerous, not only because she wished to do what she believed to be her duty—she might have disregarded that and given as her reason that she could work on the land—but because she knew that if she and Michael were meeting every day, it was inevitable that someone would—find out their relationship.

Huddersley was small—or relatively small—and tongues wagged easily. She had wanted neither a scandal which might touch her nor George, but most of all, she had determined that no breath of criticism should touch Michael.

Now, George was dead, and so far as her ostensible duty as a wife ended, she was free. Yet, it seemed that George—lying dead—in a foreign land exercised more power over Liz and her destinies than he had ever done since he married her. She stirred uneasily, wishing that the drive were over and she could settle down to think quietly in her own room, where she could make plans and decide how she would play the part assigned to her.

"Where would you like to stop for luncheon?" Michael asked.

"I don't know—somewhere we didn't go to—before."

"Doncaster—Barnby Moor—that's the place I think. Would you like to stop for a drink, Liz?"

"Yes, I'm being selfish, Mike, I'm allowing myself to be all absorbed in my own worries. I'm sorry."

"Can't I share them?"

"I don't know—perhaps, when I get them sorted out a little."

As they drank their coffee after luncheon, Liz leaned forward, her elbows on the table, her chin cupped in her hands. She spoke very softly, and Michael had to lean towards her to catch what she said.

"It's queer, Mike, isn't it, that George—dead—really affects us and will affect us more than he did when he was alive. It's as if his shadow had come between us, as if that shadow made everything lose some of its colour, robbed everything of its warmth.

"Mike, we mustn't let that shadow become—substance. I mean, we love each other, and now less than ever we are doing George harm. There'll be times when you are tired, when I'm worried and seem withdrawn, at those times neither of us must ever say or think, 'Mike's changed', or 'Liz wasn't always like this'.

"If our love is worth anything, it can stand the strain of the next few weeks——"

He said softly, "The foundations are all right, my dear. They'll stand, don't worry. I realize that we shall have to adjust ourselves, but after all there was adjustment needed when you went to London."

She nodded, Michael thought that some of the strain had left her face, she still looked tired, but her mouth was softer, and her eyes very kind.

"Remember, Mike—whatever I do or don't do—it won't be for anything but what I firmly believe to be for our ultimate good—yours and mine, but yours most of all."

"Are you certain that you know—or will know—what is for our ultimate good, Liz?" he smiled as he said it. This was the old Liz coming back, Liz with her certainty, her clear-cut ideas, her ability to make decisions. He remembered how George had said that Liz thought that 'she knew all the answers', he had admitted that she did know a good many of 'the answers', admitted it Michael had thought at the time, just a little wryly.

She smiled back at him. "I'm a conceited baggage," she said, "but you'll admit I don't make a great many mistakes, won't you?"

"Didn't someone say that people who never made mistakes, never made anything? There it is, dearest, I'm prepared to be obedient, to believe that you know best—in almost everything."

"With reservations, eh?"

"With a few, yes."

Mrs. Robbins and Ellen were waiting for them, both with restrained expressions, a kind of façade, Liz thought, which could be removed and replaced with sentiment, grief, whatever was most suitable at the moment. Not that they weren't sincere, two more genuine women never lived, but they liked to extract the last ounce of interest and excitement from such things as births, marriages and deaths.

Mrs. Robbins held her mistress's hand tightly, her eyes filled with tears. "Oh, M'um," she almost whimpered. "What a sad 'omecoming for you. You've 'ad no information as to—'ow it 'appened?"

"It's too soon, Mrs. Robbins."

Ellen said, "We've both grieved terrible, M'um. Mrs. Robbins an' me. If I've said once I've said it a 'undred times, 'Talk about a word an' a blow'—for blow it was to us as well."

"It must have been—thank you both for being so kind. Now, could you let us have tea as soon as possible?"

As Ellen prepared the tea tray, she said, "If you ask me, Mrs. R, the pore soul's frozen wi' grief."

"I'd not wonder at it."

Letters were waiting, Liz glanced at the envelopes, and pushed them aside. "I'll read them later—they're all local letters."

Michael stood drinking his tea, watching Liz. He felt that he was watching a play, criticizing the actors, waiting for new developments.

Ellen came in. "It's the Vicar, M'um, he says that he'll quite understand if you'd rather see 'im some other time."

Michael saw Liz stiffen slightly, she glanced at him, then back to Ellen. "I'll see him now, thank you. Bring another cup, please."

She walked to the door to greet the clergyman. She had always liked him, he was a well-built man of early middle age. George had said that he was sensible and practical, 'no smarm about him. A decent chap.'

"This is very kind of you, Mr. Swann."

His rather highly coloured face was grave and kind, Mike thought, but not—he was relieved to see—particularly solemn or gloomy.

"I wanted to come, Mrs. Tancred. Hello, Michael! Did you go to bring Mrs. Tancred home? Splendid. Yes, I will take a cup of tea." He sat down, and turned to Liz. "We're all terribly shocked, and grieved for you, Mrs. Tancred. I am not going to offer you—what I call 'little plasters'—if they come to your mind unbidden, they may help you, but for me to offer them to you—well, they're the easy way. These dreadful things will go on happening so long as men can find no better way of settling their differences than by killing each other.

"Death is often easier than facing acute suffering." He drank his tea and set down his cup, and rose. "If there is anything I can do—at any time—don't hesitate to send for me. Remember," he lowered his voice a little, "one of the best—perhaps the only one—solaces is prayer. Never mind if your mind is in too much of a turmoil to formulate prayers, just—think them, just let them form themselves. When ye pray—and most of us don't pray enough—we must pray as little children. There, God bless you. Good-bye Michael, I'm glad Mrs. Tancred has you to help her."

The door closed, and Liz turned impulsively towards Michael.

"There, isn't it hideous! That nice, sincere man who really believes that my whole world is shattered—and I have to listen and not disillusion him. It's the pretence! I've always hated pretence! They'll all imagine that I'm breaking my heart for George—oh, I'm sorry that he's killed, sorry for that poor girl, for the child, but why can't I say 'Sympathize with the woman who loved him'? Why have I got to listen to condolences, and allow them all to assume that I regret anyone but—a friend? A friend I'd grown fond of in an impersonal way? I had grown used to the idea, and it took a great deal of getting used to, that George had turned his affections elsewhere. At first, it wasn't easy, because I was sufficiently proud to imagine that a man would go on loving me—even if I couldn't give him children. Mavis wasn't the first, Mike, though she might well have been the last because of the child. I never wanted to *know*, I just sensed it all.

"George was never unkind, never! He was incapable of actual unkindness. George liked women, and yet—faintly—he despised

142

them. Now, I have to pretend, act lies, murmur 'Thank you—thank you for being so kind', and all the time I'm resenting, yes, resenting the fact that George, dead in Africa, can cast me for a part I hate playing—and I doubt if I can play it very well."

She stopped, and held out her hands to him. "Mike—say something."

"What can I say?" he asked helplessly, "there isn't anything *to* say. Only, Liz, dearest Liz, it's all there, the love we have for each other." He wondered if she'd ever realize the times when he had felt this same furious frustration? When men had said of her, 'Pretty woman, Mrs. Tancred. Must have been charming when she was young.' She'd never know how much he had longed to shout, 'But she is young! She'll always be young—always be adorable!' He'd had to—pretend, to keep his mouth shut, and never show by either his tone or his facial expression how much he resented their comments.

He couldn't talk like that to Liz, particularly in her present state of resentment. He understood, she was one of the straightest people he had ever met, and he understood how this play-acting was irking her.

"It will pass, darling," he said. "It's only a phase. People's memories are short. But you're right, you must get away, you must go back to London—though God knows I hate the thought of it for you. Be a little patient, and be brave."

Ellen came in, saying in a voice filled with satisfaction, "Mrs. Cawther and Mrs. Anderson, M'um."

Liz nodded, then turned to Michael. "Oh, damn these kind people! Yes, even if one is my aunt and the other your mother—damn them!"

Ellen, her tone expressing importance, said, "Mrs. Cawther and Mrs. Anderson."

Again Liz walked towards the door, Gran entered with Ada Anderson at her heels, both were wearing black clothes, more, both were wearing expressions—suitable to the occasion.

Liz said, "How kind of you, Aunt, and of you, Ada."

Gran seated herself firmly. "Nay surely we couldn't do less. I hope as Michael's been a help to you, my pore lass."

"A great help, a very great help. He not only drove up to town but he drove all the way back. I'm very grateful to him."

Ada said, "Enoch 'ud like to come and see you, Liz, if you'd like him to do so. I've never seen such a change in anyone as in him. He seems to me to have taken on a new lease of life——"

Gran said, coldly and severely, "Ada, I'm surprised, flaunting your husband when pore Liz is mourning 'ers! Nay, give over talking about Enoch, good fellow though he may be."

"I should like to see Enoch," Liz said; in some inexplicable way she felt that Enoch, quiet, unassuming and courageous, might be of help. He might stabilize her, make her feel that her feet were on solid ground again. These people who were near the soil had great stores of wisdom on which to draw. She turned to Michael, "Ask Ellen to bring in glasses and a siphon, Mike."

As he passed her Gran said hoarsely, "Sherry, Michael, always sherry for visits o' this kind."

As the door closed behind him, Gran drew a deep breath. "Liz, we have to think on—all flesh is as grass. That's life. 'Ere to-day and gone to-morrow. I did hear that the Rev. Swann had been round to see you. I only hope that he was able to offer you some comfort, and to make you understand that this blow is the will of Someone greater nor what we are."

"Yes, Gran, he was very kind, very sensible."

Ada accepting a glass of sherry said, "Well, I'm sure we're all glad that he could bring a bit of comfort. Now, I suppose you'll stay here at Cummings, eh?"

Gran sipped her sherry. "This is good sherry. If there's anything I hate it's poor sherry. You might be able to get by with port, or wine but sherry—no, it's got to be good or left alone. What's that? Stay at Cummings? O' course you'll stay at Cummings, what else 'ud you do?"

Michael, who had poured out a whisky and soda for Liz and for himself, felt that the lovely room, that room where he had been so happy, was charged with antagonism. He saw Liz square her shoulders, and face Gran, saw his mother—who must have sensed the change in the atmosphere, glance round as if startled.

Liz said, very quietly, "No, Gran, once I've seen Mr. Claygate and everything is in order, I shall go back to London."

"To that work, whatever it is?"

"Certainly. Why do you suppose I wear a uniform? Because I'm under orders."

Gran finished her sherry, and gave a slight and carefully smothered hiccup. "I'd have thought as you might have put on a more suitable dress. On this occasion, Liz. You're bereaved, same as lots of other women. Your place is here at Cummings, seeing to things, not cantering off to London to gallivant round."

Liz threw back her head—that lovely, neat head which Michael

144

loved—and laughed, "Gran, dear, don't be so silly. I'm in uniform because I've taken on a job. I have to go on with it. Michael can run Cummings, he's done it very well up to now. I don't—what was the word?—gallivant. For women like me there isn't much gallivanting in London at the moment. I'm generally too tired once my work for the day—or night—is finished."

"Gran, London must be hell in these days," Michael said.

"Then Liz has no call to stay there———"

Suddenly Liz's control broke, she turned to Michael, holding out her empty glass. "Mike, give me another drink," then turning back to Mrs. Cawther, "How much do you know about it—any of you? You read this in the papers, you hear that from some cackling fool, you read the casualty lists and say how terrible it all is. But you're safe—safe, tucked away here, miles from munition factories, airfields, and the rest of it. Oh, you do all you can, I don't doubt that—you knit, and send parcels and—oh," impatiently, "you do all you can. All right, I'm still young and I'm going to do what I can. God knows it's not much. Incidentally, will you all—all mind your own business!"

Gran rose. "Come Ada, we came filled with kindness and charity, this is what we've got. Liz, you don't want that second whisky and soda. We're going!"

Ada Anderson said, "Are you coming now, Michael? Perhaps Liz would like to be left alone."

Michael looked at Liz, her face was colourless, her eyes bright and very hard. She answered for him. "I should like Michael to wait a moment, I've some things to discuss, and I shall be away most of to-morrow. Please wait a moment, Mike."

"Very well, I'll see you later Michael."

"Yes, Mum, I shan't be long."

The door closed; Liz turned to Michael. "I'm sorry, not sorry that I snapped at Gran—she's an interfering old woman—but that I snapped in front of Ada. Ask her to forgive me, Mike."

She sat down, holding out her glass, almost untouched. "I didn't want it really. However it had the desired effect, to call forth a rebuke from Gran! Mike come and sit down just for a few minutes. You seem such miles away, as if this barrier is slowly growing and cutting us off from each other."

He sat beside her and took her hand, it was very cold. "You're overtired and overwrought," he said, "there is no barrier, and we mustn't begin to imagine one. I hoped that you'd stay at Cummings but I realize that it's wiser for you to go back to

London, even though I hate the thought of danger for you. Shall you come back for Christmas?"

"I don't think so—you'd not be able to spend it with me here, and I don't think that I should be in the mood to spend a whole day with you all—the festivities would ring a little hollow, and if I did forget to—observe a proper air of melancholy, Gran would notice it with regret and probably comment on it. No, if I don't stay in town I shall go down to Aunt Alice. Oh, Mike, I'm hating it all so! Put your arms round me, make me feel safe."

Very gently he drew her to him, she laid her head on his shoulder and he kissed her, softly and tenderly. He felt that he had grown older since yesterday, and that with that sense of increased age had come a certain wisdom. She was not only his wonderful Liz, the woman he loved so dearly, she was someone to cherish, to help, to comfort. More, she was—his future. Without her the years ahead would stretch as endless and colourless wastes.

He understood, too, that her nerves were terribly jangled, there must have been tremendous strain involved during the time she had spent in London—long hours, irregular hours, air raids, sights and scenes which must have shocked her. Now, with this new difficulty to be faced, they had snapped. She hadn't meant to be unkind, she wasn't an unkind person. He remembered how when he had told her that George was dead, almost her first words had been "That poor girl and her child". He could imagine how Gran's interference, coming immediately after the Vicar's visit—and he had been very kind, very tactful—Liz's nerves had felt taut and raw, quivering unexpectedly, resenting remarks which, had she been less tired, less highly strung, would have only roused in her a kind of amused intolerance.

"Liz, my dearest," he whispered, "you're tired out, you want rest. Let Mrs. Robbins send you dinner to your room."

He heard her laugh softly. "A little meal on a tray, eh? That's one of the panaceas a man always offers, isn't it? A cure for all ills—physical and mental. Bless you, I'm feeling better, stronger, not so terribly on edge. Will you always soothe and comfort me, my darling?"

She sat upright. "Give me a cigarette—yes, and you can give me back that whisky and soda I disdained a few minutes ago." He gave her a light for her cigarette, brought the glass and set it on a table near the sofa. Liz remembered how almost twenty-four hours ago he had done the same thing in his hotel sitting-room. How easily he moved, whatever he did was done so deftly. She thought that he had grown handsomer than ever, there was an added strength in his face, his jaw was firmer, it had lost the almost soft roundness of a boy, and had gained the power and character of a man, and a man who accepted responsibilities with courage and confidence.

He sat down near her, watching her, never merely staring at her, Liz thought. He watched her because it gave him happiness, not because he was trying to probe into her inner thoughts.

He said, "I shall have to go—they'll be waiting for me."

"Oh!" it was almost an exclamation of pain. "Mike, can't you stay and have dinner with me? I'll telephone to Anderson's— yes, I'll even say that I'm lonely, and imply that I need companionship—I know that's mean, but I do need companionship —yours. I'll telephone—yes?"

"Yes, yes, do anything that will gain me an hour or two with you."

She went out and he could hear her voice, asking that he might stay as a favour. She said that she was sorry that she had been so nervy, and he could imagine his mother's comfortable voice assuring her that it was 'quite all right, and we understood'. Liz said, "Ada, that's sweet of you." There was more conversation, he caught the word "Enoch" and knew that she was arranging a time for his father to come and see her. Then the receiver clicked into its hook and she came back.

"It's all right, Mike, Ada understands. She gave my message to Gran and Gran—I'm certain rather grudgingly—has forgiven me. Put on another log, they're apple wood. Lots of people tell you they burn apple wood, but I really do. Oh, isn't this pleasant. I was so tired, so dispirited, now—everything's clear and smooth and calm again."

"Will you do something for me?" Michael asked.

She smiled. "Anything in the world—almost. Tell me."

"I once saw you wearing a frock, black lace it was. Couldn't you go and put it on now?"

"I'll go and have a quick bath while you wash—you can have a bath if you like, we've three bathrooms. Poor George had a mania for bathrooms! Then I'll come down wearing that dress. Go and tell Mrs. Robbins that you're staying for dinner." She kissed him, lightly, and then holding him at arms length, said, "My dear, dear Mike."

Mrs. Robbins received the information that he was dining there with satisfaction. She folded her massive arms, and looked like a presiding goddess.

"An' glad an' thankful I am too," she said. "The idea of that pore creature being left alone wi' her grief—well, Ellen and me almost shed tears. It's only a light dinner, Mister Michael, for when the heart is over-loaded wi' grief it oftimes upsets the digestion. Clear soup, a roast chicken—I needn't add—with all trimmings, and as a 'follow'—angels on 'orseback. I managed to get a few oysters this morning in Huddersley. How'll that do?"

As she recounted the menu some of the melancholy left her voice, she was immersed in her culinary skill. Michael said that it sounded like a perfect dinner to him, and said, "I'll bring out the tray with the drinks—Ellen will want to clear it." As he turned Mrs. Robbins said, "Eh, Mister Michael, with all respect, what a thoughtful lad you are—for you're nobbut a lad really. One of these days you'll make a wonderful 'usband for some nice young lady, choose how."

Liz came down to find him waiting in the room where the fire danced, flinging shadows and sudden spurts of light against the pale walls. He turned from examining some small piece of china on the mantelpiece, and she saw his whole face light up as if the flames from the logs had reached it.

"Liz, how lovely you look!"

"In this?" She touched the skirt with the tips of her fingers. "It's old, my dear. It was good—once upon a time. If you like it so much I'll get another—the minute this coupon business is over."

Ellen brought in the cocktails, and noticed her mistress's change of clothes. Back in the kitchen she said to Mrs. Robbins that she thought it showed very proper feeling.

"Black, no jewellery as I could see. Just that plain black dress."

"Plain it may be, but I mind that she got it from some grand place i' London—I've forgotten the name, but it's where the Queen 'erself goes. Still, it was a nice thing to do."

Leaning back in one of the big chairs, Liz looked—Michael thought—less tense, relaxed and even rested.

He told her so, and she smiled up at him.

" 'The benison of hot water'," she said, and when he asked who had said that, raised her eyebrows. "Have you never read Brooke, or is he too old for you—I mean too many years since

148

he wrote his 'Great Lover'? I believe that you'd like him. He's the poet for—young men, romantic young men."

"I remember, I think—he was killed in the last war, wasn't he? Yes, Gallipoli or Salonika, wasn't it?"

"I'll get you his books—there aren't very many of them, he was so young. Mike, do you want to travel?"

"I've never been very far, never farther than London, or Scarborough or the Lakes. Yes—" he smiled, "I've always tried to imagine foreign places—I've read books, nearly all my pocket money used to go on travel books. You've seen those places, Liz? Venice—oh, how I long to see Venice, Verona, Paris—and Chartres with that stained glass." His voice was eager. "The finest in the world, isn't it? Dresden—only when this war's over, there may not be any Dresden left, Vienna—have you seen those places?"

She nodded. "Yes and no. I've been to them, but I shan't *see* them until we can go there together. We'll plan our journeyings, carefully, giving ourselves time to absorb everything we see. Mike, there's so much I want us to see together—so much music I want you to hear, with me—you love music? Pictures, churches, everything. We'll take time, there shall be no rushing and bustling to catch trains and work to a time-table—the world shall be our oyster!"

"And the farm?"

"Oh, we'll put an overseer in, and by that time your father will be able to direct everything. You'd like it, my dear?"

All this, Michael thought, is something that can only happen when the war is over, and even then perhaps not for years. The war! I'm going to fight, as George went to fight, what if I too don't come back, what if Liz is killed by one of those infernal bombs? All our hopes, our future ended, the curtain rung down on our play—darkness—extinction. God, don't let it happen—or if that's part of the plan, let it happen to both of us, at the same time. I'll do what's right, so will she, but it won't always be easy, maybe the time might come when it would be impossible, but we'll try—only give us a chance.

Liz spoke, "You'd like it, Mike?"

"It's like a dream, if only one day it can be reality. To see things together—to know that all this beastliness was over, and the world was sane—even moderately sane—again. To know that you were not running into danger, that at least I could be with you—even if I couldn't do much to safeguard you. God, we'd live again. Liz, you want the future to hold—both of us?"

"I couldn't imagine a future worth living that didn't hold—both of us," she said. "It will, it shall. I suppose we have to be patient, and to have patience is always difficult. Still," she smiled, "if farming has done nothing else for you, it must have taught you that—must have shown you how you have to wait and hold on to the belief that you've done your best for your land, and it will repay you."

"I was thinking something rather like that myself. I'll do my best, my beloved Liz."

Chapter Twelve

Liz returned from Bradford after her long interview with Oliver Claygate. He was considered the best lawyer in the whole of Yorkshire, and no man could have been less like the preconceived idea of a man of law. True, his voice was clipped and precise, but his size was enormous, his face scarlet, and his eyes, though very keen and clear, almost lost in rolls of flesh.

He greeted her with brief sentences, which nevertheless, held a certain kindliness.

"Mrs. Tancred—ah! Bad business, poor George. I'd known him most of my life. Good fellow. Sit down, sit down. Let me offer you a glass of sherry, it's good sherry, and a dry biscuit. And like the sherry, they *are* dry. I get them sent up specially from Bath. Yes."

He bustled about, surprisingly active for a man of his immense bulk, handed her a glass of sherry, Liz noticed that the glass was very finely cut, and then sat down in his big chair again. He sipped his sherry, savouring it with evident appreciation.

"Now, Mrs. Tancred, no need to go into matters which might be painful. Everything has been left in order—*com*-plete order."

Liz thought, 'Thank heaven he doesn't treat me as if I were a heartbroken widow!'

"The—the young lady, nice girl, very nice girl, is well provided for. So is the little girl—pretty little thing. No need for you to give that aspect of things another thought. Naturally if you wish to hear about it all—I'm quite willing."

Liz shook her head. "No, Mr. Claygate, it's George's business and not mine."

Claygate nodded his large head. "I think that you're wise. So far as George's will affects you—that's a different matter. George was a very wealthy fellow. He's left everything—except this other matter—to you. Cummings is yours, to keep or sell as you wish. There's a very sizable income for you, and no restrictions whatever. If you wish to marry again, that carries no conditions. I propose to send you a copy of the will—drawn up before he went to France. If you prefer it, I can go through it with you now."

"No, no, I don't want that!" Liz protested. "I was concerned about this poor girl—I don't know her name, except that her Christian name is Mavis."

He puffed out his cheeks. "And I don't propose to tell you her name. She has a very pleasant villa, it's hers, he bought it for her. She has quite enough to live on, comfortably, and the child's education is provided for. She's at liberty to marry if she wishes, and she would still retain her income."

"George behaved pretty well, Mr. Claygate."

"George was a thoroughly good fellow, Mrs. Tancred. If he assumed responsibilities—he accepted them, fully and completely. He—I think that I can say this to you—liked women, but he always behaved decently to them. As I say, I knew him for years, I've straightened out a good many tangles for poor old George." He chuckled. "He confided in me, and I've respected his confidence. That's why I am not offering you sympathy, because I knew the position between George and yourself. You did your duty—well, he did his, but——"

Liz said, "To quote Brooke—curiously I was quoting him only last night to a young man—'Love died long ago'."

"Exactly, I realized that." He altered his tone, it became more brisk and commonplace. "And you'll stay at Cummings?"

"No, I hope to go back to London immediately. I want to work."

"Commendable, for London isn't a very pleasant place in these days. Take—as much as is possible—care of yourself. You'd wish me to continue to look after your affairs, Mrs. Tancred? Good. I shall do my best, they're not complicated. I shall send you some statements and a copy of the will. Anything you wish to know, write to me I beg of you."

Liz rose and held out her hand. "Thank you for being so understanding. Yesterday everyone assumed that I was or should be completely heartbroken. How I hate—pretence!"

Liz drove home, feeling relieved and happier than she had been since her return. In another day or so she would drive down to see Aunt Alice, and then get back to her work. Not that she liked it particularly, how could anyone like it? You might be glad that you could offer a certain amount of alleviation to poor folk who were homeless, hungry, or terrified, but you didn't like it, it was your duty and so you did it.

It was the ugliness of it all, waste and ugliness. Houses which had been homes reduced to rubble as if some giant child in a fury had beaten them to the ground. Before she went to work in town Liz had been unfamiliar with death; she had seen her uncle, and her father lying dead—they were the only two, and there had been something essentially decent about them and their surroundings. Now that she saw people carried out from among the wreckage of bombed buildings, the decency had gone. The poor things did not look dignified, they looked tumbled, dusty, neglected.

Vaguely she wondered how George had looked when he was dead, when he lay waiting for the stretcher bearers—perhaps he looked dusty and tumbled. Poor George, with his various entanglements at which Oliver Claygate had hinted! She had never imagined that men took those affairs seriously—except very rarely—as in the case of Mavis who had a child to be considered.

She could imagine George, his face rather flushed, wearing a puzzled expression and prefacing his announcements with, 'I say, Claygate, old man, I'm in a bit of a jam—thought I'd come to see if you can straighten things out.'

Who were the women George had liked, or believed that he liked for a time? Perhaps she knew some of them! They would be pretty for George had always been ready to express admiration for pretty women. None of them, Liz felt certain, had been particularly clever, for George had never cared much for intellectual things, she remembered once quoting *The Celestial Surgeon* to him, teasing him that books and his food and summer rain had received no reply when they knocked on his heart.

He had said seriously, "Oh, dash it, Liz, no one enjoys good food more than I do, and rain—well, provided we don't get too much of it at the wrong time—I like that all right. Books—I've never been a great hand at books I admit."

Her mind went back to her talk with Michael the night before, when they had spoken of travelling. She wondered if Michael liked pictures, if he'd appreciate Venice, what would be his reactions to a great orchestra, to great singing? It would be wonderful to travel with him, to watch him forming his taste—she didn't want to form it for him, he must do it himself—and if he preferred Carlo Dolci to Bellini—then regrettable though it might be, he must stick to his own ideas. Liz smiled, she could remember when she was fifteen thinking that one of the most beautiful pictures in the world must be one which hung in her grandmother's sitting-room—a young person, Liz never quite decided upon the sex, dressed romantically in dark green velvet presumably, with lace at the neck and wrists clasping a large book, again—presumably—the Bible. The eyes were lifted heavenwards, the expression rapt, it was called 'The Soul's Awakening'. Michael should have his Dolci's if they appealed to him, he would come to Bellini later.

There would be so much to show him, so much to share, bathing in the South of France, driving along the Corniche, visiting queer, half forgotten old villages. Persuading him to try new dishes, different wine, even fruits which he had never eaten before.

Then her old practicality ousted romance and romantic ideas. Travelling with Michael—how? With him as her lover, or with she as his wife? The old problem which had been a nightmare so often when she had faced it. It was impossible that Michael, who had accepted the duties of a grown man, should not want their relationship to be something as shared by a man and the woman he loved. Respect, straight dealing, admiration—were all very well, but loving her as she realized that he did, the time must come when he would demand, however gently he might make those demands, full and complete admission of their mutual love. Or would he, filled with that over-developed romantic sense, that innate chivalry, refuse to accept whatever she might be willing to give—without marriage? Marriage with Michael—she frowned, was it possible? Could she face the fact that she would begin to fade, to wither a little while he was still at the very height of his strength and power? What would everyone say? Not that Liz cared greatly for wagging tongues, but she could imagine that some of the chatter might reach Michael and wound him, even possibly sow seeds of doubt in his mind. She heard such comments when a woman married a man who was her junior, no matter if it was obvious that they were both deeply in love.

'Her last chance, eh?' 'Cradle snatching', 'Old enough to be his mother' and the like.

Resolutely she pushed those problems away, they must wait, she would deal with them when the occasion came. She had no doubt as to her own feeling for Michael, and last night she had felt that he had grown so much nearer her own age, that he was almost bridging the gap between them.

As she drove up the drive, she caught sight of Anderson's old car, Michael must have driven Enoch over and gone off on some farm business leaving him at Cummings. She liked Enoch, liked him better than she liked his wife. There had always been a kindliness and humanity about him, and whenever Gran took

154

upon herself to be caustic, his eyes twinkled even though his face might be serious.

He rose when Liz entered the parlour, and said, "There, what d'you think o' this, my girl? Me paying social calls. If I'd had a card I'd have brought it to lay on that silver dish affair in the hall. This is a bonny room, Liz, we've gotten some nice furniture but our rooms are just—solid. You know what I mean. You've got some lovely furniture, and you've con-trived to mak' your room pro'ply elegant."

She made him sit down, told him to smoke; he said, "Nay, smoke a pipe i' this bonny room, I'd think not."

"Have a cigarette then."

"Why, I don't know," he demurred. "Tell the truth, Liz, I can't smoke cigarettes, seemly I *eat* them, chew 'em or summat. Nay, I'm all right."

He drank his tea, and nibbled some thin bread and butter, adding a word of praise about the quality of the butter.

"Prime 'utter," he said, and for the first time Liz detected the slight impediment in his speech. "Cummings's dairy is t' best i' t' neighbourhood." He paused, sipping his tea slowly and with appreciation. Then setting down his cup with tremendous care, he said, "I'm right proud of our Michael, an' that's the truth."

He began to tell her about his illness. "Mind you at first set out I knew nowt, cared about nowt, I weer just a log—useless, helpless an' handless. Our Ada was 'underful, never lost heart. No more did our Michael. I've found out since that Ada made up a sort of tale, telling folk as I was still the—well, the directing hand, as you might say. Michael spotted that, and played up."

Liz took his cup and refilled it. "Go on, Enoch, tell me."

He gave her a long, steady look, then said, "Aye, there's a lot to tell you, Liz lass. A damned lot. When you're laid aside, like I was you begin to learn to think. I did a lot o' thinking, when once my brain 'ot working agean.

"There was a lot to think about—our Ada's courage, Mike's determination never to spare himself—if I told you the hours yon lad worked—you'd blink your eyes. Gran—aye, she can be a thorn i' t' flesh can Gran, but—in time of trouble, she's a great standby. Even young Vi'let—kind, good soul. ilson, Willett, young Harry, all on 'em. I'm not all that religious, Liz, but it seemed as if God 'Isself raised me oop. Knowing that our Michael's set an' determined to go an' fight. He raised me oop so's I could take over. I know that I 'hall never be able to do what I once did. . . . Ploughin', reapin' and so forth, but m' brain's clear, and I shall be able to do—what our Ada pretended all along—and that's direct things."

Liz said urgently, "But there's no need for Mike to go!"

Enoch nodded. "I know that as well as you."

"I don't *wish* him to go!"

Again she found his clear, steady gaze fixed on her; he said very slowly, and clearly, "I know that an' all, Liz."

"What do you mean, Enoch?" she asked sharply. The clear, blue eyes never wavered, he sat perfectly still, watching.

"I mean," he said, "that I know how things are."

"I don't understand you!" there was a challenge in her tone.

"Aye, but you do, my lass. You've told me, Mike's told me —not i' words, if I'd not had that time when I was 'aid by, I might not have known, for neither on you ever saw me at the same time. But, my dear, when folks luv each other, an' when they speak of the loved one, no matter what they're talking about, there's a new note comes into their voice, aye, times even a new light into their eyes. That's why I wanted to see you, Liz——"

"You haven't spoken to Mike?" her voice sounded breathless.

"No, an' don't intend to neither. You see, things like this— in partic'lar for a youngish lad like Mike—are so—eh, what's the word I want?—delicate! It's like a lovely flower, or a peach or the wing of a butterfly—the least touch can rub off some of the wonderful bloom. I'd not do that for anything i' t' world. Yon lad's the light of my eyes——"

She said impulsively, "And of mine!"

He nodded, and abstractedly took out his pipe and filled it. She lit it for him, and he nodded again, a wordless thanks.

"We must let him go—yes, even into danger. I was reading— I do a lot of reading—about a speech Henry the Fifth made before a battle i' France. He said, 'Gentlemen in England now abed, will hold their manhood cheap because they were not here' —maybe I've not got it quite right, but that's what he meant. It went on about how when other chaps talked of this battle, the ones who weren't there would feel badly. It's true, Liz. That Shakespeare knew what he was writing, we could all do with 'eading him mor'n we do."

"But, Enoch, the danger . . .!"

Enoch shook his head. "Nay, we're all i' danger. Aye, I don't care who it is or where they live, and mark my words, we've not seen the worst of it. Planning, scheming, working, chemists and the like all trying to plan for the destruction of England. Not as they'll do it, no matter what devilment they get up to. The Spanish couldn't do it, Napoleon and the French couldn't do it—some things are indestructible, my lass—and England's one of 'em. If England is beaten, it won't be by the Germans, it won't be by outsiders, it will be from t' inside. But if every woman tried to stop her man from 'oing to fight—it wouldn't do."

"The farms——"

He laughed, "Liz, you're retreating to your second line o' defence. It's not a very 'ood one neither. The farms will be all right. I honestly believe," his voice deepened suddenly, " 'at's why t' Lord has raised me up agean. So's I can take my place in doing this job. I mind another bit o' Shakespeare—funny how once you start reading that fellow, his words come butting into everyday conversation. It's like this: 'Go say I sent thee out to purchase honour.' That's what you'll say to Mike when the time comes."

He took his pipe from his mouth and stared at it. "Luke at that now, me smoking an' filling your bonny room with the fug of tobacco! I wasn't thinking on what I was doing. Forgive me, Liz."

"Of course," then impatiently, "What do you think I care about 'purchasing honour'? Nothing! Not a damned thing."

"That's what you *think*," he said, "maybe it's 'at you believe just now, but deep in your heart you don't think that."

Liz sighed, she felt tired and disturbed. "The future, Enoch? What is that going to hold?"

He shook his head. "Nay, none of us know that, not the cleverest of us. That's hid from us, and it's right that it should be. We have to go on, day by day doing what we can. Look, that's Mike, not a word of 'at we've been saying, Liz!"

She heard Michael's voice speaking to Ellen, then he came in.

"Good evening, Liz. Hello, Dad—been talking your head off? He's a great reader since he was ill. Shakespeare, if you please, instead of sticking to his farmer's journals as a good agriculturist should!"

The cold air had whipped a bright colour into his cheeks, he stood looking at them, and Liz understood that she and Enoch were the two people who mattered most to him. There was affection in his eyes, his lips looked soft, he himself despite his height, his good shoulders, and upright carriage, seemed younger.

"Get a drink, Mike," she said, "you must be cold. Enoch, will you join Mike?"

"It's 'gainst doctor's rules and regulations, but—dash me— if I won't for once. Not spirit, Liz—is there a 'lass of port? That's it then—a 'lass of port."

She told Michael that she had seen Oliver Claygate, and when he asked if everything was satisfactory, she smiled—he thought— just a little grimly.

"Quite," she said crisply. "I'm going over to-morrow to make my own will, it's stupid not to, particularly when your father has been cheering me with prognostications that we may all be blown to bits at any moment!"

"Nay, now Liz, I said nothing o' t' sort. She's funning, Mike."

"Oh, I know," Michael assured her, "he's a regular Job's Comforter. Dad, it's time we were off, I don't want Mum to blame me for keeping you out, and taking you home tired to death."

"Will you be in later—after dinner? What about those Friesians you wanted to buy? The milk yield's wonderful, isn't it?"

Enoch set down his glass. "Milk 'ield's miraculous, but they're not a patch on plenty o' other less fancy kinds when it comes to butter. My ad-vice is to go easy with Friesians. I've said it before an' I'll say it again, they're a rich man's cattle—for that matter so's Jerseys an' Alderneys, but they're better when it comes to butter. 'Owever it's your farm, lass, an' not mine."

Liz watched him go and bring his father's heavy coat, saw how carefully he helped him to put it on, handed him the thick woollen scarf saying, "Now well up round your throat, Dad. And your gloves." Never 'fussing', just kindly, thoughtful and efficient. In a few months, he would be eighteen, the time which he had promised to stay in Yorkshire would be over. Each day brought his birthday nearer; for a moment she longed to have the strength to say that she released him from that promise, that now George was dead, he was no longer bound. It would be almost a relief to say, 'Go when you wish, Mike—don't wait for your eighteenth birthday!' then on the heels of that came the doubt if she could bring herself to speak the words.

She walked with them to the front door, Enoch turned to her, smiling gently. "Thanks, Liz, for a nice talk—not that I said half of what I'd planned to say. Don't think that I'm unfeeling about poor George, I liked George very much. I' lots of ways

158

ad-mired him. If any time there's any road I can be of help, send for me. Good-night, my lass and God bless you."

Michael said, "If I may then, I'll come in for half an hour after dinner, I won't be late."

Back in Anderson's Ada fussed about over Enoch, insisting that he should 'put up his feet on the sofa'. She admitted that she was tired, she'd been 'thrang' all day, with Christmas drawing near.

"And deliveries are uncertain. It's excuses here and there all the time."

Gran said, "Happen they're not excuses, happen the delays are part of this war business. I'd not be surprised to know that the Germans were at the bottom of it all—aye, even deliveries to Ada's shop!"

"We shall have James back at the end of the week," she said. "I don't like the idea of him spending his holidays working, but—my word!—an extra pair of hands would be a boon. Young Trench goes next week, and if you please Sally—in the silks, is going to the munition factory at Crossmoor, making aeroplanes. Two short at Christmas! Well—there's a war on, I suppose that it can't be helped."

"It's a trew saying," Gran contributed, "as what can't be cured must be en-dured."

Immediately before dinner, Ada turned to Enoch and asked if it wasn't time for him to go to his bedroom. The nurse had been dispensed with for many weeks now, but he still took his supper in bed. He met her eyes, his own twinkling.

"Nay, Ada luv, I'm taking my 'upper with the rest of the family. I'll go up the wooden hills afterwards, but I'm a hale and hearty fellow agean. Don't fash yourself, Ada."

Michael, as he bathed and changed, thought what a really nice man his father was, how he admired his courage, his determination to recover and be able to take his part in the scheme of things again. He wondered what he and Liz had talked of when they sat together in her parlour? Of George, perhaps, of the future?

With the thought of Liz, Michael knew that his mind became disturbed. He knew that his love for her was complete, was his whole life. Every effort he made, every plan which he evolved was for the improvement of her property—admittedly that property had been George Tancred's, but it was Liz—his wonderful Liz—for whom he had worked so assiduously.

He might be less than eighteen, but he had taken on a man's job, and it had made a man of him. When he met young men of his own age—except such as were already training in the Forces, and often even they—they seemed far younger than he was. What did, yes, even those who were studying gunnery, the science demanded to be knowledgeable over aeroplanes, know of the everyday difficulties which beset an ordinary farmer? There were day-to-day problems, day-to-day decisions. You were constantly speculating about the weather, you were perpetually on the watch for pests which might ruin your crops, forever wondering if this or that crop would come up to your expectations. A fine hay harvest might be made worthless by sudden squalls of wind and rain; your grain, grown so carefully, tended so meticulously, apparently splendid, giving promise of profit and satisfaction, could be ruined in a few days of bad weather.

Not only had he learned that the farmer himself must learn to adopt a philosophic outlook, but that the farmer must be able to imbue his workers—yes, even the hind himself—with hope and confidence. At the least sign of anything untoward, they would come to him with gloomy faces.

'Nay, wi' pouring rain seemly crops 'ul be ruined' or 'Measter, them peas is fair con-sumed bi' slugs! We'll have lost t' lot.'

Then summoning all your courage, and pretending a wisdom which was not yours, you did everything in your power to prophesy that the weather would 'take up', or that by dint of spraying, the peas might be saved.

He'd done it, and although he was conscious of no self-pity, Michael realized that he had fought, and fought hard. He had tried to plan ahead, he had bought stocks when they were still available, he had invested in new machinery before it became impossible to buy. He had never thought of it as a burden, but as something which he could do for his father—and Liz.

He was no paladin, he was a sane, decent-thinking young man, and he had shouldered the weight which was laid on his shoulders willingly and even happily. Now, his love for Liz Tancred had brought new problems.

He had accepted certain conventions, George had been his employer, George had trusted him. Therefore he owed something to George—conventional service at all events. He had fallen completely and desperately in love with George Tancred's wife, he had allowed himself to let his emotions get the upper hand, had taken her in his arms, been at once excited and soothed by

160

the kisses which he had showered upon her. She had occupied his thoughts to such an extent that he had by sheer mental force driven those thoughts into the background, to be replaced with plans for the four-acre field, the well-being of the calves which were born, the high quality of butter which the two farms produced. There had been times when it had been a physical effort to—literally—push the thought of Liz Tancred from his mind. Often the effort had left him feeling almost weak and drained of the strength which he needed for his work.

He had tried to argue with himself, to say that she was not really pretty, and his 'other self' had answered, 'Who cares, she's Liz.' He had attempted to convince himself that he was too young to embark on any kind of a love affair with a woman older than himself. Again his 'other self' had protested, 'You're older than your years! Liz is younger than hers—and after all they aren't so many.'

Michael Anderson was completely innocent, or as completely innocent as any boy can be who had been to a large public school. He had never had any intimate dealing with a woman—commercial or otherwise. He had never even wished to kiss—in secluded corners—the girls he had met at dances and parties. He was not ignorant, no boy brought up on a farm can remain ignorant of the facts of procreation. He had thought of it all, and had decided that there were obviously natural impulses which impelled the sexes to rush together. Because he was simple and his upbringing homely, he realized that a male and female did not automatically rush to each other with the sole desire to reproduce their own species. There was something else—there was the natural sex impulse in the animals. Then how much more was that emotion felt by people who could think, argue, and experience the mental aspect of this curious, mysterious thing called—sex?

With animals it might be—satisfaction, surely with people who loved each other it meant—fulfilment. You said all that there was to be said, you spoke softly and tenderly all the endearing words which were so beautiful, you even held the woman you loved in your arms, revelled in her softness, her charm, the scent which emanated from her. You realized that you loved her, and that she loved you, but—there was something which remained unsatisfied, unrealized after all words had been spoken, all kisses given, all the small tenderness lavished.

As he tied his tie, intent, staring into the mirror, his young face was grave, and yet troubled. Liz absorbed him, at that moment he could think of nothing—of no one else. She was his world, and while he knew that his hands shook, and that his forehead was damp, he knew that he had come to the end of the time when faithful service, the opportunity to hold her in his arms to accept her love and kindness were enough.

He was a man, everyone had treated him as a man, given him a man's responsibilities, and he in return had given whole-hearted service. He had—he remembered it as something apart—been happy in the knowledge that he was accepting the trust which George had placed in him so far as Cummings was concerned. Now, George was dead, and Liz was free. George had not denied himself a woman, George had been able to have a child by her—presumably he had loved her not only for the hope which he had of children, but for herself.

As Michael shrugged himself into his coat, he said very softly, 'I don't want to hurt her—it couldn't have been very pleasant to have to talk everything with that lawyer, but I can't go on. I've no promise that she'll marry me—one day, she knows that I love her completely, desperately, but—I know that isn't enough. Maybe I'm wrong, maybe I'm material, and carnal and a great many other things equally unpleasant, but I—I want Liz to be mine, and I want to give myself to her—entirely.

'It used to be heaven to hold her in my arms, to catch that lovely scent from her hair, to feel the softness of her cheeks—well, suddenly, for what reason I don't know—it's *not* enough. I shall still want to feel her in my arms, to hear her say that she loves me, just as I shall want to whisper foolish loving things to her, but—I've only understood completely to-night—that's not enough.'

Chapter Thirteen

MICHAEL sat down at the big desk opposite Liz and tried to speak in a voice which was brisk and completely devoid of any emotion.

"And you're really leaving to-morrow?"

Liz nodded. "First to see Aunt Alice and then back to London." He opened one of his ledgers, and laid an open note-book beside it.

"Then we'd better get on with as much work as possible. Now you realize that there are almost certain to be all kinds of new controls—eggs, milk, butter and the like. That's going to make a lot of difference to us, and it will mean a great deal extra book work. I thought that it might be a good thing if we took on a land girl who was used to doing that kind of thing."

"Of course, if it's necessary," her voice sounded puzzled, this was a new Michael, this brisk, businesslike young man with the impassive face and unemotional voice.

"I have planned out everything for the spring sowing, and I honestly believe that when I go, my father will be sufficiently strong to direct things. Not possibly to do a great deal of active work, but to give orders and see that they are carried out. I'm sure that he's right about the Friesians—milk excellent, but the percentage of cream is not sufficiently high. We want good—utility beasts. It may be that Colonel Blenkiron will buy them, the two we have now, they're both in calf to his bull, they're in splendid condition. What do you say if I see him, and then buy something good, but less—fancy?"

"If you think it's the best thing to do——"

"The tithe barn will have to be seen to this year—not completely re-roofed but partially. It's going to be expensive, I'm afraid. If it's done now it will cost less than if we wait for another year——"

Liz said sharply, "Mike, what is all this about? I'm going away to-morrow, we don't know when we shall see each other again, and you can only talk about re-roofing the tithe barn! You can discuss these things with Enoch; as you're under age I'm giving him a power of attorney, I'm arranging that when I see Claygate —do what you like about the farm and the cattle and everything else connected with the place."

163

Michael shrugged his shoulders, and quietly closed the ledger, and his thick note-book. "I wanted to give an account of my stewardship," he said evenly, "and have your instructions for the future."

"I don't want to hear about your—stewardship, Mike, and I don't want to give instructions either. Don't you want to talk to me? Aren't there a hundred and one things that we have to say to each other—our time together is so short."

She heard him draw his breath sharply, and noticed how white his face had become, his expression was set, his lips closed and hard.

"Mike," she said, "Mike——"

He squared his shoulders, and sat very erect. "Yes, there are things I want to say—about us, only I doubt the wisdom of saying them. I decided to come here to-night and to talk—business all the time. If it has hurt or puzzled you, I'm sorry, dreadfully sorry. You see, I love you so completely, so desperately—you've given me so much love, tenderness, and—yet I can't go on—as we are."

"You mean that you want to end it all?" she knew that her voice was not quite steady. "Is that what you mean?"

He shook his head. "I couldn't end it," he said, "this loving you will go on as long as I live, I shan't change, couldn't change. No, my beloved Liz, it's only that I'm a man and you're a woman, the dearest woman in the world to me. Darling, will you marry me?"

She did not answer, and for what seemed an eternity to Michael she sat motionless, her hands tightly clasped on the desk before her. He had felt tense and strung up a few minutes before, now it was as if an extraordinary lethargy had swept over him, he had made his effort, and now he had thrown caution to the winds. He waited for her to speak.

At last she raised her head and met his eyes. "No, Mike, I can't."

"Why—if you love me?"

"Perhaps one of the reasons is that I'm a coward, or that I fight shy of doing anything unconventional. People have barely got used to realizing that I'm a widow, imagine what they'd say if they heard that I was married again. It would mean scandal—we've avoided that up to now."

"Does scandal frighten you so much?" he asked.

"I don't think that it frightens me for myself, it's the other

164

people who would be affected, how your mother and Enoch would hate it, how Gran would natter and say bitter things! My aunt is more tolerant, she's travelled more, she's mixed with more people, but even she would be shocked, Mike. The difference in our ages——"

"Oh, damn the difference in our ages," he burst out, "that's a wretched hollow turnip with a light put inside, a thing to frighten old women and children. That's a bogy you've made for yourself, and now you've looked at it so often you've come to believe that it is something real. It's not! I wasn't too young to do a man's job, to carry the weight of the farm, to make decisions, but when it comes to wanting to marry the only woman I shall ever want to marry, that's all put on one side, and this blasted difference in our ages is brought out!

"Either you love me sufficiently to want, yes, *want* to give me everything, or these months have been just an—affair with me, because I'm reasonably good looking, and you'd ceased to love your husband! You can't have it all ways, Liz!"

She stared at him aghast. "Mike—to talk so—to me."

"I could say a great deal more," he protested, "and every word would be true. While you were away I was literally eating my heart out, there were times when the longing for you was so tremendous that I had to use sheer force—mental force—to try to drive it away. I managed to learn how to do it—more or less successfully, but the moment I allowed my mind to lose grip and stop thinking of crops, or wages, or the beasts, back it came stronger than ever. At first it was heaven to hold you in my arms, to kiss you—now, I've realized that it's not enough, my dear. What's more it's unfair, yes, damned unfair to me. It may satisfy you, I don't know, it leaves me like a hungry man who is given a dish of sweets to stay his hunger. No matter how delicious they may be—they're not enough."

Liz said, "I don't know you like this. I feel you've turned into someone who is a stranger—I'm bewildered."

"I haven't changed, my dear, I shan't change, but I've come to my senses and begun to understand myself a little. Liz, do you realize that never, never since I told you how much I loved you, have we been alone—really alone? Driving to London, well, the North Road is scarcely—being alone, is it? Here at Cummings, when Ellen might come in any moment, when the telephone might ring, that isn't being *alone*. It's been a series of snatches—never giving either of us time to really get to know the other. That's what has made all our times together almost feverish because we both knew they were bound to be brief. I want to have you in my arms, want to kiss you, want to say tender loving things to you, but I don't want to feel in my inner heart that—I mustn't miss an opportunity because heaven only knows when I shall have another. Liz, you must understand—dear Liz, try to understand."

"I can't marry you, Mike." Her voice sounded weary, and he wondered if she had been attempting to face her problems as he had done. "You must see that," Liz went on, "the future— who knows—but now it isn't possible. It would be wrong for both of us, it would hurt too many people—and there'd be something indecent about it, something insulting to George, who after all—whether I loved him or not—did die fighting. I do love you, I didn't know that I could love anyone so much, it was partly to safeguard you that I went to work in London."

She rose and came to where he stood, laying her hand on his arm. He looked down at her, his face suddenly softened, his mouth relaxed a little. "Dearest Liz——" he said softly.

"Mike, listen," he felt her fingers tighten on his arm, "sit down, and don't stare at me. Play with that paper knife while I say what I've got to say. There!" She paused for a moment, then went on speaking quietly, unemotionally. "Mike, my dear one, would you be happier if I said that I'd—be your mistress? Not here—that isn't possible—but I can get leave fairly easily, not for very long, but long enough for you to meet me somewhere and for us to be able to spend—more than those dreadfully brief times together. Really together, Mike—would you be happier, would that convince you that I love you, even though I can't marry you?"

Michael sprang to his feet and put his arms round her. "Liz— dearest, most wonderful Liz. But wouldn't that be a tremendous sacrifice for you?"

For the first time she smiled. "Sacrifice? Of what? The real sacrifice has been that fact that I've never been able to talk to people about you! Not that I shall ever be able to but—oh, Mike, say that you feel happier. We may not be able to meet very often, because you've got your work and I have mine, but it will mean that we can be—together."

His arms were still round her. "It will mean—pretence, my Liz, and you hate that——"

"There won't be any pretence between us, when we're to-gether."

166

He walked home under the bright star-lit sky, his feet making the frost on the grass crackle, the sharp, keen air icy on his cheeks, his mind filled with thoughts of Liz Tancred. She was leaving early to drive to Bradford to see Claygate and then driving on to London, he would not see her again, he must wait for her letters and rely on her promise that as soon as it was possible she would send for him.

"I can meet you half way," she told him, "I shall have the car and we'll find somewhere small and quiet. We'll talk and talk, and really begin to know something about each other."

"You don't feel that it is wrong, Liz?"

"Do you?" there was surprise in her voice. "We shan't be hurting anyone. We might if—other people knew—well, we must take care that they don't know. Even then, even if we did hurt—or offend—these other people—Mike, life is so uncertain, surely we have a right to snatch at what happiness we can? I've come to understand how war makes people reckless. You can only count on a day at a time—the rest well, to-morrow may come for you, or it may not. No, I don't feel that we shall be doing wrong—we're fighting for a little happiness together."

In the morning when he came in for his breakfast, Gran asked if Liz had gone, adding that she thought London was getting on her nerves, making her 'proper ratty'.

"She's gone," Michael said, "left early for Bradford, then she's going on—to London and then to see her aunt. I don't think she meant to be irritable the other day, Gran, remember it's something of a shock to hear that your husband's killed."

"I've oft-times wondered how much Liz ever cared for George, somehow they never seemed to me like folks as loves each other."

Michael wondered if Gran knew anything about the girl in Bradford, Gran had a way of getting to know things which could be very disconcerting. He contented himself with saying, rather weakly:

"Oh, I don't know. I thought they got on very well."

"There's a vast deal o' difference between getting on, an' loving."

He went about his work conscious that he was missing Liz badly, but that strangely enough he was happier than he had been when she went to London before. It seemed that there was no longer that unending stretch and limitless distance between them. He knew that he might, indeed would have to wait, but he knew equally well that Liz would keep her promise, that one day—in the not-too-far-distant future, she would write and tell him where and when they could meet.

It was good to have his father making the rounds with him, even though it meant walking more slowly. Enoch always protested that he was a 'rule of thumb' farmer, adding, "Buke learning's all right for chaps like our Michael—he had a goodish education, I got mine at the school i' Huddersley. If I tried to read bukes like what he does, I'd be fair moidered, right addle-pated i' no time. I've learnt the way of farming from t'land itself, an' taking one thing wi' another, I've not done so badly."

Michael found his advice always practical and to the point. True he rarely made suggestions which were particularly new or the result of hard thinking, they seemed to Michael to be the result of instinct, or based on experience. They were examining some machinery in the barn, when Enoch pointed to the car.

"About time yon was mended with a new one," he said. "When you drove me home in it t' other night, it fair rattled my bones."

Michael agreed. "She's been a good old bus, but she's had her day. It's difficult to buy a new car in these days, Dad."

"Aye, a new one, happen it is, but Wilson was telling me as Sir George wants to sell one of his, he's going out to fight it seems, and the place is to be turned into a hospital—aye, wounded soldiers. I might drive over and have a luke at it."

On Christmas Day Enoch said to Michael, "Mother's and my Christmas present is i' t' yard. It's mor'n a Christmas present, it's to show our appreciation of all t'ard work you've put in."

There it stood, shining with much polishing—Sir George Fowler's Sunbeam. Michael stood staring at it, the thought rushing through his mind that she would eat up the miles when he drove to meet Liz. Then he reproached himself, that when they had given him such a present his first thought was that it should carry him away from them.

James was home, grown broader and taller, filled with energy and confiding to Michael that he didn't believe that he was anxious to go into the shop after all.

"I want to be an accountant," he told his brother, "the Head says that my mathematics are well out of the ordinary. I don't want the small jobs, I want to get my examinations over, and then go on to be an actuary. I tell you, Michael, there are plums, real plums waiting for men who are able to take such things. I should be stifled in a shop—the accounts wouldn't be sufficient for me, and I'm not interested in silks and 'heavies' and the rest of it."

Michael looked at him, he was a handsome fellow, and obviously intelligent, but there was something—Michael hesitated for the right word and found it—hard in James. There was not only ambition, but there was the thought of the 'plums' which would come to him when he was properly equipped.

"I'm afraid that it will be a bad blow to Mum," he said.

James flushed immediately. "Why?" he challenged. "Why? I know that I said I wanted to take over the shop—well, I wanted when I was seven to be an engine driver more than anything in the world. You grow, your horizon widens, it's inevitable. I'm nearly fifteen, and I want Mum and Dad to send me to study accountancy when I'm sixteen. Why not?"

Michael replied, "Yes, why not—I don't say that you're not right, all I say is it's going to disappoint Mum."

"You're a sentimentalist," James retorted.

James went everywhere, he was a gregarious fellow, he liked people and people liked him. Ada Anderson had suffered qualms when Michael had been entertained by what she called 'the gentry', but Michael had never seemed to enjoy it as James did, had never been in such demand; although he was only fifteen, he looked older, and during the Christmas holidays, despite the war, he was always rushing off to some dance or entertainment.

Michael, Ada reflected, had grown 'quiet', not that he was ever quick tempered, or lacking in affection, but she felt that in some strange way, he was absorbed in himself.

It was on New Year's Day that James broke the news that the shop no longer attracted him. The shop was Ada's great and absorbing pride, and she had believed that during the Christmas rush, James might have offered to come and help her there. James had listened to her stories of the press of work, the shortage of staff and his comment had been, "I say, bad luck, Mum."

She was far too proud to ask for his help, and ask him to come and straighten out those books and accounts which her present— almost untrained—clerk wrestled with producing disaster as a result. She said to Gran, for she was still unwilling to trouble Enoch with such things, "It's a fight, a real fight. The money's coming in hand over fist as you might say, but what I'm dreading is when we've got to make income tax returns, what my auditors 'ul say, I do not know. I somehow feel that James is—growing away from the shop, if you know what I mean, Gran."

Then on New Year's Day when they sat drinking port wine after the heavy mid-day dinner, Enoch looked round the table and smiled.

"Well, here's a New Year. The old one gave us some changes, and let's hope that this new one will give us some more 'leasant ones. I'm restored to health——"

Ada said, "Thank God, which we all do, my dear."

"I can go about an' give Michael a helping hand, Muther tells me that the business is flourishing, and it's all thanks to her care an' foresight. Now, we're waiting for Jimmie to take his place and give her the assistance that she needs—aye, and deserves."

Michael looked round the table covered with its shining damask cloth, at the beautiful silver which was brought out on special occasions, and the candles which caught the finely cut-glass decanters and threw out bright prisms of many-coloured lights.

Gran, wearing her best cap, looked—he thought—a little older, but she was smiling and nodding her head in agreement with what Enoch was saying. Mum, yes, she looked tired, for the Christmas rush had tried her, but she was well, and the sense of achievement meant much to her. She had been delighted that so many of the 'quality' had come to her for their delicacies instead of sending to Bradford or even to London for them. Every evening her talk had been on the same lines—"To-day Mrs. Colonel Blenkiron—and later Lady Waring. Most affable both of them" and "Now to-day, who do you think came in? Nay, you'd never guess, the Countess herself! She said she'd heard that I stocked everything that she could want, and so, she said, 'Why send to London?' My word, an order! I'll say she did place an order! Still, there's others, old customers who can only spend a little, and I see that they get just the same civility and attention as the gentry get. I'll tell you something more—the gentry, the real gentry, like it that way."

He watched and listened, his father who they had all feared was, as he would have said, 'laid aside', sat there beaming at them all, his eyes particularly tender when they rested on his wife.

James, how he had broadened, what a good-looking fellow he was, what a good forehead, and what well-set eyes. There was determination in his mouth, and just a trace of hardness, but there was no mistake—Jimmie was a grand fellow, and a clever one.

If only Liz could have been there! Then he realized that Liz would have been there as Gran's niece, not as his beloved. There had been a letter from her that morning, filled with everything that he longed to read. She was safe, though there had been some dreadful nights. She had been given three days' leave to begin on January 5th.

That can be our New Year, Mike. Can you possibly tear yourself away from your precious farms for three days? I'll meet you at Grantham, and tell you the plans that I have made—they are too wonderful to put on paper. Oh, Mike—to be together again. . . .

He emerged from his dream to hear James speaking. "I think that I ought to tell you all that I don't feel that the shop is really my line of country. I want to study accountancy, and if I can get through the exams, study to be an actuary."

Enoch said, "And will you kindly tell us what an—actuary is?"

"The most advanced and specialized form of accountancy."

Ada said, "Nay, whatever has come over you, James. The shop's there, a living and a good living ready to your hand, as you might say. Why, that is a disappointment, seems as if I'd been working and toiling for nothing! Building for no one. Michael's filled with farming—well, I don't know!"

Gran said, "Think on, James, a bird in the hand's worth two i' the bush. How d'you know as you can pass all these examinations? How d'you know that you can make yourself—whatever it was you said. I've never heard of them!"

"If I can't," James said easily, "I can always go into the shop."

Enoch brought his hand down on the table so that the glasses rang. "Can you? Who says so? Not your Mum, not me. Anderson's as a way out if everything else fails! Meanwhile—while you're seeing about these exams and the like, your Muther's slaving away keeping the shop ready for you, if you feel 'ike it. Nay—nout o' t' sort."

James's face was impassive, he seemed completely unmoved. Enoch said testily, "Well, say summat, can't you, lad?"

"There's nothing to say, Dad."

Enoch turned to Michael. "You'll uphold me, won't you? I'm right, aren't I?"

"I'm afraid, Dad, I don't think you are right," Michael said

171

slowly. "I think that Jimmie has a right to decide what he wants to do. It's his life after all. He won't fail, you've only to read his school reports—every subject that is mathematical—he's first. It's not a bit of good trying to make him go into the shop if his heart isn't going to be in it."

Ada nodded. "Michael's right, Enoch dear. It's a disappointment, but—well, Jimmie's got a right to have his chance, and as Michael says he *is* clever at figures. I'm not so sure that once this war's over, we'd not be just as well to sell the place. It 'ul be about time then for you and me to take a holiday. Jimmie, your Dad will think about, he'll make inquiries, and we'll luke into it."

"Well, I've had my say," Enoch told them, "an' I've gotten myself prop-ly sat on for my pains. Just keep me informed," with heavy sarcasm, "of your plans and such like."

But his eyes twinkled as he spoke, it was never possible for Enoch to remain short-tempered for long; Ada smiled at him and Michael knew that the little storm had passed. Only Gran looked coldly disapproving.

"You've not changed, Enoch Anderson," she said, "just the same, no will o' your own, always ready to let others ride rough shod over you."

"Nay, Gran, I'm wise enough to know when the odds are agean me an' give in with a good grace. Any road let's start the New Year without any bad feelings, eh, Muther?"

Later when Gran had gone to bed, and Jimmie was taking his mother into Huddersley to see a film, Michael sat talking to his father. The bond between them had grown stronger, Michael felt, and he enjoyed listening to his father's comments on many things.

"So young Jimmie'll want to be leaving school when he's sixteen, I suppose," Enoch said. "We'll have to be making all the necessary inquiries about this accountancy affair. I've allus known as there were such folks, I've even had dealings with them, but I never bothered to find out how they got theirselves made what they were."

"I'll try and find out, Dad, or probably Jimmie's Head could give us all the information. Dad"—he hesitated, this was going to be difficult he realized—"would you mind if I took a few days' holiday. We've nothing that Willett and Wilson and the girls can't manage just now, and with you keeping an eye on everything it might be a good time for me to go."

"Wanting to try the new car, eh?" Enoch had seen the boy's

face flush, and the thought came to him, 'He's going to her, that's where he's going. I don't know that I like it—much, on the other hand I can't tax him with it. He'd never give Liz away, and it would only lead to lies and bother.'

Michael smiled. "I should like to try it—properly, of course."

"Where'd you think of going?"

"Honestly, I don't know." That was true anyway. "I'd only be away two or three days."

"Aye, you go, you've worked hard enough, choose how."

That night, Enoch told his wife that Michael was going off for a 'bit of a holiday'. She glanced at him her eyes very sharp.

"Enoch, do you think Michael has a young lady? Mind, I've never seen him with anyone, but last summer there were some of them—Miss Fowler and Mercy Blenkiron—always wanting him to go over for Sundays. I spoke to him about it—aye, it was when you were too poorly to be bothered. Now Mercy Blenkiron's in one of the Services, I forget which, do you think he's gotten himself entangled with her, by any chance, Enoch?"

Enoch took off his collar and tie and hung them carefully on the looking-glass as he always did. "Nay, I couldn't say, Ada. Somehow I doubt it. I only know that the girl who gets our Michael 'ul be getting a lad that's worth his weight i' gold. I'd not worry, Ada luv."

Ada twisted a piece of hair round a metal curler and snapped it shut. "That's all right, Enoch, but I can't see any of the gentry exactly welcoming one of our lads into their families. We've done all right, in fact we've probably gotten more brass than what a lot of them have, but there is a difference between the Andersons, and Fowlers or Blenkirons or any o' that lot."

Folding his trousers carefully, her husband made a littəl half-protesting noise, "Tut, tut, you women are all alike, you're always trying to make out as some ro-mance is going on. The lad wants to try his new car, he wants a bit of a holiday——"

"Did you ask if he'd like to take his brother with him?"

"No, what for should I?"

"He didn't suggest it either?"

"Oh, Ada, give over! Leave well alone. If he's running after some young lady, we'll know soon enough, or it 'ul just fizzle out."

He was growing irritable, he disliked the knowledge that he was hiding anything from Ada, he was playing a part, and he

173

only hoped that he was playing it convincingly. That was where these entanglements led—not only involving the people most concerned, but half a dozen other folks as well. Here was he deceiving Ada, Michael trying to deceive him, and Heaven alone knew how many people Liz Tancred was forced to deceive.

"Well, that's as may be, time will tell. Far be it from me to pry into anyone's business, not even my own son's, but think on, he's only eighteen—he's not eighteen yet——"

"He's got a man's headpiece," Enoch said.

"I'll tell you something, Michael writes regularly to someone, and you can't tell me that it takes him hours to write a few business letters or to fill up those forms the Government send." Enoch came to where she sat and laid his hand on her shoulders, shaking her very gently, almost playfully.

"Now, Ada Anderson, give over—do! I can remember when I was Michael's age, I ran after a little lass, I wrote letters to her, I used to leave them in the basket she took gathering eggs. It hung behind the stable door. Well, I'm damned if I can scarcely remember her name—Lucy Something-or-other. Lads falling in love is like children catching the measles—they get over it, it's nout. Now will you stop worriting and nattering!"

Michael sat in his bedroom, writing to Liz. The prospect of seeing her soon filled him with excitement; he wrote:

I am so excited at the thought of meeting you, my hand isn't really quite steady. I shall be waiting for you at the Angel and Royal on the morning of the fifth. After that, you shall decide where we go. My beloved Liz, it all seems too good to be true. I swear that I'll try to be worthy of you always, though my dearest, you are so wonderful that you'll take a great deal of living up to. I'll try, I can promise you that. Good-night, and God bless and take care of you.

Chapter Fourteen

HE drove away from Anderson's very early; the night had been a very short one for him, for he had thought so much of what the following day would hold. The previous day he had driven into Bradford, and had searched through the antique shops until he found something which he thought might appeal to Liz. A tiny clock in a case, scarcely three inches high, covered with bright enamel and figures of cupids and the forms of flowers.

The man who sold it to him said, "French. Nice piece. You'd look a long time before you found another like it. Look at those colours, as bright as the day they were painted."

The North Road had never seemed so lovely, never seemed to hold such promise of romantic things. His new car was running smoothly and easily, eating up the miles. Michael sat at the wheel whistling from the sheer joy of living.

It was still almost dark when he left the farm, but as he drove the sun came over the horizon, and slowly its rays lit up everything clear and bright in the cold, clear winter sunshine. He drove steadily, but allowed himself to watch the landscape, he marvelled at the great trees, bare and gaunt, but still magnificent. Here and there he caught glimpses of great houses, deep in their splendid park lands. Everything seemed so peaceful, so safe, only here and there did he pass a collection of Nissen huts, or an airfield with its stark runways. England might be at war, the most frightful war she had ever seen, but even the war had not penetrated into the depths of the quiet countryside.

At Barnby Moor he stopped for a quick and early breakfast. He remembered having been there with Liz, remembered how she had leaned across the table and talked to him—speaking softly and gently—when they drove up from London together. Now he was on his way to meet her again.

The waiter, still heavy with sleep, was solicitous.

"No porridge, sir?"

"No, thank you—I don't like it."

"Kippers, haddock, bacon—very good bacon."

"No," he smiled, "only toast and some coffee, please. I'm in a hurry."

Out again in under a quarter of an hour, the hard road, the stronger light; the car, he thought, pulling like an impatient horse. He drove through towns, scarcely awake, where shutters were being taken down from shop fronts, and the inhabitants were beginning to hurry off to their day's work. Then, at last Grantham, and he drove into the courtyard of the Angel and Royal, looking anxiously for Liz's car. The time was a quarter to ten.

He walked in, went into the comfortably warm lounge, and sent for a morning paper and coffee. He was chilled, even though his pulses were hammering. He tried to read, poured out his coffee then fell into a waking-dream and forgot all about both. Then slowly he began to experience panic—it was ten o'clock, had Liz decided not to come? Had she suffered some accident on the road? Feverishly he seized the morning paper, and sought for the news of last night in London. It appeared that London had experienced a quiet night. A quarter past ten, he drank his cold coffee feverishly.

The waiter said, "You've let that coffee get cold, sir. Shall I get you some more? I'll just make up the fire a bit. Are you staying, sir?"

Michael said, "No, I'm waiting for someone. They should be here any minute now."

"Lot of traffic on the roads, sir. Troop movements."

Half past ten, he paced the room, stood at the window and stared out at the passing traffic. He was standing there when a voice said, "Michael, my dear, good-morning and a happy New Year," and turning he saw her.

She stood in the doorway, her hands outstretched, her lips smiling, her eyes alight. She was not in uniform, but was wearing a suit which he had never seen before—grey, very plain and very neat.

He breathed, "Liz—you're here!"

She came to where he stood, for Michael felt that he had not sufficient strength to go to her, she took his hands, and leaning forward kissed him, very gently on both cheeks.

He said again, "Liz—how wonderful to see you."

She smiled at him, and he thought as he had thought so often, 'I may try to make a mental picture of her, but I never get it quite right, she's far more wonderful than I ever can imagine her to be.'

"Please, may I have some coffee," she said. "And may I sit

176

by that wonderful fire? I'm frozen! Oh, that drive from town—I thought that it would never end. I left at eight."

He said, "I left soon after five, it was still dark and rather mysterious. I got here far too early, and have been imagining all kinds of dreadful things which might have happened to you. Oh, my darling, how wonderful to see you!"

She drank her coffee, from time to time meeting his eyes and smiling at him. He told her about his car, he reported on the farm, quoted Ellen and Mrs. Robbins—and heard again that soft, chuckling laugh which he loved.

"And now——?" he said.

"Now, I am going to get you to drive me, in that superb car, to a discovery. It's a country inn, at a place called Witherston. I know the way. It's old, with thick walls to keep out this winter cold. It's beautifully clean, and the landlady is—simply immense. The food is quite wonderful. Not 'kickshaws'—isn't that the word?—but the nicest English food."

Michael looked at her quizzically. "How did you come to find this delectable place?"

"I know what you think I might answer," Liz said, "but you're quite wrong. I was detailed to drive a *very* important v.i.p. We came to Grantham, and he asked if I'd ever been to Witherston. The 'Great Bear'. I hadn't so we went there for luncheon. All quite proper, he was the dullest old bore, could only talk about food. And that not even well. You know the kind of thing— 'Know Venice? Food shocking I thought, except the scampi, and you can't live on scampi!' and 'Been to Marseilles? That fish soup—shocking, I thought. Quite shocking.' 'Know Larue in the rue Royale? Paris. Ah, that's where you get food that is worth eating.' I went with him on a European tour—gastronomic, of course. However, he's gone to Africa and so we're not likely to run into him. Ah, my dear, it's so good to be with you."

"You're warmer now?"

"Completely! Let's go, I can't wait to show you my Great Bear."

Michael said, "I can't wait to take you in my arms and wish you a happy New Year—properly."

They left her car, and she gave Michael directions, sitting beside him so that again he smelt that scent which she used, and of which he always meant to ask her the name—and always forgot to do so. Narrow lanes, tall bare hedges, through several small villages possessing no particular attraction, until Liz said, "We shall be there in five minutes—I can't wait!"

A straggling village, with old houses, and a market place which looked far too large for the size of the place, then an old timbered inn, with a swinging sign painted with stars.

Michael said, "Of course—The Great Bear—Charles's Wain."

Liz said, in broad dialect, "Aye, lad, t' Waggin an' 'Osses."

They turned into a wide paved yard, which had obviously been well swept that morning, for the old stones were spotlessly clean. An old man, very bent, came forward bidding them 'good-morning'.

"Will I garage 'er, sir?"

"Yes, put a rug over the bonnet, and later there's a lamp to go in. It may freeze to-night."

The old man wagged his head. "Nay, it *will* freeze ter-night."

The sight of the entrance hall entranced Michael, he had always loved old places, old beams and old floors made of the wide planks of seasoned wood as opposed to the modern narrow strips of deal. An immense woman bustled out to greet them, she beamed at them both, and said in a voice which Michael always thought of as 'fat'—it had the richness of succulent dishes:

"Welcome to the Great Bear. It's cold but it's seasonable. We always say that a green winter makes a full churchyard. Unhealthy, it is. Now, I've given you and this gentleman the sitting-room, and two nice bedrooms leadin' off of it. There's a good fire burning. Now, is there onnything as you'd like uz to send up—you've only to name it. An' I've left them nasty forms there on the writing-table. It beats me why the Gov'erment has to know everyone's business! S'ppose it's for fear of spies! Lot of rubbish! I'd like to find a spy here, I'd give him something to remember Great Bear by."

Michael said that if she would send up some sherry, it would be pleasant.

She beamed at him. "Pleasant, that's right, an' I'll tell you what, sir, the sherry will be sherry and all! Half the folk who come here don't know what sherry *is*—they're that iggorant. That's right, sherry it shall be."

They went up the polished, uncarpeted stairs where the old wood shone with much polishing, a chambermaid, only a few degrees less bulky than her mistress met them.

She flung open the door of their sitting-room, it was low-ceilinged, with a bright fire which leapt and flickered. The curtains and chintz covers were faded with much washing but spotlessly clean. There was a pleasant smell of polish everywhere.

178

She said, "An' yons your room, M'um, and t'other's the gennleman's. Though I sezs it, both comfortable. That they're clean—" she laughed, "goes wi'oot sayin'. Now is there anything I can get you?"

Liz said, "Hot water?"

"Nay, I don't have to get that, fur it's i' t' taps. It's an old inn, but the mistress had running water put in—what was it?— three years ago. Yon old Will'um, I always says he's a lazy varmint, but he stokes t' boiler pro'ply. Eh, you can scald yerself if you've a mind!" She chuckled and backed out, still laughing at her own joke.

Michael turned to Liz, his eyes shining, she thought that she had never seen him look so radiant.

"Liz, my dearest—it's all wonderful." He held out his arms, and she went to him. He drew her to him, saying, "Hotels, however good, are not places to meet the person you love best in the world. This is really where our—New Year begins."

"You love me—best in all the world?"

"For a clever—a reasonably clever—woman, what a silly question."

She said, "Mike, these forms we have to fill in. I'd forgotten about them. I don't suppose that nice old body will ask questions, but if she does—I shall say that you're my brother. Do you mind?"

"I don't really mind so long as you're here with me. Only," he touched her cheek lightly with his finger tips, "it may be difficult—one day—when we are married—yes, as we shall be, Liz, my sweet, and want to come here."

He filled in her form and his own, neatly and efficiently. She said reflectively, "You do things so—easily, Mike. I do like to see things—even stupid things like filling in forms—done smoothly."

He turned to her smiling. "Even if I'm just a—country lad, I did go to school, precious."

They sat by the fire drinking the admirable sherry which had been sent up, it was dry and wonderfully matured. It seemed to Liz Tancred that for almost the first time, she had been able to 'talk' to Michael. He was right when he had said that all their meetings had been 'snatches', feverish and filled with the consciousness that the time which they could spend together was limited, or might be interrupted at any moment. Sitting here, in this quiet, simple room, safe in the knowledge that they had—if

179

not unlimited time—at least sufficient to give them a sense of permanence, she felt that she knew what peace meant.

Michael talked easily, without the nervous inflexion which she had noticed so often; his sentences were no longer clipped, his voice seemed deeper, its modulations more full. He talked well, she decided, possibly not profoundly, but with sense and sudden touches of humour. Gradually she drew him on to talk of the books which he had read, and was surprised at the extent of his reading. Travel books, he told her, gave him intense pleasure, "because, you see, I've always longed to travel".

"You shall, darling," she assured him, "you shall."

As he talked, she watched his hands, and wondered how he had contrived to keep them so well, she knew that he was out in all weathers, she knew that he worked on the farm machinery, and did tasks which must necessitate handling rough wood, roots and the like. Yet they were well tended, brown with exposure, but with nails which were obviously given attention.

"How do you keep your hands so well?" she asked abruptly.

He laughed. "Ah you've discovered my pet vanity! Do you despise it? It wastes quite a lot of time, believe me."

"Not—wastes—" she corrected, "it pays excellent dividends. I'd hate you to have rough, untidy hands."

Later the door opened and an ancient waiter appeared. Michael thought that he must be eighty, though his face was rosy, his eyes clear, and his white hair abundant and like newly fallen snow.

"Luncheon is served," he told them, "if you're ready for it, it's ready for you." His manner became suddenly confidential. "Scotch broth and if there is anyone as can make it—like it should be made—it's Mrs. Hardcastle. Ondly one word for it— prime! Ducks, cooked while t' skin lifts off like what a lid does, stuffin', nothink missing. An' to round it off as nice a bit of Stilton as I've ever seen, an' me seventy-nine come next Shrove Tuesday."

"Shrove Tuesday," Liz repeated, "but that's fixed by Easter."

"O' course it's fixed bi Easter, M'um, what else 'ud it be fixed by? But it's Shrove Tuesday just the same, an' it's my birthday."

She said, "Yes, I see what you mean. We're just coming down."

When the door closed, Michael laughed "The old boy must be weeks out—seventy-nine years and Shrove Tuesday a different day each year!"

"I don't suppose it really matters much, do you?"

180

"In my present state of mind I can't imagine anything—mattering much, so long as you were there. Come, let's go and sample this delectable food."

They ate delicious food and it was something of a surprise to Michael to discover how hungry he was; he had imagined that the joy of being with Liz would have made him unable to eat.

She enjoyed what was set before them with obvious relish. "The food which Florence cooks is—well, as good as one can expect, but this! Mike it's a good thing that we're only here for a short time, or I should develop proportions like Mrs. Hardcastle. Then—you'd hate it, me with no 'line', wouldn't you?"

He shook his head. "It's not likely to happen, but I can't imagine anything remotely connected with you making any difference."

"Even excessive—fat?"

"It could never be excessive—with you it could only be quite perfect."

Again they sat by the bright fire, and again Liz led Michael on to talk to her about himself. She was growing to know him, growing to appreciate his work, his aspirations. He spoke modestly of what he had achieved, and did not seem to think that for a boy of seventeen he had accomplished anything unusual. He talked at great length of his father, and more than once she had the impulse to tell him that Enoch knew the relationship between them. She repressed it, it was better that one day Enoch should tell his son himself.

She found an unexpected strain of poetry in him, he spoke of his love of Borrow, of Flecker, and of—unexpectedly—Burns, almost shyly. For a time he would speak with a certain hesitation, as if he was half unwilling to talk of the things he loved, then suddenly he would forget himself, and burst out into statements of what he longed to see and hear.

"Music—I've heard none, or so little that it doesn't count. I bought a gramophone and I've collected records very carefully, saving my pocket money to get them. The first time I heard Chopin's Preludes, I thought that my heart would burst."

And, "Once at school—the Head was very decent like that, he'd often get rather special people to come and talk to us, and once he brought a pianist, called Solomon. I had never heard anything so beautiful. When it was over lots of the fellows went to him with autograph books, and although I hadn't an autograph book, I went too. He turned to me and held out his hand

—he thought I'd hand him the usual book—I just stared at him, and shook my head. I couldn't speak. He must have thought that I was half-witted."

His eyes were very bright, he stretched out his hand and took hers.

"You've heard all these people, Liz. Opera, you've heard great opera?"

"I've heard some—I don't know that I really enjoyed it a great deal. I don't think that I'm very musical——"

"You can say that! You don't mean it. I have a record of an opera by Verdi, it's called *Forza del Destino*—I suppose that means 'The Power of Destiny' eh? It's the most exciting thing I've ever heard, it begins like this——" and he drummed with his fingers on the arm of his chair. "It makes your blood run quicker, leaves you breathless. There's another opera—by Puccini—called *La Tosca*. I've read about the plot in a book I found in a second-hand shop in Bradford. There isn't an overture, just some *immense* chords. They make you shiver, you understand that tragedy is waiting, coming nearer and nearer.

"Then I found another opera by Puccini, quite different, but—grand, grand. It's called *Turandot*—whew! some of it is simply hair-raising. Was he very great, this Puccini?"

"Not so great as Verdi—but perhaps more lovable. Mike, tell me what you want most."

He smiled. "What do you want? Me to answer three questions, and on that depends my fate! Like the Calif in *Turandot*. The first thing you know—you've known the answer for a long time. That wish is far and away beyond all the others. I want to make myself a first-rate farmer, to make two blades of grass grow where only one grew before—then I want to hear music—lovely, wonderful music, played by the finest musicians. I can make music for myself when I read poetry—that's 'word music' but it's wonderful, but the other music—I can't make for myself, and I want to listen to the people who can make it."

"It shouldn't be insurmountably difficult, my dear. There, now, Mike, you see how wise we were to snatch this time together. I never knew all those things about you, never knew that you loved music—either instrumental or—just lovely words. My dear, you're going to find me dreadfully commonplace, I've heard—only just heard of Borrow, I don't know anything about—who is it?—Flecker—and Burns to me is like a foreign language."

"It wouldn't be," he protested eagerly, "if you'd read it aloud

182

to yourself and let *Burns* talk to you, here and there you'd find a difficult word, but don't take any notice, just let him—go on singing to you. Does that sound just silly rot, Liz?"

"Not to me—only I realize that you're a romantic, for all your practicality. And games—do you like games?"

"I was never awfully good at anything except tennis and fives. The tennis they play round Huddersley is—'pat ball'. I like to read that Yorkshire has won when they play cricket, I like to see that Bradford City's won when they play football. I'm no good at sport, I mean I wouldn't want to hunt even if I could afford it, I can shoot, but only rough shooting and I don't care a great deal for it. I'm not much good at those kind of things. Are you disappointed?"

She came to him, put her arm round his neck and drew his head down on to her shoulder. "Disappointed, my dearest, no." She laughed softly. "Possibly rather overcome that my lover knows so much more than I do about many things."

He laughed and snuggled his face into her neck as she leaned over him. "What, don't you follow Yorkshire and Bradford City! For shame, and you a Yorkshire woman!"

"I'm not!" indignantly, "I'm Lancashire! Never forget that."

He rose and taking her face in his hands kissed her gently. "I'll fight the Wars of the Roses with you whenever we have a spare half-hour. I was going to say that I don't forget things— but I've got to withdraw that proud boast. I had forgotten that it's half past six, that we've 'tired the sun with talking'—and that it's time I ordered a cocktail for you."

"And for yourself!"

He grinned happily. "An' if tha does ought fer nout, do it fer thesen—or a laady!"

"Do it for both. I'm going to have a bath and change, and you can do the same, then we'll drink cocktails together. Mike, you must admire my new dress. Bought especially—for you. Terribly extravagant, but quite satisfactory, I think."

He hesitated, his finger on the bell. "Do you want—dinner jacket and a black tie? I've got them——"

She smiled. "It would be rather nice—our celebration, eh?"

She left him and went into her own room, he stood by the fire, thinking how happy he was, how wonderful it had been to talk to Liz as he had never talked to anyone else. He knew that his father read Shakespeare, but felt that if Gran had heard that he—Michael—read poetry—she would have looked disapproving and said, 'Nay, I don't think I'd read over much of that—Wordsworth, or Dr. Watts or maybe Mrs. Hemens—but it's no reading for a man."

He ordered the cocktails, and then dressed quickly, he got a distinct satisfaction from the severe black and white, and congratulated himself that he had taken the trouble to tie a respectable bow, not one of the lop-sided kind that so many people considered adequate. He went back to the sitting-room, and stood waiting for Liz, she seemed to have been away from him for a long time, yet looking at his watch he found that it was less than twenty minutes. Then the door opened and she came towards him.

"Liz! The black dress I love so!" he exclaimed.

She shook her head. "Not so observant as I believed—it's as like the old one as the exceedingly fashionable dressmaker would allow, but it's new—terribly extravagant, and specially for you!"

"You look wonderful—adorable. Turn round, let me see it really properly and not just get an impression of being completely dazzled. It's beautiful, darling, quite beautiful."

"You look very nice yourself, Mike. Oh, cocktails—give me one."

How pleasant it was to stand there, watching her sipping her cocktail, the black dress showing up the whiteness of her neck, her skin looked so smooth, with a matt surface; her hair curled and lying close to her exquisitely neat head, he never failed to get a thrill of satisfaction at her appearance of always having been newly groomed. Not that she used a great deal of make-up, or if she did she knew how to put it on, and he had never seen her with the blood-coloured nails which so many women affected and which he hated.

"You're a lovely person, Liz," he said suddenly.

"I've never been within miles of being lovely," she told him. "I've learnt to make the best of myself, because I don't see why I should go about looking a sight. I've a decent figure. My skin is all right, because I've taken care of it, and my hair isn't bad. My old nurse used to say, 'There, you'd pass in a crowd if someone gave you a good push'."

"Well I think you're lovely," he persisted.

"If you do—whether you're right or wrong—that's all I care."

They went down to dinner, Mrs. Hardcastle beamed at them both, her eyes almost disappearing in creases of fat.

184

"Now that's what I do like!" she told them. "I like to see ladies and gentlemen dress—like ladies and gentlemen. I' my young days—I was in genel'man's service—yes, nobility they were. I' my young days, people would as soon have thought of setting down to dinner i' their day clothes as they'd have thought of coming down in their night attire. Things have changed, and not for the better neither, to my way of thinking.

"Well, enjoy your dinners—plain but good and wholesome. Nice drop of soup—yes, and mine is soup, neether out o' a tin or just wish-wash. A nice saddle—my own jelly, and mint sauce—the mint grown i' my own garden. And an apple pie—apples from my orchard. I b'lieve it's against the law or some rubbish, but I've served cream with it. Always have done, and always will."

Michael said, "And cheese with it, Mrs. Hardcastle?"

"Why of course! What do they say, 'Apple tart without cheese, is like a kiss without a squeeze'." Her vast frame shook with stifled laughter.

Liz said as they ate the excellent saddle, "London food won't go down very well after this interlude. I don't know how she does it! Wouldn't you like to know her history, Mike? Probably started as kitchen maid in some big house and watched the cook, and profited by what she saw.

"And the old waiter who looks like Father Time! But he knows how to wait, for all his age—and he might be a hundred—he's as neat and nippy as he can be."

"Shall we come here again—some day?" Liz asked.

"We'll reserve rooms to-night for our honeymoon," he said, and smiled as her eyes met his.

"Ah, Mike!" it was almost a sigh. "We must be content to live in the present, not the future. That's one of the terrors which come with being in love—in war-time. The hideous uncertainty of it all."

" 'The valiant only taste of death but once . . .' " he said. "I refuse to die 'many times before my death'."

"I don't believe that women in love can be particularly valiant where their dearests are concerned. They're always afraid for them."

"Aren't men afraid for their women, then?"

"I don't think in quite the same way. A woman in love grafts on to all the other things which go to make up her emotions, a kind of maternal feeling. If you were ten, twenty years older, I should still feel that, at times, you were far, far younger than I am. Women are born older than men."

"I don't know many women, I've only met girls who live round about, most of them seem terribly silly—to me. Nice, oh, quite nice, but—well, damned silly."

Her eyes, which had been grave, twinkled suddenly. "I'm quite content that you should find them so! Probably if we met them—these girls—together, I should feel at an awful disadvantage."

Mockingly he said, "The awful weight of your years, eh? Liz, you are adorable, but you talk such rot sometimes."

"I know—we can't all be blessed with your intellect! There, ask Father Time to bring coffee upstairs."

As they talked, Michael standing in his favourite attitude with his arm resting on the mantelpiece, he said suddenly, "Liz, may I ask a very impertinent question?"

"Let me hear what it is? If it is really impertinent I shall show my disapproval."

"Are you very rich?"

"It's a question of degree, comparison, isn't it? I'm a pauper compared with—with—oh, I can't remember the names of the big oil kings and so on. I'm rich compared with—Willett on the farm."

His face was very serious. "That tells me nothing."

"That's all you need to know, surely, Mike; I suppose that I am a rich woman, I could afford to live in a much larger place than Cummings, but I happen to like Cummings. Uncle Harry left me a good income, very good, George was a rich man—he's left me everything, except—some provision for—other people. When Aunt Alice dies—please God not for many years—I shall have all her money. Yes, I suppose that I'm rich, Mike. Do you mind, darling?"

"I don't know, Liz—I'd hate people to say that—I'd married money, or—well, the kind of thing they do say. I should know that money has nothing to do with it—and they'd never realize how rich I am myself, fabulously rich. I've got you, and your love —but you'd never get that into their thick heads. It's difficult—" then impulsively, "No it isn't—who cares what anyone says or thinks! You're the only thing that matters——"

Somewhere in the distance, a clock struck the hour, the sound came clearly through the cold, still air. They listened to the slow, distinct strokes.

186

"Eleven o'clock! Mike, you must be dead tired, you were up at squeak of dawn, I'm certain."

"I worked at the farm accounts until after twelve," he said. "I packed, and was up again at four. But it's been the shortest day I can remember. Tired—I don't think so. I'll carry down the coffee cups, and get a drink each, shall I?"

"Thoughtful lad, bless you. Save old Father Time's old legs."

"I hate *used* cups and things left about. Gran says that I should have made a splendid old maid."

"Old maids aren't always so tidy," Liz said. "I share a flat with one—the place looks as if a whirlwind has swept through it if she even attempts to wrap up a parcel!"

He carried down the cups, and asked for two whiskies and sodas. Mrs. Hardcastle protested, "No, sir, reely, you ought to have rung, that's what bells are for. I'll send them up, sir."

He laughed. "No, I insist, you all get quite enough running up and down. Yes. I insist. There, good-night."

They sat talking until again the village church clock struck. Liz said, "Mike, this is disgraceful. I'm going to bed."

She put her hands on his shoulders, and he drew her to him, "Liz, my wonderful Liz," he whispered. She looked at him, gravely, and tenderly, then kissed him.

"Not wonderful," she said softly, "but completely—yours." She turned without speaking again, and went into her own room. Michael stood staring at the closed door for a moment, then went to his own room, five minutes later he walked softly to the closed door, opened it noiselessly, and closed it behind him.

As he took her in his arms, she said, "You were such a long time, I thought you were never coming. My dear, dear Mike."

Chapter Fifteen

MICHAEL woke to find the pale, early morning sun slanting into his room. He had left Liz sleeping—looking he thought, almost pathetically young—in the early hours of the morning and had crept back to his own room. His first thought was 'Another day—a whole day with her.' He hoped that she'd breakfast with him in the little sitting-room, he tried to imagine her pouring out coffee while he served—whatever the dish might be. Another picture to add to his mental gallery.

He bathed and shaved, whistling with sheer happiness. He was fastening his collar when someone knocked on his door. He opened it to find the stout chambermaid.

"Madam says will you have breakfast—in bed here—well, I can see as you're one o' the early kind and I know you won't. Or will you go down to the dining-room, or will you have it with her in the sitting-room. There's a nice fire burning. And what 'ul you like for breakfast. She's having kidney and bacon—very nice too—. An' coffee—it's goodish coffee though I says it."

Michael considered gravely. "In the sitting-room, please, and I can think of nothing nicer than kidney and bacon."

"Well, come to think on it, there's not many things as is nicer."

"Is madam waiting?"

"In her bath—I don't b'lieve she'll dress, just slip on one o' those things like glorified dressing-gowns—they used to call them *peignoirs*—now they call them house-coats."

He was standing at the window, staring out at the red roofs of the old stables and coach houses when Liz came in.

"Good-morning, my Mike," she greeted him. "When I woke—I wondered if it was all a dream, you slipped away so quietly."

"You were sleeping so beautifully, I should never have had the heart to wake you." He kissed her, holding her close, catching his breath a little at the sheer delight which it gave him. "Oh, my adorable, wonderful Liz."

As they sat down to breakfast, Liz said, "This is taking an awful risk—breakfast isn't a meal when people are at their best and brightest, is it? My uncle used to say that for people to breakfast together was a barbarous business."

Michael said, grandly, self-confidently, "But we're not like

188

other people. Oh, I have a present for you—I meant to give it to you yesterday, but there was so much to talk about, I forgot."

She was as excited as a child, and insisted upon having the little clock to stand quite near her. "I want to hear it ticking——"

"Ticking away our precious minutes," he reminded her.

"You're young, you assure me that I am—we shall have millions of minutes together."

He sighed contentedly. " 'Life's very sweet, who would wish to die?' That's my beloved Borrow."

"I thought that he was a poet."

"I think that what he wrote *is* poetry, even if he used prose."

Liz said, unexpectedly, "Mike, do you think a great deal?"

He smiled. "I think all farmers do. There is so much to think about, so much to watch. You can't watch crops grow as if they were so many yards of material to be sold at so much a yard. You've got to nurse your land. Oh, I've not been at it for very long, but it absorbs me. I like to know that a day's work is finished, the beasts all comfortable and safe, and then go home and work at the wretched forms and returns, after that—to relax, to listen to some wonderful music, and read——"

"Did you like the Brooke's I sent you?"

"Some of them are beautiful, quite beautiful. 'The Great Lover'—'Grantchester'—and others; it makes you wonder what he would have done had he been given time. Would he have developed into something really great, or was that poetry the expression of his youth? So many of them, those people who wrote lovely things, you feel—unwillingly—had shot their bolt. I'll tell you who I love—" he was speaking excitedly and eagerly, "Belloc. Ah, he can write poetry for the common man—I mean not only for intellectuals. Do you know the poem which begins 'Do you remember the inn, Miranda?' It's exciting, it carries you on with a kind of rush, you can hear everything going on in the inn, 'the cheers and the jeers' and even the feeling of the 'Fleas in the high Pyrenees'—oh, it's great."

Liz watched him when he talked, she saw his eyes shine, how his cheeks flushed a little with real excitement in his subject. He had never allowed his enthusiasms to grow stale or become dulled, she could imagine that everything affected him in the same way—everything remained fresh, alive and keen. He would never lose his pleasure in small things, never adopt a bored attitude towards anything because he imagined that it appeared to show him in a more worldly light.

She told herself again, as she had done so often, that she was fortunate to be his first love, to be the first woman to know his sensibility, his essential kindliness and his innate gentleness. That he was passionate in his love she knew, but she felt convinced that physical passion alone would never satisfy him. He wanted friendship, companionship, laughter in addition to fully complete their association.

There was a sense of taste about him, although she had known how ardently he wished to make their love complete in every way, yet he had never all through yesterday shown any attempt to reach that culmination before she showed him that she was ready to do so. His embraces were full of deep and real affection, but he had always refrained from any demonstration which might have offended or shocked her in the least. This splendid lad of barely eighteen had learnt control, had cultivated tact and restraint. Liz knew instinctively that had he allowed himself the liberty which so many boys of his age, living on farms or in country places indulged in, his attitude and behaviour to her must have been coarser and more material. Boys who had experienced the rough and tumble love making of sensual country adolescents would never have been able to spend a whole day with the woman for whom they felt an attraction—much less actual love—without making demands, and showing their desire for urgent and physical satisfaction. Yet in his love-making there had been nothing prudish or crude; he had been simple, un-affected and completely natural. She had wondered as she bathed and dressed if he would appear embarrassed when they met at breakfast, if he might make some reference to what had taken place, and the thought had disturbed her; instead, he had perhaps kissed her with greater tenderness, but he had said nothing, made no allusion to their changed relationship.

He startled her by saying suddenly, "Liz—you're miles away, come back, please."

"I was thinking——"

"Of what, darling?"

"You, chiefly, wondering what went to make you the nice person you are, wondering how you come to have such poise, such a sense of—fitness."

He smiled. "I don't know that I have much poise, or any great sense of fitness. Naturally I want to show myself in as good a light as possible to you. One day you'll take me unawares and find out what a surly brute I can be. Liz, we've got the whole lay, what would you like to do? Shall I find out from Mrs. Hardcastle if there is somewhere we can drive out to, perhaps lunch there? It's a lovely morning, crisp and clear, and I've got a rug so that you won't be cold. Shall I do that, while you put on something warmer than that very attractive dressing-gown?"

Mrs. Hardcastle greeted him warmly, she was helpful and efficient. "Why, let's see, sir—there's my cousin's hotel at Wishford, that's about twelve miles away. It's a bonny little place, nice old church, they say it goes back to Norman times, though I can't say if that's true. My cousin, Jabez William Makepeace, has the George. He's as proud of it as what I am of the Great Bear. His wife—she's a Somerset woman—is a notable cook. If I was to telephone to Jabez as you and madam were coming, I'll lay any money you like, sir, that he'll have something right tasty for you."

They drove away, through the clear, crisp atmosphere, past the bare hedges and the skeleton trees, with the low, grey sky overhead. Past tiny villages, little churches, and here and there small thatched cottages. It was a typical winter scene, but neither Liz nor Michael cared. They talked very little, occasionally one of them would say, "Look—how attractive!" or "I wish that we had time to explore that place", but most of the time they were utterly content to be together, only conscious of the fact that they were snatching a few hours of close community.

From time to time Liz took a cigarette from her case, lit it and handed it to Michael, he would turn for a second and smile his thanks. Only once did he stop the car, and met her eyes—such lovely kind eyes, he thought.

"Liz—kiss me, please."

She leaned forward, and let her lips rest on his, heard him sigh, and then starting the car up again, they drove on.

They found Wishford, a long, straggling wide street, with old houses on either side, and small, old-fashioned shops, with the small window panes of their day. An old market place, with a town hall built in the style of Palladio, with pillars and a dignified porch.

"The George!" Michael exclaimed, "now to make the acquaintance of Mrs. Hardcastle's cousin—I even know his name—Jabez William Makepeace. He has been duly warned of your arrival."

Liz said, "*Our* arrival!"

He laughed. "I don't count."

An old courtyard, the house timbered and colour-washed,

with the old wood standing out almost harsh in its darkness. An old-fashioned pump, buckets standing neatly in a row—wooden buckets, painted bright green. Old coach houses and commodious loose boxes. Liz got out, stamping her feet on the smooth age-old paving stones.

"Mike—let's get inside, it's infernally cold."

He was filled with solicitude. "You're not too chilled?"

"Only sufficiently to make me feel that a cocktail will be more than acceptable."

She slipped her arm through his, and together they entered the old-fashioned inn. Copper glinting brightly, old hunting prints in frames of bird's-eye maple, some of them a little foxed but the glass in their frames shining with polishing. A huge open fire, flanked with great iron dogs, which burnt huge logs.

Liz said, "Mike, I believe that our luck's in!"

"I never doubted that mine was," he said.

The landlord hurried to meet them, he was as thin as his cousin was immense. A small man, with slightly bandy legs, who looked as if he might have been a jockey or a groom. His spindly legs encased in excellent breeches and gaiters.

"The lady and gennelman what my cousin telephoned about, I'll be bound! Now, I'll lay any money that you're both starved to death! Sit down by the fire, I'll bring summat to warm you. My wife's getting a right nice lunch for you. Ellen—that's my cousin at the Bear, said, 'No duck, Jabez', so I've got something else." Then suddenly very formal, he bowed, saying, "Ex-cuse me for a mom-ent, please."

Later they went into a long, low dining-room, the tables covered with shining white cloths, napkins which were almost as large as the tablecloths themselves, polished with much careful ironing.

Jabez Makepeace hovered near. "I have," he told Michael, "a nice Haut-Brion, sir. Very sootable for the dish we've prepared."

Michael nodded. "Haut-Brion it is, Mr. Makepeace."

It was with pride, which proved to be justifiable, that his wife brought in a dish wrapped in one of the snowy napkins.

Jabez said, "My wife's speciality, sir and madam—steak, kidney and mushroom pudding. There's folks as say larks should be included, but that's something neether me nor my wife can allow."

They lunched well, then sat before the huge fire, sipping some of the good brandy which Makepeace served in great balloon glasses.

"Now, when you get back to the Bear, Madam, make my cousin give you crumpets for tea. She's a great hand at them. I've heard," he lowered his voice to a confidential whisper, "as we shan't be able to get them much longer. Owin' to this war. When someone told me that, I fairly forgot myself. I said— excuse me, Madam, I said, 'Curse that Hitler!' It seemed to bring home to me, as you might say—the horrors of war!"

They drove back in the fading light, Liz leaned against Michael's shoulder, and more than once he turned and kissed her hair, saying:

"Oh, darling what a wonderful day!"

"Our honeymoon ends to-morrow," she said. "I must leave early, and so must you. Mike, I've been so happy."

"Then don't think of to-morrow," he told her, "let's live every minute that's left to us. No one, nothing can take from us what we've had, sweetheart."

Liz sighed, "My little clock ticking away the minutes——"

"That little clock will somewhere—somehow tick out many other wonderful minutes. Liz, won't you marry me?"

She shook her head. "I can't Mike—don't let's go into all that again, let's be content that we have snatched these two days and spent them together."

"Glad, thankful, grateful," he said, "but I shall never be content until I can look forward to the rest of our life spent together. Liz, the plans we'd make, the places we'd see, the work we'd do."

"I know, I know—but be patient, dearest."

When she watched him eating crumpets later, she felt that he was exactly what she knew him to be, a boy who was scarcely more than a schoolboy, with all a boy's appetite. He even looked younger, munching the butter-soaked crumpets.

She laughed. "You look like a schoolboy home for the holidays!"

He grinned back. "I feel like one. Would it be awful to ask for a second supply? Or does my greediness revolt you?"

"Have twenty fresh supplies if you can eat them. I told you that you were far too thin."

The stout chambermaid said as he handed her the empty dish, "Now, Mrs. Hardcastle *will* be pleased about that, she reely will! I'll have them up to you i' no time at all."

The hours slid past, Liz knew that their approaching separation was oppressing both of them. She wondered when it would be possible for them to meet again, when they could recapture the joy of being together! There were times when her determination not to marry Michael wavered, when she felt that she would fling prudence to the winds, brave the disapproval of everyone—even defying Gran's sharp tongue; then her common sense asserted itself, and she returned to her original decision. Ten years difference might not matter now when she was still young, while her skin was unlined, her movements swift and easy—but when Michael was forty he would still be in his prime, while she at fifty might have grown withered and 'look her age'. Then came those dark thoughts which so often disturbed her, if the war continued, if he went overseas, went where the fighting might grow more and more intensive every day, he might never reach his full manhood. What would she do if when he left England she never saw him again, and she had to live out her life without him? She shivered, and Michael looked at her anxiously.

"You've not caught cold, have you?"

She laughed. "No, just a goose walking over my grave!"

"What a horrid thought—imagine talking about graves with this wonderful fire and these large cups of tea, to say nothing of the fresh supply of crumpets."

"I wasn't thinking about graves—the imaginary goose was and found mine."

With a determination which held something almost grim about it, Liz set to work to drive away those dark thoughts, to concentrate on the present and refuse to let her mind reach forward to the possible future. Michael, his sensitivity sharpening his knowledge of her, had noticed the shadow on her face, the darkening of her eyes, had seen too that her mouth drooped a little. He knew that it would be so easy for him to sink into a state of acute depression at the thought of the short time which was left to them, so easy to play upon her feelings and grow importunate, begging her again to marry him, if not immediately at least before he joined the Army. He fought against the impulse and did his best to turn her thoughts and his own from the knowledge that to-morrow would mean separation. He would not allow himself to even ask when it would be possible for them to meet again, it should all be left to her, and he realized that he knew her sufficiently, was certain enough of her love for him to

194

now that she would send for him or come to him whenever it was humanly possible.

That night she lay in his arms, and he poured out all the loving, tender phrases which soothed and comforted her. This love of hers for a boy might be madness, but it was the most real and sincere affection which had ever come into her life. She had never, as a girl, indulged in flirtations however innocent, and now—looking back—she knew that although George had loved her when they married, his love was of an entirely different calibre to this love which Michael gave her. George had been uniformly kind, but extreme tenderness was something completely out of his ken. To George she had been a desirable woman, he had wanted her physically, but he had been incapable of verbal tenderness, and she remembered, too, what a shock it had been to her in those early days of her marriage, when George kissing her in a fashion which was almost perfunctory, sighed, and a moment later was sound asleep.

"Mike, you'll come and meet me again when I can get leave?"

"You don't need to ask that, darling. Aren't you coming to Yorkshire then?"

"We should be able to see so little of each other if I did—I at Cummings, you at Anderson's. When is your birthday?" He knew what was in her mind, what she meant was 'When are you going to join the Army?'

"Early in August——"

He felt her arms tighten round his shoulder. "Are you still determined, Mike?"

"Quite, darling, I feel even now that people look at me and wonder why I'm still wearing civvy clothes. It's a horrible feeling. I do look older than I am, I know, but I can't rush up to people and explain that, can't even explain that I am doing a job of national importance. Try to understand, darling one."

She moved impatiently. "You—fighting! It seems so improbable. You don't want to fight really, do you?"

"Of course I don't, who does I wonder? But—and it's so difficult to say these things without sounding hopelessly bombastic—I do want to do my duty to my country, to the people I love. Don't let us talk about it—you get hurt and half angry, and I get—oh, I don't know—it makes me feel frustrated not to be able to go now and get into uniform. Liz, remember that I love you, I shall always love you, I wish I could explain how deeply and sincerely."

195

She cried a little, and he comforted her as best he could when he crept away as the false dawn came, she was sleeping peacefully.

They drove back to Grantham scarcely speaking, the coming separation oppressed them both, words would not come easily. They went into the lounge at the Angel and Royal, and their conversation was spasmodic and trivial.

Liz said, "On that wall there used to be two engravings of Edward the Seventh and Queen Alexandra—when they were first married. I wonder where they've gone?"

"I wonder. She was very beautiful, wasn't she?"

"I've always been told so."

Liz thought, 'And what on earth do either of us care? Wasting time talking about two old pictures.'

"You'll drive carefully, won't you?" Michael said. "The road may be skiddy."

"I don't think so—and I always drive carefully."

For the first time, she felt for hours, he smiled. "Then drive extra carefully, to please me. More coffee?"

"No, we ought to go. I'm on duty to-night."

"Poor Liz——"

"Poor both of us! Oh, Mike, I don't want to go. I wish we could run away and hide somewhere, where no one could find us. Say good-bye to me here, dearest."

He held her tightly, kissing her passionately, whispering her name again and again as if he loved the sound.

"You love me, Mike?"

"Completely, irrevocably, dearest."

He stood at the door of her car unwilling to take his eyes from her until the last possible moment. Suddenly she uttered an exclamation. "Oh—Mike—did you pay the bill at the Bear?"

"Of course, did you think that I'd absconded?"

"But—I meant to do it."

"We've had this out before, precious," he smiled. "You might as well get used to it—you'll have to get used to it."

"It must have been a frightfully expensive two days for you!"

"If it had cost me every penny I have—every penny I am ever likely to have, it would have been worth all that—and more."

"Dear Mike! Don't watch me drive away, it's unlucky. Bless you!"

The Great North Road again, he tried to take his mind away from the thought of Liz driving alone; he recalled all the poetry he knew and recited it to himself—poems, long passages from Shakespeare, passages from his loved Borrow, some of the Psalms.

He turned in at the gates of Anderson's when the short winter afternoon was closing in. How peaceful it all seemed, and with that thought came another of Liz, Liz who was on duty to-night, amid the noise of London, perhaps facing an air raid. He shivered, it didn't bear thinking about.

The warm air of the big kitchen seemed to welcome him. Violet said, "Why if it's not Mister Michael! You're just in time for tea, your Gran and Dad's there an' James. Tak' a cup in wi' you, will you? Had a nice little 'olliday?"

"Very nice, thank you. I came from Grantham this morning."

Gran looked up as he came in. "Why, it's Michael back!"

"Hello, Gran—how are you, Dad? Hello, Jim."

Enoch said, "I'm gradely, thanks. I've been out and about to-day. Tired? Not a bit, us young chaps don't tire that easily!"

"Car all right?" James asked. "Tell us where you've been, give us some traveller's tales. Meet any pretty girls?"

"All the pretty girls are in the Services," Michael said, and Gran interpolated, "Pretty girls indeed! Michael's got over much sense to run about wasting his time—aye, and his money on pretty girls!"

Enoch, his eyes watching his elder son, wondered if Michael had seen Liz, if they had been happy together, and if the lad would be miserable thinking of her back in London? He liked Liz Tancred, as much as any woman he knew, she was amusing, good looking, and yet it was a pity that Mike and she should have fallen in love. Far better if he'd waited a bit and then fallen for some bonnie country lass—perhap's a farmer's daughter. He was a queer lad, a bit over-serious for his years, always had been. Young Jim now, was as different as chalk from cheese, livelier, always wanting to go here or go there, clever without a doubt—but then so was Mike. Enoch thought, 'Mike 'ul always take things harder nor what Jim will. Jim would throw things off easier. Mike—if he loved anyone—would pretty well break his heart if anything went wrong. Mike is so reliable, if he set out to do a thing—you could bet any money he'd do it, an' do it with all his might. Somehow I don't believe Jim—if he'd been Mike's age, would have stuck at anything as Mike's stuck to the farming. I may be wrong, you can't ever tell.'

James was talking excitedly. "Mum and Dad say that I can

197

leave school at the end of the summer term, and go to York to start studying accountancy, then they'll see if I pass my first exam if they can get me articled to a really big firm. That's grand, isn't it?"

"Sounds splendid, good luck, Jim."

"See as you keep your nose to the grindstone," Gran warned, "for from what I gather it's going to cost a mint o' money."

"I'll work, Gran," his tone was full of confidence, "and once I get through all my exams, I shall make oudles of money. Dad can regard me as an investment—a gilt-edged security."

Michael was in the little office when his father entered, he turned from his desk and smiled at him.

"It's splendid, Dad, to see you looking so fit. Sure you're not doing too much? You mustn't overdo it—it's early days yet."

Enoch sat down, his hands on his knees. "I can't honestly say as I'm tired, Mike. I've enjoyed feeling that I was shouldering some of my responsibilities again. I've not liked being laid by. But, I didn't come in to talk about me—I want to talk about you. You and me are good friends, I think I can say that, eh?"

"I should think you could! I know no chap ever had a father as good as mine—or a mother as good as Mum." Michael's eyes shone with affection. Enoch gave a huge, gusty sigh of relief.

"I don't know about all that good," he said, "I'm not educated like what you and James are, I've tried to educate mesen a bit, with reading good bukes and such like, but I'm—rough. Ready, I hope but—rough. I'm not a talking kind of chap, and I'm one as can keep a still tongue. I don't chit-chatter about other folks' affairs. I like to be frank wi' people I care for—I've never hid nothing from your muther—while now, and I shall continue to keep my own strict council about this partic'lar matter."

Michael said, hesitating a little, "I'm afraid that I'm not quite getting all the hang of this, Dad. Nothing very serious, I hope?"

"Well, I cut the cackle an' come to the 'osses, Mike." He drew a deep breath, then continued, "I know where you've been these last few days. Not actually *where* understand, but—well, I know who you went to meet."

"Yes, Dad? Go on, please. Are you very angry?"

"Now harken to me," his father said, "I'm not angry, for we've treated you as if you were a man, we've loaded you wi' responsibilities beyond your years, and—well, you're young i' years, but you *are* a man! I'm not going to say as I don't think it's a pity, for I do, but what concerns me most is that—I don't want you hurt over this."

Gravely his son said, "I don't think that I shall be."

"I pray you won't be. And although it goes a bit against the grain to conceal it from her, I'm not going to tell your mother. Maybe, it's wrong but I don't think it is. Anyway, I'm not saying aught."

"Thank you, Dad, I'm grateful. Dad—" impulsively, "how did you know? Can you tell me?"

"Why, aye. She told me herself."

"Liz!" the name was startled from him. "Liz!"

"Who else. The day after you fetched her back from London when George weer killed. She didn't mean to tell me, I feel sure, but we were talking about you, and there was something in her tone as made me feel—how it was between you. Something, so far as mem'ry serves me like, 'I don't *wish* him to go!' I said, '*You* don't wish——' or words like that, and then she understood that I'd seen where the wind was setting. We had a long talk, for I've always liked Liz, I've ad-mired her. Oh, I knew all about poor George and his little fancy women, aye and more than that, as I don't intend to recount to you, Mike. She knew an' all."

"I know that she did. I'm glad you've told me this, it makes us come even closer—you and me. I've asked her—more than once to marry me—she's refused. She thinks that she is too old for me."

Enoch shook his head. "Nay, there's not all that in it. She lukes younger than her years, you luke older'n yours. You be kind, and trew, loving and good to her—and if I know aught about her, she'll be the same wi' you. Don't have silly jealous feelings, don't imagine that she's got a fancy for someone else—she's all right is that lass. There—I'm going, you can get back to your work." He rose, and cocked his head on one side like a listening dog. "Yon's your muther back. Come and greet her, lad."

Chapter Sixteen

MICHAEL was back into his stride, the farms absorbed him. There was the daily routine, the planning ahead, the winter sowing, the welfare of the beasts. Controls were being imposed, and he fretted at the compulsion to send his eggs to a central depot.

"Look, Dad," he said to Enoch, "the distribution's damned bad. Eggs lying there until they're what I call—shop eggs. It's maddening—perfectly maddening."

Enoch nodded. "It's always the same wi' what's called bureaucracy. That means sticking a lot of square pegs i' round holes. It can't be helped, I mind a poem I learned when I was at school it was about an old man talking to his grandchildren about some battle. He said: 'Sooch things must be—after a famous victory.' Well, we've not had all that many famous victories as yet—but we'll get 'em."

Michael fumed and fretted, everywhere he met with forms advising him of this or that control. His eggs, his milk, even the sale of his beasts. He tried to view it all philosophically, but it irked him none the less.

Ellen and cook over at Cummings grumbled that when Mrs. Tancred *did* come home on what they called 'a spot o' leaf'— they'd have nothing to give her to eat. Michael grinned. "Who says so? I'll see that she has all she wants, even if I break the law in getting it!"

"Break the law," Mrs. Robbins retorted, "no one never ought to have made such laws, if you ask me. Flying in the face of Providence! I was always told—'The Lord will provide'—then what's all this hoarding up of eggs, an' meat, an' a dozen other things mean?"

Ellen said, "I call it fair im-pious, Mister Michael."

"I hear as we're not to be able to buy tea when we want it! Now, luke at that! I've enough eddication to know as tea comes from India—Ceylon and some from China, though that's not a kind I care for myself, well, there's no fighting in India, nor yet i' Ceylon. No, no," she wagged her head, "someone's making a pretty packet out of all this carry-on if you ask me."

Ellen said firmly, "Mrs. Robbins, never mind who's in it, I'll lay as Mr. Churchill isn't."

"Oh, 'im, bless him. He'd not soil his hands. But—" with a weighty pause, "there's others as I could name! Now, Mister Michael, have a nice cupper, you look frozen."

Liz wrote to him often, letters which were brimming over with affection, and the longing to see him, but it was not until March was 'going out like a lamb' that she said she had leave. Part of it she must spend with Aunt Alice, but they could contrive a few days together once that duty was fulfilled.

That night Michael spoke to his father. In the little office where he did his ever-increasing work, for he had been unable to find a land girl who had known something of office work, he told him.

"Dad, do you think that I could have a few days' leave? Yes, I heard to-day," in answer to his father's look of inquiry. "I know that the lambing may begin almost any time, but I shan't be away for more than three days at the most. Can I go, Dad?" he asked almost wistfully.

"I don't see why not. Look, Mike, what about buying some gelts while you're away. I don't want to encourage you to be deceitful, but we can do wi' a nice couple. Nothing over pricey, think on, but good, sound animals."

Michael went off early the next morning, the early mist hung over the fields, the whole landscape seemed to be pearl coloured as the sun gained strength and the light grew. As he drove farther south he saw that already lambs were to be seen in the fields, little creatures walking beside their mothers on their stiff, long legs, or galloping off to be recalled by them, racing back like small children being called in for dinner and leaving their play.

He saw birds busy with their next building, or possibly occupied in finding a suitable site on which to build. A magpie, like a flash flew over the road, and being a good countryman, Michael looked anxiously for a second. Almost immediately it passed him, flying to join its mate. He remembered how Gran had told him when he was quite a small boy that magpies were unlucky. "It's unlucky to see one, think on," she said, "but it's lucky to see two. So don't fash yourself that you've seen a magpie for where's there's one the other's never far behind. Just keep your eyes open."

The country never bored Michael, he loved its changes with the changing of the seasons, loved its lore, the old superstitions which clung so tenaciously; the belief that certain crops must be sown when the moon waxed, others when it was on the wane; the treatment of the beasts; special age-old cures in which the country folk had far more faith than in any medicine prescribed by the smart young veterinary surgeon. Wilson would listen to what he said attentively enough, while he visited a sick animal, there was always much head wagging, gruntings of "Aye", and "Nay". He would hold the medicine—either the bottle or the folded papers which held the powders, with a certain respect, but Michael had long suspected that later Wilson concocted some herbal mixture of his own and administered it. Invariably the animal recovered.

"He a clever chap that Harrington," Michael said, speaking of the veterinary surgeon.

"Aye," Wilson growled, " 'appen he is, 'appen he's not. If he knew all he fancies as he knows—then I'll grant he'd be clever."

But then, young Harrington was a 'foreigner', an 'off-comer', he had only been in Huddersley for five years—what were five years!

In the familiar Angel and Royal, Liz was waiting. She sprang up to greet him. "I've beaten you to it this time, Mike. I was determined to be here first. Let me look at you? You're still too thin, I believe they all overwork you."

"I might say the same about you, dearest. Oh, Liz, it's good to see you again. Where are we going? The Bear again?"

"I'm afraid so—they say you should never try to repeat anything because it's never the same, but I couldn't think of any other place that was so nice. Do you mind?"

"Mind! I don't mind where we go—as long as we're together. I've so much to tell you, about the farm, and you've got to listen!" he warned her. "Last time I wanted to talk to you seriously, you refused to listen, do you remember?"

She nodded. "I remember, the time when you came and talked like a robot. I forget whether robots can talk or not."

They drove to the Bear, the monumental Mrs. Hardcastle met them with a beaming smile. "Now this is nice, sir and madam. I was proper taken aback when that telegram came. I've given you the same rooms, that 'ul suit you, will it? And—luncheon 'ul be ready shortly—what do you say to a nice roast loin o' pork, with an 'Old wife's sod'—that's a kind o' savoury pudden. Devonshire dish it is. Apple sauce, natcherally."

"It sound like the ancient days," Liz said, "when there wasn't a war!"

"Oh, Madam, what a tedious, horrible thing it is—this war. Seems like it's going on for ever and ever amen."

Over luncheon when Michael was eulogizing the admirable pork, he suddenly asked the old waiter if Mrs. Hardcastle kept pigs.

"Indeed she does, sir. You'd not see nicer nowhere."

"Gelts!" Michael exclaimed. "I've got to buy two for my father. I see the hand of Fate in this visit." He laughed. "Killing two birds with one stone!"

"You ought to be ashamed of that remark," Liz told him.

Their two days together slipped away, Michael thought even faster than their first visit had done. He had never, he told himself, known Liz so attractive, so loving and tender. He insisted on giving her news of the farm, and she listened gravely and attentively. Once he was tempted to tell her of his long talk with Enoch, but rejected the idea, to tell her might embarrass or distress her, better keep silent.

"It's all gone like a flash," he said as they drove back to Grantham. "As if I'd only just met you and now I have to leave you again. Why is it that happy times pass so quickly, and the difficult, miserable hours drag so slowly you think they will last for ever? Liz, when will—next time be?"

"Not before May, Mike. Oh, such a long time, and so much may have happened by then."

"I go back to the lambing, then with luck the hay-making will be on us—these seasons creep up on you——" he smiled, and Liz thought as she had done so often, what a contented smile he had, that his expression was that of a man who loves his work, and—the words of some poem she had heard years ago, not a very good poem either, came to her mind—'loves his fellow men'.

"Do you like people a great deal, Mike?" she asked.

"I don't know many people. My young brother James made more friends round Huddersley during his vac. than I've ever made. I don't think that I'm really gregarious. Then," and she heard a note of regret in his voice, "most of the fellows I know— well, they aren't in Huddersley any longer. They were most of them older than I am, and they're serving."

She was conscious of that sudden constriction—of her heart —she thought. The time was coming so near when Michael would come and tell her that he had fulfilled his promise to his father, to George and to herself, and that he counted himself free to join the Army.

"It's a solitary life you live really, isn't it?" she said.

Again he smiled. "Oh, I don't know—I go into Cummings,

and that always seems to bring you a little nearer, and Mrs. Robbins and Ellen and I have a little chat about how we'd run the war, and how if everything was in our hands there'd be no shortages and no restrictions. All rubbish of course, though I don't believe that they think so. Then there's Wilson with his country lore, and Willett with his sound knowledge, and first of all there's my father. Liz, he's so wise, that man. So kindly, and so essentially good. We often sit together in the office and talk, he talks about the land, the harvests, and the beasts—it's so simple that it is—oh, it's uplifting. He's a great fellow."

The impulse came to her too strong to withstand. "Mike, do you know what he understands about—about us?"

His voice was very gentle when he answered, "Yes, darling. He told me after I went back that first time, that unforgettable first time."

"How did he know?" but there was little conviction in her voice as she asked the question.

Michael turned and smiled. "You told him, blessed one."

She nodded. "He told you that? Yes, I did. I didn't mean to, but I rather lost my head. Did he mind, Mike? He was wonderful, eh? He would be. I love—yes, love Enoch. And the others?"

"No, no, not my mother or Gran and of course not James. Dad thought it better not to let anyone else know."

Liz chuckled, "I can imagine Gran's comments on 'such goings on'. They would raise blisters on an iron bar! Do you mind Enoch knowing?"

He said, with a touch of arrogance in his voice, "No, why should I mind? I'd like the whole world to know!"

In the Angel and Royal Michael begged, "Liz, just another half-hour—please. Over our coffee, it's not such bad coffee here."

She laughed. "Then you must amuse me."

"I'm not a very amusing person, I'm afraid. I'll do my best." Sitting on either side of the fire, she said, "Now, talk to me— yes, for a full half-hour. No, don't say that you want to talk about me—talk to me about yourself, that's what I want to hear. Tell me the things that you like—things that give you happiness."

"Oh, Liz—" reproachfully, "you know the answer to the first and foremost," then thoughtfully, "What are they? One of the first, is the early celandine. So plucky, arriving so early, always so immaculate with its petals of yellow enamel. The sudden scent of violets, and you stop and search and see them, hiding under their leaves. I don't pick them because I like to go back and still enjoy their scent. Primroses—yes, they're nice, rather anæmic flowers and snowdrops always remind me of Elizabeth Browning, with their drooping heads. I'm sure they were once early Victorian ladies who lay on sofas and had long—rather dank—curls.

"Lambs, I like lambs, they're not very clever, but they do enjoy life and if you watch them you soon realize that they have a great sense of humour—rather schoolboy humour, but quite funny all the same."

"Go on," she said, "go on."

"Read *The Great Lover*," he said, "only I don't like 'the rough male kiss of blankets'—and I hate a dreadful material called *plush*. Gran once bought a tablecloth made of it, and to even touch it sent shivers up my spine. It's relegated to the kitchen now, but I don't believe that Violet ever puts it on the table. Hay-making's nice, Liz—but then any kind of harvesting is nice, you see the return for your labour. I love a hymn they sing at harvest time—'All is safely gathered in, ere the winter storms begin.' It gives you a sense of—security. I like winter, to see the land, good, fruitful, hard-working land lying resting, and when it's covered with snow, you feel that it's lying snug under its white eiderdown.

"Roses—how I love roses. Once this wretched war is over, I'd like to see your beautiful lawn restored and replanted with good turf and roses—dozens of them—planted there. Not only the new, fashionable kinds—beautiful though they are—but the old kinds—great big generous red roses, pouring out scent, a little sulphur-coloured rose—not much smell, but a lovely shape. Ena Harkness, that's a wonderful rose, and the despised——"

"Who despises them?" Liz asked.

"Oh, those superior, supercilious people who despise most simple things, the ramblers——Yes, even the rather humble Dorothy Perkins and Emily Gray. Liz, we'll have such a rose garden! With wonderful pergolas, and grass walks through them. We'll walk there in the evening, and the scent of the roses will rise up and envelop us. And—night-scented stocks—not much to look at—but the scent! Tobacco plants—not particularly handsome either, but intoxicating. A bean field—have you ever smelt that, particularly in the evening? The softest, most delicious scent imaginable. The apples, Grannie Smith in particular, Great William pears, sun-warmed apricots, even rhubarb—when it's young and an entrancing delicate pink—not that I ever eat it, I can't bear it!—and huge, purple blackberries, and sloes—we'll make sloe gin! Mushrooms too, to gather them when the dew is still heavy on the grass. I remember Wilson once told me that to go gathering mushrooms while the dew is still lying, you should go in bare feet, because there is some wonderful beneficial quality in early dew. Shall we go looking for mushrooms one day? You'll have to be up very early, and they're earlier still, waiting for you. Then to that little inn—do you remember?—the Queen's Head, and a glass of hot milk each, well laced with rum, and then home to breakfast, home-cured bacon, and—mushrooms. Do you wonder that I love living on a farm?"

She looked at him, and then said sombrely, "And yet you'd leave it—and me?"

He answered gravely, "And yet I'd leave the land and you, for a time, Liz my sweetheart, so that I should not 'hold my manhood cheap'. I'm no paladin, but I couldn't bear to face life remembering that I stayed at home. I hate the thought of going, I loathe the idea of killing or being responsible for killing anyone—or for that matter—anything. Only—my Liz, loved and adored Liz, we've got to face it. I must go, you must go—after all you're doing war service while I go and watch turnips growing—in complete safety. Bless you, my dear one, take the greatest care of yourself, and—we'll have, please God, another holiday together—very soon."

"If my leave doesn't clash with the hay-making!"

"My dear," he reproved her very gently, "you know—oh, you shouldn't have said that."

"The harvests, then the Army—both come before me!"

He took her face in his hands. "And you know that fundamentally that isn't true. Tell me you *do* know it."

"I try to believe it when you tell me."

"And you succeed?"

"Sometimes, Mike, sometimes."

"Oh, Liz, my dear—you're behaving like a naughty child, because really you do understand, and you know that I can't explain this necessity to you without sounding grandiloquent or high-flaunting. It would be so easy to rant off—even though my ranting might be sincere—but I can't do it. Liz, dearest, do believe that whatever I do you really come first—there, I could so easily say that I could not love you so much if I did not love honour more. Hell! I don't love honour more, I don't love honour within

206

a thousand miles of the love which I have for you, I don't even know that it's 'honour', but I believe that it is decency."

He watched her expression change, soften, her eyes grow misty with tears, and when she spoke her voice was very gentle.

"Mike, forgive me, darling. I know that I was wrong, but I get so damned lonely, so miserable at the thought of you——"

"Darling, it hasn't happened yet." He kissed her. "We must go."

She smiled. "I know—well, damn the harvests, damn everything that keeps you from me. Yes, let's get cracking."

He drove back, his mind filled with memories of her, conscious that the tie which bound them grew stronger with every meeting. He found so much in her character that satisfied him, she protested that she wasn't clever, but she had a shrewd ability to assess values—both of people and things. She possessed great kindliness, and in his heart Michael held the conviction that one day their love for each other would triumph, become so strong that it would sweep away all barriers and that she would consent to marry him. The details—where they would live, what would be the reaction of people who knew them, what comments Gran might make—he refused to consider.

He got home, Enoch met him, beaming that the lambing had started, and that things were going well.

"One old ewe," he said, "had two lambs, one white, the other black. T' black one she luved, the white one—she shoved the poor little thing away. I fetched it home, rubbed it with soot all over and took it back. She luved and fondled it the same as she did the other!"

It was hard work, for some of the sheep were out on the moors, and it meant constant walking even to keep a not-too-efficient watch on them.

Twice Michael came home with little shaking lambs whose mothers had died, and installed them by the kitchen range, swathed in flannel, where Violet fed them with babies' bottles. On the whole, the season was a success, and Enoch, driven by Michael to see the little creatures skipping about, looking so beautifully white beside their mother's, because their coats had not yet had time to absorb the smoke and grime of the West Riding, rubbed his hands and smiled.

"Think on," he told Michael, "it pays to feed them. It pays to watch for foot trouble—aye, times I've seen flock driven where a quarter o' the sheep has been limping. I could never suffer that on any land of mine—or thine, lad. I've seen sheep as were not watched for ticks, and dipped properly, go mad—aye, properly insane, rushing round and round while they died, because they'd not been properly watched! That mustn't ever happen here, lad."

Michael had installed an incubator. Enoch eyed it dubiously. "It's all right, but it's not natural, Mike. It's against nature. Still I suppose it's what's called pro-gress. Mind you, no selling day-olds. I read about it i' t' papers and I don't hold with it."

He showed an astonishing knowledge of the birds, it was Enoch who insisted that an old-fashioned remedy called Parish's Food should be dropped into their drinking troughs, it was Enoch who administered small peppercorns to chickens who developed the dreaded 'gapes'.

"I've been reading up," he told Michael, "about—capons. Noo, birds are going to bring a big price, restrictions or no restrictions. A good capon—I b'lieve it's reely a French word—will fetch its price. Mind, I don't know as it's all that natural, but what about geldings, for example? I think we'll have a dart at them."

It was in early April when the whole of England, the whole of the civilized world was shocked at the destruction of Coventry. Liz wrote that she had been sent there with a mobile canteen, *"on the 8th, and the bombing went on through the next day. It was quite incredibly horrible, but the bravery of the people was like a gesture of defiance to that wretched Hitler. I'm quite all right."*

Gran said, "Aye, they may have pretty well wrecked Coventry, and plenty o' other places, but it's nothing compared to what they 'ul have to pay when we get into our stride! Mark my words."

Ada came home each night tired and white faced. "It's not like it used to be—customers asking for this and that and you able to say 'Yes, Madam, certainly'. Now you've got to make excuses, you've got to ask for these blessed ration books. A lot of fiddle-faddle! That Hilda Peasly has gone off to-day, munitions! How I'm going to get on, I don't know." Then she laughed. "But I shall get on! The old Huns can't beat me no more than they can beat the rest of us."

Everywhere there were changes, Sir George Fowler's huge, stately house was turned into a hospital, and his pretty daughter was one of the nurses. Colonel Blenkiron was organizing the Home Guard, his wife had filled the house with refugees.

She said to Ada, "I never realized that people could be so dirty—forgive the expression, Mrs. Anderson, so *damned* dirty.

208

If either of those little ruffians of mine—hateful little brutes—behaved as they do—I'd—well, I'd smack them! Oh, the old biscuit for them! They don't get so many biscuits in these days, bless them."

Spring came, the fields were green once more, the lambs had grown and were becoming leggy and losing their attractiveness; the small, fluffy chickens had become rather leggy cockerels and pullets. The hedgerows were filled with primroses, and the hedges themselves showed fat buds which the country children picked and ate, calling them 'bread and cheese'. The two gelts which Michael had bought were becoming large, self-satisfied, and whenever he came near their sties, astonishingly vocal. Everywhere Michael saw signs of the rebirth of the year. Sometimes as he walked to some distant field—belonging either to Anderson's or Cummings—he found a nest, cunningly hidden, and approaching it with a countryman's caution, and ability to step silently, would peer into it, and see either the bright, watchful eyes of the mother bird, watching him as an intruder or see a little clutch of sky-blue, or light-brown speckled eggs. The sight never failed to give him intense pleasure, and in his letters to Liz he would report progress.

"*The thrush in the five acre is very observant, I think she knows me, and though her greeting is restrained and even rather icy, yet she no longer actively resents me as she did at first—opening her beak and positively hissing at me* or *The hedge sparrow of which I told you has hatched out five of the plainest children I have ever seen. They say in Yorkshire that ugly babies grow up beautiful, so I am hoping this may happen—they'll be exquisite if the old saying is true!*" In great excitement he wrote, "*I found a long-tailed tits' nest—I couldn't see any of the family, but what a case of gross over-crowding! I was so excited that I could scarcely eat my dinner.*"

He told her everything that he thought could possibly interest her, always suppressing the wish to ask her when she might hope to have leave and to meet him again. He filled his days with work, never ceased making plans for the coming year. Each day he watched his father with affectionate solicitude, and rejoiced to see him growing daily stronger and more active.

One morning Enoch had gone without taking his stick, and Gran had said, "Michael, run after him, he's forgot his stick. Run!" Carrying the ash-plant which his father always carried, Michael rushed after him, crying, "Dad, your stick!"

Enoch took it saying, "Thanks, lad, it's nobbut a habit,

209

carting the thing round, I don't damn well need it, my own two legs is good enough, time's ovver when I needed a third!"

Michael recounted the incident to his mother that evening. Ada flushed with pleasure, but true to her former belief or pretended belief, said, "Aye, he's all right, is Enoch. Not, mind you, that he was ever as bad as what the doctor tried to make out. I'll never believe as it was a stroke! A nervous break-down, through overwork, that's what it was, Michael."

And true to the legend which his mother had created, Michael replied, "By Jove, Mum, I don't mind betting that you're right."

"I know that I am," she answered, "I've known that for a long time."

"It's a great relief to me," Michael said, "to see him so well, and able to get round. I've an idea that it might be a good invest-ment to buy him a rough kind of car—so that he could drive round and not tire himself. There are such things, like the jeeps they're using overseas."

It was May before Michael saw Liz again, the whole of England was humming with the news that Hess had flown to Scotland, everyone was speculating as to why he had come, theories flew about like flocks of birds—no one actually knew anything. On May 19th, the Italians under the Duke of Aosta surrendered, and the same day Michael heard from Liz that she was coming to Cummings bringing her aunt with her.

He received the news with mixed feelings, when would they be able to be alone? Aunt Alice, Mrs. Robbins and Ellen—everything must inevitably be different from their quiet hours at the Great Bear. He found Ellen and Mrs. Robbins in a complete orgy of cleaning—which was totally unneccessary, for the whole place shone with much polishing. Their excitement was intense, and they babbled to him of what they had planned to cook, of the arrangements which they had made. "It's like having a soldier cumin home from the war!" Ellen said, and Mrs. Robbins added piously, "And let's thank God for it, wi' those 'orrible bombs and nonsense!"

He went over the night she arrived, and to his surprise found her in uniform. She explained, "I knew that if I came in civvies it would rob Ellen and Mrs. Robbins of such a lot of pleasure—they like to feel that I've been winning the war single-handed!"

"When am I going to be able to see you, and really talk to you?"

She chuckled, and tapped her forehead with her finger. "Your

Liz has—what it takes. Liz uses her loaf! I've been studying the *Poultry World*—I've come to the conclusion that we need really first-class birds. There's a place in Westmorland where they sell prize white Leghorns."

Michael ceased to be the lover and was immediately the practical farmer. "Good layers, but light—very light."

Liz countered with, "They don't go broody as the heavier breeds."

"They're not so much use as table birds."

"It doesn't matter, we're going to buy them. We're going into Westmorland to do it. Don't be difficult, Mike. I know all—well, not all but quite a lot about it. They're to be kept semi-intensive. When the ground gets fouled—I didn't mean that for a bad pun— then the houses can be moved and the ground cleaned and resown. If you don't want to come—I'll go alone."

"If I don't want to come!"

"Dearest Mike."

In the study when she made a pretence to be examining the farm accounts, he was able to take her in his arms, to say the things which were gentle, sweet and tender. She told him again that he was far too thin, though she herself was light and terribly slim in his arms.

"May," she said, "every month brings this horrible separation nearer. I don't know how I'm going to face it, Mike. I've been thinking of getting discharged, of coming back here and trying —trying I said—to run the farm. We don't get so many raids, they seem to think that Hitler's lost interest in bombing London. I think that they're planning some fresh devilry—oh, what does anyone know?"

Aunt Alice came to Anderson's to dinner—dinner which they had late, and for which Gran provided sufficient food to feed a small army. The whole thing irked Michael terribly, to be forced to speak conventionally to Liz, to know that Enoch knew their relationship, and to control his eyes, his voice, every inflexion when he spoke to Liz, made him nervous and half irritable.

Liz appeared completely mistress of herself, and announced her plans for going to buy fowls with a great wealth of detail. She had even got the name of the firm who made the type of hen-house she wanted. Michael watched her talking in her animated fashion to his father, putting forward her arguments regarding that particular breed of bird, explaining this and that with fluency.

Enoch said, "Have it your own way—I'd rather you'd go for Rhode Islands. Trew, t' flesh is a bit yellow, but they're fine birds."

Michael knew that the corners of his mouth twitched, he longed to grin across the table at Liz who spoke with tremendous authority.

"Heavy," she said, "and apt to be broody. No, I'm set on White Leghorns. Mike, could you come with me to-morrow, we've got a trailer, haven't we? We'll take that. Immediately after luncheon, eh? All right, Enoch, if I see any Rhode Islands, I'll bring you back half a dozen as a present. Is that settled, Mike?"

"I'll be ready," he told her.

He drove them back, and handed Aunt Alice out of the car and up the steps, Liz got out and was following her, when she stopped and said, "Go on, Auntie, don't run the risk of catching cold. Oh, Mike—you'll see that the trailer is ready and ought we to take a crate—and——" Aunt Alice had disappeared into the house, she threw her arms round him, saying, "Mike, isn't it plain hell?"

"We'll snatch a few hours to-morrow," he said.

"Ah, that's what I hate—this—snatching! There, my dear one, at least it's something to see you again. Good-night."

Chapter Seventeen

THE August sun was hot on their naked bodies as Michael and his friend—Gerald Calverly—lay in the long grass, stripped to the skin, except for their trousers. Calverly was the only close friend Michael had made since he came to the O.C.T.U. A tall, rather gangly lad, with a freckled face and sandy hair, but he had great appreciation for all the things Michael loved. Together they could talk for hours of the land—for Gerald was a farmer —of flowers, birds and the little beasts which were to be found in the countryside.

Now, they lay in the deep, rich grass, the scent of the meadow-sweet being wafted to them from the hedges, with cuckoo-clocks and dog daisies growing round them, basking in the heat and talking.

That morning their postings had come, with many others, but they congratulated themselves that they had been posted to the same regiment—The Stiltons.

Gerald said, "I believe they call us the—cheese mites."

Michael answered, his voice lazy, "Who cares? We get ten days' embarkation leave. I shall go home tomorrow——" in his heart he remembered that Liz was still at Cummings, she had got her discharge and was established with Aunt Alice. Hazily, for the sun was making him unbearably sleepy, he wondered what Calverly would think if he knew about Liz. He knew that he was drifting into sleep, the humming of bees, heavy with their harvest of honey, soothed him, somewhere in the sky a lark sang, as if it would burst its throat for the sheer love of living. As he lay there he watched tiny insects creep slowly up the long stalks of the grasses, and once a ladybird, red with black spots, alighted on his hand. Obeying an old childish injunction, he sat up and said to it, gravely and with an admonishing inflexion:

> "Ladybird, ladybird, fly away home,
> Your house is on fire, your children all gone!"

The tiny insect opened its wings and flew away.

Calverly said sleepily, "What on earth are you muttering about?"

Michael said, "A ladybird. It's a shame to frighten her, but it's the right thing to do. Of course her house isn't on fire, and her children aren't all gone, but—she'd better get along home to see that they're all right."

His friend said, "Anderson, sometimes I think you're a bit crackers!"

"I've never doubted it," Michael answered cheerfully, and closing his eyes drifted into sleep.

The next day he left for Yorkshire. It was a wonderful reunion, James had left school and was waiting to enter the crammers at York. He had grown and broadened, slapped Michael on the back and said, "Embarkation leave! Half your luck, Michael."

"You'll be getting embarkation leave yourself in a few years."

"Rubbish! The war will be over ages before I can get out."

"Say you're not sure!"

"I would—if I wasn't!"

His mother, Enoch, and Gran—yes, and Violet, he wondered when he would see them all again, if he might never see them, did not enter his head. For all his sensitiveness Michael was never in the least apprehensive or given to morbidity. It might be a long time, a difficult time that he would have to pass through before he was back again in Anderson's, but that he would come back he never doubted, because he never dwelt on the possibility. He felt no elation, except the satisfaction that he was 'doing the right thing', he could never have said as James did 'Half your luck!'

He had no illusions, the war was something terrible, to be fighting would be uncomfortable, dirty and—as a last thought—dangerous. That he would miss Liz terribly he did not doubt, what distressed him most was—how badly Liz might miss him. He talked long that night with his father, Enoch looked well and younger than he had done before his illness.

He said, "It's a big break, Mike, eh?"

They were sitting in the little office, and Michael was able to lean forward and lay his hand on his father's.

"Yes, Dad, but it's a break that thousands of people in England are having to face in these days—and why should I try to get out of it? I don't mind admitting to you that the very thought of fighting frightens me to death—oh, I'll behave myself, but I've never been able to kill anything in my life, and although you may be fighting with bombs and shells and all the rest of it—even if your target is too far away for you to see—you must realize that you *are* killing people, even if they're—officially—your enemies.

214

I shall hate to, the Huns may be swine, may have committed the most abominable atrocities, but they're human beings——"

Enoch said dryly, "Are they, Mike? That's just it—are they?"

"Dad, it's reasonable to believe that God made them——"

"Then," said Enoch, as if stung into sudden fury, "I reckon He might have employed His time better!" He sighed. "Nay, don't let's get started arguefying, let's change the subject. Mike, before you go overseas, are you going to ask Liz to marry you?"

Michael shrugged his shoulders. "I've asked her half a dozen times already! The answer is always the same. I shall ask her again, and the answer will *still* be the same. It's a problem—she loves me, I know that, but she will harp on this question of the difference in our ages. There! Now tell me about the farm and how things are going."

The next morning he went over to Cummings. Ellen greeted him with loud exclamations of admiration, and called for Mrs. Robbins to come and admire his uniform. They both stood surveying him as they might have looked at some fine beast.

Michael stood smiling at them, then said, "Mrs. Tancred?"

Ellen flapped her hands, "Luke at that! If I hadn't forgot that it was her you'd come to see. Forgive me, Mister Michael—or should I call you Lieutenant?"

Michael said, "No, just 'Mister Michael'."

He walked into the study and waited for Liz, she came, her eyes bright, her hands outstretched, crying, "Mike—Mike—let me look at you!" She held him at arm's length, and looked at him. She thought how almost incredibly handsome he looked in his tightly fitting jacket, how splendidly broad his shoulders were, and how slim his waist and hips. He was more than merely personable, he was quite astonishingly good-looking.

"I don't wonder the Army wanted you!" she said at last. "Mike, how much leave have you got?"

"Ten days—Liz, it's embarkation leave, my dear."

"No!" all the light died in her eyes, her face looked suddenly pale and drawn. "Mike, you're not going overseas?"

He nodded. "Yes——"

"Where?"

"There I can't answer, I've no orders, but I imagine North Africa." Liz sat down, and rested her chin on her hand, she sat staring into space, her face blank and expressionless. Michael laid his hand on her shoulder, she started as if she had been miles away and the touch of his hand had brought her back.

215

"Liz, will you marry me before I go out?"

She turned her head so that her eyes met his, then answered very slowly as if the words were dragged from her.

"No, Mike. No, I couldn't love you more if you were my husband, in actual fact that is what you are—but I understood when I came in and saw you standing there, that my first refusal was the sane and wise thing, and that nothing is changed."

"Liz," he said very gently, "if—anything happened to me—wouldn't you be happier if we'd been married?"

She started to her feet. "No, no, no! I've told you that I couldn't love you more than I do—standing before a clergyman or a registrar won't add to that love. You're young, you've got every chance of coming home, of meeting some girl—of your own age—though if you did, God only knows what I should do—but I will play fair, I will!"

"It doesn't strike you that you're being—unfair, to me?"

"No! Before you go, I'll come with you, we'll recapture some of the joy of being together, anywhere you like. That commits you to nothing, it leaves you free. I won't shackle you! If you were—no, I won't say that."

"Please say whatever is in your mind, my dearest," he begged.

"If you were lonely, if anything happened—oh, God don't let anything happen!—if something took place which made life difficult for you—I'd come and ask you to marry me. I'd throw this so-called damned modesty to the winds, I'd go on my knees and beg you to take me for your wife."

Michael listened, his face grave. "You'd marry me—because you were sorry for me—if I were blind, or had only half a face——"

Liz cried, "Mike, don't, don't, don't! Can't you see that I'm half frantic with terror? But—yes—if some such disaster should happen, so that girls would not feel your attraction, then—yes, I'd come and importune you to marry me."

He bent down and kissed her. "I believe that you would. I can't see the validity of your arguments against marriage—now, but I've told you before, that one day you will marry me. Liz, there isn't, there never could be anyone else. I shan't ask you again, darling, not if I come home on fifty leaves—you'll have to take the initiative, and apparently you'll only do that if I'm some kind of monstrosity. My foolish, adorable Liz."

His leave passed, and for the last two days Liz and he drove off to London. She had saved petrol, she could manage it. Again, with Michael still a little shaken after all the farewells, they drove down the Great North Road.

He sighed. "I hated leaving them—James, saying that he wishes he were in my shoes, Gran telling me to be certain not to get my feet wet, and to change my socks regularly, my mother—bless her—in tears, not crying noisily, but standing there with the tears rolling down her cheeks, and her voice sounding frozen with the restraint she was putting on it. My father, just stood, his face white, and kept saying, 'Noo, look after yourself!' and 'Never mind getting any medals, leave them to those who wants them'. It's hateful leaving people—who said that to part from a friend was to die a little?"

When Michael looked back on those two last days with Liz, they did not seem in recollection to have been very happy ones. He felt that they were both being feverishly intent on pretending to be happy. There was the same love existing between them, but again he experienced that sense of 'snatching'. It was as if they tried to fill every moment, resented silences which previously they had enjoyed because they felt so close, now they dared not face them, but had to fill every moment with 'things to say'.

At intervals the old sense of quiet happiness and deep content in each other returned, but such moments were rare, and by the time he left her, in a great, gloomy London hotel, he felt fatigued and over-strained.

The morning he left, Liz went to pieces. "Mike, can't you tell me where you're going?"

"Darling, I don't know and if I did I mustn't tell you."

"Surely you must have some idea, must have heard some hints dropped." Her voice had taken on a quality of obstinacy, her eyes were hard, her lips compressed at the end of each sentence she spoke. "Mike, you must know something!"

For a second he could have taken her by the shoulders and shaken her, instead his grief at leaving her and his intense pity for her inevitable loneliness and uncertainty, made him speak very gently.

"Liz, dear one, I've never lied to you, I shan't begin to now. I assure you that except that I do know we shan't go to America, or some delectable island in the South Seas, I can tell you nothing. We have been warned, so often, that we must not give information not even to our nearest and dearest. Things *do* leak out, darling, and those leakages may mean disaster. Do believe me."

He heard the strangled sob in her throat, she spoke almost

desperately, "Mike, I can't bear it. I can't let you go. Why can't we run away, hide in some little village until this bloody war is over? We *could*, you know. You mustn't go, you're all I've got."

"Did you run away and hide when London was being bombed?" he asked smiling.

At last she flung herself into his arms sobbing wildly, and he left her lying with her face buried in the pillow, her whole body shaken with heart-rending sobs.

He stood watching her for a moment, thinking of all she meant to him, wondering if this parting might have been easier if she had consented to marry him. When would he see her again?—months, it might be years, it might be that he would never see her again. He stooped and kissed the back of her neck where the hair grew to a little point, he had called it her 'drake's tail'. She made a convulsive movement, stretched out her hand blindly, he took it and held it.

"Go now, Mike," she said hoarsely. "Go now."

★   ★   ★

The rest of his immediate days seemed to Michael like a series of vivid pictures; the embarkation, the miseries of those who were sea-sick, the convoy making its way through long, hot days, and stifling dark nights, the whispers that the Germans were waiting to attack them and the varied reactions of the soldiers to the news. The change from ordinary uniform to drill, and the whispers—"It's Africa we're bound for!"

Disembarking, a North African town and two days' rest. The smells—Belloc poem came back to him—'The smells and the yells.' Women with veiled faces, and dark, inquisitive eyes watching everything. Of the Arab quarter which was 'off limits', strange tales were told of British soldiers who had entered the *Kasbah* and never appeared again. A swarm of locusts, everywhere. At first Michael tried to avoid them, but they lay too thick on the ground, and his heart twisted with disgust when he knew that he was crushing them underfoot. Then the order to go forward.

His first experience of actual warfare. Calverly said, "Windy?"

"I'm too windy to know whether I'm windy or not!" Michael said. He had imagined the desert as being miles and miles of sand, rather like the sea-shore at Scarborough, it wasn't a bit like it. It was stony and shifted as you walked. Everyone talked of Rommel and his brilliance as a leader. They took some prisoners, tow-headed where you could see any hair at all for their heads were shaved, sulky and yet sullenly defiant. Mail was irregular, though he tried to keep a diary which he sent to Liz from time to time.

Then came the news of Pearl Harbour—Michael thought how strange it was that when we—the Allies—contrived an unexpected attack, everyone said "Jolly good show!" If our enemies made one, we all said "Damned skunks!" On December 8th England and America declared war against the 'Little Yellow Men'.

"The war's as good as over!" men declared.

Others said, "Don't you believe it! It's only starting!"

Russia and Germany, having been allies, now declared war on each other. The O.C. said, "This damned war makes you giddy—very soon we shan't know who is on one side or the other. Now Hitler's going to take command of the German army in Russia. Tell me what does that infernal house-painter know about commanding an army?"

He felt that the whole life was unreal—he thought that he had forgotten everyone. He realized that it was difficult to visualize his mother's face, Gran's or his father's—even Liz seemed to have become indistinct, though when he read her letters it became vivid again as he read. Then—it faded, and there was just—war, and desert sores, and once he contracted sand-fly fever and was sent to hospital. He spent Christmas in hospital, it was a rest and it was pleasant—in spite of fever—to feel clean again—clean and free from the abominable sand which seemed to permeate everything.

Calverly came to see him, Michael said, "What's the news?"

He said, "Siam declared war on England and America," and the two of them rocked and shook with laughter. You laughed easily, and lost your temper with equal ease. Michael felt in a perpetual state of nervous tension.

At the end of January he was back with the regiment, there were gaps, men he had known had gone, both he and Calverly were given their second pips. They were desperately bored— officers and other ranks alike. They all hated the desert, hated the flies for even in the cooler weather there were still—flies. At the end of March the adjutant sent for him.

"How long have you been out, Anderson?"

Michael grinned. "I could answer that, sir, briefly and quite correctly——"

The elder man, he was scarlet-faced, no amount of sun or exposure seemed to tan him, though his eyebrows and scrubby moustache were bleached almost white, laughed.

"Too bloody long, eh?" he said. "Well, what about a spot of leave?"

Michael wondered why everyone always said 'a spot of leave'?

"Much obliged, sir. When?"

"I think that I can get you a flight—mind it won't be particularly comfortable. Air travel isn't luxurious in these days. Yes, I think I can get transport to fix you a place in three days. Fourteen days."

Again Michael grinned, when he smiled like that he looked, the adjutant thought, very young. "Without the option, sir?"

He had never flown in his life, and had only heard of the comforts of air travel. When he stepped on board the plane, and saw the two lines of aluminium seats, polished with the impact of many posteriors, he felt that certainly luxury could be counted out.

A bumpy flight, and the windows so small that you got a crick in your neck trying to look out, great rolling banks of clouds like cotton wool, sudden glimpses of mountains, lakes, huddles of houses which were towns, and finally the order, "Put on your Mae Wests! No smoking!"

On March 28th—when the first commando raid was made on St. Nazaire, Michael stood again on British ground. He felt strangely unexcited. A little dizzy from the flight, he made his way to the buildings—all looking curiously impermanent, and went through the usual formalities. It was a cold, grey day, with sudden gusts of rain sweeping over the airfield. He found a man he'd met in Africa, who said, "Hello, Anderson, going to town? There's a car here if you like to share it."

"It's jolly good of you, thanks. London?"

"Where else? Back to the 'Smoke'. Fourteen days—think of it!"

They drove back to London, and slowly Michael felt that the sense of unreality was passing, that his excitement was growing. He must send telegrams, then he would catch the first possible train, and go North. Liz—to see Liz again! Now when he thought of her, he could visualize her face quite plainly. He could almost smell the scent which she used—could they still get scent in England?

Somehow they would contrive a few days together. He'd go to a tailor and order a new uniform, his excuse could be that he must come up to town for a fitting.

"How's the petrol situation?" he asked his companion.

"Pretty sticky, I believe. My father manages quite well, he's got some Government job. Pretty tight though for the average chap."

Later he asked, "Where shall I drop you, Anderson?"

Michael thought for a moment, then remembered that George Tancred had bought his clothes from a tailor in Conduit Street.

"Conduit Street, if it's not taking you out of your way."

"Not a bit, delighted."

He ordered his new uniform, and the tailor assured him that he would make a special point of having it ready for a fitting in ten days. "Then we can deliver it two days later. Uniforms have preference, sir. Let other people excerise a little patience. The Services can't wait. Yes, sad about poor Major Tancred, very old customer of ours. Very good, sir, we'll be ready for you."

He went to send off telegrams. The girl said, "I should warn you there will probably be four to five hours' delay. Priority telegrams—go first."

He said very gravely, "Obviously, that's why they're called priority."

She nodded. "Quate."

The great, gloomy station depressed him for a moment, then he found the R.T.O., obtained his voucher, and sat down in the corner seat of his carriage, conscious that he was desperately tired, and also that he felt abominably dirty. The train was not full, and he managed to sleep. He changed at Leeds, and shivered a little in the sudden cold. The porter, an ancient man with a face like a withered apple, said, "Noo, 'Uddersley. Nay, that 'ul mean changing at 'Olbeck. After that Ah'm not all that certain—ou'd better ax someone theer."

Michael grumbled, "Holbeck! Oh, damn it. Any chance of getting a taxi?"

"Cost a mint o' money, I reckon. Still, you young chaps 'ave it ter fling aboot seemly. We can but ondly try. Cum along."

The wind whistled in the big station yard, again Michael shivered. The usual traditional conversation took place between the porter and a taxi driver wrapped in a huge coat, and with a muffler which reached to his ears.

" 'Uddersley—nay, that's a tidy way. Petrol's bad to cum by. Nay, Ah doot as Ah can do it."

The porter said, "Aye, it's a longish way, but this young chap's ready ter pay. On leaf, bean't you? Ah thought so—" he grinned, " 'appen there's somone waiting, eh?"

Michael nodded. "True enough!"

The taxi driver smiled broadly. "Ah'd be the last one to want ter part tew luvin' 'earts. Can you manage a fiver, Captain?"

"I think so."

"Then let's be off. Shove the bags inside, William."

The day had faded, the country looked sad, Michael thought, familiar places looked unfamiliar in the half light. Villages through which they passed showed scarcely a chink of light—of course, he remembered, the black-out! The driver slid back the window, letting in a blast of chill air, and shouted, "Joost aboot theer!" and shut the window again.

"The first pair of gates," Michael said, sliding the window back again, "they'll be open, drive right in." He could never remember the time when those gates had been closed.

As they swung through them, a boy on a bicycle shouted, "Hi, joost a minute!"

A telegraph boy, held out a telegram to Michael. He thought, "I bet it's my own telegram, saying that I'm home."

They stopped, and Michael asked the man if he could do with a drink. "Something hot, eh?"

The fellow, an elderly man, nodded. "A drop o' mulled ale 'ud go to the reight place. I don't mind if I do."

Michael pushed open his door, a heavy curtain hung behind it. More black-out, even here in the wilds of the country. Violet called, " 'Ooever is it? Nay, pull t' curting on one side. Frame, 'ooever you are!"

Michael, the driver following on the heels, disentangled himself from the folds of the curtain, and walked in. Violet screamed.

"It's Mister Michael 'iself!"

"Complete with this Good Samaritan, to whom a hot drink would be welcome. How are you?"

"Nicely, we're all nicely, yer Grannie's had a touch o' the screws but it's better nor what it was. Sit down, mister, while I get you summat 'ot."

Michael paid the man, adding a generous tip, and bidding him good-night walked down to the parlour. He halted and knocked.

His father's voice called, "Come in," and Michael knew that his heart was beginning to beat faster. He swung open the door, saying as he did so, "Here's a telegram for you."

He might never have been away, there they were—his father in the big chair on one side of the fire, Gran—glancing up from her knitting—on the other, while Ada sat sewing busily at the round table covered with its smooth red cloth.

Enoch ejaculated, "I'm damned!"

Gran said, "Why it's our Michael. Is t' war over then?"

His mother sprang to her feet, and flung her arms round him, crying, "Michael—eh, dear lad, this is wonderful. Let me look at you? I believe you've grown! But you're thin, luv."

Enoch got up and caught his son's hand. "Nay, this is a right do, this is. Wheer have you come from?"

"Some place wheer he's left his manners seemly," Gran said. "Can't Grannie have a greeting, and me knitting socks for you at this very moment!"

He kissed her soft cheek, saying, "I left the best to the last! Last stop, Dad was Leeds. Last night I was—over the seas and far away. I flew over."

"And you've got leave for a bit?" Ada asked.

Michael grimaced. "A *bit* is right. They would have liked to have given me more, but they were afraid of what might happen to the Army if I wasn't there. Oh, here's your telegram! It's to say that I'm arriving. Dad, I don't think much of your Yorkshire hospitality. I could do with one!"

"Dammit! I've been letting my wits scatter!"

"That needn't mak' you scatter bad language, Enoch," Gran warned.

For the first and last time in his life Enoch Anderson was rude to his mother-in-law. "Oh, for any favour, *give over!*"

He bustled off to return quickly with glasses and a decanter of whisky; while Ada was making inquiries as to when Michael had last eaten, what he would like to eat now.

"Depends on what you've got, Mum?"

"As nice a cut of cold roast beef as you've ever seen, or some of Gran's brawn, or eggs and bacon—just give it a name, Michael."

"Just to be awkward," he said, "have you got a cold sausage?"

223

"We have!" she almost shrieked in her triumph. "I'll have a tray here in no time. Sausage—well, it makes you think that Providence arranged for me to have them cooked for tea. Then somehow none of us fancied one."

Gran said, "I'd not presume, Ada, to imagine as Providence —wi, a war to luke after, concerns Hiself greatly wi'—sausages."

Chapter Eighteen

was wonderful to be with them all again, to sit in the warm
rlour, with the bright fire throwing gleams of light into the
om. Wonderful to see his father looking so well, his mother—a
:le stouter, Michael thought—sewing away but glancing up
ery few moments to meet his eyes and smile broadly; Gran,
are as always, never failing with a retort which held something
.d in its quality, but all the time his thoughts were turning to
z—when could he make an excuse to hurry to her?

He had asked after his brother, and Enoch had said, "Doin'
ll, seemly, doin' very well." He had asked about Wilson and
ung Harry, about the land girls, about the prospects of the
y harvest.

Only after all this did Michael bring himself to ask after Liz.
was Gran who answered. "She's away at 'Arrogate with her
untie Alice. Seemingly Alice is taking one of these fancified
res. They went first thing this morning. I'd not know rightly
w long they've gone for——"

Michael knew for the first time what it felt like to be dizzy
th disappointment. He had imagined their first meeting, he
d longed to be able to take Liz in his arms again. Surely this
ne she must realize that the difference in their ages was bridged.
: had seen so much, experienced so much. He had seen men at
e moment living, shouting with excitement, filled with vigour
d youth—and the next moment, lying—shattered wrecks of
man bodies.

Now—Liz was with her aunt in Harrogate.

He said, and in his own ears his voice sounded mechanical,
hope the cure's successful. Rheumatism, is it? I believe their
ters are wonderful."

While his heart cried, 'Liz . . . you couldn't have got my
egram, or I know that you'd have been here.' Some of the
ightness had died, the dancing flames no longer seemed to light
the whole room. He looked at the clock, then compared it
th his own watch.

"Half past nine," he said.

Enoch started up. "We'll get the news at ten. You'd like to
ar the news, eh?"

225

"Yes, Dad, of course." He knew how little he cared about t
news! Liz was in Harrogate! Then he upbraided himself, curs
his own ingratitude. His own people—they were so unaffecte
glad to see him, they were ready to go to any lengths to make h
happy, and yet—at this moment, his heart must go straying af
Liz Tancred. He mentally shook himself, and began to ta
rather rapidly about the desert, the Germans, the Italians. I
felt that he was listening to his own voice, and wondering he
the devil any fool could imagine that what he was saying cou
possibly be amusing.

He was talking mechanically, his brain working in two separ
parts, one burbling on about things he had seen, things he h
done, the other thinking that his telegram to Liz must have be
delivered. Either Ellen or Mrs. Robbins would have eith
opened it or posted it on to Harrogate. When would it get
Liz? How soon after its arrival could she leave for Hudders
How soon could she be at Cummings?

Gran was staring at his leg, his trouser had slipped up a
there was a patch of flesh showing between the bottom of I
trouser leg and his sock.

He said, "Anything wrong, Gran?"

"What's that mark on your leg? Nay, there's two on 'en

"The remains of a desert sore, Gran."

"What in the name of pity's a desert sore for any favour?"

"Sores you get in the desert, dear. I don't know why—sa
or flies or a combination of both."

She snorted disapproval. "Ada, take a luke at the lad's l
Small wonder we're not winning the war! Haven't they enou
sense to put some primrose ointment on it?"

Michael laughed. "I'm sure they would do, only there a
no primroses in the desert, Gran."

"Tch! They could send home for some! I'll get you some
mine, yon place still lukes angry to me. Desert sores!"

She hurried out and Ada said, "It is a nasty place, Micha
Mind you, Gran's primrose ointment is wonderful. M
healing."

His momentary distraction had passed, and again his mi
was turning to Liz Tancred. He might telephone to her—th
he realized that he did not know the name of her hotel. He mi
go over to Cummings, they would be certain to know it the
But—at ten o'clock at night—he could imagine his father's lo
of disappointment, his mother's gentle comment that surely

uld wait until the morning, and some acid remark of Gran's
out people never being able to stay in one place.

So he did his best, and was rewarded by his father's smiles
d his mother's obvious content. Gran returned with a pot of
er primrose ointment, and insisted upon dressing his leg. It
as useless for him to protest that the sores had healed long ago,
e persisted, and was only happy when she had swathed his leg
bandages, saying, "Healed it may be, but a bit more healing
l do it no harm, choose how."

That night he lay in his own bed, and smelt the scent of
vender in which the sheets had been laid. This was something
e had not known for months, the room which held the smell of
rniture polish, the crisp curtains, and the smooth linen. He lay
ere relaxed and almost happy, had his mind not been twisting
d turning, wondering when he might see Liz. To-morrow,
rely, he could go over to Cummings, and there gather some
formation from the servants. Fourteen days would slip past so
ickly, and he had planned to spend two of them in London
ith Liz. Fourteen days—and after that—who could tell? It
ight be months before he saw her again!

Then slowly the deep sleep of youth overcame him, and when
is mother came in, opening the door very carefully, he was
ing with his arm flung out, looking almost pathetically young
d defenceless.

Ada longed to kiss him, but told herself that it might 'break
is rest'. She murmured very softly, "Aye, God bless you, my
arling lad, and thank Him for bringing you home to us." Then
osed the door softly and went to her own room.

"Sleeping like a baby," she told Enoch. "He looked a
icture."

Enoch said, "Aye, yon's a good lad, and it's grand to have him
ome, even if it's only for a bit."

Mike woke with that sense of unreality which a strange bed
ways produced. He rubbed his eyes, and reorientated himself.
le was home—to-day he felt certain he would see Liz, the thought
ade him feel faintly giddy with excitement and longing.

His mother brought him a cup of tea, saying, "You don't get
rly tea in the Army, do you?"

"You do if you have a batman like the one Calverly and I
ave, he can 'win' anything."

"The private soldiers don't get early tea, do they?"

Michael grinned. "Of course, the sergeants bring it to them."

227

"You're teasing! Well, I must be off—my work's waiting f
me. You'll have to arrange to go over to York to see James o
day. He'd not like to miss seeing you. There—have a nice day
she kissed him.

He bathed and dressed in a leisurely fashion, then came dow
to the kitchen. Violet said, "The missus give orders as you we
to have it in the parlour, Mister Michael. Oh, and they've be
on the phone from Cummings. Mrs. Tancred will be back abo
half past eleven and she'd be pleased if you'd take lunch with her

He went to the telephone and spoke to Ellen, "I'll be ov
for luncheon, Ellen, tell Mrs. Tancred. How are you all?"

"Eh, fancy you being back, Mister Michael. We telephon
to Mrs. Tancred as there was a telegram. She said we was to op
it and read it. Mrs. Robbins read it, her hands was fair shakin
'Eh,' she said, 'what a relief, it's ondly to say as Mister Micha
'ul be 'ome to-night on leaf.' So the missus is leaving her aunt
in 'Arrergate an' driving back."

"Splendid! And you're all well?"

"Never better, thank God!" Ellen assured him piously.

He went out later with his father, Enoch as excited as a b
at the praise Michael lavished on the farm and the beasts. T
prospect for an excellent hay-making was good, the lambing h
gone well, there were two new litters of pigs—"all likely do-ers"-
Enoch assured Michael.

"And it's not too much for you, Dad?"

"Not a bit, mind I take a bit of a rest after my dinner, t
doctor ad-vised it. Just go off for twenty minutes or so, and I'
as fresh as a daisy. Wilson's doing fine, so's young Harry, y
girl as does the writing job—filling in forms and such like, she
a good lass, so's the other one as helps wi' pigs and hens. Min
Mike, Liz does a good job over at Cummings. Remember how s
she was on Leghorns? She's going to do grandly with them an
all. Up early every day, keeps all the management in her ow
hands. Comes over sometimes and borrows bukes about farm
ing, stock and the like. Mind, Willett's a great help to her, he
a goodish farmer is yon."

Then lowering his voice, and glancing round to see that r
one was within earshot, he said, "How's things wi' you, Mike-
I mean regarding what we once spoke about."

Michael folded his arms on the top bar of the gate and stare
out over the fainting waving grass, away to the moors in t
distance, and the range of hills against the sky. He drew in de
228

breaths of the cold, sweet air, then turned his head and smiled down at his father's intent and rather anxious face.

"Things are just as they've always been, Dad. I asked her to marry me before I went overseas, she refused—as I knew she would—so I told her that I'd never ask her again, that if she wanted to marry me—she must come and tell me so."

Enoch shook his head, "Nay, lad, I can't see Liz Tancred doing that! Does she write reg'lar?"

"Wonderful letters, sends me more cigarettes than I can smoke, what with Liz's parcels, and Mum's, they regard me as the luckiest chap in the regiment. Well," he laughed, "so I am without a doubt."

Enoch filled his pipe carefully, scrutinizing the packing of the tobacco as if the fate of the nations depended upon it being done properly. He cleared his throat, then said, "Women—out there?"

"A few, mostly Arabs. I'm not a prig, Dad, but I'm damned fastidious. I don't believe that I could go to bed with a tart—whatever her nationality, however entrancing she might be to look at—if you paid me."

"I'm glad to hear it. I've never held with all this mullocking about—and I'd say out in those foreign parts—it's damned dangerous."

Michael looked at him affectionately. "It's not only the danger. The Army looks after its chaps pretty well—only some of the silly fools won't *be* taken care of. No, it's that—well, I don't expect Liz to go, as you said, mullocking about, and she has the right to expect the same of me."

Enoch's pipe was going nicely now; between his contented puffs, he said, "Aye—well, I'm right—pleased to hear you talk—that road."

They wandered about the farm, talking in a desultory fashion about all things appertaining to the growing of crops, the various inroads made by rabbits and foxes.

Enoch said, "I can do wi' rabbits, if a chap has a gun he can keep 'em down all right, and have summat for the pot an' all, I don't hold wi' traps—and them gin traps are inventions of the devil—damn' things! It's rats and foxes as get me wild. Rats coming after chickens and eggs, and foxes carrying off the goose you'd had your eye on for Michaelmas. If hunting folk can't keep foxes down, then they ought to be shot. That's what it 'ul come to, Mike. If you shoot rabbits—why not foxes?"

Pleasant, easy talk, which Michael found very soothing, for

his father's voice held all the softness and open vowels of the West Riding. As they walked over fields, well tended, well fed, where the hedges were beautifully laid, where the gates hung evenly on their sockets, where the loose stone walls had been watched and repaired after every heavy gale, his heart swelled. Looking over the broad lands through which the busy little river flowed, purling over the stones, flashing and glinting in the spring sunlight, the words of some song he had heard—he could not remember where—came to him.

This is worth fighting for. . . .

Enoch pointed to the river with the stem of his pipe. "Remember the trout you've caught there, Mike? Nothing like a freshly caught trout."

They had turned their steps homeward, Michael looked at his watch, the time was a quarter past eleven.

"I'm lunching at Cummings, Dad," he said. "Liz is coming back from Harrogate this morning. I spoke to Ellen on the telephone. I'll have to go."

"Aye, lad," his father said, "get along," then almost wistfully, he added, "Get happiness while you can—and Mike, if you want any brass don't hesitate to ask for it, I can spare it all right."

"Thanks a lot, Dad. I'm all right at the moment."

He reached Cummings very quickly, his long legs making short work of the distance. Ellen beamed at him as she opened the front door.

"Well, this is a right joyous day, Mister Michael. No, madam's not here yet, we're expecting her any minute. Just come and have a word wi' Mrs. Robbins, she'll be that pleased."

Mrs. Robbins—larger, Michael thought than ever, greeted him with effusion, her large, pale-blue eyes overflowing with tears.

"I never thought to see you again, not once you got there wi' them nasty Germans. But God's spared you to us—aye and to England, for which we must be thankful—as indeed we are. I've a luncheon I hope you and madam 'ul like. A clear soup, lamb—aye, it's real lamb and all—cutlets, it's early for peas, but I've managed to get some of them tinned things and if you know how to cook 'em they're not too bad, a few right little potatoes—don't ax me where Willett got 'em from for I don't know, and a nice apple pie, with a drop of cream and a bit of Wensleydale. How's that?"

Michael, looking suddenly very young and boyish, said, "Prime!"

There was a sudden stir, Ellen exclaimed, "It's madam!" and flew out of the kitchen, Mrs. Robbins followed her and Michael was left standing there alone, longing to see her, aching to take her in his arms, to feel her lips against his cheek; he stood —motionless. He had dreamed of this moment, and now that it had come he felt drained of all strength. In the distance he heard voices, Liz's very clear and distinct.

"Mister Michael is here?"

Then a murmur from Ellen, and Liz speaking again. "I'm in the parlour, tell him please, Ellen, and bring drinks."

"Mister Michael, it's the mistress. She's in the parlour."

His strength seemed to flow back, the blood to circulate in his veins, he nodded, and walked to the parlour.

She was standing near the fireplace, holding out her hands to the flames as if the long drive had chilled them. He came forward, and said in a voice which he did not recognize as his own, "Liz——"

She turned, her beautiful head which he loved so much, thrown back a little, her eyes filled with tenderness and expectancy.

"Mike—oh, my beloved Mike—such a long time!" then she was in his arms, and he was holding her tightly, wondering how he had been able to bear the long separation.

She pushed him away, laughing. "Darling, Ellen will be here in a second. Let me look at you! You're still far too thin, and Mike—here and here," she touched the hair on his temples with the tip of her finger, "grey hairs!"

He laughed. "Give the war another year or two to run, and I shall come home and everyone will say, 'But, Liz, to marry that old, old man, how can you?' "

In horror Liz said, "Another year—or two! You don't think that, do you?"

"I refuse to even think about it. Liz, you're lovelier than ever. That darling head, your nice, long, slim neck, the whole *shape* of you—oh, it's sheer, unadulterated joy to be with you again. Dad tells me that you've done marvels, that you're up early every single morning, that you've got the whole of the business of the farm under your control. Splendid! There's Ellen coming—Liz—quickly—kiss me again!"

She wanted to know everything, he had been ill, was he really better? What exactly was sand-fly fever, and what were desert

231

sores? Did her parcels reach him, and the cigarettes? Did he get enough to eat? Was it eatable when he did get it?

"I doubt if Mrs. Robbins would think so, but—" he laughed, "there's a war on! Some of it's pretty foul, most things are served with a dressing of sand. The flies are abominable—but it's not too bad."

She sat, her hands hanging between her knees, watching him intently, her fine eyebrows drawn together in a frown.

He smiled at her expression, and said, "Yes?"

"Mike—women?"

He came and sat beside her on the sofa, and took her hands in his.

"Darling, what would you say if I asked you—Liz, men?"

"I should be furious! Naturally."

"I shan't get furious, darling. Only I give you my word of honour that—well, it's just not my game. You need have no fear, Liz—if I did—slip up, I'd tell you, and ask for your forgiveness. Now is that stupid bogy laid for ever?"

She laid her head on his shoulder. "Oh, Mike—I get so afraid sometimes. I look in the glass and see my face tanned by the sun, I wonder how long it will be before it begins to look—weather-beaten. I look at my hair——"

"Your pretty, charming hair——"

"I think it looks dull and lifeless. I *am* extravagant, twice a month I go to London, and I have everything done to make me presentable. Face packs, massage, shampoos, sets, manicures—the whole bag of tricks! Tell me, reassure me that I don't look too awful."

He took her face between his hands. "I think that you are a positive danger to the peace of mind of any normal man. When do you go next to London? I'll tell you—in ten days from now, when I have to go there to be fitted for a new uniform. While I'm at the tailors, you can visit your beauty specialist."

"But it takes hours!"

"I'd wait," he told her calmly, "you're worth waiting for."

Liz shuddered. "Another awful separation——"

"This time, I shall see you safely off in your train for the North. Now—talk about other things, we've got days and days—a long stretch of wonderful hours. I want to go to York to see my young brother, you'll come with me?"

He exerted himself to amuse her, to tell her of incidents which he felt might amuse or interest her, he even told her of Gran's primrose ointment, of Mum's offered selection of dishes and his own final choice. Slowly the tension eased, and by the time they went in to luncheon her smiles came more easily, and a little colour had come back to her cheeks.

She watched him eat with wonderful appetite, pressing him to eat more new potatoes, more cheese, more apple tart.

With her chin propped on her hands she watched him sip his coffee with appreciation. She sighed, Michael looked up, his eyebrows raised in surprise.

"It's nothing," she said, smiling quickly, "only how nice it would be if we didn't have to realize that there is always a—time limit. Shall we ever, Mike, be able to look forward to a long—really a long—time together?"

"I can think of one way in which we could——"

"You said that you were never going to talk of that again."

He shrugged his shoulders. "Darling, I've said nothing, only told you what was in my mind, and that vaguely."

He saw her every day, and counted the hours between. He loved his father and mother dearly, but the love which he felt for Liz was something which consumed him. He knew that he dreaded having to leave her when he returned to the Army, he remembered so vividly the last time when he had left her sobbing wildly. Could still imagine that he heard her agonized voice, "Go now, Mike, go now!"

She drove him to York to see James, James who seemed so much older and more sophisticated than when Michael had seen him last. He liked his work, found that it came easily to him, but he was longing—he told them—for the time when he could join the Air Force.

"Only the whole thing will be over by that time, worse luck," he grumbled.

"Don't worry," Michael told him, "we've only been at it since '39. There's plenty of time, Jimmy. You'll make it all right."

"How long do you give it?"

"Three years—in Europe, God knows how many in other parts of the world."

Liz cried suddenly, her voice sharp, "Mike, no!"

Michael saw James glance at her as if her protest puzzled him. He caught her glance and hoped that she saw the warning in his eyes. She said more quietly, "Three years—it's an eternity, or it seems like one."

As they drove home, Liz said, "Sorry I allowed myself to get startled when you were talking about the war. I must be more careful. Forgive me, dearest."

He spoke very gravely, very gently, "Angel, can't you see that it's practically inevitable that we must give ourselves away—sooner or later? My father knows now—he's safe as houses, keeps his own counsel. But suppose my mother realizes—about us, what then?"

"Does she know?" Liz asked.

"I don't think so, she has said nothing to me. But—well, you know how chaps' mothers *do* know things, as if they possessed an additional sense. Then I've either got to lie—or," he gave a short, mirthless laugh, "tell the truth. If I do that she will think me a cad because I've not married you."

"You can blame me, Mike. I'll take it all."

"Then she'll dislike you because you don't want to marry her precious lout of a son. No, we should get it in the neck—both of us, if Mum did find out. Never mind, dearest, we'll build our bridges when we get to the river. Don't worry your adorable head about it, you've got enough to think about."

It seemed that he had only been home for a few hours, and there was Mum, packing his bags, and dropping tears on to his neatly folded clothes.

"Don't cry, Mum dear. It won't be long before I'm back again on another leave, I might get some nice, cushy little wound, somewhere where it didn't hurt too much and get sent home. I might get jaundice, they often send fellows home when they get that. Shall I try and get jaundice? Perhaps Gran has some herb brew that induces it, eh?"

"Oh, Michael, don't try to joke. It's dreadful. You who have never been the fighting kind—going out to kill men that you've no quarrel with. At this moment their mothers maybe are packing their bags like I'm packing yours, thinking the same things that I'm thinking."

"I agree, it's all a mad business, Mum. But it's here, and it's got to be settled—let's hope once and for all."

"I don't believe all this awful killing and blowing each other in pieces ever settled anything. Still, it seems that wiser heads than mine think it does." She paused and laid another shirt carefully into the bag, smoothing it with the tips of her fingers. Then she twisted round to face him. "Michael, tell me something, will you?"

He thought, 'It's come! She knows,' then said quietly, "Yes, if I can, Mum."

She flushed, the unbecoming flush of middle age. "What about women out there?" her voice was flat and without expression.

Michael said, "Mum dear, make your mind easy, I leave that kind of thing alone. There are no—women out there, for me at least."

"Then," she paused, and he saw her hands clench, her eyes were hard, "then—there's someone over here in England?"

He met her eyes, his own steady, his face impassive. "Yes, there is someone over here."

"Shall I tell you her name?" Ada spoke the words crisply.

Michael answered quietly and smoothly, "No, Mum, I don't think so."

Ada rose to her feet, a little clumsily for she was growing stout. "You can't marry her! Michael, she's ten, eleven years older than you are! She couldn't give a bairn to George Tancred—she can't give one to you. Darling, she's my own cousin, I know her age to a day."

Still remaining very quiet, he said, "My dear, I've never mentioned Liz Tancred, have I?"

His mother's comely face was scarlet. "You don't need to. I've heard her voice soften when she spoke of you, I've known that you go over to Cummings every day. Michael, do you truly love her?"

He spoke very gravely, "Mum dear, I'm not going to lie to you—I love her better than anything or anyone on earth."

"Have you asked her to marry you!"

"I have, many times. She won't."

Ada relaxed a little, sighed and said, "No, and I should think not! You, the best-looking lad here—about to marry a widow woman nearly old enough to be your mother! Nay, Michael lad, find yourself a nice lass of your own age. Marry her and have some lovely bairns."

She turned back to her careful packing, saying, "Mind, I shan't speak a word of this to anyone. You can trust me."

Michael bent down and kissed her cheek. "Bless you. I do trust you."

"Mind you," Ada continued, laying shirts and vests carefully into the bag, "mind you, I'd find it hard to forgive anyone who hurt you, willingly hurt you."

235

"I don't think that Liz would do that," he said quietly.

"They do say that Sir George fancies her——"

Michael sprang to his feet. "That scarlet-faced monstrosity! She'd never look at him." He felt his heart contract, had Fowler been hanging round Liz? His impulse was to rush off to Cummings and put the question to her.

Ada said, "Give me those other shirts. Well, that's what they say, and he's got a rent roll of going on for 7,000."

"Let him have it," Michael retorted, "that won't matter to Liz. She's a rich woman in her own right."

In a voice which sounded to him suspiciously pacific, his mother said, "I don't know—that's just what they say."

His control left him, he paced the room, his hands clenched. "Damn and blast the lot of them, what bloody business is it of theirs—whoever they are! Liz—to even look at Fowler! The thing is impossible. An attractive widow—and with money, mind that—is a mark for every busybody in the place. How dare they? The bastards!"

Ada sat back on her haunches. "Michael, I don't care for all that bad language if you don't mind. So—" very slowly as if the words were wrung out of her, "Liz is your mistress, eh?"

"I never said so——"

"You don't need to," Ada said still placidly. "Michael, you've told me as plain as any words could do. No man goes raging off —as you did—unless, well, no need to say more. I don't reproach you, I've no hard feelings against Liz—I think it's a pity, but well, the world is upside down any road. When this war is over—what then?"

He said, stolidly, "I don't know, Mum."

"That's about all any of us can say, luv. It's all in God's hands. I won't say that I don't wish it was different. We've never had anything like this in my family." She sighed heavily. "Nay, the whole business is beyond me. God bless you," she rose from her knees and said. "There, strap it up. Eh dear, I wonder when I shall pack for you again. Mind, Michael, I shan't mention this to your father—not a word, nor to Liz. My God!" with sudden intensity, "if she's not good to you, I'll—I'll—well I don't quite know what I'll do."

He slipped his arm round her ample shoulders. "You needn't worry, Liz plays fair, and you go on being your own dear and sweet self."

"Nay," she said, "it's all past me!"

236

He left the next morning, Liz had gone to Harrogate and from there was to meet him in London. He scarcely knew whether he longed for the time they would have together, or dreaded it. He left them at Anderson's—Violet sobbing into her apron, while Gran admonished her, "You daft thing! That's a bonny way to send a man off to the wars, give over—do!" while the tears ran down her own cheeks. His mother, white faced, but with dry eyes kissed him and murmured, "God bless you, my own lad!" while his father, looking, Michael thought, older, gripped his hand and said, "Good luck, lad, s' long."

Chapter Nineteen

Two days in London, days which they filled feverishly, as if it was necessary that neither of them should have time to think of the approaching separation. They fought against mentioning it in any way, and yet both of them were acutely conscious of the hours slipping past. Michael kept his word, and resolutely saw Liz into the train which would take her to Harrogate. They scarcely spoke, Liz was white faced, her lips set tightly, Michael felt that his heart was cold and constricted.

"Don't wait to watch the train out, Mike," Liz begged. "It's unlucky. Go now, darling."

He kissed her, her face was cold against his lips. "God bless you, dearest, dearest Liz."

"And you—and watch over you."

He turned and walked away, squaring his shoulders, walking in a haze of misery. Liz—she was everything he had ever dreamed of, she could be dynamic, completely practical, gentle, demanding. He longed to go and see lovely things with her—statues—he had seen pictures of the 'Moses', he had treasured for a long time a postcard which some friend had sent him from Edinburgh, of a picture there—by some Italian called Tiepolo. 'The Finding of Moses.' He had heard of wonderful things at Ravenna, read of the glories which were enshrined in Dresden—they'd probably be either bombed to hell or stolen by that fat brute who was said to be ambitious to make a collection which should stagger the world. That the exhibits were stolen would not affect Goering!

He wanted to see 'The Winged Victory', the Acropolis, Saint Peter's. Wanted to see them—and with Liz. He was not an intellectual young man, but he had an inborn sense of beauty. First came the land—which he loved, then the ardent desire to see the beauties which the world offered so generously. At school, and he had given sufficient time to games to win for himself a place in the eleven, and to be chosen for the fifteen—he had saved his pocket money to buy books about travel, and he imagined what his feelings would be when he stood for the first time before the 'Gioconda', or the 'Sistine Madonna'. Those had been his dreams, and they were still his dreams, but he wanted Liz to be there with him when they were made realities. He longed to hear music—real music—the voice of Gigli, to hear the orchestra under the direction of Toscanini, to listen to great musicians—in the flesh—not only over the radio. But Liz—Liz must share all these things, without her they would lose their glory.

He walked on, out of the great, grimy station with its roof showing scars of the blitz, into the gloomy street. He walked on, mechanically, making his way towards—he neither knew nor cared—where. To-morrow he would be on his way, back to the discomfort, the sand, the flies, and the monotony. He didn't mind, it was a job which he had taken on, a job which he could have evaded, and he wasn't grumbling at having to get on with it. He dined somewhere, he would have been hard put to remember what the place was called, the food tasted, to him, of nothing. He went back to his hotel, where the bedroom seemed tragically empty. He sat down and wrote to Liz. He wished that he could have known how to express all that he felt, but it had always been difficult for him to put his thoughts into words.

He posted his letter, and warned the night porter that he must be called early.

"Going back, sir?" the man asked.

"Going back—get me another drink, please." He felt slightly drunk and was glad of it, it dulled the sense of loneliness.

He offered the porter a drink, he accepted, it gave him the chance of talking to someone. "Yes, going back, so—call me early mother dear." Where was Liz? Was she lying alone in that room at some hotel in Harrogate, feeling as lost and desolate as he did?

"I'll call you in good time, sir. You'll want a taxi?"

Michael heard his silly, rather high laugh. "Of course, can't walk to—what's the station?—Victoria. Yes, Victoria."

The porter said gravely, almost severely, "Forgive me, sir, I think it's Liverpool Street. It's Africa you're bound for, eh?"

Michael nodded. "Qui' right. Liverpool Stree'. Yes, Africa——"

The porter watched the good-looking young man who had obviously drunk more than was good for him, and sighed. He had two sons of his own fighting, both older than this fellow. He said, "It might be as well, sir, if you'll let me have a look at your railway voucher, there mustn't be any mistake. Thank you, sir. That's all right, I'll see that you're called and that a taxi's waiting. Best get a good night's rest, sir."

He slept heavily, and woke to find a chambermaid with a

large cup of tea standing by his bed. He drank it gratefully, for his throat was as dry as a lime kiln. That was the beginning of his journeys, he wondered when he would get leave again, not realizing then how long it was to be before he saw England again.

Libya, and later El Alamein, Tunis and Bizerta, and on May 13th, 1943, the surrender of the German and Italian forces in Africa. Catania, the Americans at Messina, Sicily looking shabby and battered. Michael went down with malaria, a mild attack, but sufficient to earn for him ten days' sick leave at an officer's convalescent hospital at Toamina, where he was bored and irritable. Then on September 3rd, the crossing to Italy, and less than a week later, posters appearing in Italian towns and villages, announcing, 'Italians, for you the war is over!'

Calverly said, "Wish to God it was over for us! I'm getting fed up with the damned war."

"We might get a spot of leave," Michael said.

"Not us! They gave us that other spot to keep us sweet, now if we get any there'll be no available transport to get us home—we're not ENSA band leaders or V.I.P.s."

Naples, filthy and swarming with beggars, Salerno—and the beaches. News coming through of the increasingly heavy air attacks on Germany, the *Union Jack* read eagerly, more for the pleasure that the 'Two Types' gave than for the news. No one was very interested in the news, it was all so far away, war on any other front seemed vague and improbable.

Christmas came and went, the winter passed, spring was in the air, Michael thought how he and Liz had talked of coming to Italy in the spring some day—so long ago. The days lengthened, men said, "It won't be so damned dull when we get to Rome," but Rome seemed a long way off. There was much talk of 'our offensive', they said that it was a bloody long time starting, that the Germans were withdrawing a little, but only to entrench themselves firmly on their Gothic Line.

On June 4th they entered Rome, the pavements were hot with sun, the roads seemed to burn your feet as you marched. Michael moved in a half dream, this was another place he had longed to see, had read countless books describing its beauties and wonders.

"We'll see it together one day, darling," Liz said.

He had read of the countless Roman fountains, now they were dry, their basins filled with dirty bits of paper, cigarette ends, and general litter. Not that the cigarette ends remained there very long, they were pounced upon by ragged urchins and fought over for they had a market value.

He wandered about Rome, stared at the balcony from which Mussolini had launched so many of his pronouncements, ending with that final declaration of war which had ended his career as a leader and ruined his country. He went with Calverly to an audience at the Vatican, they asked one of the interpreters, "Is it all right for us to go—we're not Catholics."

"All ri'—don't metter," the man told them, "Il Santo Papa 'e bless alls, 'e doan't mind 'oo 'e is."

Michael stared at the fine, worn face, with the large, luminous eyes, saw the beautiful hands raised in blessing and knew that his eyes smarted and that his throat contracted. He had heard so many stories concerning this man, his bravery during the German occupation, it was said that by his orders the persecuted Jews had been hidden—even in the Vatican itself.

Then Rome was left behind and they were marching towards Florence. Florence was liberated, the Germans withdrew to Bologna, over the Pistoia and Futa Passes. The Americans fought like tigers, the Germans contested every inch of the way, death and destruction were everywhere. Whole villages were brought to ruins, homeless peasants sat among the ruins of what had been their homes. Nineteen forty-four faded, Michael said, "How many years more is this flaming war going on?"

Calverly said, "Have a bit of patience, man, only about another ten or twelve years."

Spring came again, and seemed to make the destruction look additionally horrible, and with the spring they marched into Bologna and reached that great grey, slow moving river—the Po. Everyone expected that there the Germans would make a determined stand but except for bursts of fighting here and there they seemed to have lost heart. They had strewn mines as they went, and outside Bologna, when Michael was leading his men over a piece of open land, they found one.

There was a roar, he felt something hit his face, knew that blood was flowing, then he fell and darkness seemed to overtake him.

He thought that he was dead, for it felt that he had been completely blotted out of existence for ever. He recovered consciousness temporarily, tried to speak and knew that he only made indistinguishable sounds. Then darkness descended again. Slowly the periods of consciousness grew longer and more

241

frequent, and with them came such pain as he had never known existed.

He knew that his head was swathed in bandages from forehead to chin, but there was another pain, which nagged and stabbed, sent sharp blades of pain through him. He was too tired to attempt to discover what it was, he only knew that it filled the nights and made the days hideous. Sometimes nurses with cool hands came and lifting his arm, pressed something which pricked sharply, into it. Then slowly the violent pain receded, though the persistent ache remained. Slowly he drifted away into unconsciousness.

Once, making a supreme effort, he asked a nurse, "Do they know about me at home?"

She nodded. "Oh, yes, they knew a long time ago. Don't worry."

"And Liz—does Liz know?"

She replied, "Oh, yes, Liz knows, she sends you her love"; his sensibilities might be blunted, dimmed, misted, but he realized that she had not the faintest idea who 'Liz' was. He moved his head impatiently, so that new stabs of pain racked him.

In Yorkshire the telegram from the War Office arrived when Enoch was out on the farm, Ada was at the shop, and Gran was cooking a baking of bread.

Violet, took it from the boy, and held it out to Gran.

"Is't for me? Nay, it says Anderson. Best leave it lie while t' measter comes in."

"Should I tak' it to him?"

"Nay, leave it be."

Enoch came in whistling. He didn't whistle very well, almost always off the note, but he enjoyed whistling, it took his thoughts off other things. Michael had been eighteen when he went out— he had been home once in '42. Now it was '45, and James was chafing to be into the Army. Years were slipping past, Enoch thought, lads losing their youth, missing the joy of living. Mike has spent his twenty-first birthday 'somewhere in Italy', now they were to see Jimmy go as well. No wonder he whistled to keep his spirits up!

As he entered Gran nodded towards the telegram. "Telegram's come for you, Enoch."

He snatched at it, "Maybe it's a spot of leave Mike's gotten."

She said, "Maybe it's not!"

Enoch tore open the flimsy envelope, he read it with an agonized concentration, then said, "Aye, it's not leave. He's seriously wounded. Oh, my God!" then suddenly, "Can't they tell you mor'n that? Can't they—spending millions every day on this bloody war, tell you about what it is? Seriously wounded! What does it *mean*? If it was their own lads they'd want to know mor'n that!"

Gran said, "Nay, Enoch lad, try to keep calm. There'll be more news shortly. Come, come, bear up. Someone's got to tell our Ada."

"Aye, Ada must be told," he said, his voice devoid of any expression. "I'll telephone to her, quicker nor driving over."

Gran warned, "Be a bit careful what you say, Enoch."

He moved as if he were walking in his sleep. "I'll be careful." He said, "Mrs. Anderson? Oh, it's you is it Ada luv? I'm afraid I'm going to upset you, my dear. It's Mike. No, no, it's not the worst—only he's been wounded. I thought, maybe you'd like to come back home, luv. It's upsetting but happen it's nothing all that serious."

He went back, and taking the telegram crumpled it and shoved it in his pocket.

"No sense in telling Ada as it says—seriously," he said. "Just forget it, and we'll say it said—wounded only. Happen we'll get some good news in a day or so. Mind you, Violet, just watch what you say. I don't want her upset mor'n's necessary. Think on."

Ada came, white-faced and calm. "Where's the telegram?"

Enoch said, "Dash it! I b'lieve I put it on the fire."

She met his eyes squarely. "You did nothing of the kind, Enoch, and I've a right to know. He's not killed, is he?"

"No, luv, no. I swear he's not."

"Then what did it say? I'm his mother, I've a right to know."

"It said—seriously wounded, luv."

Ada Anderson nodded. "I see—and how'd we know what that means? Well, we must pray and have faith that God'ul spare him to us. My dear, good lad."

Gran said, "Amen," loudly and fervently, while Violet sobbed into her apron; Gran added, "V'let, for any favour—stop it!"

"I'll just slip over and tell Liz," Ada said.

Gran said, "Why, telephone to her—no call to go rushing over."

"No," Ada said quietly, "I'd rather go over, the car's here, it won't take a minute."

Enoch watched her grave, white face, and thought, 'So our Ada knows too. I wonder how she found out? Trust Ada to keep a still tongue.'

243

She found Liz working in the study, she looked up as Ada entered. "Hello, Ada, this is nice. Oh, these endless forms! And I'm such a fool about figures." Suddenly her voice sharpened. "Ada, there's nothing wrong is there? Michael's not—not——"

"He's wounded. Liz, it says—seriously. I thought I'd like to come over and tell you."

"Where is he? Does the telegram say? In Italy, I suppose." She pushed back her hair, her hands were shaking, her voice came in gasps as if she were breathless. "When can you get news? When can we get in touch with the hospital, the doctors—when can we hear how badly he is wounded? They must fly him home—God, I'll buy an aeroplane to bring him back. I could do that—couldn't I?"

"And then," Ada said, "when—if—we do get him back—what then, Liz?"

She watched Liz tilt back her head in that characteristic movement of hers. "Then—I'm going to ask him to marry me—I don't care how badly he's wounded——"

"I'd not like to think anyone married my lad out of pity, Liz."

"Pity! Don't be a fool, Ada—I worship him, have done for a long time—— Pity!"

"I know," Ada said, "I've known it for a long time. If I hadn't known, well, you'd have told me this afternoon." She went to where Liz sat and laid her hand on her shoulder. "Be good to him, won't you? He's the kind that it's easy to hurt, is Michael."

"You needn't be afraid, my dear. I know there is the difference in our ages—that's why I refused to marry him before—he's asked me often enough. I was afraid that one day he might look at me and think—'She's old—old—old.' Now," she seemed suddenly charged with energy, "now we've got to do something. Wait—let me think. I've got it! A friend of Aunt Alice's and Uncle Harry's—General Sir John Cockermouth. He's some kind of big-wig at the War Office. I'm going to London—they'll have to listen to me! I'll telegraph to you fully, Ada. Just be patient, know that I shall do everything possible to get him back."

"God bless you, Liz."

Grimly Liz said, "I only hope that He will."

They waited for long, restless days, then Liz telegraphed.

Michael arrives Brotherton Leeds to-night reserved room at Queen's afraid terribly ill but at least alive come over on receipt of this direct to hospital. Liz

Liz watched them carry him in, he looked like a dead man except for the long purple scar which ran from his temple down to his chin, and looked as if someone had laid a thick, ugly coloured cord drawn and puckered down the side of his face. Liz stood leaning against the wall, feeling that her blood had changed to ice. His eyes were closed, his face seemed shrunken, and the thick, brown hair was completely grey.

They carried him past her and she followed, dragging her feet as if they were weighted with lead. At the door of the room which had been reserved for him, the nurse turned and said, very gently, "I think you'd better wait, Mrs. Tancred—while we get him into bed. Look, sit down there — I'll come back immediately."

Liz sank into the chair, and sat there with her hands clenched; her ears alert for every sound. The wreck of a man was her Mike, changed, battered, and grey-faced—so different from the gay and gallant young man who had left her last at King's Cross Station. Yet she knew that she had never loved him so much, never longed to hold him in her arms as she did now. Her whole body ached with the intensity of her devotion. She thought, 'Giving birth to a child must be like this—oh, Mike, I'll be so good to you, my darling.'

The nurse came back, "I think you can come in now, Mrs. Tancred. I don't think that he'll know you, and don't try to talk too much to him. He's had a dreadful time, poor man."

Liz said, her voice thick, "Man! He's only a boy."

He was lying propped up on pillows, his eyes closed; his face seemed more bloodless than ever, the dreadful scar only showed any colour. His breathing was quick and shallow.

She stooped and kissed his cheek, the eyelids fluttered and then his eyes opened as with a great effort. His lips—those colourless lips—moved.

"Liz—darling Liz." The sound was a mere thread and she had to bend down to catch it.

"Mike," she said, "*fight* my dear one, fight!"

"I'll—" there was a long pause, "try. Liz."

Then the eyelids came down again and he seemed to drift away. Ada and Enoch came, they stood in silence watching him. Enoch had tears running down his cheeks, Ada's eyes were dry, though her face was a mask of agony. They kissed him, but he had drifted away and made no sign of recognition.

They saw the matron, kind and capable, trying to make everything easy for them.

"It's not just the wound on his face, is it?" Ada asked.

"It's the amputations, Mrs. Anderson. They had to take off his leg, three operations—now it's off right up to the thigh. They're afraid of—I'm so sorry—gangrene. We shall do everything possible, do believe that. It's all so heartbreaking. All you can do is to—hope and be brave. Yes, in the morning—whenever you like. At the Queen's? If it's—necessary, we shall telephone to you."

All night Liz sat waiting in a chair, listening for the ring of the telephone. She felt unutterably weary, drained of strength, and yet sleep had never seemed so far away. As the daylight came, and the electric lamps seemed to have lost their power, she could wait no longer. She bathed, changed her clothes—if he were conscious she must look well groomed for him. Her hair must be exactly as he liked it, even her scent which he loved and of which he could never remember the name, must be used.

She drove to the hospital, it was barely eight o'clock. She asked to see Michael, and the nurse, her face showing the weariness after a night's watching, nodded.

He did not seem to have moved since she left him last night. She knelt beside his bed, and said, "Mike—it's Liz."

His eyes opened slowly, she saw the fingers of his hand move, and took them in hers very gently.

"Mike—I've come to ask you to marry me. Will you? I want it more than anything in the world. Please, Mike."

"Darling Liz," the grey lips moved slowly, "I've asked you so often—you know the answer. I'm very—proud, dear Liz."

"I'll be so good to you, Mike."

"You always have been—oh, darling."

His eyes closed; very softly she spoke the lines which he loved:

"The wind on the heath . . . all sweet things . . . life's sweet, brother . . . who would wish to die."

Michael sighed, but his eyes did not open again. As the door opened and Ada and Enoch entered, Liz laid her finger to her lips.

"He's asleep," she said, then for the first time in her life, she slipped to the floor and lay there unconscious.

Enoch said, "Leave her be, Ada. Aye, he's asleep—our dear lad. He can do with his rest—God bless him."

Gardone Riviera.
September 1955.